Zara Stoneley is the *USA Today* bestselling author of novels including *The Wedding Date* and *The First Date*.

She lives in a Cheshire village with her family, a lively cockapoo called Harry, and a very bossy (and slightly evil) cat called Saffron.

Born in a small village in the UK, Zara wanted to be a female James Herriot, a spy, or an author when she grew up. After many (many) years, and many different jobs, her dream of writing a bestseller came true. She now writes about friendship, dreams, love, and happy ever afters, and hopes that her tales make you laugh a lot, cry a little, and occasionally say 'ahhh'.

🅕 /ZaraStoneley
🅧 @ZaraStoneley
🅞 @ZaraStoneley
www.zarastoneley.com

Also by Zara Stoneley

Stable Mates
Country Affairs
Country Rivals
A Very Country Christmas
The Holiday Swap
Summer with the Country Village Vet
Blackberry Picking at Jasmine Cottage
The Wedding Date
No One Cancels Christmas
Bridesmaids

Four Christmases and a Secret

Zara Stoneley

OneMoreChapter

One More Chapter a division of
HarperCollins*Publishers*
The News Building
1 London Bridge Street
London SE1 9GF

www.harpercollins.co.uk

This paperback edition 2019

First published in Great Britain in ebook format by
HarperCollins*Publishers* 2019

A catalogue record for this book
is available from the British Library

ISBN: 9780008363161

Set in Birka by Palimpsest Book Production Ltd,
Falkirk Stirlingshire

Printed and bound in Great Britain by
CPI Group (UK) Ltd, Croydon, CR0 4YY

For everybody who has felt at some time in their lives 'not good enough'.

Believe me, you are!

Prologue

MISTLETOE KISSES

24 December 2004

'Iflung open the curtains and shouted look at my hedge-hogs!'

Oh my God, I knew it. My mother is going to totally embarrass me. Here, at Uncle Terence's Christmas Eve party, in front of everybody.

Want to be able to embarrass your kids as they get older? Get your own back for every little slip up? Well, bring them up in a village where everybody will know them, and nobody will forget anything they have ever done. And never ever move house.

I am eighteen years old, for heaven's sake. I need to stop coming to family and friends' parties so that I can avoid total embarrassment.

Nine months, that's all. I just have to stick it out for nine more months and then I'll be free.

I love my parents to bits, I sometimes even like them, but I cannot wait to go to university. My own place, nobody watching my every move and I will be able to snog who I like, when I like, where I like. I will be able to leave crumbs in my bed, read until 4 a.m., spend the weekend in my pyjamas.

I straighten my antlers self-consciously, set my jumper to 'flashing' mode as a distraction and glance at Dad, who just shrugs apologetically, because we both know that mother in full flow is unstoppable.

'Wendy, darling?' He does try, but like I say, she's unstoppable.

'And Stuart switched the patio light on and there they were!'

'Hedgehogs?' I hear somebody say, hopefully.

I edge back, try to sidle behind a bookcase before anybody notices me. One more step and I'm heading towards the 'Narnia' display. Another step and I'll be safely hidden behind a giant White Witch.

'Oh no, no! Our Daisy and a boy. Horizontal on the lawn, searching for slugs they said! I didn't even know Joshua the postman's son was interested in hedgehogs. I never even realised that Daisy knew the boy, she'd definitely not introduced him, had you dear? Daisy?'

I lean back against the bookcase and close my eyes. I am mortified. I mean, wouldn't you think that when your parents are holding a dinner party, you'd be safe having a quick snog in the back garden?

Four Christmases and a Secret

If Josh had had his way, we would have been naked and have more in common with rabbits than hedgehogs, but the full moon, dew sodden grass and nip in the air had dampened my ardour (as well as my best jeans) a bit. I mean he's okay, he's quite a lot of fun actually but I'm not about to marry him. And I'm not a hedgehog. Or a rabbit.

He's a bloody quick thinker though, he probably would have said we were doing some kind of druid-dance to summon up snails (I bet Mum would have fallen for that, not sure about Dad). While I just stared wide-eyed like a rabbit in the headlights then scampered for the safety of the summerhouse.

Anyway, having your parents and four of their friends (who you've known practically from birth) all staring out at you with glasses of wine in their hands totally chills off the warm feeling between your thighs and deflates your nipples. It does, believe me, so don't do it.

Josh went home, and I went in for a discussion about why slugs come out at night, and what kind of beer you should put out for them, before I managed to escape to bed and my 'A' level revision. Thank God for revision, it will get you out of practically any social occasion where your parents are involved.

I quite wish I could do that now.

Except I do actually love Uncle Terence. Once I've put my Christmas jumper on and we've set off for his rather posh bookshop (which actually looks more like a wine bar when he's got it fancied up and makes it a brilliant

3

venue for a party), then Christmas has officially started. And I love his bookshop with or without its festive vibe. It's a bit of an Aladdin's cave if you're a bookaholic like I am. I've been going in there since I was in a pushchair and I'm still discovering new books and book-related knick-knacks and pictures.

Uncle T is not actually my uncle, but I've always called him that. And he lives in Stockton Hall, which is definitely not a hall. So, it could be confusing. But he is however hilariously funny and has a very impressive collection of waistcoats. He makes a mean cocktail and changes his girlfriends and wives more often than I have my hair cut. I was going to say change my knickers, but that's not quite true. Close but not true.

'*Psst.*'

I jump, stumble, and nearly topple into a life-size Harry Potter cut-out, adorned with tinsel. I'd rather collide with the White Witch to be honest.

Uncle Terence has popped through an opening between the book shelves, like a genie out of a bottle. He's looking very dapper, as normal. But that is less important than the glass he is holding out to me. 'It's the Bee's knees!'

I stare at him.

'The cocktail, my dear! I thought it would suit the occasion, a nice drop of gin, something tart and a hint of something sweet.' He winks. 'And not a hedgehog in sight!'

He puts his arm round my shoulders and gives me a hug. 'I will miss you when you fly the nest, my darling

4

girl. You have become part of the fixtures and fittings in my little shop. Now, take a break and put your feet up for a second. I've got a wonderful stock of new and slightly racy books in your favourite corner.' He puts a finger to his lips. 'Our secret though, or else your mother and Vera will be here in a shot! I'm expecting an invasion by the playgroup mothers when the news gets out. Over there, between original editions and Spiritual Healing.'

He gives me a gentle shove, but I don't need the encouragement. What could be better than a cocktail and a book?

'Thank God, you're still here!' Ollie Cartwright flops down onto the small leather sofa nearly taking my eye out with his sharp elbow. Then stretches his long legs out, squashing me into the corner and nearly sends my book flying. 'Thought you'd managed to come up with some excuse to escape and I was the only person here under forty! God, I hate these things!'

'Why would I want to escape?' I raise an eyebrow at him, cross that he's come to annoy me, but also vaguely pleased. 'I love Uncle Terence!' And his book shop I could add. I really love his bookshop. And the books. I give this one a quick once over to check it's not been damaged by Ollie's arrival. Okay, I admit it. I'm a bit anal about books – unlike Mum who bends the corners over instead of finding a bookmark and bends the spine.

'So, what are you doing hiding in a corner with a book?'

'Well it is a book shop!'

5

'It is a party!' He grins.

We stare at each other. Impasse.

'I needed to check something.'

'Check something? What is that anyway?' He makes a lunge for the book, but I am quicker, and I'm leaning back over the arm of the sofa, clutching it to my chest. '*Riders?* Ha-ha, the school swot Daisy Dunkerly reads porn!'

'Don't call me a swot! You're just jealous I got a higher mark than you in Chemistry.'

'I am.' He chuckles. It's quite a nice deep, rumbling chuckle that makes me want to smile stupidly back at him. But I try to resist, despite the fact that he's leaned in and lowered his voice to a confidential level. 'My mum will never forgive me for giving yours some extra ammo. I can hear it now: '*Well, my Daisy came top in Chemistry! Can you imagine it? Isn't she clever? When I was at school the girls thought chemistry was just what you felt when a boy tried to get in your knickers!*'

I can't help it. A grin escapes. It's a pretty good impression of my mum, if a little high pitched.

His mum, Vera, and mine are best friends. She's nice enough but honestly, the pair of them can be so competitive and embarrassing. I swear it started when they were both on the same maternity ward and Ollie weighed 3lb more than me (a win for Vera), but Mum was in labour for two hours longer (a win for her). From there it got worse, first child to say a word (shit from Ollie, but Vera insisted it was sheet), first one to poo on a potty (me, yay!).

6

They're still at it. God knows what they'll talk about when we leave home and go to university in the autumn. They'll both have to get a puppy or something.

'She doesn't talk like that! Anyway, it's not porn! Well, not *that* kind of porn! It's Jilly Cooper.'

He shrugs, and sags back onto the sofa. Which leaves me feeling a bit cold and abandoned, even though he's still only inches away.

Ollie Cartwright reads books, but only school books and weird geeky stuff based in alternative realities. He's a bit of a smart arse.

'And I'm not prim and proper!'

He raises an eyebrow. 'S'pose not, not according to Josh the slosh anyway.'

Joshua, my fellow hedgehog hunter, is unfortunately in the same class at school as Ollie. My cheeks burn. 'Why do boys have to be so immature?' I will kill him if he's been talking about us to his mates.

Ollie shrugs and looks faintly embarrassed, a tinge of pink along his high cheekbones. 'One-upmanship I guess.'

It's my turn to roll my eyes. 'You're eighteen for heaven's sake! You'll be going to uni in October! Don't you have anything better to talk about than sex?'

'Who said anything about sex?' He laughs and leans in closer again, then frowns and touches my arm lightly. 'You do know what kind of rep he's got, don't you? I mean I know he's gobby but ...'

'Oh, shut up! I know exactly what he's like!' I move

7

away a bit, because the touch of his hand is bringing out goose-bumps on my arm and making something deep in my stomach flutter. I can't remember feeling that funny sensation with Josh, even when we were so close our hip bones clashed. The only goose-bumps I'd had was because it was bloody freezing.

In a strange way it would be nice if Ollie carried on, just to see what happens, but he doesn't. He moves back as though I've swiped him away, not just retreated a bit.

'So,' he clears his throat, and points at the book, 'what are you checking? Bet I can tell you more than a book can!'

'In your dreams.' I snap the book shut and sigh. Rupert Campbell-Black and Jake will have to wait another day. I mean, I know *Riders* has been about a while, but I read in a horse magazine that it is one of *the* books to read. So as soon as I spotted it was one of the new books Uncle T was stocking, I thought it was a good opportunity to try it out. 'Anyway, why are you hiding in a corner, bothering me?'

Ollie rolls his eyes. 'If I have to hear your mother saying one more time, '*Well, my Daisy is going to be a vet, isn't she clever?*' I will stick my head in the vat of mulled wine.'

'Ha-ha, well I have to listen to your mum going on about you.' I do. Uncle Terence's Christmas eve party seems to bring out the worst in both of our mothers. 'Doc Ollie, ha-ha. Suits you!' Ollie isn't particularly cool, he's a bit studious (that might be the glasses), a bit geeky. His hair is a bit too long, and he's very (and I mean very) lanky.

8

'That Christmas jumper suits you!' He grins again, his dark eyes twinkling.

'You look a bit of a twerd to be honest, where the hell did you get yours?' I say and giggle in a very stupid girlish way, to deflect the churning feeling that has just started up in the base of my stomach, and the desire I've got to kiss him.

Kiss him?

Now where the hell did that come from? I don't kiss Oliver Cartwright! He's the son of my parents' best friends for heaven sakes. And he's annoying and a smart arse, and always trying to compete, and, well, and quite gorgeous actually. In this dim light. But he's got a silly jumper on.

'Twerd?' He's closer again. Not grinning now though. In fact, he's staring into my eyes.

I swallow.

'Mix of a twerp and a nerd? My brain couldn't decide before it came out of my mouth.' God, my mouth is dry. And his mouth is so close.

'Whereas your jumper is the height of festive fashion?' He laughs and leans in even closer. He's acting pretty chilled and relaxed by his normal standards. I think he might have been hitting the whisky with my dad, his own dad and Uncle Terence.

Whereas I have only Uncle T's cocktails to blame.

'Definitely.' I swallow again. I've gone to town this year. Found a very smart jumper, with two robins, whose chests light up. Ollie has a giant reindeer head with a big flashing nose. Not original or new, I'm sure he wore it last year. Except now it's a bit tighter, stretched over his chest which I'm sure is broader, and a bit tight over his flat stomach, and ...

'It'll be weird next year, won't it? We won't have seen each other for months!'

'Ha-ha, there's a good side to everything!' I laugh, to cover up my embarrassment. Because it will be weird; in fact, it'll be very strange to not see Ollie at school, at parties at his parents' and my parents'.

He's staring down at the book I'm still holding. 'You didn't bring Josh tonight, then?'

I shrug. 'It's nothing serious. Just a bit of fun, why should I bring him?'

'Just wondered.'

'It would be daft to get serious, I'm off to Edinburgh Uni, he's going to Bristol or somewhere daft, I mean who gets serious with somebody when they're still at school?'

'Yeah, you'd have to be mad, wouldn't you?'

'Totally.'

I suddenly realise that he's stopped looking at the book and he's staring straight into my eyes.

His mouth is only inches from mine. His thigh is warm against my bare leg. I feel all fluttery, not-quite-sure what to do. Whether to pull my skirt down, shoot off the chair, or say something clever. Instead, I just stare back. My breath catching in my throat as he raises a hand and touches my cheek.

'Mistletoe.' He mumbles glancing up.

'Oh, yeah.' I look up as well, then back down.

Our gazes lock, and it's like I'm seeing him for the very first time. I don't want to look at anything or anybody else, not even my book. All I can see is him. All I can feel is the soft imprint of his fingers against my cheek, his warm breath fanning my skin.

My heart is hammering, and I'm trembling inside and out. But I know this is going to happen.

I lean in. I can't help myself.

'We should ...' Then his lips brush over mine. It's the lightest of touches, but it sends a shiver down my spine.

I freeze, and then I can't help it. I close my eyes and I kiss him back.

His lips are soft, his hand warm on my waist, and I'm tingling all over, nervous but weirdly excited. He tastes of whisky and mince pies. And something else, something that is Ollie and nobody else. Something I want more of. And a small part of me deep inside, that I didn't know existed, has woken up leaving me all breathless and shaky.

I've never kissed Ollie before. Well, I have, or rather he kissed me. But we were six years old, and he was Joseph to my Mary in the school Nativity, and he was showing off.

But this is way different.

I mean though, we're not like this. Are we?

'Daisy, Daisy, where are you hiding?'

'Oh God, it's Mum!' I pull back, my lips feeling bruised and swollen, and I just know I'm flushed and flustered.

'Right, er, well.' Ollie blinks at me.

11

I cough and glance up. 'Bloody mistletoe, he puts it everywhere.' The stupid giggle comes out before I can stop it.

We both stand up abruptly at the same time, collide, lose balance and sit down. Then he stands up, holds out a hand and helps me to my feet.

'Well, er, see you at school, I guess.' His hand lingers on mine, and we're close enough to kiss, again.

I nod, swallow. 'Yeah, you sure will.' I sound embarrassingly like a cowboy and do a thumbs up which is totally uncool.

'Have a good Christmas, Dais.' We both look down at our still-joined hands then let go awkwardly.

'You, too, Ol. Happy, er, Christmas. Just, er, going to check out the other books.' I edge up the aisle one way, and he sidles the other way.

'Good.'

'Er, right fine.'

'Think I'll get another drink, find out when we're going.' He points. 'Might have drunk too much whisky with Dad.'

'Sure.'

'That was, er ...'

'Cool, cool, whatever.' I do not want him to say 'mistake', 'silly' or anything like that. 'Just for the mistletoe!'

'Nice.' He blushes bright red and is off before the word has even settled in the air.

I look at the books, not seeing them. Then shake my head. In a few months' time I will sit my exams and then head off to Scotland and a brilliant, exciting few years at uni. And Ollie will move to London and meet a whole new set of friends.

Our futures lie ahead, separate futures.

'Fine, nice, bye.' I stare after him. My fingers rest on my bruised lips, and I blink to try to get rid of the taste of him, the feel of his hand on my waist, the sensation that prickled through my body as his teeth clashed with mine, then his tongue skittered over my teeth.

Oh. My. God. I just kissed Oliver Cartwright, and it left me all wobbly and weak-kneed in a way that Josh's never did. But it meant nothing. Definitely nothing. It is Christmas. We are drunk. It was a goodbye snog.

But an amazing snog.

I shouldn't have done it. We're mates, he's always been just like an annoying brother to me. But now we've kissed.

I'll never be able to look at Ollie in the same way again.

In fact, I'm not sure I'm going to ever be able to talk to him in the same way.

Is it a good or bad thing that we have new and exciting lives ahead of us – in different places?

ACT 1 – MUST TRY HARDER

Chapter 1

24 December 2017

'Oh. My. God! Look at this place!' Frankie, my friend and flatmate is standing in the open doorway of the bookshop and staring in as though she's just discovered an alternative reality. She throws her arms wide as though embracing the whole place. 'This is so fucking quaint. I didn't know places like this still existed!'

'You sound like a tourist who's just discovered Stratford-upon-Avon.' I can't help but laugh, despite my nerves. 'It's a bookshop.' Uncle Terence's bookshop to be precise.

'Well yeah, but look at those proper wood bookcases, and wow, cute nooks and crannies, and ... cocktails!' She leaps on Mabel, Uncle T's bookkeeper, who nearly drops her tray in shock. 'Oh my God, I'm going to orgasm, this is the best Dirty Martini I've had in ages.'

Mabel gives her a horrified look and scurries off to the safety of a nearby cranny. Dumps the tray and then heads for the protection of Uncle T.

'Stop, please stop.' I'm trying not to laugh. I think Frankie must be on some hallucinogenic drug. I mean, she's not got much of a filter, she says what she wants, but she's not normally this full on.

Frankie's sheet of long black hair swishes in my face as her slim fingers spin the martini glass, and the look of mischief in her eyes is positively dangerous. Most of the time she's cool and languid, but tonight she is positively buzzing.

She's had a bust up with Tarquin, her boyfriend, which is (1) why she begged me to let her come tonight, and (2) why she's ready to party with a capital P.

I am now beginning to realise that agreeing to let her tag along with me to Uncle T's Christmas Eve bash could have been a mistake.

After all, this is not some swish cocktail bar, this is a bookshop, and I use the word 'bash' loosely – it's more a close friends and family do. I will undoubtedly have known everybody here for most of my life, and there's a fair chance I will be the youngest attendee by a country mile.

Which is why I agreed to wear the customary Christmas jumper and antlers. No chance of making a fool of myself in front of an attractive man tonight! Only the opportunity to once again be a slight disappointment to my mother, who would very much like a daughter to be proud of. A daughter with an impressive career, a handsome partner, and preferably a bun in the oven. Or at least the knowledge that said oven is nicely warming in preparation.

I have a job on the local rag, Frankie, and an empty womb. Oh, and Stanley – my four-legged date.

Therefore, I am still hovering on the doorstep. I am not ready to party, with or without a capital P. I'm taking a deep breath and pulling my metaphorical big girls pants up, preparing for the onslaught.

'Here goes, Stan!' I shoot him a pensive smile, which he ignores, plaster a grin on my face and follow her in. I've not got any choice. She's grabbed the front of my jumper and Rudolf's nose is being stretched to its shiny limit.

You know how you go in some shops and it hits you, the warm air and soft music, the bright clothes yelling out 'buy me' even though you're broke? Well, Uncle T's shop is like that. But with books not clothes. And mulled wine and mince pies. And much, much better.

The warmth of happy people, *and* the sounds and smells of Christmas wrap themselves round me like an old familiar blanket.

Christmas has arrived, it's officially here. Uncle Terence's party marks the start of the festive season. The hum of happy people chatting away, the smell of mulled wine, holly and warm pastry assault us and it's a bit like walking into a Christmas-past time capsule. But with cocktails and canapés.

It takes a moment to adjust to all things festive and nice, after all the chaos that's led up to it. I'm still adjusting when I'm assaulted. By my mother. My mother is the downside to Uncle Terence's party. I do love her. Honestly. In controlled situations (i.e. my parents' home). In small doses. Uncle Terence's party does not bring out the 'small dose' side of her though. It brings out over enthusiasm. She treats me like exhibit 'A' – something to be paraded and boasted about. Which was strangely apt last year, when I was working as a barista and she insisted on telling everybody very loudly and proudly that I was a barrister.

Uncle Terence, who knew better, thought it was hilarious and kept asking how the coffee bean interrogation was going, and whether I was dealing with many mug-*ings*, and if the serial killer liked his coffee like his victims – all ground up. That last one was a bit *eurgh*, but it kept him entertained all evening.

Anyway, unfortunately, I am not exactly an overachiever on the career front (unlike Ollie Cartwright – but more about that later), do not yet own 'property' (unlike Ollie), and am a total disappointment on the getting hitched and producing offspring side (Ollie hasn't done that either), so Mum struggles, over exaggerates or makes things up.

Since leaving school with a crap set of exam results to my name, I've always left the party feeling that my card has been marked 'could do better'. This is not a jolly start to the festive season.

'Daisy, darling! You're here at last! We thought you'd got lost!' I get a quick hug, and a *mwah-mwah* kiss. Frankie grins over her shoulder at me. Mesmerised. I think it's my mother's new 'pink rinse' and animal print jumpsuit that has done it. Or the fact she's already downed two cocktails.

'Love the outfit, very on-trend.' Frankie manages to sound genuine. She winks at me.

My mother preens. 'Thank you, dear.' She gives her an up-and-down who-are-you look that confuses some people but doesn't faze Frankie at all.

'We're not late, Mum!' Anybody would think I hadn't spoken to her for months, rather than earlier today. 'And how can I get lost? I come here all the time.'

'Where is he, then? Where's your young man?' Mum peers around me, almost shoving. See, it has started. She wants to mentally measure him up for his morning suit and see how he'd look framed on the mantelpiece.

'Stephen, isn't it? Stephen?' She shouts his name as though she expects him to appear like a genie.

'Simon! He's called Simon, but I told you he's not coming!'

'Not coming? Oh yes, yes, silly me, I forgot! It's Frank now, isn't it? I can't keep up with you and all these men! Well, where's Frank?'

'Frankie not Frank!' I point at Frankie. Luckily, she is distracted and is staring across the room so doesn't notice my mother's disappointment.

Mum, just to be sure Simon isn't lurking on the pavement, or hiding behind a lamppost, pushes her way out of the door to peer up the street. Treading on Stanley's paw (sorry, I might not have mentioned – Stanley is a dog) and trapping me against the door jamb.

'Oh buggering, flaming ...'

'Language, darling!'

The plate of sausage rolls, which I'd very cleverly balanced in one hand, goes flying one way as the dog dives between my legs and my mother dives the other side.

'Oh my God, who the fuck is that?' Frankie is oblivious to flying pastry, and the blob of lightly herbed pork that has landed on her head. 'Fuck me. Well, him, well, oh my God, I think I still believe in Father Christmas!' She clutches her throat melodramatically with one hand, and my arm with the other. Did I mention she's a bit hyper tonight? 'Ditch those canapés, girl and introduce me, so I can go and hang my stocking on his tree! I need to make babies with him!'

'Frankie!' I laugh and forget all about Mum for a moment, because this is weird. 'Who, where? What on earth are you going on about?' I'm sorry, but nobody in their right mind would want to shag *anybody* who attends Uncle T's party. Unless he's smuggled in a sexy bartender this year, instead of relying just on Mabel who isn't as young as she was.

'There!' She does a low wolf whistle, then blows the tips of her fingers. 'Smoking. Hot!' He must be, because she seems to have forgotten she still has a boyfriend.

There are never hot men here though. Ever. It is a family and friends party. In a bookshop, in our village.

I look where she is pointing. At a man who is vaguely familiar, and admittedly quite attractive, in a Robert Downey Junior earnest-with-glasses kind of way. He reminds me a

22

bit of Ollie's dad, Charles. He must be some distant relative I've never met.

He has the faintest of smiles on his face, tugging at the corner of a generous mouth. Which would be slightly effeminate if he wasn't so definitely male. Oh yes, he is definitely all male. For the first time ever at one of these parties, I wonder if the antlers might have been a mistake.

'Oh, that's Oliver. Silly girl.' Mum stops searching for my missing date and chuckles. I gasp, and the mood music in my head grounds to a halt.

'What?' I think it came out as a screech, because the conversation nearby has a hiccup. Then they go back to talking. Luckily the sound doesn't appear to have reached his side of the room though, that's the advantage of a bookshop – those thick pages swallow up the sound. 'No way. That is *so* not Ollie!' The last time I saw him was at very close quarters. I was snogging him. 'It can't be.' I think this comes out as a pathetic whine. Buggering hell, Ollie can't be here. Not in person. And he can't look like *that*.

This makes it even worse than normal – we'll now be plonked side by side, like we were as toddlers and compared *in real life*!

I've not seen him for absolutely ages, thirteen years to be precise. He's been in Africa, or America, or Coventry. Well he's always somewhere miles away. Doing good on a global scale. Well, he's not been at Uncle Terence's parties anyway. Which has been a bonus. At least while Mum and Vera have been going on about his virtues, I've been able to imagine him in my head as a pimply, fat arsehole.

'Of course, it is, dear. Isn't it lovely to see him?'

Fabulous.

Kill. Me. Now.

He will pity me, not want to snog me. Or he will laugh.

'He's got a girlfriend, you know.'

'Hasn't he always?' I say, slightly sarcastically. I can't quite help myself. Part of Ollie's upward trajectory is his ability to date gorgeous women. Ollie always has a girlfriend, and I always have to be told about her. Just like I've been told about every step of his career since he went to uni.

My mother, and therefore, I, have lived vicariously through every one of the five years at medical school, followed by his two years of placements. I have heard every 'Oh he's been so brave when faced with mangled people in agony, I couldn't do it!' from his mother Vera, and lots of 'oh he's so clever' and 'so sad you didn't do something like that' from my mother. I have then had to endure 'speciality training' (hearing about it, not doing it, but believe me it's just as bad), and face-fanning (Vera and Mum) when she speaks about the conferences and courses he's attended. Since he qualified it's been worse. I haven't seen the bloody man for thirteen years, which has suited me fine. How could being face to face with the demi-god who I can never match up to help my self-esteem?

Thirteen years is a bit scary though. That makes me old.

Well at least old enough to be a responsible adult. Which I most definitely am not.

'Wow, that's Ollie the pompous prick?' Frankie drags her gaze away from him for a second and stares at me. I heat up like an electric blanket, my cheeks positively glowing, and Mum frowns.

I could just go home now.

I might have called him that. Once or twice. To Frankie. 'He's, er, changed.' The endless stories from my mother and his about how well he's doing, and how many girlfriends he's got, and when he's going to become pope (made that bit up, but it's close – he deserves a sainthood, apparently) have really got on my tits, and definitely made him sound like a pompous prick. And anyway, he might still be a pompous prick, just a hot one.

'The one who felt you up when you were four?'

'I never said that! We were six, Frankie, I said he kissed me not felt me up!' My cheeks are burning. If I blush any harder I'll be hotter than a chestnut roasting charcoal burner. Thank God I didn't tell her about the drunken face-eating when we were eighteen.

'Felt your what?' My mother has a puzzled expression, which I ignore.

'Well, whatever he did, he is mine! 'Scuse me, ladies!' Frankie steams off in pursuit of her prey and doesn't hear my mother's plaintive, 'Well, actually, I think you'll find he's Juliet's, dear!'

Grrr. How can Oliver Cartwright be *gorgeous*? Be bloody

25

perfect in every way. He wasn't when we were kids. He was a bit lanky, sweet and maybe a bit cute, but all arms and legs, and the odd spot, and voice that hadn't decided how low it was going to be, and a 'did it at home' haircut. And bad jeans. Yeah, he had bad jeans.

Frigging hell, he had all that and was still worth some lip action? I must have been very drunk.

I am not going near the man, he will be totally insufferable.

'You two can have a nice chat, you must have so much to talk about!' says Mum.

It is all wrong. I'm exhausted, and the party hasn't even started.

And now my toes are warm and damp.

I glance down. Stanley is nibbling bits of sausage roll from between them.

The last couple of days have been disastrous.

Chapter 2

The lead up to Christmas, and Uncle Terence's party has gone like this ...

9.30 p.m., 22 December

Things I have to do before Tuesday evening at Uncle Terence's:

1. *Find my red nosed reindeer Christmas jumper and antlers* (urgent or will stand out like sore thumb).
1. ~~*Make*~~ *Buy sausage rolls to take to buffet* (can do this in my lunch break tomorrow then if M&S have run out can always go to Greggs and cut large ones into small canapé size. Added advantage of this option – can buy vegan ones which will score points).
1. *Send boyfriend message about what time to arrive and tell Uncle Terence I will have a plus one!*
1. *Buy new festive lipstick that Sunday supplement said was 'guaranteed to make you smile'* (v. important when

spending Christmas with my family, hope have time in lunch break to do this, might have to queue jump in Greggs. Which is top priority, lipstick or sausage rolls?).

1. *Find wrapping paper. And sticky tape.* (Urgent – top priority!)

My mother is bound to raise my shortcomings at Uncle T's party, but she will soon be distracted by the scandal of how young Terence's latest girlfriend is. Even better if he's married her by now, which he might well have done, it is very hard to keep track. He's had so many girlfriends, and even more ex-wives, in the last ten years even I can't remember all their names. Uncle T's a 'bit of a one' according to Mum, but he seems to bring out the fun and twinkly side of Vera. I'd never say this out loud, but Ollie's dad Charles is a bit scary. It's hard to believe he and Terence are brothers. I can quite understand Vera needing some light relief.

Charles is a consultant. In fact, the whole family, apart from Vera (who was named after Vera Lynn), are pretty intimidating. They are total over-achievers. Ollie's got a brother who is a barrister and a sister who is an opera singer. I think I'm the only one that has noticed that Vera has called her children after characters in Oliver Twist, they're Oliver, Will and Nancy. I suspect she has done this on purpose and it's her little secret joke. I'll know for sure if they ever get a dog and name it Bull's Eye.

I don't know why we go to the party really, but it can be rather fun, and it is a firmly entrenched family tradition (my father's words not mine, I don't talk like that) which only death or marriage will excuse me from (another thing Dad said). Personally, I think getting married is a bit of a drastic solution, and I do love Uncle T, this party less so.

The only negatives to kicking off Christmas with Uncle T are (1) my mother will be there, (2) she will compare me constantly to the hugely successful and perfect Ollie Cartwright, even though luckily, he won't be there (he never is), and (3) dodging the mistletoe can be a health hazard. Terence hangs it everywhere, as he seems to want everybody to snog everybody else. If he wasn't so nice and jolly, I'd suspect he had some weird fetish, but instead I will believe him when he says 'love makes the world go round'.

It was bad enough when we were eighteen. Just the thought of that drunken totally unplanned snog with Ollie is making me feel all hot and bothered.

The only good thing has been that Ollie has not turned up at a single party since our embarrassing encounter. Which is good, and bad. I mean, back then, we actually might have got on, but we live on different planets now. He has ticked every success box going, I have to look back with fond memories of beating him in a Chemistry exam. Since then my life seems to have taken a dive and whilst he lives on planet-perfect, I meanwhile inhabit a galaxy far, far away where everything is disorganised and success can be measured by how many nearly-passed-their-sell-by-date bargains you manage to grab just before the supermarket closes.

Which makes point (4) on my list – the perfect smile part – even more essential. To be used when my mother asks if I've changed my mind about marrying Ollie Cartwright yet (as she knows I haven't seen him since we were students, then how on earth can she still be dreaming about our happy ever after?). I know she will ask though (probably in front of Vera), even though I will have my own, actual boyfriend with me. This is a win, this is the first time in years that I've had a boyfriend who has actually agreed to spend Christmas with me and my family.

7 p.m., 23 December

I have had a truly shit day. Christmas has already got off to a dismal start. I already need to strike (3) off my first list. Simon, my boyfriend, rang me at work.

'Dais?'

'Simon?' This is odd. It sounds like Simon, but Simon never calls me at work. He also never calls me Dais.

'Slight change of plan, darling.' When he calls me 'darling', he's either after sex, snacks, or is about to say something he knows I won't like. It is one of his whee-dling words. 'Have to cancel your Christmas dinner with Mom and Pop.'

'Why? *Oh no!* What's happened, are they okay?'

I try to stop staring at the photo of a missing cat on

my screen. It's tricky, it's got a weird squint that is hard to ignore. I fear for its safety, a cat like this would not remain missing for long – it would be impossible to ignore.

'They're fine. Why wouldn't they be?'

'Well, if we're not ...' I blink, his words have sunk in. 'Hang on, you said cancel *my* dinner?'

'I thought you'd be pleased, far too much food in one day. I mean who can eat two Christmas dinners, ha-ha!'

'But you're still going?'

'Of course, I am, they're my parents! Look, nothing personal, it's just there's not enough room. Lucy,' his little sister, 'has made up with that boyfriend of hers, Ralph, Rafe, whatever he's called, so he'll be coming.'

'But ...'

'They don't really have enough table space for everybody, and you'd make it an odd number.'

'Why? That's two extra, Lucy and Rafe.'

'And Grandmother! Cancelled her cruise cos of her dicky hip. Can't expect Mom to turn away her aged parent, can you Daisy? Be reasonable!'

'Of course, I don't. I didn't know about that!' It's not fair to suggest I'm being unreasonable.

'Sorry sweets, but Mom's all excited about a possible engagement announcement so Lucy's man has to be there! And be fair, she knows them all far better than she knows you, they're family!'

I'm sticking my lower lip out, I know I am. But the whole point was she would get to know me, but she obviously considers me a 'a passing fancy' (he doesn't say that last bit, but I have assumed it from his tone).

'Oh right. Fine.' I'm not sure it is fine. 'But you are coming to Uncle T's party tomorrow?' He has to come, he just has to. I've got to prove to Mum I can get at least something right.

'Probs with your Christmas eve party as well now. It's a bit awkward but Ralph—'

'*Rafe!*' He doesn't even remember the name of the damn man who will be tucking into my Christmas dinner.

'Lucy's boyfriend asked me to go the local with him, got to chat to the potential brother in law, ha-ha, think he wants to discuss man stuff, proposals and all that.'

'But you don't know anything about proposals!'

'Sorry and all that but didn't think you'd be bothered.'

Bothered? I can feel my jaw tighten. I'm about to grit my teeth, which the dentist has told me not to do. 'But I've got you a present!'

'We can swap tonight. It's only Christmas after all.'

Only Christmas? How can he say that? And how can a pub-date with a potential brother-in-law be more important than coming to Uncle Terence's with me?

I therefore informed Simon that I no longer wish to meet him this evening as I have far too much preparation to do, and no longer wish to swap presents.

This led to full scale hostilities and him complaining about all kinds of things, including stinky Stanley (he doesn't stink). 'It's me or the dog.' Simon had actually said, in the midst of our heated conversation about Christmas lunch, when I asked if he was at least going to pop in to Mum and Dad's for pre-dinner drinks. I'm not sure if he was being funny or not.

I no longer have a boyfriend.

Git.

I cannot believe it. I was so close to being able to stun my mother into silence. To turn up with a proper man-date, but Simon has spoiled it.

Also, just remembered other disadvantage of breaking up with Simon – I didn't have time to shop at lunch time as I was too heartbroken to buy sausage rolls for party. Who can think of food at a time like that?

Looking on the bright side though, this year for Uncle T's party, and Christmas dinner, I still have a plus-one. Stanley! He snores, passes wind and likes to try to stick his tongue in my mouth when I'm talking, but you know what? I love him. Sometimes a dog is a way better bet than a man.

2 p.m., 24 December

Disaster! Point 1 on my list is not looking good. I cannot find my flaming Christmas jumper anywhere, despite urgent search last night and again this morning before setting off for work.

I think Uncle Terence started the obligatory Christmas

jumper tradition because he knew that we would all get hot and need to strip off at some point. When I was at junior school I thought it was funny, now I'm over thirty having a red nose adorning my boobs isn't quite as hilarious. However, not wearing said jumper will leave me feeling naked and exposed – I will be the centre of attention, which must be avoided at all costs.

I have left it a little late to buy a new Christmas jumper. I've been in every supermarket and clothes shop and I am now in the pound shop. I might have to settle for a hot-chick T-shirt, or a 'bargain buy' Rudolf that looks like a cross-eyed donkey. Decisions, decisions. I have never been good under pressure, plus the only antlers left are the ones in the pet shop (I checked in there in case they had a jumper that would fit an Irish Wolfhound or some other giant breed, that could be modified for human use). Said antlers are more suited to a Labrador. I might have to buy some for Stanley instead.

4 p.m., 24 December

Stanley has just wolfed down half of the sausage rolls that I had home-baked (well, shop-bought from the late shop next to the beauty salon. They were a bit scuffed up which makes them look more authentically homemade, but also meant they were reduced to a bargain price). We are all expected to contribute, and in the past I have stuck to multiple bottles of bubbly and cut price stuffed dates, but this year I am rather skint. This is mainly because (1) I lent Simon the snake the money to buy his father a rather expensive bottle of malt whisky, and his mother a ridiculously expensive bottle of perfume, and (2) I bought him a gaming station. It was in the sale, but still cost way more than I'd ever spend on a toy, but I don't think they will take it back. I see a New Year filled with trying to work out what *Call of Duty* is actually about, and then settling for a romp with Sonic. As I no longer have a boyfriend, snogging Sonic could be as good as it gets on New Year's Eve.

Frankie says I'm too generous, I've always retorted that the giving not receiving is the best bit about Christmas. I'm beginning to think I might need to rethink that one.

So, anyway, I bought two bottles of Prosecco on offer, one as a reward for surviving Christmas, and one to take. Plus some savouries. Half of which have been scoffed.

I now don't have time to nip down to Tesco Extra to replenish supplies, and wash and iron my hair, and get dressed, so I am going to have to cut the remaining sausage rolls into halves and pretend they are sophisticated snacks.

I'm also going to have to check for teeth marks.

Maybe a dog date isn't a much better bet than a man?

6 p.m., 24 December

Yay! I have found my jumper and antlers! I've just dug out the spare Christmas gift bag that I kept in case of emergencies, and *voilà!* There they were. Along with some leftover stuffed dates (last year's disaster) and some shrivelled up mistletoe.

I've also come up with perfect reason to keep away from fresh mistletoe! I just googled, more out of desperation than real hope, and it is poisonous to dogs, and I have Stanley. We don't want vomiting, drooling and diarrhoea in the vicinity of Uncle Terence's first editions, do we? I never thought I would say this, in response to those three words, but ... *result!*

'What the hell is that, Daisy?' Frankie is lurking in my doorway, a drink in her hands, pointing at my list which is pinned to the wardrobe. Along with a photo of Simon with a heart shaped hole cut out of his stomach, and a big cross over the 'sausage rolls'. She is looking very *Ab Fab* and is struggling to sound indignant, she's laughing too much. She starts to pull my list off the wardrobe, then pauses and spins back round to stare at me. 'Fuck me, you really do take this family party thing seriously! Great jumper, not so sure about the twigs growing out of your head though.'

'Antlers!'

'I need to come and see this!'

'No, you don't. And you haven't got a Christmas jumper.'

'And does this,' she peels Simon off the door, prods her finger through the hole in his chest, then rotates him slowly, 'mean you haven't got a date?'

'Well, yeah.'

'Well, nor have I.' She grins, wickedly. 'I can be your date!'

'I'm taking Stanley.' Stanley dives under the bed.

'Who the fuck is Stanley? Have you been two-timing Simon?' She gives a low whistle. 'Dark horse!'

I sigh. 'Stanley is the dog I've agreed to foster over the holidays.'

'Oh.' She looks disappointed, then frowns. 'How did I not know about this?'

'I smuggled him in, I knew you'd like him once you got to know him.' It's her flat, and I really should have asked her, but I couldn't risk her saying no. Stanley can't spend Christmas in a kennel.

'Whatever.' Frankie suddenly smiles. 'Well, you can take me too then! Pleeeeeeease!'

'Where's Tarquin?' I look at her with suspicion. She had a night of lust planned, like you do on Christmas eve if you're a normal person and have a boyfriend, which is why she's glammed up.

'I told him to fuck off.' She downs her drink. 'He started a sentence with 'if you really cared about me', and it all went downhill from there. He needs to get a life.'

She sounds a bit sulky.

'He is trying to, Frankie, with you.'

'I'm not ready, I'd be bored within a week and so would he. Can I come?'

I look at Stanley, who is peeking out from under the bed. He stares back, resignedly.

'It's full of old people, and books.'

'You should get a career in sales, oh hang on, you have! Please, it'll be fun. I can do old people.'

I'm sure she can. 'You'll have to promise to behave and not put a straw in the vat of mulled wine.'

'Promise. I won't.'

She probably will.

'And not propose to Uncle T?'

'Is he rich?'

'Very, but he's probably married at the moment. I can't remember. You mustn't try and steal him!'

'Okay.' She puts on her sweet and innocent smile. But I know she's not either.

'Come on then,' I sigh, I haven't got time to argue, 'I'm taking my car and getting a taxi back.'

'Cool. Can I wear your antlers?'

Chapter 3

So, I have arrived at the party minus a boyfriend, and plus a dog and a flatmate. And now Ollie frigging Mr Perfect Cartwright is here.

Brilliant.

'Oh my, how lovely to see you, Daisy, sweetheart!' Uncle Terence manages to catch the plate (minus most of the sausage rolls), put his foot on Stanley's lead, flick most of the pastry off my jumper with his silk handkerchief and kiss me on both cheeks without breaking into a sweat. 'Splendid jumper, by the way!'

Stanley is so shocked he stops licking my toes, sits down and stares.

Uncle Terence is a bit of an enigma. He's rather debonair, the only man in the village who can pull off a bowtie and is a kind of cross between a cuddly uncle and a London man about town. Yes, I know, it's hard to imagine until you meet him. I've also absolutely no idea how old he is, except he's older than me and not as old as my mother. I also know he used to run a literary agency which he thought he'd hand over to Ollie (he actually is *his* uncle) until Ollie's dad persuaded his son that the medical profession was a much worthier cause.

'Thank you! Looking forward to the party!' I flash my new-lipstick smile, and he looks impressed – it looks like the magazine was right, it was well worth spending all that money on. I reckon it cost more than the entire contents of my make-up drawer.

'Oh, my goodness, they look a bit pasty, don't they?' My mother picks up a sausage roll and eyes it suspiciously, before dropping it behind a pile of books and finally forgetting about Simon and my pompous prick comment offers her cheek for a kiss.

At least she's been distracted from the lack of boyfriend.

'Oh darling, what happened to your boyfriend? Tell me again!' Bugger. Spoke too soon. Mum peers around me, as though I might actually have brought him and forgotten.

'He had to cancel, I told you, things came up!'

'Oh no. Such a disappointment.' For a moment her face falls, then she chirps up. 'Never mind, we'll find you another nice young man. Sadie at Number 17 has a lovely son, he's a dentist, always handy to know a good dentist! Don't you think so, Terence?'

'Far too boring for a bright young thing like our Daisy.' Terence winks at me. 'No hurry is there my dear? Get your career up and running before you go for all that nonsense, eh?'

'Oh, my goodness, yes, we forgot to tell you.' He's now set Mum's mind off in a new direction, which I'm not sure is a good thing. 'Daisy has got another job!' Terence raises an eyebrow. 'She works for the *Hunslip and Over Widgley Local Guardian*, she's in charge of promotions and marketing you know. They headhunted her, a proper job!'

'Really?' Uncle T whispers in my ear.

'Small ads, not exactly proper.' I whisper back, as my mother carries on regardless.

'No?' Uncle T studies me for a moment, then smiles. 'Well, what is proper, my dear? What would you really like to do?'

'I'm not quite sure yet.' I scan the room and am quite relieved that Ollie seems to have disappeared from view. With any luck he's gone home. It's just so bloody embarrassing, the way my mother still keeps trying to throw us together when our lives have gone in totally opposite directions. Why on earth would the hugely successful Ollie, with his glamorous girlfriends and on-track life even want to talk to me, let alone father my babies?

'Oh, she'll soon be editor, won't you Daisy!' My mother has high expectations. Terence merely raises an eyebrow.

'You can do whatever you want my dear, you know. You're awfully clever, you always were such a bright girl.' He pats my hand, then hands me the end of Stanley's lead back. 'And who needs a date, when you've got a dog?'

'Exactly!' I told you Uncle Terence was nice. Very nice.

'Back in a jiffy, just going to stir the mulled wine dear girl, then I've got a gorgeous original edition to show you. Quite a find, a real gem, and I know you of all people will appreciate it!' He winks.

'*Fab!*' I grin back at Uncle T.

'Ollie has a proper date, you know!' Mum nudges me in my ribs.

'What a surprise.' I mutter. Ollie has a date for every occasion apparently. How does he do it? Every year, according to my mother and Vera, Ollie flaming Cartwright has a different woman in tow.

'Vera thinks he might even marry this one!'

I frown. This raises the stakes as far as my mother is concerned.

'Such a shame you two couldn't get together, we were so sure you'd get on well when you were little, your first kiss!' She's gone a bit swoony. 'I hope you haven't missed your chance!'

I admit it. Ollie and I have snogged more than once, it wasn't just that drunken fumble under the mistletoe thirteen years ago.

He kissed me when we were six years old, when he was Joseph to my Mary in the Nativity at the village hall – egged on I think by our mothers. Honestly, what kind of parents encourage that kind of behaviour in innocent children? So, I battered him with the baby Jesus. A plastic version, obviously. I hit him pretty hard, though to give him his due he didn't cry or hit me back, but he shouldn't have kissed me.

He didn't try again for another 12 years.

He was a pain in the backside when we were kids. He once pulled my bathing suit down and tried to drown me when we were semi-naked in his paddling pool ('Just playing, how sweet,' said Mum), then progressed to blowing out my birthday cake candles before I could ('Hilarious,' said his mum).

These days he is even more of a pain, though at least I haven't actually had to see him in person. Well, until now. When Frankie spotted him across the crowded room and pointed out that not only is he successful, rich and has his life in order – he is also a tiny bit dishy. How did that happen?

Ollie passed all his exams, attended the medical school at Oxford University and is hugely successful and well thought of (according to my mother). He is very serious and always has an attractive, clever girlfriend with him whenever he comes home (according to his own mother – who then passes the information on to my mother).

I, on the other hand, buggered up my exams, did a rubbish degree at a university I'd only heard of through Clearing, still live within the same postcode we were brought up in, lost my job at the local vets after behaving irresponsibly with a scalpel when they tried to euthanise an incontinent cat (I think threatening to report me for GBH if I didn't leave the building immediately was a bit OTT though), and so foster rescue dogs and have just managed to get a pretty naff job on the local rag.

How can my mother possibly still think we're compatible when he's everything I'm not? Have it all Ollie pleases his parents, is smart, has a life plan, a partner, but absolutely no sense of humour (from what I have observed), whereas I have no idea what I'll be doing tomorrow, let alone in five years' time.

'You were such happy, chubby, little things.'

'We were toddlers, Mum. Toddlers are always fat and happy.'

'Well, you're not now, are you! You need to do an egg timer test.'

'What?'

'I was reading all about them when I was having my car serviced, they have a wonderful set of magazines in there you know! Not just about cars, although there were car ones as well for your father, and a golf one.'

'Why do I need to do an egg timer test?'

'To see how much longer you've got before they go off dear! Then you can decide if it's worth freezing a pack for future use.' She pats my hand. 'I mean, now Ollie is off the market.'

'Mum,' I sigh. 'Ollie was your fantasy, not mine.' Well, he was my fantasy for one brief night after that snog. Well, maybe several nights if I'm honest. But that was all. I mean, at eighteen it doesn't always take much does it? 'There are other men, and anyway, I might not want one.'

'Not want a man?' She frowns. 'Oh my! That explains everything! You're a lesbian! Oh, darling, why didn't you say?' She hugs me. 'Everybody loves a lesbian these days.'

'No, I'm not.' I struggle free.

'How exciting! Is it that Frankie girl?' She frowns. 'Is she bi? She's still bothering Ollie, you know!'

'No, Mum, she's not, she's straight, she's got a boyfriend and I—'

'And you can get a sperm donor these days, you can be Mummy and Mum, or Ma, or Mom!'

'Mum, stop!' I lower my voice to a hiss, as everybody else has stopped talking – just not her. 'I am not a lesbian, but I still might not want to get married, and I might not want a baby!'

'Oh rubbish.' She shakes her head. 'Of course, you want a baby. And you need one while I'm still young enough to push a pram, and your dad can still play football with him!'

We seem to have made a massive jump here, from egg testing to kids hurtling round the garden kicking a ball. There also seems to be an assumption on sex. 'What if it's a girl?' I say, which I shouldn't have done because it suggests there *might* be a child in my not so distant future.

'They play, too! Honestly, I thought you youngsters understood all about equal opportunities, you kicked a ball around at school, you know! I mean, you weren't exactly George Best, but ...'

I'm about to ask who George Best is, then decide it might be best not to.

Zara Stoneley

'Daisy, how lovely to see you!' Vera kisses my cheek and hands me a glass of mulled wine. 'Any idea who that tall girl with black hair is? She's rather monopolising Ollie!'

'Oh don't worry about her,' says my mother, 'she's bi, she's already got a boyfriend and a girlfriend!'

'Back in a jiffy, Stanley needs a drink!' I take this opportunity to run off, before my imaginary (and rather more interesting than in real-life) sex life is dissected.

'Oh my God, I need to do something, I can't go on like this for the rest of my life, can I Stan?' I pass Stanley the sausage out of the mini toad-in-the-hole and pop the rest in my mouth. He takes it off me delicately, puts it on the floor than examines it for signs of poison. 'I mean look at me, and you!' He looks straight at me, munching his treat, a sadness in his brown eyes. 'Sorry, I love you, you know that, but you weren't supposed to be my plus one.' I sigh. 'You're not even mine, you're on loan.'

I am over thirty, and I've brought a dog to Uncle Terence's Christmas Eve party. And he's not even my dog. I'm fostering him until a suitable home can be found.

It isn't the fact that my boyfriend ducked out of Christmas, and my life, at the very last minute. He was just the straw that broke the camel's back so to speak. It is everything.

My mother will, of course, be disappointed that Simon isn't with me. And that I still show no signs of getting engaged, let alone married or with-child, and she won't waste any time in telling me and everybody else in hearing range. But it's not like a man is the missing piece in the jigsaw of my life. The whole bloody jigsaw is a mess, it's a mishmash of several different puzzles at the moment. Or at least that's how it feels. And I need to work out what the finished picture is supposed to look like.

'Oh God, Mum is heading this way again!' I adjust my antlers, straighten my rather fine Rudolf jumper and take a swig of mulled wine. 'Brace yourself, Stanley, this is my "must try harder" moment!' Stanley stares at me, his lovely brown eyes look worried. 'Me, not you, there's nothing at all wrong with you.' I reassure him. 'Well, there is, but we can talk about that later. Minor point!' He doesn't look convinced.

Stanley and I are huddled together in the corner of the rather lovely bookshop. It's cram packed with old furniture, books and antiques that have seen far better days. The air is heavy with the smell of leather, of new and old books, of dust, and potpourri. And mulled wine and sausage rolls.

On any other day it would be heaven, but I know that all my shortcomings are just about to be broadcast. One of them being Stanley.

'Long time no see, Daisy!' I am so focused on watching my mother approaching that I haven't noticed Ollie sneak up on the other side. 'On your own?'

'No, I've got Stanley!' I wave my glass a little too enthusiastically and splatter my reindeer.

He glances around, looking puzzled.

'Stanley!' I point at Stanley, who wags his tail rather

too enthusiastically for my liking. I was sure I'd explained to him that Ollie was the enemy. A huge part of my 'must try harder' problem.

Ollie glances down. 'Ah, a dog.' He raises an eyebrow and the corner of his mouth twitches. If he laughs I might have to throw my wine at him, which would be a shame as I have already wasted quite a bit of it and it is rather fine wine. 'Lots to be said for sticking with a dog.' He tickles Stanley behind his ear, and the traitor wiggles his body in ecstasy.

'So good of you to make it this year! No lives that need saving in the Third World?'

'I'm sure there are, but I'm based back here now and I'm not on call.'

'Oh.' There's an awkward silence.

'Room for me?' He nods his head at the space on the seat next to me, and I'm suddenly feeling all hot and bothered. I've just realised that I am sitting in the very spot where we had our drunken snog all those years ago. Where he plonked himself down without asking. Oh Lord-y. I shift up a bit, and before I can object, he's plopped himself in the gap, his warm thigh pressed against mine. 'Bit of a squeeze these days.' He grins.

'We've grown.' I swallow. Not quite sure where to look, but unable to not look if you know what I mean. My thighs have spread, his have kind of muscled up and gone all firm and take up more space. His chest is also broader, his jawline squarer, his lips still ...

'No mistletoe, then?' He glances up and grins, hopefully he's not cottoned onto my under-the-eyelashes sideways staring.

'Oh no, ha-ha, Uncle T must be slipping, thank heavens for that, eh!'

He raises an eyebrow.

'Seeing as you're practically married and everything.'

'And everything?' The eyebrow quirks higher and his dimples deepen. I'd forgotten about his dimples, right next to his full lips, nestled there in a very tempting, kiss-me kind of way.

Oh bugger. Pull yourself together Daisy. 'Babies, weddings, saving lives and all that! You're a responsible adult now, aren't you?' I try to shift up a bit, but there is absolutely nowhere to go. The seat has shrunk, it has to have done. I was never that skinny. Although he was, with lanky long legs.

Shit, he's thrown one arm along the back of the sofa. I really do feel hot now. He is quite sexy, and he seems to be sending waves of testosterone or some other kind of hormone out in my direction. Along with fingers, which seem to have accidentally brushed against my shoulder. I blame my oversized jumper, which keeps slipping.

It must be something they teach them in medical school. I mean, I know I did snog him last time we were sat here, but we were hormone-ridden teens with alcohol-laced blood. This is different.

Flaming heck, I need a fan, or something.

I hike the jumper back onto my shoulder.

'And what about you?' His voice is deeper than it was. Unnerving.

'Me? Me?' I fan myself with my hand, trying to just make it look like a casual wave and not a life-saving manoeuvre. 'Oh me, I'm the same, you know, no babies, no saving lives, unless you call a *'would like to meet'* ad a public service, ha-ha.'

'No boyfriend with you tonight?' He chuckles. 'What was his name? Josh, Josh the slosh, that was it!'

It's like somebody has grabbed me around the chest and is trying to squeeze the life out of me. The gasp escapes before I can stop it.

'Daisy?' Ollie is giving me an odd look. 'Are you okay?'

I am not okay. I am *so* not okay. My forehead is clammy and I feel sick. I stare at him and try to hold it all in.

Luckily, I do not feel at all like snogging Ollie now. Kissing is the last thing on my mind. I want to thump him. Or scream and run away.

Josh is history, Josh is a name I never want to hear again. My lust has flown, now all I feel is mild panic.

'Daisy?' He prods me, so I swallow down the horrible taste in my mouth and try to think of a witty retort.

'Oh, there you are, darling! I wondered where you were hiding!' Whilst I have been distracted, my mother has sneaked up.

'I'm not hiding, Mum.' This has to be the first time in my entire life that I have been pleased my mother has barged into a conversation.

'You're never going to find another man if you're hiding next to,' she squints so she can read the books on the nearest shelf, 'Ancient Relics and Wonders of the World!'

'I'm not going to find another man at Uncle T's party, anyway, am I?'

She ignores me. 'Look who I've found!' She hustles Vera into our little group. 'And you've already seen lovely Ollie of course!' She beams at Ollie in a proud mother kind of way and pats his shoulder. She should adopt him. 'Vera was just telling me all about your new girlfriend!'

'You have got a *new* girlfriend?' I have to ask him.

He shifts uncomfortably. Probably because of the way he's sandwiched into the seat with me, and that fact that when I turned slightly to face him, I nearly elbowed him in the nose.

How the hell do I get out of this seat without being too obvious? I feel like the last sardine in the tin, the one that has been squashed into the remaining tiny space that is too small for it. I need prising out with a fork.

'Daisy is on her own again, aren't you dear?' Mum has carried on oblivious. 'Single and independent, she might be gay you know!'

'Mother, I didn't say ...' I glare at Ollie, daring him to snigger. He doesn't. He's not really a sniggering type these days it would appear.

'Might be? You don't know?' A tall, slim blonde girl is peering at me as though I'm a particularly fascinating first edition. 'How interesting! Are you bi?' Then she glares at Ollie, who has his elbows squashed against his sides, after trying to remove his arm discretely from the back of the chair.

'Oh, have you met Juliet, dear? Ollie's girlfriend!' Vera announces this as though he's just won the sack race at school (strangely appropriate, but I beat him hands down at the egg and spoon) and he's now showing off his trophy. 'This is Daisy,' she drops her voice to a confidential level, 'she's young, free and single again! Aren't you, dear? Or are you having a thing with that girl?'

'No, I'm not, she's my flatmate. I am lovely and single, free to do what I want, shag who I want, get drunk and ...' They are all staring at me. Bloody hell, it gets hot when you're wrapped in a jumper and squeezed between a man and the arm of a leather chair. 'Well, obviously, I don't shag around, but I am free to kiss anybody I want under the mistletoe this year!'

'Terence?' Questions Ollie, drily. Did I mention that he appears to have turned into a very 'dry' type? I'm not quite sure if he's still got a proper sense of humour, it seems to have evaporated as he's got older, I suppose it isn't allowed now he's a consultant. And it is not hip.

'Definitely!' I don't actually mean this, but there really aren't many people at all at his Christmas parties that you would want to snog, or touch, or even air kiss.

Juliet smiles, and looks down her long nose at me. She has perfect long, blonde, sleek hair and a long, slim, sleek body. Long has never been my thing.

She leans forward, well down, as though she's greeting a child, and air-kisses.

'Lovely to meet you, Daisy! How cute!' *Mwah-mwah.* 'Well done! I work in medicine, what do you do?' It's not just the words she uses, it's the way she says them – in a very posh and very serious tone, that makes me feel like a child.

'Oh, how lovely.' I have a bad habit of imitating people's accents when I'm in awe. 'Medicine, fancy that!'

'She works in communications,' chimes in Vera.

'And you're a doctor?' My mother frowns.

'PR!' Adds Juliet. 'In medicine!'

'Smashing, ha-ha, how clever!' I say.

'Christ, so you're the one they wheel out to apologise when there's a cock-up? Unexpected deaths and all that.' Frankie has arrived and is now perched on the arm of the chair next to me. She drapes her arm round my shoulders, though she only has eyes for Ollie. She's like a cheetah, waiting for her moment. I'm not sure if it's the moment to leap on Ollie, or the moment to slay Juliet.

My nervous laugh is met with stony silence. Juliet is twitching, Frankie is positively purring.

'We issue statements to the press, if that's what you mean.' Her tone has cooled.

'Ah that's what they call them!' Frankie grins, then glances at her mobile phone, which has launched into a rendition of 'Stop The Cavalry'. 'Duty calls!'

'Splendid.' I say, to fill the gap as we all watch her sink into a leather armchair, her phone to her ear.

Juliet is not mollified. 'I spearhead the PR campaigns.'

'A bit like your job, Daisy, but people adore you, you're not trying to wriggle your way out of being sued for incompetence!' Chimes in my mother, who is using a plate of mini burgers as her way into the conversation. Sometimes I could hug her. 'Daisy's a journalist now! Canapé?'

'Ah! Super, thanks.' I grab a handful and try to move the conversation on from my sadly lacking career. 'You're in medicine as well, aren't you Ollie?' He raises an eyebrow, which is fair enough. He knows I know what he does, my annual date at Uncle T's makes it impossible to avoid his accomplishments. But I was just trying to shut my mother up before she started to expand upon my not-so-wonderful career.

'I thought you were in law?' A faint frown lines his brow. How is it fair that frowning can be attractive on a man, but a disaster on a woman? 'A barrister?'

'Oh no, no, you must have misheard.'

'Maybe father was confused. I swear he said ...'

'Oliver's on the specialist register now, so clever, aren't you, darling?' Juliet buts in, which is rather fortunate. 'That's how we met, at work.' She giggles and tries to link an arm through his, which is tricky. 'And what did you say you did, Maisie?'

'Daisy, it's Daisy.' I might have to thump her. 'Oh, nothing so highbrow!'

'I wouldn't say it's highbrow, just making a living like everybody else.' Says Ollie. He shifts self-consciously and manages to extricate himself from Juliet's grasp. 'Just part of a team. Not exactly rocket science.' He gives a self-depreciating laugh and Juliet nudges him.

'More like brain surgery, ha-ha!'

'Not exactly.' He looks uncomfortable, and finally manages to lever himself up off the chair. Released, I nearly slither off onto the floor but manage to grab Frankie on the way and scramble to my feet.

'Nonsense, darling! It practically is!' She sounds a bit like Vera, I can see what drew him to her.

He has gone highbrow though, all home counties.

'That's enough about us though Maisie, what about you?' She is not to be distracted, even though I swear she's not listening to a word I say.

'Daisy works for the *Hunslip and Over Widgley Local Guardian.*' Uncle Terence has crept up unnoticed and pats my arm protectively. It's getting pretty packed in my little corner now, soon our elbows will be squished against our sides and we won't be able to drink out of our glasses. 'For now! She's quietly planning world domination though.'

'What a mouthful!' Juliet's eyes are wide open.

'Known as *HOWL* for short.' Ollie looks amused, and I'm not sure if I should punch him or smile. I smile, then Juliet guffaws. Well, it's more like a neigh.

What on earth were they thinking when they named the paper that? Why not *Over Widgley and Hunslip*? Or ditch the *Local* bit?

'Oh, my goodness, how hilarious!' Juliet is gasping for breath, wiping tears from her eyes.

I want to tell her it's not that funny, but that would be rude.

'Oh, I'm going to have to tweet that! I really am! Are they on twitter? I'll tag them!'

'Still dogging?' Ollie raises an eyebrow, and glances down at Stanley who is now lying on his back, legs akimbo. The *HOWL* thing was his fault, so I can't exactly forgive him for deflecting the conversation.

'Dogging! They do that here?' Juliet pauses, mid tweet. 'Oh my God, I need to tweet that as well! Do they like, advertise in your paper? Or is it really hush-hush?'

'Ha-ha!' I can feel myself going red, but I am not going to be belittled. I also would quite like to punch her on the nose or point out to everybody her unusual level of interest in potential dogging sites. Instead I decide to take a mature attitude and ignore her. 'I help out with animal welfare.' I tell Juliet, who I don't think is actually that interested. She's too busy brushing imaginary fluff off her boyfriend's shirt. It's like watching a monkey groom its mate. But at least it is stopping her tapping on her mobile.

'Oh, you rescue rhino's, do you? That's so brave, so, so visionary!'

'Dogs.'

'Dogs?'

'I foster rescued dogs, street dogs, well I don't actually go and rescue them myself, I help rehabilitate them and foster. I do have an actual job as well you know, I can't just go racing off round the world.' Although right now, that might be an idea. In fact it could be quite a good idea. I must make a mental note to think about this one later.

'Oh. Like woof-woof dogs?' She looks at me blankly, as though a rhino is every day, but a dog is harder to comprehend.

'Like Stanley!' I point to Stanley, whose sleeping on his back routine was a ruse so that I wouldn't notice him sneak off. He is now skulking under a table with what looks like a turkey leg in his mouth.

'What is it?'

'Erm, a dog.' Surely, she's not so fixated on safari animals that she can't recognise a dog?

'What type?'

'Stanley is a street dog.' I say proudly. 'From Spain. I think. He had fleas, ticks, mange and worms!'

'Oh.' She stares, then wrinkles her nose. 'Have you thought about having him groomed? My mother takes her dog every week.' She looks at me, horror dawning and takes a step back. 'You don't have fleas, do you? I'm allergic.'

'No! He was sorted when I met him. But I have helped rehabilitate him!'

'Maybe not a very good example.' Says Ollie, with a twitch of smile.

'Part rehabilitated. He's a work in progress.'

'So, no rhino's then? Tigers?' Juliet says hopefully.

'They wouldn't fit in my flat.' I point out.

'No garden I suppose.' Says Ollie, and I'm not sure if he's taking the piss out of me, or Juliet, or being serious.

'Very small balcony. There would be health and safety issues. Ha-ha!' I wish I could stop laughing nervously but being shoved in front of Ollie seems to have that effect on me. I'm perfectly normal in other company. Just not Christmas party company.

'So, you still live *here?*' Juliet sounds incredulous. She sips her drink delicately and I resist the urge to neck mine. I am well aware that my life is pretty crap at the moment, but ten minutes in the company of this pair and I feel worse than ever.

'Yep.'

'Ah,' she looks as though she's struggling for something to say, then suddenly smiles triumphantly, 'so you play polo! Everybody does, don't they in the countryside! My step-brother lives in Cheshire, plays polo all the time, so exciting!' As she is excited it seems a shame to disappoint her.

'Oh yes, polo! Great! All that galloping, hot men, chasing a ball! Yes, of course I play, ha-ha! Definitely.'

Ollie raises an eyebrow. 'Wow, you have been busy, I thought you hated horses.'

'Hated horses? Me? Never!'

'I'll have to challenge you to a chukka or two next time we're up this way then.'

'Splendid.' What the hell is chucking?

'My brother plays in Argentina a lot, do you?'

'Oh no, no, not enough time. Dogs to rescue! Oh sorry, phone buzzing! You know what it's like, all work no play when you're a journalist!' It isn't, well not here. Unless there's been a mass food poisoning incident and half the village have been rushed to hospital. But I cannot take this much longer. Just hearing about fabulous Ollie and his fabulous life has been bad enough in previous years, but actually being in the same room as him and his silly girlfriend is making me want to scream. Or run away and hide in a corner. With a book. A book never lets you down, a good book, bad book, any book, I don't care.

I'm just about to dash off, when there's a shriek.

'Oh my God, Maisie!' For a moment, I think Juliet is about to collapse, her hand is on my arm, she's grasping, long polished nails sticking in. I stare down, slightly aghast. It's a bit like being grabbed by a bird of prey wearing nail varnish.

'Daisy.' I say it automatically.

'My God!' She clasps her throat melodramatically. 'How absolutely awful.' She flashes her mobile in front of my face, then waves it in front of Ollie's.

His reactions are quicker than mine. He grabs her wrist, so that the phone stills and he can read it. 'That can't be right. I'm sure it can't. Never read anything so ridiculous. Don't worry, Daisy.'

I wasn't worrying, until he said don't worry.

'What?' I grab the phone from her, but as I'm reading, she's shouting out.

'How absolutely awful, to lose your job on Christmas Eve! What on earth will you do, poor Maisie?'

'Job? You've lost your job?' Mum has heard and scurried back over to my side and is trying to extract the phone from my frozen fingers.

I stare at Ollie, I can't breathe. There's a massive lump blocking my throat.

If I'd thought the last couple of days have been rubbish, this is the cherry on top of the bloody cake.

Shit. How low can I go? I've cocked up my career plan, been dumped, and now even lost my crap dead-end job. I'm overweight, live in a rabbit hutch, and I'm staring at the man who has it all worked out.

I hate him.

'Even my hair's a mess.' My voice has gone as wobbly as my legs.

'Hair?' He looks very concerned, and it makes me want to cry.

'Come and sit down, you poor girl.' Terence puts one hand on my elbow and the other in the small of my back and steers me towards the corner of the shop where he houses the special editions. 'You're in shock. Somebody get a brandy.'

Even feeling like I do I have to take a deep breath and let the smell of old leather and special words (yes, they do have a smell) filter their way into my body. I'm not sure if I want to cry, or curl up with a book and escape, pretend I'm somewhere else.

I also feel a bit heady, which could be dust, words of wisdom, or the goldfish-bowl sized brandy glass he's pushed into my hand. The fumes alone are making me splutter.

He gently prises the phone from my fingers and hands it over to Ollie wordlessly.

'You've not been sacked, Daisy.' Ollie crouches down in front of me and looks into my eyes. He's got the lovely warm brown eyes he had when he was Joseph to my Mary. Before they turned naughty and he kissed me. He was mischievous then, he's not now, he's all earnest and caring, but he actually looks a bit like the Ollie I knew. He looks like the eighteen-year-old Ollie with the luscious lips and the nervous smile. Maybe I don't hate him.

'But Juliet said ...'

'It says here,' his tone is firm. It's quite commanding and authoritative, I can see why he's so successful. 'That the three local newspapers are merging. The office is closing, but there will be opportunities for all staff to apply for jobs and no compulsory redundancies are expected. None.'

'Well, that's okay then, none!' My voice sounds pathetic and all wavery to my ears, but it's the best I can do. I say it again, trying for a stronger tone. 'None.'

Uncle Terence pats my hand absent-mindedly, but he's frowning at Ollie. 'How the hell can they not have announced it in the office, that's not on is it? Downright underhand if you ask me. No emails, nothing, Daisy, darling?'

'Erm, maybe I might have missed a meeting while I was writing a missing rabbit ad. It explains why David was avoiding me when I left.'

Something nudges my left leg. Something damp lands on my left knee. It's Stanley, with a slice of ham.

I stroke his ears and stare at Ollie. 'It definitely says there are jobs?'

He nods. 'Definitely.' Our gazes lock and his is so intent I'm spun back to that Christmas all those years ago. When it was just him and me, and nothing and nobody else mattered. When all I could see were his eyes, when he tasted of whisky and mince pies, when the scent of cloves and cinnamon mingled with the citrus of his aftershave. And now I'm not sure what is past and what is present. I just know I'm glad he'd here.

'Mince pies, anybody?' I blink my way back to the present feeling a bit unnerved, just as Mum waves a tray under Stanley's nose, so I cover his eyes.

'He's not allowed dried fruit, it's poisonous!' She waves one tantalising close and his nose twitches. 'Don't you dare, Mum!' I kiss Uncle Terence on the cheek and down the rest of the brandy in one gulp. Which could be a mistake. The fiery liquid burns its way down my throat and insides and brings tears to my eyes and makes me cough and splutter alarmingly. 'Thank you.' I blink like an owl in sunlight.

'You're welcome, my darling. You're okay?'

'Definitely.' I nod vigorously to prove the point. 'Sorry, it was a bit of a shock, but I'm fine. All ready to party!'

Uncle T smiles. 'That's my girl. Oh look – mistletoe!'

Ollie blushes, and just like that he's the teenager I used to know. Except the grown-up Ollie is even more gorgeous.

He glances at me, the corner of his mouth quirked up into the hint of a smile. A shared secret, and my stomach does a little flip of anticipation.

I want to touch him, kiss him, see if he still tastes the same.

I mustn't!

I scoop up my dog and take a hasty step away from Uncle T. 'Come on, Stanley, let's mingle.' Then I flee.

Chapter 4

'Sorry, Dais, I'm going to have to whizz.' Frankie is hugging me as she speaks, she's all flushed and smiley. Or maybe it's me that's flushed and her that's just smiley. 'Thanks so much for letting me come, not had so much fun in years, but Tarquin just called.'

'He did?' Frankie and Tarquin have quite an explosive relationship. She's always so controlled and restrained, right up until the moment she screams at him or throws something heavy. I think he winds her up on purpose, their relationship seems to thrive on the emotional highs and lows.

'He's sent a car, and roses! He's booked a hotel for the night to apologise.' She winks. Break-up make-up is the way they roll.

'That's nice.'

She glances across the room at Ollie. 'Shame he's got that

cow in tow, he seems nice.' She sighs. 'Well he's dishy so who cares if he is or not? You'll have to give me his deets!'

'Frankie! You're just about to make up with Tarquin!'

She grins. 'He's an orphan, he'll have nobody to eat Christmas dinner with if he doesn't make up with me!'

'Really? That's so sad.'

'Sad? Cheeky cow, what's sad about having to spend Christmas day with me!'

'I didn't mean that, you know I didn't.' I glare at her. 'The orphan stuff, not having anybody. That's horrible.'

'He's not an orphan, you dork.' She rolls her eyes. 'He just chooses not to see his fam. So don't go all drippy and nice to him when you see him. I know you, you'll be helping him move in!'

'Oh.'

'Have a great Christmas if I don't see you.' She winks. 'I'm hoping to be tied up on a four-poster bed! I might text your Ollie and see if he wants to make a foursome!'

'Frankie!'

'*Oooo!* You want him for yourself, don't you?'

'No, I don't! You're worse than my mother, anyway he's almost family.'

'Too sexy for family.' Her voice has got that dreamy edge to it again. 'Admit it, he's a hunk.'

'He's a hunk, and he's got a girlfriend! A nearly fiancée. And it's not all about looks you know.' She's being ridiculous. Totally. I do not fancy Oliver Cartwright.

'Ha-ha. Says who?' Frankie smoothes her hair down, the heavy jet-black fringe would make anybody else look like a vampire having a bad day, on her it's cool. 'Me thinks you doth protest too much.'

She doesn't give me time to correct her quote, or protest that I'm not protesting too much. I just don't want to shag Ollie. End of.

Well, okay, there might be a tiny bit of me that wonders what it would be like. Just a tiny bit. Just out of curiosity, because after all he was a bloody good kisser. And now he's cuter than ever. And kind, and I was so tempted to go in for some lip action a few minutes ago.

Frankie strides out of the shop, letting a waft of cold air in, then I hear her whoop and there's a clatter of high heels on the paving stones as she spots the posh car and Tarquin.

The rest of the party passes in a bit of a blur. At one stage, I lose Stanley and rediscover him sharing a chaise longue with Mabel. They look rather sweet, and they're both snoring.

I think I have had a vat of mulled wine, enough mini food to make up a banquet sized portion of full-size offerings and several unscheduled stops under the mistletoe.

Ollie goes back to being boring, stiff Ollie with Juliet – who keeps giving me patronising sorry looks, until Uncle T tempts her to try the mulled wine, and she falls into a pile of *Great Expectations*.

Which makes me snigger, and when Ollie catches me at it the corner of his mouth twitches with what could be a smile. Or wind. Either way, it cheers me up.

Then he and Terence prop her back up and she tries to kiss his face off and plucks at his shirt like a hungry kitten as he steers her out. Probably for a night of passion, if she stays awake.

I bet he's good at that as well. Bugger. Where did that thought come from? I do not want to think about Oliver and his sexual prowess. Not at all. I do not want to even consider the possibility that I have missed out on some brilliant bonking. Not that he would have been that good when we were eighteen. Or even wanted to. It was just a kiss.

She's too tall for him though. I mean, look, she's had to wear ballet pumps and I'm sure she's a high heels girl at heart. Not that he's short, he's just normal height. But she's definitely too tall. It will never last.

Half an hour later, everybody has gone so I prod Stanley awake and let him hoover up crumbs while I'm waiting for my taxi to arrive.

'Don't worry about the job dear girl, that can wait. No checking emails tonight, it's Christmas.' Uncle Terence kisses me on each cheek, continental style.

'Of course, I won't!'

I will.

'Next year will be better, my dear!'

'Of course, it will.' It has to be. If Ollie can do it, then I bloody well can, too.

I hug Stanley close. Ollie has everything, Ollie has the type of life I had assumed I would have. Seeing him tonight has been a bit of a kick in the gut if I'm honest, it's hit me just how much I've been avoiding facing up to all the things that are wrong with my life.

All the things I could make right, if I tried hard enough.

I've let what happened to me when I was eighteen define the rest of my life, define me.

I've let one sad, horrible failure stop me from trying. I've been kidding myself that I'm happy coasting along, accepting what I've got, rather than risk failing again. And even though I can never change what happened in my past, I can change me. What's going to happen in my future. Can't I?

I've got to get my act together, I really have. I deserve so much more than I've got.

I am going to show them. I am going to show bloody Ollie Cartwright, and my mum that I am not a complete failure.

I'm going to prove it to myself.

Chapter 5

Very, very late p.m., 24 December (or early 25 December)

I think not knowing about my imminent loss of job could partly be my own fault. Because my data allowance had nearly run out this morning, I was very sensible (this is part of my sorting my finances out strategy) and turned my mobile data off. Then turned my phone off, because what's the point if you can't check on Twitter and Facebook? Then forgot all about it as I had so much to do (and the lady in the beauty salon won't let me near my mobile until my nails are definitely dry).

This is why I have had no notification of my possible change in circumstances i.e. jobless status. Though I have to admit that I was slightly concerned that nobody *at all* had messaged to wish me a Happy Christmas. I hadn't thought I was *that* unpopular at work, or in general.

There is a delay when I switch my mobile back on, while it fiddles about in hyperspace looking for the Wi-Fi, then it goes berserk. Honestly, it is bleating and tweeting like a sheep that has suddenly spotted its lost flock.

I stare, rather drunkenly, as it bleeps and flashes. It is just like cooking popcorn, gradually the time between bleeps gets longer, until it is safe to open the bag.

There's an unread email. Lots of emails.

There are texts.

Voicemail messages.

I am rather drunk, but I need to read them all, listen to the messages.

Have I really been sacked the day before Christmas? Am I going to start the new year destitute and homeless, relying on my mother (oh my God) to provide shelter and food? Will I have to live in a stable like the baby Jesus (fine, I know he didn't live in a stable, but I'm drunk, and upset, okay?)?

This is so unfair. Even before seeing Ollie at the party tonight and realising just how pathetic my life really is in comparison to what it should have been, I had decided something has to be done.

I was going to kick off next year demanding a better job, or at least a pay rise, so that I could find a better flat. I do love Frankie, but honestly, my room is so small I end up piling all my books in the corners like mini towers of Pisa. One day they will all lean in so far they'll meet in the middle then collapse and kill me in my sleep. I had been determined to be more organised, to budget, to change my life.

And now this.

70

I won't panic. I will be logical about this and start at the beginning – and not with the most recent, and most eye-catching email with the subject HELLLP MAD COLLIE ON MY HANDS. This one is from Carrie, who runs the dog re-homing centre and is Stanley's official guardian. She is slightly unhinged, but very well meaning, and I would normally put her top of the queue. I want to help her, and I want to help any dogs that need helping.

I will also prioritise and ignore Frankie's text '*Oh my fucking God, send ambulance, won't be able to walk tomorrow, make up sex is the best! P.S. Did you get the pompous prick's number just in case?*'

No, I can't ignore it. '*In case of what?*'

'*Injury.*'

This is cryptic. I'm not sure if she means hers, or Tarquin's. I suspect the second, she might be calling on a substitute if he runs out of steam (or something snaps) before she does.

It is very hard to concentrate on possibly life changing emails when all I can think of is Tarquin's dick snapping off, and I am drunk. But it's essential. I need to know the worst-case scenario before I tuck into my Christmas turkey a few hours from now.

The first unread email (after one asking if I've considered a penis extension, another selling support underwear, and the mad collie one) was sent by my boss David approximately five seconds after I left the office. No wonder he was cross with me – it wasn't that he was grumpy about

Christmas, he was waiting for all staff to leave so that he could drop his bombshell.

He'd had his finger poised over the send button as I was waving and wishing him a happy Christmas.

Twat.

Not only is he a bit of a sex predator, he is also spine-less and pathetic. And rude. And a terrible manager. I am sure (given his age) he has been offered a fabulous early retirement package that will mean he can jet off to Spain and never have to face any of us again. Our village is quite small, he would have to face up to all the mutterings and turned backs, the funny looks and rotten eggs. He might well be the headline in the free local newspaper, and he won't want to hang about for that.

I take a deep breath, clutch Stanley to my pyjama clad breast, and click on the email.

It is very brief; he regretfully wishes to inform us that in the New Year the *Hunslip and Over Widgley Local Guardian* will cease trading as an individual entity. He has accepted a retirement package and is moving to Kent (not Spain) and will miss our camaraderie (I won't miss his). A caretaker boss has been appointed and will oversee the operation for the next three months, after which we will have an opportunity to apply for a job within the new organisation. The office will be unavailable from 24 December as the lease has come to an end, all belongings will be packed and sent to a new temporary location for the New Year. Full details attached blah, blah, blah.

Oh my God! You have got to be kidding me? Not only have I lost my job, somebody will be rummaging through my drawers! Have I left anything incriminating on my desk, or anything I'll miss? There were definitely spare tights, spare knickers, a packet of festive Pringles, a collection of pens that clients have given me. Who has been touching them? Has David himself packed the boxes (*eurgh* – I do not want my undies back!)?

Good luck team! Have a great Christmas.

How can he expect us to have a good Christmas now?

There is a very long forwarded message from somebody called James Masters who wants to welcome us to publishing house HQ. There are a lot of words that concern me, like merger, consolidation, and acquisition which I think are best left until the morning and a clear head. I am more than a trifle concerned about the bit buried between the welcome and the Christmas wishes that mentions 'slimming down' and the need for some roles to go during the reorganisation (isn't it a shame it's not so easy for a person? A company can just chisel off and bin the bits it doesn't want. I don't want to be binned, but some parts of my bottom may benefit from this approach as I am rather pear-shaped). The words 'voluntary redundancy' and 'flexible attitude towards suitable positions' have also set my pulse pounding – should I take a redundancy offer and seek out a better job, or risk 'flexibility' meaning I could end up with the promotion I deserve?

There are also lots of attachments, including one

ominously titled 'Application Form'. I think it's time to move on and look at my other messages, I am not in a fit state for attachments.

I also have an email from Eva, who sits across the desk from me. She excels at passive/aggressive and manages to reassure me that there will be a place in the new organisation for such a young dynamic person as myself, whilst making it clear that if I really was dynamic, I'd be working somewhere else already. Brian (desk in the corner) chips in with an invite for drinks between Boxing Day and New Year's Day – for us to discuss strategy and possible legal action (think he's jumping the gun a bit there), and there is a rather formal email hoping I got home safely, wishing me well and offering his services from somebody called Oz, which confuses me. Am I being headhunted? Should I move down under? Is he a stalker? Then after blinking a couple of times I realise it is from O. Z. Cartwright. Ollie.

It is rather nice of him to get in touch, but I'm not quite sure how he can help.

And why isn't he busy bonking his girlfriend? Maybe she passed out before he had chance, unless sex is the one thing he's not good at and it only lasted thirty seconds. Which would be tragic but explain the rapid turnover rate.

Bugger, I have to stop thinking about Ollie and sex. But what the frig am I going to do now?

Apart from wondering what the 'Z' stands for? I never knew Ollie had a middle name, if he ever comes to another Christmas party, I must remember to ask what it is.

I can't help myself, I can't wait until next year! I fire off an email thanking him for his good wishes and asking if his middle name is Zebedee or Ziggy. Either would be quite funny.

I decide it is time to close my laptop and go to sleep. My last thought as I pull my duvet up to my chin, is that I'm bloody glad I didn't suck up to David this morning and beg for a better job before he dropped the bombshell.

5 a.m., Christmas Day, can't sleep

Reasons this newspaper merger is a disaster:

1. The new office is miles away from the old office, and therefore my flat
2. My savings are practically non-existent and will run out soon so if they don't take me on, I am screwed
3. Winter has to be the worst time of the year to find a new job if I fail to keep my job (or apply for voluntary redundancy)
4. I am rubbish at filling in application forms and interviews. (I tend to start to answer a question, veer off course and forget what it was. I also get panic attacks, sweaty palms and hiccups when under pressure.)

Reasons this merger could be a triumph (always be positive):

1. I could get a pay rise
2. I could get a new, better role
3. I no longer have to work with letchy David, though pass-agg-Eva and Brian-the-pessimist might also apply for their jobs back
4. This could be a new start, a start I choose rather than one that has happened by accident. And there will be more openings.

Issues – the triumph bit is littered with 'could's; I could quite easily end up with no job at all, or one even worse than the one I had up until yesterday.

I put my mobile down and curl up under the duvet again. The flat is quiet, Frankie will be with Tarquin, in some luxury hotel, celebrating in style.

'We'll be doing that next year.' I tell Stanley, who is curled up against my feet. He wags his tail lazily, to show he's listening. 'Well, you'll have your *fur*ever home, in some big house with a massive garden. I'm not quite sure what I'll have.'

I lie back and close my eyes, but I can't stop thinking about my job. Or lack of it. So I pick my phone up again.

There is a new email from Ollie: 'Sorry to disappoint, nothing as amusing as Ziggy – it's Zane. Rgds Ollie.'

I wonder if he always writes such formal emails?

'Not a disappointment!' It is. 'Is it a family name? Best

wishes, Daisy' – I did write 'Love Daisy', but then decided that was a bit too familiar for somebody who says 'Rgds'.

'No idea! Night. O'

'Good night!'

I wait a few moments to see if he sends any more messages, and when he doesn't I open the email from James Masters.

Maybe my first step in proving to everybody (including myself) that I can be a success, is to challenge my caretaker boss and demand better a better job immediately?

5.30 a.m., 25 December

Still can't sleep. Keep wondering about what might have happened if there had actually been some mistletoe in my snug in the bookshop when Ollie had squeezed in beside me.

This is not a good way to think.

1. He has a girlfriend (can't see it lasting though).
2. I still kind of have a boyfriend, I think. Not sure if cancelled Christmas = cancelled relationship, or if he might want to see me again.
3. Our lives have gone in different directions, we are no longer compatible. At all. Whatever my mother thinks. He is smug and insufferable, and I hate him. Though he was very kind earlier.

Bugger! How can he be so annoying and taking up so much of my head space when he has *nothing to do with me and my life*? I pull the duvet right up to my ears, feeling stroppy.

He was very kind though, and I was tempted to kiss him.

I curl up, and realise I'm smiling.

It was the way he looked into my eyes, as though he understood me. As though he knew. For a moment I was the old Daisy, the teenage Daisy, the one he'd snogged.

He really does have very kissable lips, and a cute dimple, and eyes I could lose myself in ...

Chapter 6

'Y ou'll find something.' Mum says, even though I haven't
mentioned my possible jobless state. 'You always do,
you're resourceful, and your adverts are wonderful, they'd
be silly to let you go. Stir the gravy will you, darling.'

I stir the gravy. 'Everybody has to relocate though, to
the head office. Ours is closing.'

'How sad, I wonder what it will be?'

'What, Mum?'

'The office! I wonder what will happen to your office
when it's closed, they'll turn it into a trendy bar I imagine.
Stir harder darling, there are lumps.'

'I could sieve it?'

'See, I said you were resourceful. Now, sprouts, will they
make Stanley smell?'

'Stanley?' He looks up hopefully at the sounds of his
name, he's been lurking in the kitchen since we arrived
and doing his best to trip Mum up.

79

'Well I'm serving him a dinner as well dear, he is your plus one after all!' She's being rather upbeat about all my shortcomings today. I give her a quick hug and she gives me a bigger one back. 'Now where did I put that slotted spoon, where is it then?'

'Here.' I pick up the spoon which she's placed ready in front of herself.

'Oh, not that, silly. I meant where is the new office?'

She does this, jumps between conversations. She'll leave one unfinished, then half an hour later carry it on as though there's not been a break.

'The email said most of the jobs will be in Stavington.'

'That's a long way, darling. Who do we know there? I'm sure we know somebody who lives there. It will come to me. Just pop that cranberry sauce in the microwave, will you?'

Stavington *is* a long way. If I carry on living with Frankie and commute all the way to Stavington, I'll be spending nearly all of my paltry salary on train fares – or polluting the countryside with my car.

Which means moving there, if the pay is good enough for me to afford a flat, because I haven't a clue who my mother is thinking about. We don't know anybody who lives in Stavington.

Oh my God! I'll be finally leaving home if they offer me a job.

I mean, I know I don't actually live at home, I do live with Frankie. But I'm practically on the doorstep.

This is different.

I'll be moving on with my life, like I'd always thought I would. I put the sauce into the microwave with a clatter and press a few buttons. I won't be living in this village any longer, it will be a fresh start somewhere else. This is a positive I hadn't thought about.

A scary positive. I will be totally independent, a proper adult.

'Daisy, Daisy, darling, I don't think it should be bubbling like lava should it?'

'Oh shit, sorry, no.' I ping the door open and stare at the sauce, mesmerised as it flows over the top of the bowl.

'Is everything okay, darling?' Mum presses a dishcloth into my hand and squeezes my shoulder. 'It will be okay, I know it will. You'll sort it all out.'

I glance at her, and she nods encouragingly.

If I move away, I'll be further from Mum, just as she's started to support me more, just as I've started to realise that despite the competitive banter with Vera, she does really care. She does believe in me.

I'll miss her.

'It's not that far away really, just far enough.' It's almost like she's read my mind, like she used to when I was little. Well, at least I thought she was a mind-reader back then. 'It's rather exciting, isn't it? Do you think I've done enough sprouts?'

I nod, then smile. It is. My stomach is churning a bit, and I do feel all jittery and nervous, but it *is* exciting. This could be my turning point, my fresh start.

'Now if you don't wipe that up quickly it'll be stickier than a flypaper!'

'Sorry?' I frown at her.

'The sauce darling! It will set like toffee, you'll have to scrape it off the sides, oh my goodness, the gravy!'

The rest of Christmas day passes in a bit of a blur. It's hard to fully appreciate cracker jokes when your future is held in the balance. Although I have to admit I had totally forgotten how much fun pin the tail on the donkey can be after two brandy and Babychams, and a snowball consisting mainly of Advocaat. Maybe retro really is the way to go.

ACT 2 – NEW YEAR, NEW ME

Chapter 7

11.57 p.m., 21 March 2018

The last few months have been a bit of a nightmare, I feel like I am dangling in hyperspace. My life has been suspended, while I wait to see what Guardian HQ has in store for me.

In January, we were moved into a much smaller office, just up the road from our old office, with a much bigger temporary boss. She's enormous, has chin hair, and is very stern and serious. I think she'd rather be in Stavington reporting on speeding offences and petty crime, than here featuring the village fête and looking for lost gerbils.

She also isn't that keen on my funny small ads ('Is humour really necessary?') or enquiries about my future ('We've all been there, just cope. Is that really how you spell Chihuahua?'). In fact, let's face it. She's a grumpy cow.

I did in fact mention this to Ollie, who has been sending me the odd email (and some of them are very odd) since Uncle T's party, asking how things are going. It's a bit like when we were kids and he'd leave a note in my locker saying 'I'll beat you next time' if I'd got a higher test score than him. Except now he says things like:

Hi, Daisy,

I hope you told her that humour is always neces-sary. A Daisy without her cheeky, funny side, is like a cow without an udder – there's something essential and life-affirming missing.

Oll.

Hi, Ollie,

Did you really just liken me to an udderly useless bovine?

Dais

Daisy,

Ha-ha. I did. Did I ever tell you Uncle T used to have a Jersey cow called Daisy? It was a creature of beauty.

Oll

No, but I'm not sure where this is going. I think you should stop before I get moo-dy. Aren't there any lives you need to rush off and save right now?

Daisy

Daisy,

You're no fun. If you'd have known her, you'd have

loved her. Your namesake. I think I'll press the mooote button now though!

Oll

You've been looking these jokes up on the internet haven't you? D x

I'll have you know they're all my own work! O x'

Followed up swiftly by:

Unlike the list of one-liners you helped me compile in Year 1 so I could woo Jasmine Smith. You're the only person I've ever known who solved everything with a list and a military precision plan! Sorry, bleepers gone off, need to don my cape and save lives. Good luck with the interview, not that you ever needed luck! O x

I think they might have sent the caretaker boss in so that we all quit our jobs, but I am made of sterner stuff.

Okay, I did think about it briefly. But as I've only been here a few months, have zilch experience and might appear to be jumping ship before I'm sacked, I have decided that my immediate future might lie with the newspaper. Although if they refuse to give me a better job, I might need a rethink. But I have been gritting my teeth and waiting to see if my new boss, James Masters is going to give me a job. And not just any job, but a better job than I had before. I am going to demand it, and I am going to get it.

All I have to do is survive the small matter of an interview.

After a bottle or three of wine with Frankie this evening, though, I do now know how to sort my life! It's simple.

1. I must be more organised; and
2. I must try harder; and
3. I must be more like Frankie – who definitely has her shit together. When Frankie decides to go for something, not even an apocalypse would stand in her way.

4 p.m., 22 March

I look down at what I was sure (last night – after rather large quantities of wine) was the solution.

Books.

I have downloaded lots of books.

Now I am not so sure.

I mean, I'm sure about books in general. I have lots of them, I could start a library. But they are fiction. These are different. These are self-help books. I mean, self-help, that's exactly what I've decided to do, isn't it? Help myself. But this is going to be like scaling Everest when all I need is a few highlights, a few challenging peaks that I can fit into a mini-break.

Reading this lot will take me hours, and that's before I even start to implement the suggestions.

I drop my e-reader and flop back on my bed and stare at

the ceiling. Why do non-fiction books have so many words in them? There is obviously a gap in the market, people need *How to get your shit together in 3 easy steps – with pictures*! If I ever do get my shit together and have time, I will write this book. It will be a bestseller and help millions of people.

These bloody books have actually made my situation worse and I have just wasted another two hours of my life flicking through them on my Kindle, when I could have been planning my interview strategy. According to the books, a strategy is important. I need to write it down and then visualise. I totally get the strategy bit, I'm pretty sure the teenage me had a plan and strategy, as Ollie said, for everything. A subconscious one. But the visualisation is a new one on me.

And on top of the books, yesterday's email from Ollie didn't help either. It pushed me to the edge and made me think something more drastic was needed. Well, that and knowing that I would soon have to go for my interview, and then face my family and all their expectations. And Ollie. Who wished me luck at my interview. I'm not sure how he even knew, but you know what my mum is like, she tells Vera *everything*.

Anyway, seeing his perfect life was made ten tons worse at Christmas. And not only has he totally got his shit together, and it's not parental exaggeration, he is also still quite nice. If he'd been a twat at Uncle T's party, I could at least have consoled myself with the fact that being perfect comes at a price.

But he isn't. And it doesn't.

I can't carry on letting everybody, and myself, down

though. I am going to do whatever it takes to succeed at something truly boast-worthy!

I am going to stay calm, I am sure that 'calm' is key, in my bid to conquer this year (and possibly the rest of my life). It will be my year, the year I stop disappointing everybody (including myself) and be the me I am supposed to be. I am in fact going to conquer the rest of my life.

I've realised that I am allowed to fuck up, to be sad, angry or unsure, but I am also going to be a better me. The me I knew I could be when I was still at school – with a few adjustments of course. The one with a flat of her own (or at least a proper sized room), a wardrobe with more than two items that match, tamed hair, and a career plan. I am going to be an adult and commit (where possible, as living on a shoestring because of a crap salary does *not* help me in being more like Frankie).

I *do* have the answer to all my problems. The books have indirectly helped, so they weren't a complete waste of money, as has Ollie.

The answer is simple. It is something I already knew. It is better lists. I have always been a fan of lists and have never been able to break the habit. But I can see now that they need to be more detailed. And I need plans. They will be prioritised and have timescales. This year I will be planning Christmas in July. I will be rediscovering my inner teenage geek – the one who always had a plan, even if she didn't realise it at the time.

Chapter 8

The final countdown has started, and I have *far* too much to do before my very important interview. Once I put my newly purchased interview outfit on, there is No More Time Left.

Things I must do before my interview

My new improved lists are definitely the answer, my brain already feels less scrambled. This is my first significant list, it is phase one of my preparation for the interview. I am already becoming *more like Frankie.* She is so together even her wardrobe is organised by colour and type. She can actually find co-ordinating stuff and doesn't have to root in the wash basket, under the bed and through drawers to find the top she's after. Then iron it. Ever. She also has a good job, and the big room in our flat. Because it is actually her flat, and I rent a corner. I need to work towards a proper flat share.

1. *Hair – 1pm, booked*
2. *Nails and eyebrows – 3pm, booked! These two are very important, because if I look and feel professional and confident, it will come across in my interview. Everybody says this, including my mother*
3. *Read through CV every day*
4. *Find photo of James Masters online (done) and visualise interview – visualisation imperative according to books*
5. *Prepare intelligent questions – done*
6. *Wash S—*

9.00 a.m., 4 April

'Oh, you are there, Daisy!' Mum says this as though she's been desperately trying to reach me for the past few hours, when the truth of the matter is that my phone has rung out six times.

'I was in the middle of something!' Point 5 on my list actually, and I'd have forgotten what it was if I'd stopped. The phone ringing was so annoying that I did have to stop in the middle of point 6, but I know I'll remember what that is.

'I'm sure it can't have been that important, dear.' Mum thinks it's rude if you don't answer within three rings. 'Oh no, I'm not interrupting anything am I?' She chortles in a horribly suggestive way. Not that I mind people being suggestive, but my *mother*? 'You're not busy with your young man, are you?' I've got a suspicion she's crossing her fingers and giving Dad the thumbs-up.

'No, Mother, I was writing a list!'

'Oh.' She sounds disappointed. Honestly, I know she's menopausal, but living vicariously through your daughter's sex life is so not on, is it?

'Simon and I have consciously uncoupled.' I say primly. I have to admit at this point that I have not been entirely honest with my mother. After our big argument at Christmas, Simon and I had been on a slow fade. Honestly, that man is such a jerk I don't know why I dated him at all.

'You've unconsciously what dear? Is that a euphemism for sex with your eyes shut?'

I sigh. 'We've split up.'

'Oh dear, that's a shame, but never mind darling I'm sure you'll find a proper boyfriend one day.'

I am going to ignore that comment, skimming through the free excerpt of *How to be the Zen you* has taught me that inner calm will help with outer chaos, or something like that. At the moment lists seem more practical though. 'I don't want to seem picky, but shouldn't a girl your age at least be in possession of an en-suite? Delia's daughter has a lovely two bed roomed flat and they're both en-suite!'

'Who is Delia?' I try not to sigh because that will make her worse. She already thinks I'm dysfunctional, sad and lonely. Incomplete because I am over thirty (just), single, have a crap career and rent a room. I don't even have my own dog, he just lodges with me.

'Next door, darling. The new people? They've got two children and they've both got their own places even though they're single like you are! And as for Oliver, I was talking to Vera only the other day, and did you know he has—'

I might have to scream. 'Mum. I am rather busy, I'm trying to find you a perfect birthday present.' I'm not, I haven't even thought about her present yet. Need to put that on a list, pronto. It's a 'significant' one this year, (but nobody is allowed to mention numbers) and Dad has arranged a party. At Uncle T's. Partly because Uncle T is much better at arranging things like that than Dad, and partly because it is supposed to be a surprise. But Mum of course found out, because she is exceedingly nosy. 'Really going to have to go!' I do not want to hear about the *perfect* Oliver Cartwright. I like the version I get in the emails he sends me, the non-bragging, funny, sweet Ollie. Not the version our mother's report back, the blemish free, high achieving Ollie who shows up my imperfections. Well, that's not entirely true. I am a tiny bit interested in everything he's been doing since I saw him at Uncle T's party. But I'm not sure why, I must have inherited the nosy gene from Mum.

'Oh well, I won't keep you. I'll tell you all about Oliver when I see you! You are coming to Uncle Terence's party in July, aren't you? I don't think you've RSVP'd!'

'Yes, Mum.' Yes has to be the answer, if I said no I'd get the Spanish inquisition. 'How could I not be coming to your *surprise* birthday party?' Why is she talking about *this* now? It is months off, I have an interview to prepare for!

'And are you bringing a plus one?'

'Not yet, but I'll tell him if I decide to.'

'If he asks you to bring food, you won't bring those stuffed dates, will you dear? And I hope you're not spending too much on my presents, I know you're hard up!'

'I won't, haven't. But the party is ages away yet!'

'I know dear. That's not why I called, you just distracted me! I wanted to make sure you weren't planning on staying up late on Wednesday, you won't go out with that Frankie girl, will you? You know you turn into Miss Grumpy, if you're tired, and you have to be bright and breezy, don't you?'

'Yes, Mum.'

'You've got your interview!'

'I know, Mum.' Does she honestly think I might have forgotten? I go to sleep each night dreaming about my interrogation and wake up each morning feeling slightly sick. I think it's a bit like when you're expecting a baby, you're excited, but just want it to be over, and you wish people would stop asking about it.

I mean, this has been dragging on for ages. According to our regular updates from James Masters things are progressing as envisaged, but in the office we think this is business-speak for, 'We've been waiting until we've sorted out all the voluntary redundancies and know how many of you we've got left.' Anyway, Brian-the-pessimist went into a huge slump after the merger was announced and declared he was too old for change and that he'd rather bite the bullet now, rather than be shot with it later, and took what he decided was a rather satisfactory redundancy package (he had been working for the newspaper for eons). Pass-agg-Eva stuck it out for a month, then realised that in our caretaker boss she'd met her match and managed to find a job stacking shelves at the village supermarket, and quite a few other people who didn't fancy moving to Stavington headed off to pastures new (as Brian called them). So I think the HQ holding-fire strategy has worked out quite well for them.

I'm hoping it has also worked out well for me. I have applied for the job of advertising manager, which is a big step up the ladder – but as Frankie pointed out, it is much better to aim high in the area I already have expertise in, rather than be star struck by some of the roles in journalism, which would mean starting at the bottom again. And now, with so many people leaving, I'm sure I've made the right decision to hang on. There is hardly any competition!

'That's why I called! Now, you will ring me the instant you come out and let me know what you'll be doing, won't you?'

'It doesn't work like that, Mum. They won't tell me on the spot.'

'Oh, I'm sure you'll get an inkling! It's so exciting. Now, I better go, lots to do!' I love the way she always manages to turn things round, and it's her who is busy and has to dash. 'Good luck, darling! Your father says good luck as well, he said you need to picture the interviewer dressed as an Easter bunny and it will work wonders!'

'Dad really said that?'

'With ears! Well, not exactly, he said picture them in their undies, but that seems strange to me. Goodness knows how *he* ever got a job! I'll speak to you on Thursday, I've got flower arranging tomorrow and I'll be watching my TV series on Wednesday, so I thought I better call now. Love you!'

I put the phone down feeling strangely happy. When I was at school, Mum was never exactly a pushy mother, but I always knew she was there for me, a reassuring voice in the background saying she knew I could do it – where 'it' was practically anything and everything. After 'it all went wrong', I'd felt only the disappointment, the weight of expectations that were never going to be met. But I'm beginning to wonder if it was all in my head. I'd been disappointed in myself, hadn't thought I could do anything right, and I think maybe I only let myself hear the bits I wanted to, the 'could do better's the 'not good enough's (which she never actually said in so many words) and blanked out the tentative encouragement, the support she'd always offered me.

Mum has always had my back, never stopped the hugs even when I had my fingers in my ears and was refusing to listen to her. I mean, yeah, she is always going to be in competition with Vera, but she never actually stopped singing my praises, did she? Even when it was a struggle to find anything – full marks to her for turning my dog-fostering into a Nobel Prize-worthy venture and my small ads into a work of literature.

I do love her. It's just a shame she's always going to be disappointed on the man and baby front!

Oh bugger, I have forgotten what I was going to put on my list. What on earth does 'wash s' mean? Socks? Shirt? I'm sure it will come to me, after all it must be important, or I wouldn't have been adding it to my list.

As my brain is so overloaded it is refusing to co-operate, I put my summer sunshine playlist on and empty the entire contents of my side of the fridge – a mini bottle of cava that I have been saving for a special occasion. Surely this counts as such an occasion? I am about to have an interview that will hopefully change my life!

And the butterflies in my tummy are telling me that something good might be on the horizon. I think this strange feeling inside me is positivity!

Chapter 9

Bugger, bugger, bugger! It's gone. How can a list just disappear? Unless I dreamt my whole 'getting organised' thing.

I am sure I will work out where it is once my brain has been recharged with coffee. Coffee is the answer to everything. Some people think tea is, but they're mistaken.

Although it appears it is not. The fridge is the answer.

It's there! On the fridge door – my list! What on earth? Is Frankie on some kind of paper diet now?

'I hope you're not nicking my milk again!'

'Borrowing. In exchange for coffee.' I shove my mug in Frankie's direction, and she waves a frantic hand as though it may pollute the air she's standing in.

Frankie is a walking, talking advert for green tea and kale smoothies. It's a bit of a surprise that she isn't green-tinged; she isn't, she's a slim and sleek bronzed goddess

99

with glossy hair and perfect skin. If she was a dog she'd win best in show at Crufts. I put this down to the fact that she balances out the healthy living with wine and nachos – and goes abroad a lot.

'What on earth are you wearing, Daisy?'

I look down. 'Too much?' I admit it, I have dressed in rather a hurry (as I have lots of stuff to do), but this is my favourite skirt and top. They are also very bright and positive, and the colours according to the Sunday supplement are bang on-trend. And surely wearing what you love makes you feel better?

'I know lime green and orange are 'in', but together? You look like a mouldy orange. The orange Christmas forgot.' She laughs, a full hearty, kale-sponsored laugh, which means I am not at all offended by being compared to a Christmas leftover. She might also have a point about the whole combo. I've never actually worn both items together before. 'Which makes sense seeing as it's April!'

'Did you nick this?' I wave the list.

'Soz.' She grins, not looking sorry at all. 'Wicked list! I put it there so I wouldn't forget to ask you why Uncle Terence's Christmas Eve party is happening in July?'

Frankie likes to know what's going on in my life.

'It's not. This is for my Mum's surprise birthday party, it's in July.'

She pulls an 'eek' face, that involves wide eyes and a pulled-out mouth. 'Wow, July! That is still ahead of the curve! Can I come?' She tilts her head on one side.

'No! You hated the Christmas Eve one, and it's the same people, same place!'

'I didn't hate it! It was a laugh. I want to come next Christmas as well! Think old Terence will let me?'

'If you come again, you'd have to dress properly, and you wouldn't be seen dead in a Christmas jumper, you also hate mulled wine—'

'But those cocktails were to die for, and as for your mum, she is amazing!' She probably is, if you don't happen to be her daughter. Well, okay, she is pretty cool (though amazing might be pushing it, I mean she's my *mother*, you don't think of your mother that way do you?), but other people think she's amazing because of her flamboyant choice of clothes (that must be where I get it from), and her hilariously tipsy behaviour at parties (embarrassing if you are her daughter).

'And you'll be far too busy shagging Tarquin this year.'

'True.' She smirks and lifts a knee to her chest, presumably to stretch her hamstrings, then pauses, perfectly balanced on one leg. 'How come you're up so early, Dais?'

Frankie is always up early. Right now she's limbering up and is encased in perfectly fitting designer Lycra. If I wore it, I would look like one of those safety-wrapped suitcases you see at the airport, or a vacuum-packed hi-viz pear – either way it would not be a sexy look. I, however, do not get up early to experience the dawn light and bracing unpolluted fresh air. Life is too short to suffer that much. And we all know it can bugger up your knees in old age, don't we?

'I'm busy. I've got stuff to do before work!' I grab my granola and head back to my room and stick my *Christmas in July* list back on the wardrobe door and get another sheet of paper. It's probably easier to start again.

Then my phone beeps with an incoming email, and I very nearly tip the contents of my coffee mug over it.

I'm a bit jumpy. I'm pinning nearly everything on this interview, and I keep thinking that any second now I'll be told it is cancelled. That they've changed their minds – there are no jobs.

It is not an email from James Masters, it is from Ollie.

Daisy, I've had a chat to Uncle T. We've got this – forget the party plans, concentrate on your interview. I know how important it is to you!

Oh my God. This is the first completely non-jokey message I've had from him for ages, and I'm welling up. Mum's party really is a distraction I could do without right now, and he's offering to help!

Apart from the pooch prob. No idea how to stop him eating off the table, sitting on the table, or stealing anything edible or otherwise from the table or from people's bags or pockets. That dog is a demon, you sort scrounging Stanley, we'll sort the rest. Is there such a thing as a dog counsellor?

Speak soon – I'll take you out for a celebratory glass of bubbly, if you fancy it?

Ol x

P.S. Don't worry about replying, get that interview prep done!

'Stuff? You never do stuff before work!' I try to ignore a shocked Frankie, who followed me and somehow managed to squeeze into my room unnoticed whilst I was reading my email.

This is nothing short of a miracle. I mean, she is pretty skinny, but I rent the smallest room (I'm probably breaking the trade descriptions act or something calling it a room, it's more of a cupboard, or even more accurately a very large box, perfectly suited to the term box-room) in the flat. As life choices go, this is marginally better than still living with my parents but means if I want to have a sex life it's got to be (a) with somebody who is vertically (and horizontally) challenged or (b) with somebody double-jointed or (c) with somebody with their own place. It also means I don't have room for a bookcase. I think I might be able to cope better with no sex than no books.

'Oh. You've got a lot of lists.' Luckily, she is distracted by the lists, and doesn't notice that I have gone all mushy and dewy eyed and am clutching my phone to my chest with relief. Ollie is lovely, as lovely as his mother says. I owe him for this. 'You really are trying to get your shit together at last, aren't you?' Frankie has flopped back on my bed, which makes her hard to ignore.

'Shouldn't you be going for your run?'

'Even a temple gets a day off now and then. So?'

'Yes, Francesca, this is how I am going to get my shit together.' I answer in my prim, telephone voice.

'Awesome, told you that you could do it! Expecting another shitty day at work?'

Frankie is a landlady/counsellor rolled into one. She is scarily good at working out why I've had a bad day or am acting out of character. She also swears a lot.

'Has psycho-boss stand-in been checking your grammar again?' She knows all about my temporary boss. But has obviously forgotten all about my impending interview, which is tomorrow and worrying me A LOT because it is SO IMPORTANT. So important in fact that I am thinking of it in capitals and feel like it is stamped on my eyeballs.

It is however also making me feel a bit queasy.

'It's not just her.' I squeeze onto the edge of the bed, next to Frankie, and stare at the lists. 'My whole life's a mess.'

'Is it?' She frowns at me.

'It is. I'm over thirty—'

'Only just!'

'I will be thirty-two soon! And, One' – I tick it off on my forefinger – 'I haven't got my own place—'

'You live here! Without you, I'd have to let Tarquin move

in.' She does a pretend grumpy-face. 'Don't make me let Tarquin move in. Per-lease!'

Every time Tarquin, her boyfriend, stays over he tries to leave something behind – move in by stealth – Frankie always spots things, puts them in a carrier bag and hangs them on his 'peg'. The only thing he's allowed is a coat peg, Frankie reckons that schools let kids have them so it can't do any harm, it's not permanent.

I ignore her and carry on ticking things off on my fingers. 'And, Two, I haven't got a career—'

'You have! You're a journalist!'

We both know that this is stretching the truth a bit. 'Writing ad copy for the *Hunslip and Over Widgley Local Guardian* doesn't exactly qualify me for a roving reporter of the year job.' I shoot her my serious look.

'It's a start, you'll work your way up in the new place.'

'It was an accident.' It was. It is the truth. I didn't exactly decide to be a journalist. I had sent the newspaper what I thought was a witty advert in a last-ditch attempt to re-home Gerald, the ugliest and smelliest dog at the re-homing centre that my friend Carrie runs.

Somebody at the paper had majorly cocked up. My witty prose and the more sombre words that had been submitted in remembrance of the dearly departed Gerald Jones, late of this parish, had been mixed up. I mean, how? Not even I can cock up on that scale.

The 'Obit.' column had described the deceased as tooth-less, balding, with a bark worse than his bite but with unique charm, and 'Pets and Livestock – Home wanted' had declared that a short service would be held for Gerald at the local crematorium on Wednesday.

Luckily (or not for him), Gerald the deceased did not have any living family, and his friends managed to see the funny side once a full apology had been printed and a free wake (all the pies you can eat and pints you can drink) offered at the village pub. Most of them had actually thought it was a real obituary, because it did fit Gerald quite well. They'd just been confused about the 're-homing' bit and wondered if the crematorium had a new policy.

There was one positive side to the story – the re-homing centre was inundated with callers keen to save Gerald from imminent death.

Anyway, the editor had rung me to ask, 'you don't fancy a few hours work fiddling with the classified ads each week do you?' And I have been fiddling ever since.

I mean, it is a positive that they thought I was smart and had initiative, but bad because I really do not want to spend the rest of my life writing ads for the occupants of what is not much more than an overgrown village. I have known for a long time that I need to develop a proper career, with a proper salary and prospects. Or at least something challenging and enjoyable. What do I do if James Masters only offers me a role doing much the same? Fiddling. Demanding something better is all well and good, but what if he says no? I will have lost my chance of a very nice redundancy package and be even worse off than before – as I'll have to travel miles to work. What if I don't get the chance to 'work my way up'?

I need to be positive. Definitely. If he is not prepared to recognise my skills, I will look elsewhere.

'But you've reported on stuff as well.' Frankie prods me. 'You'll be fine once you start the new job. There'll be more opportunities.'

This is easy for her to say. I am petrified and excited in equal measures. The last week has been like living on the big dipper, one moment all I can think about is what will happen if I don't get offered a position, the next I'm wondering what will happen if I do. My looming interview has taken on an importance out of all proportion – it is the first day of the rest of my (much better) life.

It is not just the fact that all I do is write small ads that is bothering me. I know I'm earning way less than my male equivalent because some fool left the salary list on the printer the other day, so I nicked it and took a photo on my phone. And I am going to demand equal rights, equal pay. I hate confrontation, and bigging myself up does not come naturally so I am going to have to practise this bit in front of the mirror at least one zillion times (which I don't have time to do – though handing over my party planning will allow me to do it at least ten times more). I've also been studying the pay grades for other jobs at the newspaper, jobs I know I could do if I buckled down. Jobs with salaries that could change my life. Maybe only in a minor way, but it would be a start.

Frankie props her chin on her fists. 'So, what would you do if you weren't at the paper? What if ... you don't get the job you are after at this interview?' Frankie is kind, and has a way with words, but this is something I'm too scared to think about.

I do think I need to compile a list though, so that failing at this particular obstacle does not completely derail my life again. I need a Plan B. This time round things have to be different. One failure cannot be allowed to ruin my future.

I need a list of all the things I am good at, all the things I want to do. Books and dogs are top of the list, but as I have no plan to write a book about a dog (though *A Street Dog Called Stanley* would surely be a best seller), I need more to go at.

I frown at her.

'Why are you frowning?'

'I'm thinking.' I've always frowned when I think.

When I was at school, I'd always planned on being a vet. I hadn't even considered an alternative, I just knew that was what I would become. It was all going to plan until a skeletal, scared horse was dumped in the field behind our house and I had to hand feed it grass and practically sleep with it, which screwed up my schedule and cut back on revision time more than it should have. I was in the middle of working out how to make up for lost time when Josh happened. Josh (slug boy), who I did actually sleep with (big mistake), and who was supposed to be a casual boyfriend but who turned out to be something much more complicated. Josh impacted my revision time far more than the horse did.

Josh left me with a void in my life and a feeling that I'd never be able to do anything right ever again.

Even thinking his name is making me feel sick.

I try not to sigh, sighing will make Frankie suspicious and I don't want to talk about Josh. But things took a drastic downturn just around then, not long after my festive lip-smacking with Ollie. And, I couldn't find a way back, a way to make things right. In fact, I don't think I've really wanted to until now.

Anyway, I flunked my 'A' levels, my parents were 'disappointed' (ballistic would have been so much easier to deal with, disappointed is just plain cruel), and I accepted a place on a biology course, because biology was the only exam that I'd got a remotely good grade in. My dreams of going to veterinary college were completely screwed, I was going to study for a degree that prepared me for absolutely nothing I wanted to do in life.

I think that I have recently hit upon the crux of my problem. Since leaving school after everything went horribly wrong with Josh, I have let things happen to me, I haven't chosen them. I have been acting like a victim.

I really need to pull my big girls' pants up and take control, don't I? The old, confident me never let insecurities hold her back.

I'm not exactly sure what has made me realise this, but I think a lot of it had to do with seeing Ollie after all these years. He wasn't the cardboard cut-out I'd invented in my head, based on the stories his and my mother told me. He was real. The real I was supposed to be, and it made me realise just how much I've let things drift.

The Josh thing will be something I can never forget, but it was a mistake. It is something I can't change, that was never meant to happen, but did. Just because I'd spent days wishing it would all go away, doesn't mean I made it happen. It wasn't my fault.

Shit, as they say, happens. Now deal with it.

I'm going to. Mum has never stopped believing in me, and I shouldn't have done.

Moving on doesn't mean I've forgotten. I think it means I'm finally coming to terms with it.

No more accidents, no more things just happening to me. I'm going to make sure I'm in control.

To be honest, even my name was an accident. I didn't have any say in that particular part of my life, obviously, but I was going to be called Heather. Then I was born with a bad case of jaundice, and when I was passed to my mother, swaddled in a white blanket with just my little yellow face visible, she (delirious from gas and air she claims) shrieked out, 'She's the colour of Daisy! It's a sign – we'll call her Daisy!' Despite my father's best attempts to persuade her to sleep on it, she'd waited until he'd gone then sneaked off to the registrar, who was visiting the hospital that day, and insisted that was what went on my birth certificate.

'I'm not quite sure exactly what I do want to do for the rest of my life.' Doesn't that sound far too long a time to commit to something, a whole life? But I do know that I am determined that my immediate future is going to look very different to the last ten years.

'Oh sugar.' Frankie suddenly spots the time. 'I've got a breakfast meeting, and I need to go and collect my Amazon delivery from the locker in the supermarket.' She waves a finger at me as she rolls off the bed. 'We'll talk about this later!'

'Do you want me to collect your Amazon stuff?'

'Oh *wow*, that would be brill—' She stops, and glares at me. 'Have you got time?'

'Well, no, I've got to get ready for my interview, and have my—'

'Exactly! Daisy, how the hell are you going to sort your life if you keep offering to do stuff for people?' She holds a hand up to stop me interrupting. 'You need to be assertive, you need to be less nice and helpful. You need to not let yourself be distracted!'

'Aren't you going to be late, Miss Biggest Distraction of All?'

Frankie laughs. Frankie is never late. 'Aren't you?'

I just smile. This morning, for the first time in ages, I got up super early. This morning I have accomplished everything I intended to, and I have my plan ready for the rest of the day. I am leaving nothing to chance. In fact, I think I am even more on the ball than Frankie!

Chapter 10

3 p.m., 5 April

Bugger and double bugger. I was supposed to finish work at 12 p.m. sharp, but I had call from a bereaved relative who wanted to know how much it would be to put a notice in the obituary column. Before I knew it, I was discussing poor dead Alice with her sister Mary, and was weeping buckets as she asked me how she was going to cope, knowing that the lamb she ordered for Easter Sunday would be far too big for her to eat on her own, and she had far too many hot cross buns in the freezer.

It was all so tragic, the thought of her eating dinner all alone on Easter Sunday. I searched out the telephone number of the village community group for her (they advertise a lot with us), promised I'd pop in and see her soon, and advised her to take it one day at a time.

It was 2 p.m. before I put the phone down, and everybody else was out on late lunch – apart my stand-in boss who I think was stuck in her wheelie chair and so refused to meet my eye when I waved goodbye. She was probably waiting for the office to be empty then would try to upturn herself so she could escape.

I am definitely going to face up to my new permanent boss, if I ever get one. I am going to demand equal pay, and the chance to contribute articles on a regular basis. This will be my number one priority once I have a contract; point one on my life list.

Not that I'm having much luck with my current lists. I had to text and cancel my 1 p.m. hair appointment whilst I was on the phone to Mary. This is bad news.

My hair needs professional help. Unfortunately, a quick iron on a low setting is going to have to suffice.

Things have got even worse now. All my pratting around with finding phone numbers for Alice, plus helping out a woman in the pound shop who had lost her mobile phone (it was not lost, it was in her coat pocket where she *never* puts it) has meant I am late for my appointment at the beauty spa and now have a choice. According to the cross girl on reception desk, I can't have 'artistic varnish' *and* my eyebrows done.

Beetle eyebrows are a very bad look, mine are verging on slugs. Mum always says I should do them myself, but I'm one of those people who can't colour in between the lines, or trace around things without getting bored halfway through and going all wobbly. If I pluck my own eyebrows, they will have holes in and be a total mismatch. I tried it once and if I covered up one eye with my hand I had a slightly surprised look, if I covered up the other side I looked like a mangy squirrel.

I can't *not* have my eyebrows done. My interviewer will be staring me in the eye, interrogation style, and they will be inescapable. I will look unprofessional. I will also feel shit, and I am determined never to feel that way again.

Cross girl is tapping her very artistic nails on the desk and gazing at her tablet pointedly.

'Well?'

'Eyebrows!'

'Fine. Sit down and I'll tell Eloisa you're ...'

'But nails are important, aren't they?' How can I not have my nails done? Mum is bound to add it to her 'reasons you can't get a well-paid job' and 'reasons why you can't keep a man' lists. 'I need my nails doing!' I need to look polished, and I can't wear gloves in April. Unless I wear surgical gloves and say I have a skin problem? No, definitely not. Totally not. What am I thinking?

I'm not thinking, I'm panicking. I need to be the best version of myself I can be for this interview. If I think I look good, then I will feel good. I will be confident and able to kick ass. I am visualising a lot of ass kicking in my immediate future.

'Artistic?'

'Yes, definitely! Artistic and summery. Glitter!'

She dramatically strikes out 'eyebrows' and taps on the tablet. 'I'll tell Emmi that you're—'

'Hang on, hang on!' I stare at the price list.

114

She sighs dramatically.

'I will have my eyebrows done and a basic manicure!'

'Basic.' She taps away, emphasises the word as though nobody in their right mind would ever want a *basic* manicure. Not when you could be artistic or glossy.

Maybe it isn't perfect, but basic says business-like, not flirty.

'Sit down. Suzy will sort it out in a minute.'

'Suzy?' Isn't Suzy the one Frankie said never to have, not under any circumstance?

'Our junior. It's basic.'

Ah. 'Will my eyebrows be safe with er Suzy?'

'Well, she's got plenty to work with.'

Some people don't know the meaning of customer service. Or maybe she's just annoyed that she's working late and has decided to take it out on the annoying clients who have decided to book late appointments.

I did comment that eyebrow shaping surely only takes a matter of minutes, leaving plenty of time for other things, but there were muttering about deforestation and major reshaping, so I shut up.

Right now, all that matters is looking good for my interview.

Chapter 11

'Daisy Dunkerly? Hi, I'm Tim.'

I could have sworn he just said 'Tim' not 'Jim'. This is worrying. All my correspondence has been with James Masters. Jim. Unless I misheard.

Tim, or Jim, is holding his hand out. So I shake it.

He has a very firm handshake. Firm and dry, not clammy and a bit furtive like David's was.

'Sit, sit. Sorry, I'm standing in for James, last minute thing. He had to dash off, family emergency.'

I can feel the scowl forming on my face, though I am really trying to stop it. But I've had all this stress, then come all this way for my interview, and the boss can't even be bothered to turn up.

Commuting to Stavington is going to be even worse than I'd imagined – as in practically impossible. It is either car, or very slow bus that stops everywhere, and makes you feel slightly seasick as the bored driver sees how quickly he can fling it round the blind bends on a single-track road. The public transport solution would also cost a ridiculous amount and would mean I'd have to get up even earlier than the milkman.

And I mean, we all know what 'family emergency' means, don't we? Hangover, cold, or can't be bothered.

Not that I can really blame him.

'Dog ate a bone, splintered, nasty.' Tim pulls a face that suggests nasty happenings. He seems to talk in shorthand, missing out unnecessary words. It must be because he's used to tight word counts.

'Oh no, poor thing.' I can now perfectly understand James not being able to be here. His poor dog is probably laid out on an operating table as we speak. A vital organ pierced, a studious vet shouting at orders to a hassled nurse who has been dragged away from her stash of Easter eggs (it is Good Friday tomorrow, after all, so early chocolate eating is allowed). 'Is it? Will it?'

'Okay, I think.' He winks. 'Post op care at home.'

'You really do need to be careful with cooked bones you know.' Bugger, I'm already criticising the absent boss. 'Though I'm sure he is.'

'True, the bone thing. Probably better not to have them at all.'

'Dogs?'

'Meat. Chickens.'

'Chickens?' I am confused.

'We don't need to eat meat to survive you know. Never touch it myself.'

I look more closely at him. He is the proof of the pudding as my mother would say. She says a lot of strange things and when I was little I thought the proof was something you found at the bottom of the bowl, after you'd eaten the pudding. Like the syrup at the bottom, a little lake of something called proof. Anyway, he is the proof that you don't need to eat meat, he looks surprisingly well and bouncy.

'Right, er.' He coughs as though he's realised we've strayed away from his interview script and shuffles some paper around. It's rather endearing. If an interviewer can be endearing. 'Thanks for coming in today, sorry you've got me, James didn't want to leave people hanging any longer, didn't want to reschedule. Not fair, you know.'

I nod. I do know. Definitely not fair. I quite like Tim, and James. I just wished they were nearer to my home. And had done this in January, instead of sending psycho-boss in for three months.

'Am sure you'd much rather be home breaking out the vegan Easter eggs; know I would.'

'Not sure about the vegan bit, but I'm with you on the chocolate!' I smile, then realise the error of my ways. This is not going to get me a job. 'Though it's brilliant of you to do this, and I don't mind at all, and there's hardly anybody on the roads so it was really easy to get here.'

I'm rambling, I know I am. I clamp my lips together and force myself to wait.

Tim grins very disarmingly. Although he'd be disarming even without the grin.

I was expecting someone older. Or somebody like psycho-boss stand-in.

Somebody youngish, good looking, who is not staring at my boobs or leaning into my personal space has thrown me. God, I hadn't realised just how bad working with my old boss was. Maybe this is all going to work out for the best. As long as I do get a job. 'Now, sit down and tell me a bit about yourself.'

I hover, mid sit. Tell him about *me*? This hadn't featured in my pre-interview prep. I have a whole spiel prepared about why I changed career, how satisfying working with the public is, how I am more than a classified ads supremo and aspire to having my own feature, how enthusiastic I am, how co-operative and how much I like to collaborate – the perfect team player, no 'I' in team, ha-ha. But at the same time how I take initiative (though this isn't proven – answering the phone all by myself isn't exactly hitting the heights, is it?).

'Please, sit.'

I sit. Rather heavily, and flounder. 'I, er, write the ads.' Shouldn't he know this bit? Is he so underwhelmed by his act of swallowing our little newspaper up whole that he hasn't actually read my bloody application form? I spent bloody hours writing and rewriting and deleting stuff

119

when I wasn't sure if my grammar was right and trying to think up interests that might actually seem interesting to somebody else. He might be bloody good looking, but we deserve better!

'Sure, I get that.' He raises an eyebrow. 'But I want to know about you, from the horse's mouth as it were.'

Oh.

I stare at him. My horse's mouth dropping open.

He's actually quite attractive in a freckles and mussed up slightly ginger hair way, and staring is no hardship, but probably won't help in the getting-a-job stakes. His eyes are a soft brown flecked with green, and his thinnish lips are strangely mobile and attractive. And it's hard not to look at him and try to pin his features down.

If I don't stop staring and get my brain into gear though, then writing small ads is all I will ever do.

'Don't look so worried, nothing too personal.' He laughs. 'Though I am all ears on that one, but work wise? What do you do, what do you want to do, what brings you here?'

'Well, losing my job brings me here.' I might as well start with the easy one, and he has wound me up a bit with his cavalier attitude to my application form.

'Not losing.' He sits back, relaxed. So I cautiously let my clenched fists relax slightly, but I stay perched on the edge of the seat trying to look professional and interested, and not slouch. His voice has softened. He really is rather nice. 'James doesn't want anybody to lose jobs. We're one big family here, and we're getting bigger. Know that sounds a bit like marketing hype, but we are. Honestly, not bullshitting! He wants to slot people into the right spots though, not shoehorn you where you don't want to be.' He shrugs. 'And if you'd rather not move here then that's cool, too. He knows this is quite a move and people have responsibilities, homes, kids.'

'Not me! Young, free, single, well not free in that way, I mean free to take on work responsibilities, to move.'

'Great! So ...' he leans forward earnestly, rests his forearms on the desk. He's pulled his sleeves up, showing off tanned, toned arms that have a mist of soft blond hairs over them. 'So where do you want to be?'

His fingers are steepled under his chin. His hair has got the hint of curls to it. He's also staring at me as though he's genuinely interested in what I have to say.

'Well, I er, I write the ads and, er, well,' I swallow. 'I have done the odd article here and there, on demand. I'm versatile.'

He suddenly smiles broadly, and he's gone from earnest to pretty damned attractive. If Frankie was here now she'd be talking about column inches in a totally inappropriate way.

Mum would love him.

'You've taken adverts and notices to a totally new level.'

I was so on edge when I came into the office, I hadn't noticed all the sheets of paper he'd got on his desk. I was also too busy staring at him, which doesn't help. He picks a sheet up.

I think I might be grinning. 'In a good way?'

He chuckles. 'Definitely. Particularly the pet ones.'

'I love animals, I wanted to be a vet, and now I foster dogs.'

'Ah. Figures. What else do you love?'

What am I supposed to say now without sounding daft? Pizza? Pringles? A night in with a good film and my pyjamas? G&T, cocktails? All those things most of us would like to admit to, but instead we say 'tennis' or 'the opera'.

'Honestly?' I do want to be honest. I want to get the best job I can on my own merits, not just made up guff. 'Books!'

'How much?' His eyes twinkle. If I didn't know better, I'd say he was flirting. But the nervous tension in my shoulders is taking a hike and my stomach doesn't feel quite as upside down and empty.

'Oh God, I can talk about books all day.' And I can. I think it all started when Uncle T offered to look after me in his bookshop, while Mum did her Christmas shopping. It was magical, I'd never been anywhere like it – and Uncle T was just like a character out of one of the books on the shelves of the shop. It was like having my own personal library, and as each year passed, he guided me round from genre to genre, continent to continent, from this world to others.

'Classics?' He frowns slightly, as though he's thinking. 'But you didn't do lit at uni?'

'Oh no, no. I mean I have read some of the classics, I loved the stuff we read at school, but I read anything really.'

'Totally anything?' He starts to throw out titles. Some

I've read, some I want to, some that would be like inviting somebody to poke my eyeballs with needles.

Tim laughs, I think I said that last bit out loud. 'You know what you like!'

'Oh yeah, I mean some of the hyped-up ones are fantastic, others just aren't my thing.' Terence treats fiction like mothers treat food, he's always encouraged me to try a taster, even if I was sure I wouldn't like something. I mention a treasure I found hidden in the bookshop a couple of weeks ago, the amazing dust jacket of a book that's due out any day, Uncle T's habit of sneaking psychological thrillers in with romance, and the odd romcom in the fantasy section.

He smiles, and twiddles with a pen. 'Fab! Films?'

'Definitely. All kinds of films, I love a good movie. Though not the really nail-biting stuff, that makes me want to hide behind the sofa. I have to peep out and pretend I'm not watching, but I can't help myself.'

'Art?'

'Proper art, not weird stuff that you're supposed to say clever things about.' I'm getting into this now, he's so easy to talk to. 'You know that black canvas with a red dot kind of thing that supposed to represent the dawning of humanity, or aliens visiting from another planet? Crap! Sorry, I mean it's rubbish. To me.'

He chuckles again. It's the type of chuckle that warms you up on the inside and brings out goose-bumps on the outside.

His long, elegant fingers are steepled under his chin, his gaze locked onto mine. 'Looking at the stuff you've done I reckon you like people, don't you? You like to help, get involved?'

Is this a trick question? This is nothing like an interview. Especially not an interview for an advertising manager. I'm not sure I'd consider helping Mary sort out her sister Alice's funeral really counts for anything at all in this situation.

'Well yes, but ...'

'Great.' He leans back suddenly and fishes out a second sheet of paper. 'I'd re-home this dog in a jiffy if I hadn't got a cat that would torment it then eat it for breakfast.'

'Really? You've got an evil cat?' Sad. I had him down as a dog person. A definite dog person. Not that I have anything against cat people, but I'll always have a dog. Our relationship is already doomed.

'I have.' He puts the sheet down, and the smile fades. He leans back. Face of regret on. 'Sadly, I've got a bit of an issue here. James is cutting back on staff in that department, more and more people are subbing adverts online, so I can't make any promises. It's not my call, it's his.'

'Oh.' Shit.

'Have you ever thought of doing something other than ads?'

I am not going to clean the office. Or just make coffee. No way. I have got standards, I have fallen as low as I'm going to. So he better not bloody suggest that!

I take a deep breath and spit the words out before I

have chance to back down, like the old pre-life-changing-catastrophe Daisy would have done. She would have owned this. 'Well, yes, actually.' Frankie had told me to aim for advertising manager. To work my way up, but inside I know it's not my passion, not what I really want to do. And chatting to Tim about books has lit some kind of fuse inside me.

'Go on?'

Oh God, what have I done? My insides have gone all jittery. What do I say now?

'Well apart from the fact that I'm underpaid,' I seem to be on some kind of uncontrollable auto-pilot, 'I think my skills have been overlooked.' Bugger he's raised an eyebrow. But I'm not going to let him put me off. 'I love books, obviously.'

'Obviously.'

'But I also love people, like you said, I want to help people.'

'I can tell that.'

'You can?' I blink. He nods, an encouraging kind of nod. 'I've written the odd column for the paper, nothing much, but I'd really like to write some human-interest stories.'

'What kind of stuff were you thinking? We do have a style, and ...'

'Look, there's lots going on in villages like ours, and even here.'

'True. And we'll be covering your old stomping ground as well as a few other areas when we get going properly.'

'Exactly! There are lots of invisible people who make

a real difference to the community. Local newspapers are important, local people are, I could cover stories like that. I know the people, the places.'

'I'm sure you could.'

'I mean just because we're going to be based here doesn't mean the small stories aren't important.'

I run out of steam a bit and burn under his silent appraisal. Then he smiles. 'True.' His voice is soft. 'The paper's not lost sight of that with the merger you know.' He's gone into auto-professional mode. I get the impression he's repeating some of the things his boss has said.

'Well yes, but—' You need somebody like me, I want to scream. But I don't.

'You've got a natural empathy. You're genuinely interested in helping people,' he pauses, grins again, 'and dogs.'

'Well yes, I did write a—'

'Jimmy read the pieces you've done and was pretty impressed.' He shrugs, suddenly boyish and cheeky. 'They're not bad at all. You've got a way with words.' He smiles. 'You're funny.'

There's a strange sensation in my tummy. A fluttering.

'He agrees with you, he thinks you've been under-utilised. Look, nobody wants to put pressure on if you don't want to—'

This is positive. He's not saying no! 'I do want, I do!' I'm not quite sure what I'm committing to here, but I need a job. I can worry about what type of job later. Although, I did vow to set my life in order. Take control, stop letting

126

things just happen to me. 'Probably. I mean I am more than happy to look at,' I pause, 'any jobs you think I may be suited to.'

He raises an eyebrow. The fluttering slows to a flap.

'Spreading my wings.' Flying. Right now I want to fly out of the window, I think it's time to shut up. I'm talking rubbish. What kind of newspaper editor is interested in employing somebody who spouts nonsense?

'Good.' His eyes narrow and he studies me for a moment, then suddenly seems to make a decision. He leaps out of his seat. And all that nice feeling of anticipation drops with a thud to the bottom of my stomach. 'Leave it with me. Great.' He glances at his watch, then shoves out a hand. He's rather tall actually, towering above me. 'Sorry to rush, but I've got another appointment. I was supposed to be helping James by splitting the load, but,' he shrugs, 'all down to me now. Thanks again for coming in though, I'll report back to the boss,' he grins, 'and he'll be in touch. I'll walk you to the lift.' And just like that I'm dismissed. Very effectively.

Shit, shit, shit. I've blown it. I've blathered on about diversifying and flapping my feathers, whilst digging a hole.

I'm a funny copy-writer who always dreamed of becoming a vet, not a journalist. Bugger, I didn't even mention my aspirations, my lists, my new positive attitude.

The office is deserted, apart from the receptionist and a couple of other people. Which means 'next appointment' didn't even exist.

God this man is smooth.

I hardly notice Tim's running commentary as we walk to the lift about who's who. I don't need to know who is who, I'm never going to meet them.

'I'll take the stairs, thanks.' I force a smile onto my face and ignore the funny look he's giving me.

'Great! Nice to meet you, Daisy. See you soon?'

There's that awkward moment of silence, then a strangled 'maybe' emerges from my mouth and I dive into the stairwell before I get a chance to clutch at him and beg him to tell Jimmy Masters they need me.

I plod down the stairs, I need to work off the eight Easter eggs and giant box of Maltesers that I intend to devour as soon as I get home. Sod waiting until Sunday!

It's cold and damp when I step out onto the near-deserted street.

Bloody hell, we didn't have any snow at Christmas, just ice, rain, plenty of slush and a cold wind, and today of all days, when it is nearly Easter, festive weather has arrived. But I don't feel festive at all. I just feel sad. But I know I need to ignore this if it's the setback it might be. I need to buck my ideas up, plough on. The new Daisy is not going to give up.

Carrie still needs me to help her walk dogs as she's given her staff time off over the Easter break. Stanley needs me. And Frankie will have to let Tarquin move in if I can't pay my share of the rent.

My phone beeps and I'm tempted to ignore it, but there is a big chance it is either Mum (will you be coming back home to stay, darling? I need to know, so I can make up your old room) and if I ignore her she'll ring, then actually drive over here and demand entry to the office, or it is Frankie (please don't tell me I've got to let Tarquin move in), or it could be important.

It is.

Important that is.

It is an email from Tim, who has copied in James Masters, bloody hell he's quick off the mark.

He must have had this email already prepared, ready to whizz off as soon as I'd left the building.

Dear Daisy,

Many thanks for your application for the role of Advertising Manager.

Unfortunately, as I mentioned, (oh fuck, fuck, fuck. I knew Frankie was wrong when she insisted I aim high. I should have stuck with what I know, worked my way up later. Now I've screwed up and will end up with nothing. Do I run up the stairs, batter down his door and insist he reconsider? Maybe I could be chief coffee maker after all?) *we are currently in the process of amalgamating the advertising and promotions teams across all our titles, we would however like to offer you the position of junior reporter here at head office, with specific responsibility for our review column. There would be a trial period of three months after which your performance would be reviewed, and if a future vacancy for a feature writer came up you would be welcome*

129

to apply. Full details are attached in the offer letter and accompanying terms and conditions.

It was lovely to meet you, I do hope we will be able to welcome you to the team.

It was lovely to meet me! Bloody hell! Tim thought it was lovely to meet me – and he's offered me a job! I stand outside the office in a daze, blinking away the tiny snowflakes that are landing damply on my eyelashes, my heart pounding like billy-o. It's not miserable and cold – it's snowing!

Shit, what do I do? It's a proper job, he's offered me a proper job! But I'll have to move, find a new place, and let Frankie down, or hitch to work, and I'll have responsibilities. I'll have to buy proper work clothes. What will I do with Stanley? Will I still have time to help Carrie out at the re-homing centre? Oh my God, a proper grown-up job, a career! My palms have gone all sweaty, my hair, damp from the drizzle is sticking to my face, my nose and ears are bloody freezing, and I can't stand still. I think I need the loo!

'Hey, Daisy! Daisy?'

I look round, there is nobody looking my way.

'Daisy!'

I spin round and my feet slide from under me, so I somehow manage to end up wrapped round a lamppost, like a spiralised strand of cucumber, hanging on tight. It's the laugh that does it though. Helps me pinpoint where the voice is coming from. I glance up, my feet slip-sliding away so that I pirouette round and end up on my bum, gazing upwards.

'What do you think?' Tim is leaning out of the office window, a broad grin on his face. Those fabulous forearms on display, even though it's frigging freezing out here. At his age he should know better.

'Better point out you'd have to put up with me if you say yes, you'd be working here in Stavington.'

I laugh, not sure what to say.

'I know it would mean moving, and you'll only be on a junior's salary. It's lousy pay.'

'How lousy?'

'Not as lousy as you're on now! And it could be worth the risk?' There's a definite question at the end of that sentence. I swear his eyes are twinkling, and the corner of his mouth quirks up in such a cute way I can't stop staring. 'I'm not that bad a boss.'

'You'd be my boss?'

'Guiding the way?'

This isn't sounding bad at all. Better by the second. He would be a tons better boss than David. He's actually quite nice. And a tiny bit sexy.

'Not expecting an answer now, think about it, I've emailed over a job description and terms and conditions for you to look at.'

'Thanks!'

He gives me the thumbs up, then rubs his arms. 'Bloody freezing out here! Happy Easter!' And he ducks back inside, slams the window shut, then re-opens it. 'Don't want to be forward and all that, but you wouldn't fancy seeing me

131

sometime next week for a drink even if you don't want the job?'

'I might be.' I've come over all coy, I think I'm hugging myself.

'Great! Text you, your numbers on file, is that okay? Don't want to break any employment laws!'

'It's okay.' I nod. More than okay.

'Happy Easter!' He backs out of sight and I'm pretty sure he doesn't hear my 'Happy Easter' back.

I am grinning. And I have wet knickers. From sitting under the lamppost, not because I wanted a wee.

Who'd have thought that doggie obituaries could be witty enough to get me the promotion that might solve all my problems – apart of course from the housing one.

I also appear to have a date.

Which is cool. Yeah, definitely cool.

A snowflake lands on my nose, dissolves as quickly as it appeared. I am still musing over cats and dogs when I realise my phone is ringing. I answer automatically without looking at who it is.

'My darling girl, come for a hot drink, hot cross bun and a chin wag! I have a proposition.'

'Sorry?' The word proposition immediately makes me think of Tim. But it isn't him. 'Uncle Terence?'

'That's me!'

'I'm sorry, I'm not at home, I'm—'

'In Stavington! Vera told me you'd be here.'

'Vera?'

'We had lunch.'

'But how did ...'

'Your mother told her. I'm looking right at you – tiny coffee shop across the road. Hurry up before you catch your death. I've got hot chocolate with extra marshmallows at the ready and a pile of hot cross buns. Rather yummy if I say so myself!'

He rings off before I get chance to ask the where, how, why questions that are on the tip of my tongue.

12.30 p.m., 6 April

The warm air hits me as I step into the coffee shop, and I spot Uncle T immediately. It's hard not to. The word that springs to mind is dapper. Uncle Terence is the only person I know who thinks wearing a waistcoat and bowtie at this time of day in a village coffee shop is normal. He has a waistcoat for every occasion, tweed ones, linen ones, and in this case a rather dazzling brocade version, which it's hard not to stare at. He wraps me in a hug and kisses my cheeks, and a waft of very fine aftershave catches the back of my throat. 'Well, isn't this splendid? Just the three of us! Happy holidays, dear girl!' He holds me at arm's length, and I blink.

Then it hits me. 'The three of us?' I still can't drag my gaze from his waistcoat.

'Teal!' He taps his chest and grins, ignoring my comment but noticing my admiring look. 'Bought it when I married

133

Emma because it matched her eyes. Seems a shame not to wear it again. Ah, here's our number three!'

I turn, half expecting to see his latest girlfriend (Emma was two wives ago, and since then he's had more girlfriends than I've had hot cross buns). But it isn't. It's a man, in a very expensive looking well-fitted black coat. He's dusted it down, taken it off, put it on the back of a chair, shook hands with Terence, brushed the snow out of his thick hair, and I'm still doing an impression of a goldfish.

Ollie is wearing a soft looking sweater. Cashmere, I reckon, or something expensive. He looks all soft and stroke-able. And he also looks suave. It's not a word I'd normally use, but it suits him. As does the sweater, and the rather close-fitting jeans. And the slightly tentative smile.

I suddenly feel all hot and bothered, so I sink down onto a chair.

'Oh, my dear girl. Are you alright?' Terence places his hand over mine and looks concerned. It's so touching tears well up in my eyes. 'You look pale. You're not telling me they've not offered you your job back?'

'No, no, I'm fine.' I sniff and try to get a grip. 'I'm happy.' I sniff again. 'It's just the heat in here, and everything.' God knows why I've suddenly come over all emotional. It must be the shock of good news after all the shit. Although I do wish Ollie would stop looking at me in the way I imagine he looks at a patient who he can't find a diagnosis for. I fan myself with a hand madly. 'I don't want to be rude, and it's so lovely to see you, but what are you doing in Stavington?'

Uncle T chuckles. 'I've got a little place here, didn't you know?'

I shake my head, and spoon marshmallows off the top of my drink. 'Oh, Mum said she was sure somebody she knew lived here!'

'Well not exactly live, but more of that later.' He winks, and Ollie shifts uncomfortably in his chair, and frowns.

'Not keeping you, are we?' I don't want to be rude, but I can't help it.

Ollie ignores me and pours his tea.

'Now, tell me, how did it go? Though from the look on your face when you were staring up at that chap from under that lamppost, I'd say things are on the up!'

Ollie makes a funny spluttering noise, which I ignore.

'Definitely.' I grin, I can't help it. 'Definitely on the up. Tim interviewed me and he was so lovely!'

'Your mother will be so pleased. That's why we're here, to celebrate!'

'But what if I hadn't got offered a job?'

'Oh nonsense, your mother was convinced and so was I, she has total faith in you, you know. We all do.' He pats my hand, 'more than you know. That's why she asked Vera to mention it, to sort things out!'

My mother's vote of confidence makes me feel all warm and cosy inside. I think my grin has got even bigger. I am so happy that finally I am starting to prove that her faith has not been misplaced. It's a bloody good job she was right though, or this would have been 'totes embarrassing' as a friend of Frankie's always says after four vodkas. Especially in front of Ollie. But it's not, it's brill!

I laugh self-consciously. My mother has taken bragging to a whole new level.

Uncle T taps the side of his nose. 'But more of that later. So, you're advertising manager!'

'Er, no.'

'Oh. In charge of the small ads?' Uncle T smiles encouragingly, managing to inject the anticipated demotion with positivity.

'No.' I pause and take a deep breath, then carry on quickly before he has chance to move even further down the career ladder. 'They've offered me a better job.'

'Splendid! I knew it!'

'Junior reporter, I'll be writing reviews, books, films, art.' I wave a hand airily.

'Wonderful.' I'm not sure if Ollie is being genuine or not, but he looks sincere when I dare look over my hot chocolate at him.

But his sincere look suddenly gives me the collywobbles. Shit, I haven't actually got a clue about art or how to review. This is real. I've been offered a job I know nothing about.

'What do I do?' I look from him to Uncle T, and back again. 'I don't know anything about it!'

'What do you mean, what do you do?' Ollie's frown is back. He frowns too much, his forehead will be thoroughly furrowed by the time he's forty – like a potato field.

'I've only ever had articles about dogs and cats printed,

and I don't like all art, I told him I don't, I hate all the pretentious stuff and all the deep meaning, and ...' I think this is why I felt emotional when I came into the café. It had begun to dawn on me that I might not be able to do this. 'All I can do is write normal.' I blink at Ollie. The corner of his mouth lifts.

'That's why they offered you the job, you twallop.'

'Really?'

'Really.' He nods. 'And you can spell, can't you? Honestly Daisy, no way is this beyond your capabilities, you could do it in your sleep! It's just saying what you think.'

My cheeks are starting to burn, and I'm squirming about a bit in my seat. Nobody has said such nice things for years! Ollie really does still believe in me, it's not just Mum.

I grin back self-consciously as it hits me just how important it is to me that Ollie thinks I can do it. He's been helping me out because he thinks I can do it, not because he feels sorry for me. Which would have been the absolute pits.

'And you know exactly what you think about books!' Says Uncle Terence. Which is true and makes me feel even more positive.

'Definitely. I do. But' – this is the bit that's starting to worry me – 'I'll have to move, and I don't have any money, my place is really cheap. Frankie hardly asks for anything.' I wish I hadn't said this bit, Ollie will be totally unimpressed that I can't even afford a room in a flat. Although I will be getting paid more. Slightly.

'Well, that's why I'm here darling Daisy.' Uncle T is beaming. 'I have the answer!'

'You do?' Ollie and I say in unison.

'As your mother rightly said, I have a place here.' Yippee, my homelessness problem is solved! 'Ollie uses it when he's in town at the private hospital, don't you dear boy?'

Bugger, no way am I sharing a place with Ollie. He'd hate it. He'd have a spreadsheet for the bathroom and tut at my untidiness. 'He's not there much these days, are you?'

'Well no, but ...' He looks a bit shocked, which is probably more or less how I look.

'So, you'd be more than happy to share with Daisy, wouldn't you?'

'Well, I ...'

'She's excellent company.'

Ollie nods. 'Excellent.' His voice is tight. He's probably thinking about the other excellent female company he usually keeps.

'You know each other so well!'

'Yes, but ...' Oh. My. God. I can't live with Ollie. What if I get an uncontrollable urge to snog him over his cornflakes?

'Well, there you are!' Terence sits back, looking pleased with himself, and I hate to burst his bubble. 'Problem solved then!' He claps his hands together, thrilled that he has provided an answer.

'Well, I'm not sure it ...' Frankie will never believe this, in fact she'll probably want to move in with me so she can keep an eye on Ollie. Once she's stopped laughing about the fact that I'm living with the 'pompous prick' who has been helping me ruin my self-esteem for the past few years. Though, to be fair, it was unknowingly. It's not his fault. Most of it is of my own making.

'Nonsense, it will work perfectly! Won't it, Ollie?' Ollie doesn't comment. 'You can live there for now Daisy, and Ollie can slot in when he needs a place to crash.' He chuckles. 'Don't look so alarmed, there are three bedrooms!'

'One for me and one for Stanley then!' I say, jokingly.

Ollie doesn't seem to see the joke. He frowns. Again.

'Don't you like dogs?' I've heard the 'me or the dog' line before, and I'm prepared to stand up for Stanley again.

'Oh, Stanley. Dog. Yes. No, no that's fine.'

'Wonderful! To new beginnings then!' Uncle T raises his hot chocolate.

'Right, er, new beginnings!' It's a bit weird sitting in a café toasting my future with Uncle Terence, Ollie and hot chocolate. But then, what about my life hasn't been a bit weird lately? 'And,' I say, smiling, 'maybe a new boyfriend!'

Uncle T gives me quite an old-fashioned look, which is not what I expect from him at all. 'Not that I'd let him stay over or anything. It's just a date. A maybe.'

He smiles. 'Wonderful.' He fishes in his waistcoat and doesn't bring out the fob watch I am half-expecting, he brings out a key. 'Ollie can show you round, and if it's not to your taste let me know!'

'Oh, I'm sure it will be perfect.' I'm still not sure about the Ollie angle, but it will be fine. At least short term.

'Thank you.' As long as he doesn't have a shagathon in the next room every time he's there.

'You're very welcome my darling girl. Oh, this is totally splendid, I do believe you might have found your niche, my dear.'

'Niche?'

'Books! I have never known a child devour books like you did when you were little, and now you get to read them for work! You have made your vacation your vocation, as they say! How splendid is that?'

'I have.'

'Right little bookworm you were.' Ollie grins and I grin back. It's good to be friends again with the boy who knows me better than any other man in the world (except Dad). Swapping emails over the last few weeks have made me realise how much I've missed him.

And I have to admit that I like the grown-up version much more than the annoying child. In fact, every now and I again I can't help myself wondering whether we'd have repeated that kiss under the mistletoe last Christmas if we'd both been single.

I blush. I really shouldn't be thinking this way at all – we're supposed to be sharing a flat. Purely as friends!

No snogging. Just friends. He will have his girlfriends, and I have a potential date.

'Splendid, splendid.' Terence grasps my hand in both of his, gives it a squeeze, and stands up. 'Now if you'll both excuse me, I have a wonderful woman to propose to!'

1 p.m., 6 April

'Fancy lunch and a glass of something fizzy? You know, to celebrate? If you've got time?'

'I've got the rest of the day off. What about you? No major surgery planned?'

'Nope. And the sun seems to be coming out, funny kind of weather for April.'

'It's Christmas, delayed. Because I didn't have anything to feel good about in December.'

'Oh? You arranged it?' Ollie grins. 'What do you mean, nothing to feel good about, you saw me for the first time in years!'

'Hmmm.'

'What is that supposed to mean? According to our mothers you've missed me!' His grin slips, probably because I'm not smiling back. Well, I'm trying, but I bet it's a pretty weak attempt.

'Well, it was nice to see you.' I sigh. Ollie and I were always honest with each other. 'But you're a bloody hard act to follow.'

'You were always harder!'

'Were being the operative word. I've been flapping about for a bit.'

He frowns. 'But you're sorted now? The job sounds good.' He's watching me carefully, which is making me wriggle in my seat a bit, and forget all about my job offer, and the lovely Tim. 'Don't you want it?'

'Job, er, yes. Yes, I reckon this could be good for me.'

'It should suit you, something you really want to do.' There's a pause. 'Better than writing dog obits and trying to re-home old people.' The corner of his mouth twitches.

'You read that!' I can't help but grin back.

'I did. Excellent piece of reportage.'

'Small ad, not reporting. Poor Gerald, the dog that is.'

'Close enough. You can write my obit any time.'

'Well you probably will expire before me.'

'You reckon?'

'Statistically, and,' I say, pausing, grinning, 'if you call me a twallop again, or leave the toilet seat up, well, who knows ...'

'Please don't tell me you're going to hit me over the head with Jesus again. Or a book. God, what was it you slapped me with? War and Peace or something? All I did was beat you at spelling!'

He chuckles, it's a grown-up chuckle that starts somewhere deep inside him and warms up something deep inside me. I glance down and study the bubbles in my glass.

It's odd being together like this. Just the two of us. Totally different to swapping jokey emails. When he laughs like that it feels intimate. And I'm back to that 'wondering what it would be like to kiss him'.

'I'd forgotten about that! It was Black Beauty.' I frown. 'That was ages ago, we were still at Primary school.'

'Then you rapped me on the knuckles with a ruler when I beat you in the algebra test.'

'You never did beat me! You cheated. I saw you and Jordan copying each other.'

'Never.' He shakes his head. 'We were collaborating, important part of development, not that you'd know Miss Competitive.'

'I was not.' I was though. Especially where Ollie was concerned. Oh God, I'd forgotten just how determined I used to be to be best at everything. But it was fun, I'd enjoyed the challenge, the hustling. I'd been motivated, and just look at me now. I've let myself become even more of a wet lettuce than I'd realised. It really is a good job that I've finally given myself a talking to and taken the first step along a new path. 'I was just cleverer than you, and I worked harder.' I laugh, a slightly nervous laugh, to cover up my embarrassment. Because I am embarrassed. Truly.

'Dais?' He looks me in the eye. His long fingers twirling the stem of the glass. There's a long pause. I just know he's going to say something I don't like. 'Tell me if it's none of my business.' Another pause. I've got a feeling that whatever he is about to ask will indeed be none of his business.

I stare out of the window. The sun is breaking out from behind the clouds, sending beams of light to warm the flower buds that had never been prepared for the chill. 'The sun's coming out!' I smile, but don't dare look at him. 'I hope the cold doesn't kill the magnolia.' My own gaze is fixed on the beautiful tree that grows just outside the café. Its branches laden with large, open white flowers that are tinged with pink at their centres. 'The tips of the flowers will go brown.'

'They will. Daisy, I can't not ask, can I?'

'Can't you?'

I do look at him now, and his warm brown eyes hold questions that I'm not sure I'm ready to answer.

'No.' His voice is soft. 'What happened? Why did it all go wrong?'

Uh oh. He's no idea what he's asking, how massive a question 'why' is. 'Shit grades.' That's the easy answer. 'Go directly to Clearing, do not pass go, do not collect two hundred pounds.' We used to play monopoly together, he'd get the reference. I try to make light of it, but inside my stomach is clenching.

I can't tell him what happened. Not the full story. I've not told anybody. For a long time I just tried to pretend it never happened – I pushed it out of my head, pushed anybody who wanted to talk about it away. Then I got angry, angry at myself for letting it happen, angry at Josh. And then I just felt sad.

I try to push it out of my head every time it threatens to pop up, because I know if I let myself think about the past the waves will hit again. I don't understand what happened, why it happened, it just makes me want to cry. It makes me feel empty inside, useless. A failure. Out of control, all of those things I don't want to feel.

I've got this now, I really feel like I've got this and am

moving on. I'm scared to talk about the past though, unless I jinx the whole thing.

'Clearing?' Ollie is staring at me, he looks shocked. Which is good, because he'll just put my hopeless-years down to a slip up on the revision front. He never knew just how bad my grades were, just how much of a mess I was in. We'd hardly seen each other after that Christmas snog. We had different friendship groups, different teachers. It was a big school.

'Clearing.' I nod. 'They were seriously shit grades.' Concentrating on the grades is a good distraction. It's black and white, no emotion involved – apart from humiliation.

'But, why?' He looks mystified, though not disappointed. Seeing him disappointed would make me feel even more of a loser. It would hurt, big time. I don't want Ollie to feel sorry for me, to pity me. 'You were such a swot, you were cleverer than me, than all of us.' The corner of his mouth lifts gently, not a smile, a nudge. It shouldn't, but it's making my stomach churn, my palms are suddenly clammy, damp. 'If we're going to be living together, surely we should be honest with each other?'

I shove my hands between my thighs, out of sight. 'Ha-ha, don't push it. We're not living together, we are inhabiting the same apartment. Well it'll be mainly me doing the inhabiting.'

'Dais?' He's not going to let me wriggle out of this one, any more than he used to let me wriggle out of his armlock when I nicked his last sweet. Even as a boy he was as tenacious as a bloody terrier. 'Please?' It is soft, not demanding. And that's why I feel the barrier start to crumble. He's not trying to knock it down, he's just chipping a little hole. Just asking for a glimmer.

'Okay.' I draw the two syllables out, down what is left of my Prosecco, and he tops the glass up. I take a deep breath. 'Josh.'

'Josh?' He looks at me as though I've just sprouted an extra head. 'You flunked your exams because bloody Josh didn't want you to go? You did it for him?'

The way he says *him* makes me blink. I'd never realised he didn't like him. I mean he did warn me off when we were eighteen, but I'd just taken that as a casual comment. 'No, not exactly.' This is awkward. Harder to say than I thought it would be. Humiliating, sad, embarrassing.

'You're not trying to tell me you just didn't want to revise? I don't buy that, Daisy.' He's giving me a reproving look. 'You wouldn't. You were conscientious, you were the person who always did your homework.'

I look back down at my drink and watch the bubbles clinging to the side. They daren't let go and rise. I can sympathise. 'It wasn't that I didn't want to revise, I couldn't. I just couldn't concentrate.' He leans in, because I'm mumbling.

There is a silence. It stretches on so long that in the end I glance up at him. He's waiting for more. But I can't do it. I can't give him more.

'I think I better go now, if that's okay, thanks for the ...'

I wave my hand at the drinks and grab my coat. I'm halfway to the door when I feel his presence behind me.

'Daisy, stop, don't run off.'

'You need to pay, go back.'

'I've paid. Daisy?'

'I have to.' I've been running from my catastrophic past since it happened, but I just can't do it right now. I can't turn around and face it.

'Daisy, please.' He grabs my arm and it halts me in my tracks, I spin round and stare at him, but he's blurry. Everything is blurry.

Even thinking about what happened back then makes me feel queasy, makes me want to bawl like a baby. Part of me wants to tell him, part of me wants to share. But I daren't. He wouldn't understand. What the hell would he think of me if he knew what happened?

Ollie and I are two totally different people these days.

Who have to now find a way to live together.

Bugger.

'I've got to go.' I tug my arm free, and he lets me. To be honest I don't quite know how I feel now I've told him the tiny bit of the puzzle that I have.

I think I feel scared.

Scared of what he'll think if he finds out the rest.

I was quite enjoying getting to know the grown-up Ollie. I was quite getting to like him. I want him to like me too. I don't want to ruin whatever this is between us.

Chapter 12

2.00 p.m., 8 April

'You are shitting me?' Frankie stares. I haven't seen her since she went off to celebrate her birthday with Tarquin, and now she has returned looking slightly less good-living goddess, and slightly more queen-of-shag.

I have been so bursting to announce my news, I've leapt on her as she comes through the front door. Which is probably why she's so taken aback.

'No! They offered me a job! Just like that. I could be chief reviewer by next Christmas! And maybe even start doing features!' I grab her hands and do a little jig. She doesn't join in.

'Wow.' She frowns. 'Look, you know I'm not one to rain on your parade, hun, but is this what you want? Telling the world to watch shit movies?'

'And books.'

She raises an eyebrow. 'Books?'

'Yeah, you know, those things that are piled high in my

148

room! I didn't mean I have to tell the world to read shit books, I meant I'll be writing about them, books as well as movies, though obviously not shit ones. It's about telling the world not to watch the shit ones, just the good ones.' I think my lower lip is sticking out. 'I like watching movies and reading books.'

She suddenly grabs me in a hug. '*Aww*, sorry, I didn't mean to be off. That's great!'

'It is?' I stiffen.

'If it's what you want, then it is! It was just a bit of a shock, I thought you were going to be advertising manager, you know, start at the top!'

'Oh.'

'But if this is what you want, that's fab. Starting over is good, it just seems a shame to waste what you've achieved. But let's celebrate!'

I'm not sure an entry in the obit column has ever been much of an achievement. 'I know it's starting at the bottom, but there will be opportunities this time, I'll get proper training. I'll have a career, rather than a dead end, ha-ha.'

'Brilliant! You'll get there, I know you will.' For the first time she smiles properly. 'Oh, ignore me, I'm so knackered, I so need some space, Tarquin has been on me twenty-four/ seven! Literally!' She leers. Then hugs me again. 'I'm so pleased for you. Honest.'

'I, er ...' I need to get this all out at once, I cringe a bit hoping for a minimal reaction – 'will be working in Stavington, so I'll have to move out I'm afraid.'

'God, you mean I'll have to let Tarquin move in?' Her eyes open wide in mock horror.

'Afraid so.'

'You really are getting your shit together! You go girl! Don't forget me, will you as you zoom to the top?'

'Never! You can't get rid of me that easily, I need you.' I grin, but I mean it. Frankie is good for me, she makes up for the positivity I lack.

'So have you found new digs? I can ask around.'

'No need, Uncle T's got a place he lets out, he said I can stay.'

'Cool.'

'With Ollie.' If I don't tell her, and she finds out (which she will) I'll never hear the end of it.

'Fuck me,' I knew she'd say that. 'I'm not surprised you took the job!'

She is gone before I can protest and tell her that living with Ollie is not the reason I took the job. But I'm sure she's kidding.

She sticks her head out of her bedroom door. 'How about I come there every week?' She wiggles her eyebrows suggestively and I can't help but laugh. Even though I'm still smarting a bit about the job comments. 'Get my feather duster out?'

'He's hardly ever there!'

'Oh yeah, pull the other one, it's got bells on.'

I'm not quite sure if she's pleased for me, or pissed off with me, until she pops out of her room one more time and blows me a kiss. 'What are you waiting for? Get your glad-rags on babe. There's no way are we not celebrating this. It is MEGA.'

'It's only two o'clock.'

'I need to keep partying, if I stop now that'll be it for the day. Maybe even for the week.'

1 p.m., 16 April

'Hi babe! Cool Easter?'

Stanley's back end is flapping about like he's a fish on dry land. He is ecstatic. Carrie has this effect on dogs.

'Great thanks. What about you?' I say this slightly hesitantly. She declared a few years ago that she wasn't going to do any kind of celebrating any more, especially not if it has religious connotations. Which pretty much rules the majority of bank holidays out.

She started up the re-homing centre after her girlfriend Evie died of breast cancer, and she decided that dogs were nicer than any of '*the stupid twats who tried to pick me up while I was still in bits*'. They'd been madly in love, and for a long time she was too broken to do anything but hug the puppy that Evie had handed over to her when she knew she only had days left. She still refuses to date, she says she gets enough love from the dogs. The kind of selfless love that no human but Evie had ever given her.

So I don't push the issue. She needs time, not turkey and tinsel, or chocolate Easter eggs.

'Not bad.' She mumbles from her position on the floor, covered in dog. Stanley is currently trying to French kiss her, which makes talking difficult. 'Stanley been behaving himself?'

'Oh yes, he's brilliant. Everybody loves him. Do you want a coffee?'

'I'm in a bit of a rush to be honest.'

She stands up, lifting Stanley into a cuddle. He's still licking her face. 'Sorry to spring this on you, but those peeps that came to see Stan just before the hols are definitely up for adopting him. They check out, great house, garden, the lot.' She hugs Stanley harder. 'You're such a lucky doggie.'

'Fab!' I try to smile, but my face feels stiff. Stanley is going, somebody has offered him a home, we'll only have a few days left together.

'I suppose it fits in great for you, now you're moving?'

'Well I would have—'

I was about to say, 'taken him with me', but I don't get chance.

'I am really soz to spring this on you, but the sooner he settles in with them the better.' She squeezes my arm. It's then I realise she's still holding Stanley.

'You're taking him now?' What about our private goodbyes I want to say, his last chance to wee on next door's tree, our last walk by the canal, our last shared supper of cheese? What about all his belongings – the tin full of his favourite treats, and the bouncy ball he's totally mad about?

I don't know what it is about Stanley, but I don't want to let him go. When I foster, I always know I'm a stop gap, and I've always been thrilled for the dogs when they find a permanent home. But this time it feels different. I just hadn't seen this coming, some part of my brain thought he'd be with me forever.

'Sure, he'll be off your hands, you'll get the bed to your-self tonight!'

Carrie is happy, but I am not. It's her job to find good homes for the dogs, and she's done it. I'm glad for Stanley, but I'm so, so sad. I love him. I want to cry.

'I'll be in touch next week?'

Oh my God. I mustn't cry. I really mustn't. It will make Stanley sad, he won't understand.

Why does life have to do this? Everything was going so well. I'm friends again with Ollie, I've got a brilliant new job. Things are amazing.

And now this. This is crap. This is so unfair.

I don't want the bed to myself. I want Stanley on it.

'Daisy?'

I nod, then give Stanley a last hug and kiss and whisper in his ear telling him how much I love him, before Carrie eases him back into her arms and he's carried away from me forever.

Then I go back to my room. Throw myself on my bed and have a bloody good full-on snotty cry.

Chapter 13

3 p.m., 22 April

'What are you doing here?' I know this is not the usual way to greet visitors, but I'm a bit shocked when I answer the door expecting to see Tarquin, and it is in fact Ollie. 'Sorry, I mean, hi!'

We stare at each other. This could be awkward. The last time I saw him was over a glass of bubbly, and then I ran away.

But then he grins. It's a bit of a boyish grin, rather than a senior consultant serious grin. 'Hi to you too! Uncle T told me to come and help you move. Not that I wouldn't have offered anyway, I mean I didn't just come because ...'

'I'd shut up now if I was you.'

'I will.' He smiles again, then motions behind me. 'Can I come in? Hard to help from here.'

'Sure, sure.'

'Which way?'

I point towards my room, feeling hot and bothered as he squeezes past. 'I don't actually need a hand though.'

'Oh, sorry, you've got help?' He looks around, as I obviously haven't. I don't need it.

'No.' I wave a hand indicating all my worldly possessions – most of which are piled on the bed. 'I've got very little to move.'

'Ah. Right. Well, I can help you shift this.' He lifts up one end of the chest of drawers, and the muscles in his arms bulge slightly. I didn't expect him to have muscles, in my head he's never been that type. I'm dying to prod them though, see how hard they are. I would have done if we were still kids, now it would seem odd. 'I meant to say last time we met and forgot. Also, whilst I'm thinking about it, I want to apologise for Juliet at the Christmas party, she can be a bit of a cow.'

I didn't expect to hear him call anybody a cow. We share a smile. His arms are beginning to quiver a bit. 'Other end?' He indicates with his head. The quiver is more of a tremble now.

I can't believe how fast this is all happening now, it's a bit like an unstoppable torrent. Once I'd confirmed that I'd be delighted to accept the terms and conditions of the new job, the wheels were set in motion and within what seemed like only hours I'd got a start date, a confirmed salary (much better than my old one, and with a rise after three months!), had agreed with Frankie when I'd move out, and had boxed up my stuff in the office.

'It's fine, fine.' Juliet is the least of my worries and I don't know why he's brought her up, unless he's bothered that I'll be rude to her when she comes to *our* apartment. 'I'm sure she's nice.' Underneath a heavy layer of sarcasm and bitchiness.

'She was out of order. Nobody wants to hear they've lost their job at a Christmas party from a stranger.' His arms are practically shaking now, from bearing the weight of the furniture, and he's gritting his teeth a bit.

'Well next party I'll be able to tell her I've got a new much better job!' I have totally decided I can do this job. I am finally taking charge of my future.

'Maybe not.'

'Not?' I frown, does he know something I don't? How can I have cocked up before I start? Or does he actually have no faith in me doing this job after all?

'We've gone our separate ways.'

'Phew. Sorry, not about you and her, phew about something else, phew it's hot in here.' Ha-ha. Thank God for that. He wasn't talking about my shiny new career being in jeopardy, he was talking about Juliet.

Wow, Juliet! He's split up with Juliet. He's a single man. Why am I grinning and have an (almost) uncontrollable urge to run round the flat jumping about with glee? This is weird, and totally out of proportion. It is also a bit mean, he could be heartbroken, but he doesn't look heartbroken. I tilt my head on one side and study him more closely. 'Did you know you've gone a bit red in the face?'

'Of course, I've gone bloody red in the face, woman. This is heavy! Are you going to?' He tips his head, indicating the other end of the cabinet again. He's gone *very* red, I think I spot beads of sweat.

I fold my arms and smile. 'Not mine. I don't own furniture. It came with the room.'

He drops it, looking embarrassed. Then he starts to chuckle. 'Why the hell didn't you tell me! You did that on purpose!'

'It was you who picked it up, I never asked you to!'

He shakes his head, still laughing. 'You always were a bit of a smart arse Daisy Dunkerly!'

'And you always were ...'

'Oh my God it's the pomp—'

I am going to die. Frankie has just burst into the room and is going to call him a pompous prick. Luckily, she is stopped in her tracks when somebody grabs her from behind. Tarquin.

'Door was open, so I came in, baby!' He kisses her neck and I roll my eyes. They are just so over the top touchy-feely. It gets obscene at times, depending on where they touch and feel. This is something I am *not* going to miss.

'Sorry, I think I forgot to shut it.' I was too busy holding my bits in as Ollie squeezed past.

Tarquin was so thrilled when he found out I was leaving, that he started to try to move his gear in straight away. It's been a battle, him dropping stuff in random places in the flat, and Frankie moving them back to the bag on his peg. I'm not sure at this point who is going to win, they're both pretty determined. And the bag is pretty near bursting point.

'God, I am going to ravish you in every inch of this place you sexy witch.'

'Go!' I push Frankie back out of my very small room. 'Both of you, you pervs. You could at least wait until we've left!'

Lordie, this is embarrassing. I glance at Ollie who has grabbed a random cushion and is looking at my OTT flat-mate, and her lust-filled lover with a dazed expression on his face. It's like when you're watching a movie with your parents, then the stars unexpectedly strip off and go at it like rabbits. Awkward.

'Right. Well. Just cases then?' Ollie puts the cushion down, picks up a carrier bag in one hand and is reaching for a case.

'Just cases. And cushions, and my duvet. Stick your arms out.' I start to pile things on top until he's stacked up to his nose, so I figure he can still see. 'Oh, and books, but I've already put them in boxes in my car. They're the most important thing!'

'Where's Stanley?'

'Gone.' I say it quickly and turn away, checking there's nothing left under the bed. Giving my face time to straighten itself out again. Ollie will think I'm ridiculous, crying over a dog.

Stanley has gone, and I am heartbroken. He was the best furry little buddy I've ever had. I'll also be sad to leave

Frankie of course, she's been my hero and my hand-holder. But not as hot on the cuddles, listening and warming my feet up front.

I'd been tempted to beg Carrie to let me keep him. But this is going to be my year. I am going to have a bigger room, more money, a new career and, and this is the real biggie: I am going to be organised!

And I'm sure Stanley's new home will be much better for him. Even though I'm missing him so much it hurts. The flat has seemed so empty without him, and just looking at the spot where I used to keep his toy box makes me well up. I am heartbroken but I have to think of Stanley. Stanley is lucky. I have done my job and helped him on his way and I must be brave about it.

I glance round my room for a final time, then pull the door closed. It feels strangely symbolic, as though I am finally shutting the door on a not very successful part of my past.

Then the thought pops back into my head again, Ollie is single! And I'm pretty sure I've got a stupid grin on my face and I've just giggled. God knows why!

4 p.m., 22 April

Ollie throws the door to the apartment open and I am stunned into silence. Well, not quite stunned, or silent.

'Bloody hell, this looks like some kind of show apartment!'

'It is a bit ordered I suppose.'

159

'Ordered? It's, it's unreal.' I have never really believed minimalistic exists in the real world. It is an illusion, something to aspire to. It is glossy magazine, it is not real life. Well, it is now. It is very smart, very tidy (as in there is nothing that isn't totally functional) and strangely like the inside of a space capsule. 'Has your mother never told you about soft furnishings?' Vera does the lived in and cosy look very well. Smart but welcoming.

'I'm not here much, but I suppose it could do with somebody giving it a bit more of a lived-in look.' He tosses one of my cushions on to a chair.

'I can make it look lived in.' I can, I really can. But this is worse than I ever imagined. I still thought underneath it all, Ollie and I were *slightly* similar. But we're not. He might as well be an alien from another planet. I think after we left school he must have been abducted and re-programmed.

He is going to *hate* living with me.

'I'm sure you can soon put your stamp on it.' His laugh is slightly nervous.

Oh yeah. A stamp of dog hairs (Stanley might have gone, but there will be other dogs that need me), books, clothes, cushions and general clobber. He will hate it. He will hate me. Living with Ollie (even if he is never there) will never work.

'You'll hate my stamp.'

He shrugs. 'Try me. I'm tougher than I look,' then a cheeky grin breaks out, 'and I can always kiss you again if you annoy me too much.'

Oh my God, this is awkward. What's he doing talking

about *that kiss*? I spend a lot of time trying not to think about that kiss. Does he think about it as well? Or is he talking about when we were six years old? Eek this could be awkward. He might have completely forgotten the second time. I swallow hard to dampen my dry throat and try not to squeak. Casual, I need to be casual. 'Is that why you did it? To shut me up?'

'The first time?' He raises an eyebrow. 'Or the second?' I blush. He does remember it! This is the closest we've ever come to mentioning that drunken kiss, the second kiss. Which is probably best forgotten. Well, I haven't forgotten it, it has somehow lodged in my memory banks and refuses all efforts to erase it. And pops into my head every now and again when I think about him. Not that I want to erase it, because it was nice, but we shouldn't have. Not a full-on snog. We're not like that. We're friends.

'First!' I squeak.

'I guess so. It did shut you up, though the violence was a bit uncalled for.'

'Ha-ha.' It's okay, he's not going to dwell on the one-that-shouldn't-have-happened. Though I wonder what he thought about it? Has he ever been tempted to do it again? 'I'm even more dangerous these days, I've got a much better left hook.'

'I bet.' He backs off. 'Guess I better go before you get tempted to try it out. Give me a call if you need anything, or the central heating plays up, cooker doesn't work.'

'I will. Thanks for the lift.' This is fine. Not awkward

at all. He has brushed off the second kiss like an expert. Which is slightly disappointing if I'm totally honest. But good. Perfect. How it needs to be.

'No probs.'

'Guess you better get back to saving lives.'

'Guess so.'

'I'll look for my own place as soon as I can, then you can have some peace and quiet.'

'No rush. I'm not here that often, and who knows,' he shrugs, 'I might get to like a homely touch.'

The apartment is strangely quiet when he's gone. So I rifle through his CD's, put some music on and start to put my stamp on things.

8 p.m., 22 April

'Just thought I'd check you know where everything … bloody hell, you've made it, er, different.' Ollie is standing in the middle of the living room and his head is practically spinning 360 degrees.

'What you mean is, I've got stuff.'

'Where the hell did all this come from? You didn't have anything!'

'In my suitcases, I know how to pack.' I see a small space as a challenge. Well, apart from when I'm expected to live in it. I have tried every variant of packing, from the stuff it in and hope, to the fold it, to the roll and wedge and I can honestly say that a combo wins every time.

I don't actually have *that* much stuff. Ollie is exaggerating. He's just not used to cushions. And throws.

'You did say you were sure I could put my own stamp on the place. So I have.'

So now he's back and is admiring my stamp. Or not.

'Just a few cushions and throws.'

'And flowers, and photos, and,' he pauses, picks up the framed photo I'd put on the windowsill. 'Bloody hell, it's Mary and Joseph, before you gave me a black eye!' He chuckles, and the laughter reaches his eyes. 'You kept this, all these years?'

'Well, we had some fun times, and actually my parents framed it for me so I can't hide it away. It would be rude.' It is actually quite cute as well, but I'm not going to say that.

He laughs. 'We did, even if you were a bossy know it all, and I was,' there's a long pause, and he looks me right in the eye. 'A pompous prick.'

Oops. Embarrassing. I didn't realise he'd heard Frankie say that. She can be so mean, and loud, at times. 'Oh, you weren't a pompous prick then, you were just a pain in the arse.'

'But I am one now?' He tilts his head on one side, but his gaze never breaks. Which is making me feel a bit hot and bothered. Awkward.

All I can do is shrug. 'Well, in my head you were, cos I hadn't seen you for years.'

'Why?'

'Because you don't come to Uncle T's parties!'

'Not that, why was I a pompous prick in your head?'

'Well, it was either that or a demigod.'

'I'd have preferred divine rather than dick.'

'Wasn't your call. Wine?' I wave my glass at him, it would seem rude not to, after his help, and drinking alone isn't brilliant.

He nods, and follows me to the kitchen, getting a glass out of the cupboard and waiting for me to pour.

'So what's your problem with me, apart from,' his eyes are twinkling, our fingers brush as I pass the wine back to him, and I feel a bit hot and bothered again. I'm sure I'm far too young to be menopausal, maybe this place is over heated. Yes, definitely, toasty warm. My body isn't used to toasty warm. 'Apart from my perfection?'

'That's the problem! Have you any idea how much of your brilliance is shoved down my throat by my mum and yours? I think Mum wants to adopt you and disown me.'

'I'm sure she doesn't, on either count.'

'I flunked my 'A' levels, took a crap degree—' Oh God, I shouldn't have mentioned that again. He's giving me a look. That type of look that says it's going to be hard to get out of explanations this time.

Would it be rude to grab his glass back off him and push him out of the door? Or at least into his own room. Or make a run for my own? Which might involve a sliding rugby tackle and sliding between his legs, seeing as he's blocking my exit.

'You *always* wanted to be a vet, you had it all planned

out from the time you were twelve or something daft like that, didn't you? You pulled your dog's baby teeth out!'

I'm surprised he remembers. I can't remember for the life of me what he wanted to be, apart from rich, popular and sophisticated. Like the rest of his family, apart from his mum who is just plain nice.

I nod.

'You were always the school swot, you were clever. Bloody hell, in those days it was *your* brilliance that was shoved down my throat. You win on the pain in the arse stakes.'

'Not any more!'

'Oh, Dais, can't you tell me what happened? I'm not going to judge you, I'd just like to know.'

'I grew up, fucked up and fu—' I was going to say fucked off, but I didn't. I stayed right here.

'Come on, Dais! It's me you're talking to.'

I study him for a moment in silence. It's almost like we're back in those days when we could say what we liked to each other, try to drown each other, see who could climb the highest up the tree his mum had said we should never climb.

Almost. Except now he's not gawky, pale, pimply and with knobbly knees that looked like Bart Simpson's if you squinted.

He's toned, tanned, and well Frankie's right, he's hot. Not that I should go there. We're mates. Always have been, always will be (well apart from for the past thirteen or so years). And not that I know about the state of his knees,

165

not at all. Not seen his knees, don't want to see his knees. Ever again.

'Well?'

He's still bloody annoying though.

I sigh. 'Okay then, a poorly horse, daft dog, sex mad boyfriend, take your pick.' I shrug. 'End result is the same, didn't revise, crap results.'

'Really?' He doesn't believe me. 'I thought you just couldn't concentrate?'

'Stop giving me the evil eye! Really!'

'Okay, so why didn't you retake? It was what you really wanted to do!'

I down my wine and top up our glasses. This is one question I've never really found an answer to. Well, okay, I've never honestly tried. It never occurred to me to do resits. I just accepted my failure. I wasn't in a fit state to go back and live those few months over again, it wouldn't have changed anything.

I'd needed time. Time to come to term with things.

'Didn't you want to? I mean, it's okay to not want to, exams aren't everything.'

'It wasn't that simple, Ollie.' I hadn't been able to get my head around what was happening to me in that winter term after I'd kissed Ollie. It had made it impossible to concentrate, thrown up so many questions about my future. Then, just as I'd thought that maybe I had a plan, it was all thrown up in the air again. And when the pieces came down they fell in a totally different place to where I'd expected.

Ollie is watching me, and I realise that I do actually want to tell him. I want to explain. I don't want him to think I just gave up on everything for no reason.

I don't want him to think I turned my back on the person I used to be, the ambitious, confident teenager he'd once kissed.

I put down my glass I am clutching before I either break it, or end up spilling the drink all over myself, because my hands are trembling so much. Take a deep breath and look him in the eye.

And something about him is so open, so honest, so concerned, it helps me speak with hardly a trace of a wobble in my voice.

'If I tell you this, you mustn't tell anybody. Not Uncle Terence, not your parents, nobody.'

He stares back, confused. But nods.

'Especially not your Mum.' Though I suspect she might know.

'Daisy, you're worrying me here.'

'I couldn't concentrate because,' I summon up the courage, my blood is pounding in my ears, my voice sounds distant, then it comes out in a rush, 'I found out I was pregnant.'

I've not spoken about that pregnancy, that baby, for years.

Since I was eighteen years old, and doing it now, putting it into real spoken out-loud words is weird.

I definitely don't feel unburdened and light though.

This is why my mother's plans for me and perfect Ollie are so, so way off the mark. I don't deserve a family, I don't deserve a sparkling life, and I don't deserve a man like Ollie. A man who can have it all, when I know damned well that I would never be able to give him the baby he'd want. I couldn't. I couldn't face that again.

And from the look of shock on his face he's just realised how different our lives now are.

But I do deserve a better life than the one I've got. I do deserve to get back on track, even if that track is a different one from the one Ollie is on. From now on we need to live parallel lives, in the same apartment.

I swallow. He doesn't say anything for a long time, just studies my face. Then he slowly puts his own glass down.

'Oh, Daisy, why have you never told anybody?' He puts his hand over mine, and I can't help it, I snatch mine away. I don't want to be touched. Not right now. Because I don't want to cry, I don't want to think about that stupid pregnancy test, that stupid blue line that I'd not been able to fix. Up until then I'd had a solution for everything in my life. And suddenly, I hadn't. 'What happened to—'

'Do you mind if we stop?' My throat is scratchy, the words stilted. 'Talk about it another time, please?'

He nods.

I blink away the prickly sensation in my eyes. 'I couldn't concentrate, I tried, I really tried but my brain just didn't work, I couldn't do it. But I still thought, I still hoped that I'd somehow wing it, that I'd get the grades. I'd still been shocked that I'd cocked it all up.' I sip my wine and frown down at the glass. 'Seeing those results on paper completely threw me.' My words swirl around in my mouth, my head, then slowly sink in.

I had felt like I'd lost everything. I'd got nothing. Was nothing.

It completely derailed me, I can see that now. When I was young, everything had always worked out okay for me, I'd just drifted along without questioning things. I'd never for a moment considered failure. It wasn't that I thought I was too good, it just didn't really exist. And even though I had struggled over some of the questions on the exam papers, it had still never occurred to me that I would end up with nothing.

Failure and loss had left me feeling steamrollered. Squashed and useless. I'd always succeeded, then I'd failed at the most important point of my life so far. 'Then I guess I started to question what I wanted.'

'Which is?'

'I dunno.' I look down, avoiding his earnest gaze. Trying to keep my voice even. 'I really didn't have an answer.' The question was too big, too difficult. Too unexpected.

I thought I'd known what I'd wanted, then in a blink of an eye my future life had been swept away by a pregnancy I'd not expected and a set of crappy exam questions I hadn't prepared for.

I flap my hand in front of my face and bite down on my lip to stop the emotion bursting free. There's a long pause, then he seems to realise he needs to change tack. Save me before this gets messy.

'I thought you did actually work at the vets? With, old what's his name Hanford, Herbert?'

'How do you know that? You were in Borneo or Bosnia or somewhere.' I laugh awkwardly, relieved he's moved on.

'Bristol probably.' His tone is dry, but there are dimples at the corners of his mouth. 'I've only done a couple of stints abroad. But Mum told me.' He raises an eyebrow. 'She tells me quite a lot about you.'

My God, has he been regaled with every detail of my crap life, in the same way I've had the minutiae of his success?

'He let me go. The vet.'

'Because?' He tops up our glasses.

'I threatened him with a scalpel when he tried to put a cat down for no reason.'

'No reason?'

'Well it did wee where it shouldn't, well not just where it shouldn't, pretty much everywhere, but he might do that one day! Incontinence shouldn't be a death sentence!'

Ollie is chuckling, I heave a sigh of relief. I'm on solid ground again. 'He's a stupid git anyway, haven't liked him since he called our rabbit weird.'

'Well, Hoppity was a bit weird.' I try to keep a straight face and serious voice. He was, I think in a previous life he had been a lamb or kid.

'So? There's plenty of room in the world for weird.'

'True.'

'How did you end up writing small ads then?'

'I was headhunted.' I wink, and he laughs again. I quite

like making him laugh. In the old days it was the other way round, he used to enjoy nothing better than pinning me to the ground and tickling me until I felt sick. That kind of behaviour is perfectly acceptable when you're under the age of ten, less so when you are grown adults like we are now. If he did it now it might lead to all kinds of things it shouldn't. I must stop thinking these inappropriate thoughts. I really must. 'They loved my witty prose. I sent in ads for the dog's home.'

'Ah, right. Sorry you lost Stanley.'

'So am I. I miss him.'

'I missed Hoppity.' He says it with such a straight face, for a moment I think he's serious. Then the fan of fine line lines round his eyes deepens, and his dimples reappear.

It's sickening to admit, but I'm not surprised Vera goes on about him so much. He's a son to be proud of.

The laughter dies from his face. 'But you're good now, you want to do this job?'

'I do.' As I say it, I realise I really do. I like writing. I like the slight air of chaos in the office, the buzz of activity, the tension as deadlines approach. It's good. It's fun. 'It's just a tiny bit ...'

'Terrifying?'

I nod.

'I'm terrified every time I go into surgery. But what do they say? Feel the fear and do it anyway? You can do this, Dais, you know you can. Any girl who can beat me at arm wrestling has to be a winner, even if she did cheat.'

171

'Who are you calling a cheat? I just used my initiative. Anyway, you just want me to do it so I start earning and can get out of your hair.'

'You said it!' He's got that cheeky grin on his face, the one I remember from years ago.

'I will be rich and famous.' I wave my arms about. 'And worth boasting about, people will read my column and gasp!'

We both laugh, and then he stops first. Probably because he is less pissed than me, this wine really has gone to my head.

I think talking about awkward stuff made me neck it quicker than I should have.

'Stuff all that, you will be *you*, Dais, the old you. The one we love.' He's looking at me so intently I've come out in goose bumps, maybe he *is* as pissed as me. It's all a bit intense.

There's a loud buzz and for a moment I'm confused, then realise it's the intercom. We both dash for it at the same time and have a messy wine incident when we clash.

'Yes?' Ollie has beaten me to it.

'Oh, er, not sure got right door.'

Even though it's distorted, and I don't know his voice very well, it has to be Tim. Nobody else misses so many words out. 'Looking for Daisy?'

'I'm here!' I yell under Ollie's armpit, he's too tall for me to shout over his shoulder even when I stand on tip toes. I press the entry button, and a second later he's at the door.

'*Ta-dah!*' Waggling a bottle of wine. 'Welcome gift!' He

stares at Ollie. 'Not interrupting anything am I?' It is then I remember that I said he was welcome to pop in any time.

'Nothing. Nothing at all.' Lovely, funny Ollie has gone, and stiff, formal Ollie is back. Shame. Although better to be interrupted before I drank more wine and was tempted to rugby tackle him, which could go badly now we're both grown up. 'I'll be off then, don't want to get in your way.' He picks up his jacket. 'Stay in touch, and er good luck with the job, though I know you'll smash it. Fine, right.' He is suddenly awkward, which is unexpected.

'Yes, sure, thanks for helping, and for dropping in, and everything.'

He smiles, a soft, gentle glance that is less sympathy, more understanding. Could I ever tell Tim, or any other man, what I've just told him? My cheeks are burning.

'Oh,' he takes a step then pauses on the doorstep, 'Uncle T said if you need any help give him a shout. I'm the muscle man,' he flexes his arm and I can't help but smile, 'he's the literary expert. For God's sake don't confuse us and ask me about books.'

'She's got me for that!' Says Tim, shrugging off his coat. Making himself at home alarmingly easily.

'Sure.' Ollie gives him what only can be described as an assessing look and is gone. He'll have to be careful or I'll put him back in the pompous prick category.

I smile at Tim, and for a brief moment feel a little bit miffed that he arrived just as my goose-bumps burst out. It was just like old times chatting to Ollie. But better.

Actually, he's not pompous at all. I'm a little bit sad he's gone now – it might have been quite nice to spend the whole evening together.

7 p.m., 29 April

'Let's drink to surviving a week!' Tim raises his beer bottle and plonks his feet on the coffee table. I'm not sure Ollie would approve.

'Oh my God, yeah!' Frankie who is sitting on my other side raises her glass. 'Here's to the end of shitty adverts and a whole new beginning for the critic of the year!'

I decide not to mention the fact that only a week ago she was telling me that advertising manager was my way forward, and I was compromising my ideals by starting at the bottom again. I was actually quite miffed at the time, and if it hadn't been for Ollie agreeing that my job was totally the right thing, I might have started doubting myself again. I try not to sigh. Frankie is lovely, Frankie is amazing, but sometimes she isn't exactly encouraging – in fact she can put quite a dampener on things. I've started to wonder if Frankie actually preferred the old, accepting me, and might not totally have my interests at heart. She's been more comfort blanket (sympathising with my lack of success) than Mrs Motivator.

'How's she doing?' She talks across me to Tim.

'Acing it.' Tim gives a thumbs up.

I am actually. Acing it. I have written my first bunch

of reviews and if I say so myself, they were rather good. Tim also took me to a very good vegan café for lunch and kissed me on the way back. It wasn't completely toe-curlingly good, but it was more than passable. It stirred up feelings in my nether regions that hadn't been stirred for quite a long time. I had been a bit concerned that more than my abs would have been declared redundant by my 32nd birthday, but I am now cautiously optimistic that a full bodily work out is on the cards.

'You haven't snogged him, have you?' Hisses Frankie in my ear as I open the front door for her.

'Might have.' I think I have a silly grin on my face.

'But he's a vegan, what if he doesn't eat—'

'Go away!' I push her out of the door before she finishes her sentence, which I have a feeling is going to be very rude.

'Are you allowed to shag your boss?'

'Out!'

'Call me tomorrow, report on the meat situation!' She cackles and dodges my swipe.

'Miss you, Frankie!'

'Miss you too, hun. But boy is Tarquin trying to make up for my loss!'

Chapter 14

8 p.m., 10 July

'I thought you'd want to know, it didn't work out for Stanley.'

'How? What? Hang on Carrie, let me mark this page.' I stick an envelope between the pages and drop the book I'm trying to read.

To be honest, I feel like my brain is on fire and my head is about to explode. I don't normally read anything scary, as there are far too many nasty things in real life and I like my fiction to cheer me up, but I was told (by Tim) that this was a *must read*, we couldn't not review it. It is scary, I am holding my breath, but also flicking the pages as fast as I can. Partly because I just have to know what happens, partly because the quicker I can get it over with the more chance I have of sleeping tonight. It's a love hate relationship, God only knows how I am going to review it. The words 'not for the faint hearted' definitely need to be included.

'The vet called us after their cat got totally cheesed off with being chased and nearly took his eye out.'

'Oh no, poor Stanley.'

'It's not just that.' There's a long pause. 'That's the story they told him, but he said there are other cuts and bruises and he's got quite nervous. I mean, can you imagine Stanley diving for cover when there's food on offer?'

'No.' It comes out as a little squeak. I feel a bit queasy, my stomach all hollow. Surely nobody could harm gentle little Stanley.

'That's why he called me. I picked him up, and he's definitely not himself, but now the bloody people want him back, they said they'll sue us if I dare re-home him with anybody else, said he's theirs now and they can do what they want. How could I get it so wrong?' She finishes on a bit of a wail.

'Oh hell, Carrie. It's not your fault, it really isn't, you're so careful about checking people out. The sods. Do you want to bring him here? Poor little Stanley, he wouldn't hurt a fly.' A sausage roll maybe, but not a fly.

'No, I can't.' She sighs. 'He needs to be here until this is resolved, or God knows what they'll accuse me of. I can't afford solicitors or anything like that.'

'I'll have a think. Maybe I can get somebody to run something in the paper?'

'I'm not trying to stir up trouble, I don't want you to do anything, Daisy. I just wanted you to know, I know how fond of him you were.'

'Okay, thanks. But if there's anything I can do.'

'Thanks, hun. I'll call you. I just thought you should know, that's all.'

9pm 10th July

I can't concentrate on my book. How can my head deal with a duplicitous psycho killer when poor Stanley is in danger? What if they go and smuggle him out when Carrie isn't looking?

Or, I put the book back down, what if I do it first?

I blame the story for making me think this way. But it is a brilliant idea! Carrie doesn't even know where I live now, so she'll have no idea where he is if they call in the heavy mob. They'll never find him!

But I can't do it on my own.

I'll call Tim.

I can't call Tim. We decided to rethink (his word not mine) our relationship after a mega row by the water cooler at work yesterday. It started with chocolate. I'd tried to snatch a quick snog the night before after committing the felony of eating *milk* chocolate. It was still on my teeth, or tongue, or breath or something. Apparently, it completely ruined the kiss for him, and made him feel a bit off all the way home, so he just *had* to bring it up at work, he couldn't not as it was preying on his mind.

Oh God, he is *so* not perfect for me. How can I go out with somebody who doesn't like chocolate? But he's kind, and nice, and keen to help my career. And it would be so lovely to take him with me to Mum's surprise party, and maybe even Uncle T's Christmas Eve buffet, and show everybody how far I've come this year.

And I do like him.

Even if when I mentioned that feeding me tofu under false pretences was worse than chocolate-breath, it all escalated from there and came to a head when our boss happened to walk past and tapped his watch. We were on a deadline.

To be honest though, I've never been sure about the whole going out with somebody from work thing (though it is where I've met quite a few boyfriends), so we decided like mature adults that we should take a step back. So we have. Which is a bugger as far as the party goes.

He's not spoken to me since, apart from to throw the scary book at me.

I could ask Frankie to help me rescue Stanley, but she might give the game away if Carrie goes over there. It needs to be somebody independent.

'You don't know where the bottle opener is, do you?'

'Shit!' I jump. 'You scared me, I forgot you were here.' Ollie isn't here often, and when he is, he's a bit like the invisible man. Especially if Tim is around. He doesn't seem to like him much, he comes over all stilted and formal, and apologises for interrupting.

Which actually makes living with him much easier than I thought it would be. Not the stilted bit, the not being there bit.

I've actually got this massive place all to myself most of the time, but it's quite nice when Ollie is here, it somehow makes the place feel more like home. Which is a bit weird, but it does. I guess we've known each other so long we're like brother and sister, even if I do sometimes have very un-sisterly thoughts about him. But no way am I ever going to act on them and kiss him a third time (not that he'd want me to), I'd be losing one of my best buddies. But I am bloody tempted at times, just so that I can see if his snogging has improved. That's all. No other reason.

'Are you okay, you look a bit pale?'

'It's Stanley!' The words spill out before I can stop them. 'He's in danger!'

'What?' He looks startled. 'What kind of danger?'

'Sorry, I'm being melodramatic, it's that book, and the way you made me jump, and, well they've hurt him, well the cat did, but the vet thought it might have been them not the cat, and I need to kidnap him and make sure they can't have him back.'

'Who's hurt him?' Ollie picks the book up absent-mindedly, opens it at the page I've marked and skims over it. 'Bloody hell I'm not surprised you're jumpy, this is enough to give anybody nightmares.'

'Even you?'

He grins. I've got used to his grin, it's the grown-up version of the one he had as a kid. 'Well obviously not me, but for a girlie-girl like you.'

I throw a punch, and he laughs, and easily dodges it. 'See what I mean? Lightweight!'

'You watch it, I'll come and sort you out in the middle of the night!' I wag a finger at him.

'Promises, promises.' There's silence as his laughter dies and he puts down the book, as we both realise what he just said. Awkward. Even more awkward is the fact that I'm pretty sure I am now the colour of a pickled beetroot.

'I didn't mean, I meant, I ...'

'Reading this for business or pleasure?' He's better at recovering than I am.

'Business, definitely business! Oh God, yeah, that book is horrible. Well in a good way, a brilliant way, it is brilliant, it's just ...'

'Scary?'

'Terrifying.'

'Work going well then?'

'Brilliant, apart from this book. I'll just find the bottle opener for you.'

'Why is it there?' He looks perplexed as I fish it out from the drawer next to the sink.

'I've rearranged things.' Work really is going brilliantly, and somehow because I have to be more organised in the office it seems to be seeping into other parts of my life. Not only am I now filing things in the right folder on my laptop, I am also now filing kitchen utensils in more appropriate places. It's confusing Ollie a bit, but he hasn't complained. Yet.

'Uncle T said you'd been in touch a couple of times?'

'Uncle T has been ace!' He really has. He's dropped in the apartment a few times, when Ollie has been in far flung places, to check things are okay. 'Did you tell him I was stuck with that romcom?' I'd been trying to compare a modern day romcom with the classic novel that it mirrored, and the words just hadn't flowed. Ollie had popped home to find me lying on the floor, staring up at the ceiling, the book open on my chest – waiting for some kind of inspiration, or divine intervention. I was easy either way.

'Might have done.' He smiles, slightly abashed. It makes him look cute, vulnerable.

'He's read so many books.' I swallow away the dryness in my throat and bash on, talking rubbish, to cover my embarrassment at thinking of smart-arse Ollie in that way.

'He sells them, guess it goes hand in hand.' Ollie grins, as he pours us both a glass of wine. Luckily, he doesn't look as cute now, just his normal self. I have to say through he does have very capable looking hands. I can quite imagine him leaning over a patient shouting 'scalpel please nurse.'

'Well not always, he really loves books, with a passion.' I wonder if Ollie loves operating with a passion? 'He's quite a passionate person I think.' I now realise that I hadn't known Uncle T at all well before, but our regular grown-up chats since the start of the year have shown a whole new side of him. He really is a passionate person, he embraces life head on.

'He has to be, with all those wives.'

'I think he's a true romantic.'

'Really?' Ollie raises an eyebrow.

Before, I used to laugh about Terence's many wives, it's a bit of a family joke. But I think it's because he really loves, well, the idea of love. I've also started to think he's chasing some ideal that he can't find. He likes all his wives, and they all like him – even after divorce – but it's almost like every relationship falls at some hurdle, leaves him slightly disappointed. I actually think Uncle Terence is like some tragic hero who found and lost true love and has been searching for something as good ever since.

But I don't think I'm going to say this out loud to Ollie.

I also don't think I'll mention what I found hidden amongst Uncle T's special editions, the ones he keeps locked in a cabinet, when I was rooting around for inspiration last Saturday. I'd been minding the shop for him, while he popped out.

I wasn't snooping, honestly. It just felt out of a first edition of 'The Great Gatsby'. I'd only picked the book up to stroke the cover, and a yellowing sheet of paper drifted to the floor.

It was a love letter. A love letter that brought a lump to my throat, and tears to my eyes.

My darling V,

Today is the day my heart was shattered into a million tiny shards.

Exquisite love brings exquisite pain, and exquisite is the word that has always suited you best.

Today you shone, your eyes alive with a joy that

extinguished a light inside my soul. Today the diamond that flickered for the first time on your finger, was the dagger that tore my heart asunder.

Today I was transformed from lover to slave, when you chose another man over me. How did I not know that my time had run out? What kind of fool let's another step in, because he has feared to step boldly into commitment?

I am no longer master of my emotions, I can no longer express my ardour, my pain, I must obey your wishes, admire your beauty from afar. Watch you with another.

Sorrow is not sweet, love in the shadows is no love at all. But my passion for you, my darling, is my purpose. Beneath my façade of indifference, the man that watched you go without a murmur, lies only my agony. You must know my sweetheart, that my soul, my essence, the very core of me can do no other than love you for all eternity. Without my passion for you I am lost. Without that I am nothing. An empty vessel of no use.

A life without you my darling, is a shadow of a life.

Darkness has fallen.

But still, I am yours for eternity, T xxx'

Oh my God, it was almost like a suicide note. A thwarted lover, a man whose lover had got engaged to another! And it had to be from Uncle T, surely? But he'd never sent it, which was confusing. Had he thought better of it? But why not throw it away? Or maybe he'd written it purely as a way of pouring out his emotions – like a diary.

Whatever, it was, it was obviously private. And I shouldn't have read it. So I slipped it back between the pages, gently wiped the book down in case of incriminating fingerprints, locked the cabinet and pretended I'd not been anywhere near it.

I mean, how embarrassing would it be for Uncle T to discover his heartbreak was common knowledge? It's the type of thing you share when you're ready, isn't it? And I've never heard anybody mention this before. And definitely not Uncle T himself.

And it was to V, which made me colour up when he came back and asked if I'd found anything of interest. V! V couldn't possibly be Vera could it? If it is, this is scandalous – something you definitely wouldn't expect from Ollie's family.

But I mustn't jump to that conclusion. Lots of people have a forename starting with V. Lots. Vera, Violet, Victoria, Vanessa, Vera. Bugger. It can't be Vera.

Anyway, Uncle T has been a huge help with my book reviews. He's not written them for me, but when I've been stuck he's asked me questions about how the stories have made me feel which have made me understand so much more. He's not so good with the movies though, he laughingly told me to talk to Ollie about that.

'Really, he is. He's in love with love I reckon.' Terence also told me that he thinks Ollie is a romantic at heart, and that he picks girlfriends that he knows aren't for him as a way of protecting his heart. They are opposite sides of the same fragile male coin.

They make a right pair if you ask me.

Ollie raises an eyebrow. 'Only you could come out with something like that, in love with love!'

'Huh. Maybe I should ask Uncle T to help me with Stanley, except he's probably not into this type of thing at his age and he's got a reputation to keep.' I look at Ollie through narrowed eyes. 'Actually, you might be able to help.'

'And I haven't got a reputation to keep?' He looks amused.

'Oh, forget it, it was a daft idea.'

'What? Come on, what are you up to?'

'If I told you you'd either have to help or I'd have to kill you.'

'I think you need to stop reading that book. Come on, spill. What's happened?'

'The people who adopted Stanley have been ill treating him.' I pause. 'Allegedly.'

'Allegedly?'

'The vet called Carrie because he was concerned. She's taken him back, but she's worried they'll insist on her handing him over. They've already rung and had a go at her.'

'So?'

'I was thinking,' I look him straight in the eye. I'm pretty sure I can trust him. 'Of kidnapping him. That way, they will have to go through the proper channels and prove they'll look after him properly to get him back and can't just do a grab and run. And Carrie won't know where he is, so they can't bully her into telling. Obviously, I'll give him back if she says it's the right thing to do.'

'Obviously.' He grins. 'And Carrie will tell you this, why? If she doesn't know he's here?'

'She will tell me, because she may have her suspicions. Are you up for it or not then?'

'Now?' He looks at his watch. 'I've got a flight to Barcelona first thing in the morning, medical conference, so it's now or never.'

'Well when you put it like that, I can't just leave him, can I?'

'Sure. See you back in here in ten minutes, I need to get changed.'

Well I hadn't expected super-conservative, very sensible Ollie to react like that.

'What if Carrie gets into trouble over this?' Ollie as ever is being the sensible one. Though he is now dressed in black, ready for anything I'd say. He actually looks quite lean and sexy, maybe I should take a photo and send it to Frankie. She'll never forgive me if I don't.

'She'll understand.' Deep down I've got this niggling suspicion that Carrie would be disappointed if I didn't do this. And she didn't actually ask me to, did she? So it can't be her fault.

'Got everything? Rope, torch, crampons?' We are sitting in the car parked outside the rescue centre. He opens the door and the security light flicks on, his eyes are twinkling in the dim light.

'Key!' I hold it up and grin.

'Maybe we shouldn't have parked right by the entrance? Not exactly acing this undercover lark, are we?'

'There's nobody around for miles.' I point out.

He shakes his head. 'You could at least pretend we are on a dangerous mission!'

'Shh!' I put a finger to my lips. 'You'll set the dogs off barking and wake Carrie up!'

'What about the light?'

'She's used to the lights coming on, they're always being set off by cats and foxes. Come on.'

We tip toe over towards the entrance door, Ollie's warm breath making the hairs on the back of my neck stand up and sending a shiver down my back. 'Stop it.' I giggle, I can't help it. It must be the adrenalin, the excitement, the danger of being caught – even though it would only be a very cross Carrie catching us.

The night air is still.

'What's that?' Ollie hisses clutches my arm. 'There's a big dark figure!' I shoot in the air and drop the keys.

'Where, what?' My heart is pounding, my voice sounds odd in my ears.

'It's okay, it's a tree.' He laughs.

'Git! Sod off! You did that on purpose.' I kick him on the ankle.

'Ouch.'

'Serves you right, God you haven't changed one bit since you were six!' I bend down to get the keys at exactly the same time he does, we bang heads, both glance up and our noses are practically touching.

He has changed. He's changed lots. He's got a hint of stubble, his nose is longer, leaner, not the funny little button nose he used to have. His chubby cheeks have disappeared, and now he has proper cheekbones.

'Sorry.' His word is soft, his fingers warm as they cover mine as we both blindly grope for the keys. 'Sorry again.' He pulls back as though he's been burned and straightens up.

I must be overdosing on adrenalin, because my blood is buzzing in my ears and there's a trembling in my body that's making me feel all light headed. And I can still feel the touch of his hand on mine, even though I saw him snatch it back.

'We better ...' I fumble with the keys, finally get them in the lock, 'get a move on.'

You don't need a torch to find your way round the centre. I've been here before to help Carrie tuck the dogs in at bedtime, and she has more nightlights than you'd find in a nursery. I think she must have been traumatised by the dark in her childhood.

'This way.' I motion him to follow me as I walk through reception, and down the first corridor. 'Shit.' I bang my knee on the fire extinguisher that I'd forgotten was there. This bit is really badly lit as there are no dogs in here. One dog barks. We freeze. Ollie breathes down my neck. He starts to hum the twangy bit from the James Bond theme tune in my ear, his warm breath bringing me out in goose bumps, the noise making me giggle. 'Shh!'

I open the next door and can see the dimly lit dogs. Some are curled up tight, ignoring us. One or two are at their doors, wagging their tails, a collie has its head cocked on one side with a quizzical expression on its face. 'Now, where's Stanley? Stan, Stanley?' I whisper into the gloom.

'Christ!' Ollie jumps as a terrier launches itself at the front of the pen barking furiously. He careers into me and I stagger backwards, falling against the pen on the other side of the corridor, where what looks like a massive St Bernard barks. The sound echoing around the room.

It's like a domino effect, all I can see as I glance down the corridor between the pens is mad terriers leaping in the air, and spaniels madly trying to dig their way out to get at us.

'Shit.' We clutch each other. Then I can't help it, I start to giggle again.

Ollie puts his finger on my lips, which makes it worse. Then all the dogs start to bark.

My God, it's like meal time.

We spin round, back to back, as though we're in some action movie surrounded by the baddies. The barking gradually dies away, a small terrier having to have the last word.

Then a Chihuahua adds a comment, and the terrier has to retaliate.

All is quiet.

No lights come on. No doors open.

'Shit security here, isn't it?'

I nod. Trying not to grin. I reckon Carrie has seen us on the CCTV, turned over and gone back to sleep. But I'm not going to tell Ollie that, I'm having far too much fun.

We tiptoe our way down the corridor, peering at the ghostly dogs – some have gone back to bed, some are watching us warily, one or two are pressed against the front of the pens.

'They want cuddles!' I want to, I really do. 'I want to let them all out and have a mass love in.'

'Don't you dare!' Ollie has his stern, business-like look on.

'Bossy doesn't work with me.'

'Don't I know it!' He rolls his eyes. 'Back to Bethlehem, are we?'

'No.' I shake my head, trying not to laugh. In my head it's worse, my past and present have alarmingly collided – and I'm not even drunk! I can just imagine him in his white coat, stethoscope at the ready as he peers at a patient, and it's me. He leans even closer, too close for a consultant, and kisses me. So I hit him over the head – with a bedpan.

'I know that look on your face. I don't want to know!'

A yelp reminds me why we're here.

It's Stanley! His little skinny body is squirming like I've never seen it do before, he's panting, spinning in circles, so excited he can hardly bark.

'Oh my God! Stanley! Come here, you.' I shove Ollie out

of the way, open the door and clamber into the pen with the little dog. He's in my arms, licking my face, nibbling my ears, kissing my lips and then he's off. He hurtles out of the pen, down the corridor, then spins round, his legs going in all directions and he speeds back up, past us, does a wheelie at the end then starts to chase his tail.

I want to cry. I think I am crying.

'*Aww*, Daisy.' The look on Ollie's face isn't humour, it isn't horror at my outpourings, it's so gentle and warm it sets me off again. He gives me a quick hug, rests his head against mine briefly, then pulls away. 'Come on, we better be off.'

We do not make a dignified, stealthy exit. Stanley is wriggling like crazy and trying to jump into my arms – but when I lift him up, he jumps down again, weaves his way around my legs and sends me crashing into Ollie, who falls against that flaming fire extinguisher, before somehow ending up sitting in the fire bucket which is full of sand. 'I really am going to have to tell Carrie to tidy up her fire precautions.'

Ollie pulls himself back to his feet. 'And her security.'

'I think she turned it off tonight.' We share a smile, then Ollie gets into the driving seat of the car, and I get into the back seat with Stanley. No way, can I stop cuddling him and drive.

We're back home in minutes, and I still can't stop hugging and kissing Stanley as Ollie opens the front door and ushers us in.

'I better get some shut eye, I need to set off for the airport at 4 a.m.'

'Thanks for helping.'

'No probs. Night, night Stanley.' He ruffles my hair, fondles Stanley's ears and heads for his bedroom.

'You don't er mind having a dog here?'

He stops, turns to look at us and frowns. 'He can't stay here, we were just rescuing him, that's all.'

'But.' A hard lump forms in my throat so quickly it shocks me, as do the tears that are already brimming over.

'Joke!'

'Oh.' I gulp the lump away, wipe my forearm across my eyes and try to smile.

'Oh, Daisy.' His voice is suddenly gentle, and he's at my side, wrapping his arms round me and Stanley. He drops a kiss on Stanley's head, and gives me a squeeze. It's nice. 'Sorry, I didn't mean to upset you, it was only a joke.'

'I think I'm a bit wound up, being silly. Sorry.' I step away awkwardly feeling very silly.

'No, I'm sorry. It wasn't funny. Take care of each other eh? I'll see you soon.'

'Thanks again.'

'No problem, it was fun, wasn't it?'

I nod, feeling strangely emotional, on the verge of asking him to stay and chat a bit longer. 'Maybe you're not such an arse after all!'

'And maybe you've got more guts than you think you have.' He grins. 'Night, Daisy.'

Stanley comes to bed with me. 'Love you Stanley.' I kiss him on the nose. I do love him and snatching him from that pen made me realise just how much I've missed him.

I feel all warm and fuzzy inside. I have accomplished something important.

Stanley doesn't curl at my feet where he always used to, he creeps up until he's close to my chest, then he lays his head down so that we're practically nose to nose, gazing into each other's eyes. Then, with a heavy sigh, he closes his eyes and he's asleep.

I don't fall asleep quite so quickly.

Tonight has felt a bit of a rollercoaster. Even though it wasn't really a proper rescue mission, there was no danger. No chance we couldn't pull it off. But it was nice to share it with Ollie. I've not had so much fun in ages. He's not a pompous prick at all, he's lovely.

I roll onto my side, my body curled around the warm dog, then I drape my arm over Stanley.

Having him back in my arms has made me realise, I've been with Stanley longer than I've ever been with a boyfriend. He's the biggest commitment I've ever made.

My new job, my career is going to be the next commitment. And then my own flat. I am on the up.

Chapter 15

2 p.m., 16 July

Tim and I are getting on amazingly well. I mean we do have our differences, mainly to do with food (Stanley is on my side as far as that goes), but I'm so glad we kissed and made up the day after we shouted and broke up.

The day after breaking Stanley out from Carrie's I turned up to work with a scrape on my elbow and a plaster on my hand (okay, I know it wasn't that difficult, I did have a key, but it was dark and I fell over the planter by the door on the way out because I was giggling so much).

'I thought you were staying in to read that book?' He'd managed to look cross and concerned at the same time, then dragged me into the corner next to the photocopier and just looked concerned. 'Are you okay, Daisy? What on earth happened?' He tucked my hair back behind my ear, then lifted my hand up tenderly.

'It's top secret, I can't tell you. But I'm fine, Ollie helped me.' I said in a hushed whisper.

'Ollie?' He frowned. 'Daisy, you should be able to tell me anything, I'm your BF!' He often abbreviates things like that, I think it's because he doesn't want to say the word 'boyfriend' and he says he doesn't like being a 'partner'.

'Are you?' I was confused. 'But, yesterday, you said ...'

'Of course, I am. Don't you want me to be?' He kissed the tip of my nose and managed to look hurt at the same time. 'Christ, so sorry about yesterday, don't know what got into me. Just meant we should cool it at work, not professional and all that. Can't keep away from you though! We are still okay?' His worried gaze met mine and I wanted to snog him there and then. But I didn't, it wouldn't be professional.

'Of course, we are!' Bloody hell, I really would be better sticking with Stanley. But I do like Tim, and I quite understand the remaining professional at work thing.

He winked. 'Great! Fill in at lunch?' Then he walked off in one direction whistling, and I went back to my desk with a big grin on my face. It was even better when I spotted an email from the big boss congratulating me on another brilliant review.

8 p.m., 17 July

'Oh my God, I miss you!' I launch myself at Frankie, who is dressed in a halter-neck black velvet jumpsuit that plunges at the sides almost down to her waist. If she had big boobs they'd be planning an escape, but she doesn't. She has clothes-friendly tits that make designer gear look fab.

Frankie somehow managed to wangle an invitation to Mum's surprise party from me, and even though she knew we'd be in a bookshop, with the mainly elderly inhabitants of the village, plus my family, she's never been one to worry about being overdressed.

'Hello darling, my goodness, you're early!' Mum has appeared from nowhere and managed to jump between us, which means she gets the slobbery kiss intended for my friend. She's so taken aback she's speechless for all of two seconds.

I have actually managed to arrive before my mother for once though! This is mainly down to the fact that I left work on time, Ollie had very kindly packed my food for the buffet into a posh hamper and taken it with him earlier, and I had hours on my own to shower, change, dance to my summer schmoozing playlist with Stanley, get dressed and pick up Tim. He doesn't drive as it damages the planet, but he's quite happy to be driven. He's also quite happy for me to use up petrol and go on a detour for him, only to find he's left a note on the door saying he's been called on urgent business and will see me at the party later. I text, asking why he couldn't have let me know, and he said it was because he'd left bubbly (for Uncle T), and flowers (for Mum) with his neighbour and wanted to be sure I'd got them. Which was nice.

Anyway, it was quite hard to not be early actually, seeing

as these days I am so organised. I truly am in danger of getting my shit together, I've got a boyfriend, *and* a career!

'Well, you do look lovely!' I think it's shock that is making Mum so nice.

Frankie winks at me over her shoulder. She is towering above both of us (even more than normal) in her ultra-high heels. Her black fringe has been cut at a daring angle so that it dips over one eye, and she's gone for the type of bright red lipstick that only people like her can pull off.

'Quite sophisticated.' Somebody should explain to Mum that sometimes less is more, she should stop at the 'lovely' and not add 'quite's'.

Sasha, who writes the fashion column for the newspaper has an amazing eye for fashion (she used to be one of those personal stylists) and is also very generous. I've managed to totally revamp my wardrobe with a combination of freebies she's pushed my way, and advice she's given me on shopping trips. I am now looking stylish, rather than bag-lady. I am going to stop at *quite* sophisticated though, I think the natural me is more casual than smart.

'Oh my goodness dear, won't your breasts burn?' Mum has just seen Frankie's reflection in the glass door and spun around to stare. 'Would you like to borrow a cardi and cover them up?' She turns back to me, looking puzzled and slightly disappointed. A look I know well. 'I thought you were bringing a boyfriend to my party, not a girlfriend?'

'He's going to be late, he went to interview some guys who've chained themselves to trees.'

'Saving the planet? Is this a vegan thing?'

I laugh at Frankie. I can't help it. 'No, they've just chained themselves to trees, but they're naked and the allotment is on one side and the school dipping pond on the other.'

'How frigging stupid can they be? Don't they know there's a heatwave? Their bits will frazzle and drop off!'

'Oh, my goodness, it doesn't bear thinking about!' My mother clutches her hand to her throat melodramatically. 'Those poor oldies who grow their own veggies will think they've got a bumper crop of beetroot, they'll be trying to pull them off!'

Frankie is laughing, in fact she's laughing so hard she'll fall off her heels if she isn't careful. 'As long as they don't try and chop the stalks off!'

'You two should form a double act!' I shake my head at them. 'Tim should be here later, and he'll be coming for Christmas as well Mum.'

'How lovely. Ah now, you ladies will have to excuse me, I need to go and chat to Vera and tell her all about your new man and your job.'

'I can tell her myself, Mum.'

'Oh, don't bother yourself dear, now where is your father? I'm sure he was with me a minute ago!'

Dad had winked at me, blown a kiss and mouthed 'catch you later' before sneaking off in search of a whisky bottle the moment Mum had leapt between me and Frankie. He's not daft. I imagine he is now safely hidden between some bookshelves with a tumbler, Uncle T, and Ollie's father, Charles.

'It is brilliant to see you again.' I give Frankie a proper hug, now that we are on our own and have a drink in our hands.

'I only spoke to you three days ago, you daft bint!'

'Talking on the phone isn't the same and you know it.'

'Maybe not, you only give me the highlights. I don't get the down and dirty on the luscious Ollie, all you talk about is Tim and his hairless sack, back and crack.'

'No, I don't!'

'Yes, you do!'

I might have mentioned it once, in passing, because I've never been out with a man who is so totally obsessed with reducing drag.

'He wants to swim faster, he's competitive!'

'He's a bloody reincarnated fish if you ask me.' She laughs and plonks herself down on a chair. 'Fuck, these heels have to have been designed by a man.' The one green eye I can see glints as she gazes round the bookshop with mild interest, and rests on Terence who has just walked over to join us. 'No insult intended.' She winks at him, and he laughs.

'My darling girl, I totally sympathise but they really are glorious I have to say.'

I'm not sure if, when he says he understands, he means he's done the heels thing (oh please, no, the image of Uncle T in bowtie, waistcoat, a skirt and heels is terrifying), or he's just spent so much of his life with women that he can empathise. He is an empathetic type anyway. He's lovely. With or without heels.

And he writes the most beautiful love letters. I so want to mention the one I found, to tell him it nearly made me cry, but I can't. I shouldn't have found it. Although he had said I could look in the book cabinet any time I wanted. I wasn't snooping.

'Wonderful to see you again Frankie, and of course you, my dear Daisy. You are positively glowing!' He gives me a big, whisky-infused hug. 'No Stanley?'

'He's not really keen on the hot weather, so I left him flopped on the kitchen tiles dreaming about Christmas.' He really doesn't like it when it's hot, and he doesn't like the bad weather either, the first sign of rain and he hides under the bed when I get his leash out, and he sulked for hours when he discovered that the white stuff outside wasn't warm sand, it was icy snow. He's a funny dog.

'Well I don't know about Stanley, no pompous prick either?'

'Don't call him that!' The words are out before I stop to think.

'Really?' She laughs, her amused gaze resting on me in such a way that I can feel myself going bright red.

'Ollie's fine, quite nice actually.' I mumble. 'And he is here, well at least I hope he is, he promised to bring my nibbles.'

'And you'd know, now you live with him.' She drawls. 'And is the lovely Juliet here?'

'Oh, good heavens no.' Uncle Terence shakes his head,

and whisks a cocktail from the passing Mabel, who shoots off in alarm when she recognises Frankie. 'Juliet is old news.'

'Thank fuck he saw sense! I mean, what was he doing with somebody who makes up excuses for a living? Who's he dragged along today then? A cardio nurse who'll jump in and resuscitate me when I swoon at his feet? Or will he do mouth to mouth himself?' She licks her lips in anticipation and I don't know whether to hit her or laugh.

'He's single.'

'Single?'

I can positively see Frankie perk up and start to search for him with new intent. She's always making remarks about Ollie on the phone, calling him an arse, but I'm pretty sure she still wants to make babies with him as much as she did when she first saw him last Christmas. All the insults are a cover. She's been round to my new home a few times and the disappointment positively rolls off her when she realises he's not there. He's never there when she is. Which is good as far as I'm concerned, I don't want to watch their mating ritual.

'But you're not single Frankie, you've got Tarquin! Haven't you?' I feel strangely possessive of Ollie, I don't want him to be another of her conquests. And I *think* she's still got Tarquin, although it's hard to keep track of Frankie at times.

'Oh God, Tarquin. It was so much frigging easier to live with you than sarky Tarqy.' She rolls her eyes dramatically.

'God you have no idea how much room that man takes up.' She throws her arms wide to demonstrate and nearly empties her bright blue cocktail over a pile of thrillers. She puts the glass down, and I can feel relief wave off Terence. 'Stuff here,' she flings one arm, 'stuff there,' she throws the other out, 'game controllers, tablet, phone, they end up everywhere! Then he can't find stuff. And his guitars.' Another dramatic eye roll.

'Guitars plural?' Asks Terence.

'Three! He dances round the living room semi naked—'

'I thought you liked him semi-naked?' She likes most men semi-naked.

'Not with a Strat strapped between me and his vital parts! He is just so,' she pauses, searching for the word, 'big. Even though he's only average size.'

'Like a terrier, that bounces about so much you might as well have a Great Dane?'

'Not sure about that analogy.'

I laugh. I do miss her. 'Where is he then?'

We had agreed to meet up here as a foursome. She'd said Tarquin had been complaining they never went out as a couple (Terence was quite keen to add him to the guest list, I think he thought she'd be easier to manage with a man in tow), and I'd said I'd bring Tim. She has a thing about Tim. She likes to needle me about him. I sometimes think Frankie's expectations are higher than my mothers. Mum just wants me to have an escort, Frankie wants to be sure he's the right one.

To be honest, right now I'm siding more with Mum, I just want somebody who will come out with me, who will be nice and will not invade my apartment, or life, or upset my dog. And Tim might fit that bill. I don't want to get to that stage where you take each other for granted, get upset when lids get left off and snipe about who finished the wine (me) and who forgot to turn the bathroom light off (him). Is it too much to just want a bit of romance and a laugh?

'Tarquin? Oh, he's got a nasty nettle rash that makes it hard to sit still.'

I raise an eyebrow, they're really not the woodlands-walk type, and she sniggers.

'It was something we read in a book about the power of stings, a quick whipping can do wonders, apparently. It's important to keep the spice in a relationship. So' – she seems keen to move on from that quickly – 'where's Ollie, then?'

'I do believe he is with his parents, although I'm sure he will mingle later.' Uncle T gives me a sideways glance. I think this is his code for '*I've warned him Frankie's here, so hide in a corner*'. I do like Uncle T's company, we've grown even closer over the past few months. He is a complete film and book buff, he's funny and he's kind. He's also incredibly close to Ollie, I hadn't realised just how similar they were until recently. I think Ollie actually finds Uncle T's gentle humour and manner easier to deal with than his own father's gruffness. I guess we have parental high expectations in common.

'Oh, I do hope so.' Frankie grabs a bottle of bubbly from the passing Mabel and fills her cocktail glass to the brim. 'So, Tarq has got a nasty rash, what's Timbo's excuse? Have you been nibbling his nuts?'

'Frankie!'

Frankie has gate-crashed a couple of times when Tim and I have been having a night in, and they've got on okay, but she has made the odd dig about him. It's almost like she's been jealous of him taking my attention away from her when she's been expecting a girlie night in. So, this evening was partly my way of stopping her little jokes, I just knew once we had a proper night out together, that would be it. I mean, I don't exactly want her fancying him (like she does Ollie), but it would be great if they were friends. It's a lot easier to manage when everybody gets on, isn't it?

'Have you met him, Terence?'

Terence nods, and orders dirty martinis all round. 'He's a nice boy.'

'But not her forever man?'

He chuckles. 'More a spring fancy.'

'That's turned into a summer warmer?'

'Hey, you two, stop ganging up on me!'

'I'd never gang up on you, Daisy.' He pats my hand. 'But sparks don't exactly fly, do they? You need passion in your life!' He says the word passion with gusto and a punch to the air.

'Damp squib.' Mutters Frankie. 'Not enough lead in his pencil.'

'I heard that! What have you got against him?'

She tilts her head on one side, as though she's thinking. 'Maybe it's the beard? Maybe he'd look more he-man if he had a chin?'

'He has got a chin! And I wouldn't care if he hadn't, he's nice!'

'So are strawberries dipped in chocolate my dear,' Terence takes the bottle of fizz from her and tops up all the glasses, 'but they're not very satisfying, are they?'

'Oh, I don't know.' Frankie gazes beyond us and sighs. 'If you've got a man who knows his way round fruit, a punnet of strawberries can last all night!'

'But a strawberry without passion is just ...'

'Soft fruit,' finishes Frankie, and stares at me. 'Squelchy.'

'Stop it. He's not soft and he's not squelchy.'

'Good. I just want you to be happy, hun. You know I do! I'm only teasing, I didn't mean to upset you.'

'You haven't upset me.' I glare at Uncle T. 'He *is* passionate, he's passionate about all kinds of things, about the planet, plastic, animals.' I don't know why I'm being so defensive, I think it's because Frankie is attacking him in a totally unfair and personal way. Why does she have to comment about his chin, and call him squelchy?

But to be totally honest he is lacking a bit in the passion department (not that Frankie needs to know that), when he kisses me it's perfectly pleasant – but is perfectly pleasant really good enough? He needs lessons from Ollie, Ollie just gives me one of his looks and I'm feeling all hot and bothered. And as for that teenage kiss ... 'He loves Stanley so much.' I say something quick, before I get too diverted comparing him to Ollie. Loving Stanley is a huge plus in my book. 'He's brilliant at his job, he really cares, and he's passionate about the future.' Am I overdoing this?

'Whose future?'

I am stunned into silence by Uncle T's interruption, for a second or two. 'Sorry? *The* future. Everybody!'

'My darling Daisy.' Uncle T pats my hand. 'You deserve somebody who is passionate about you, your future!'

'He is!'

'Well then that is all that matters.'

'Lordie you should see your face.' Frankie is grinning at me. 'We're teasing, lighten up! This must mean it's serious.'

'I like him.' I say, like a sullen child. 'He's fun and he's clever, and I wish he was here as well because I need you all to help me.'

'Help?' Frankie stops twiddling with a breadstick and her eyes light up. She can be a pain in the arse, but she likes to help. And she's good at helping.

'Carrie's been threatened with eviction.'

9.30 p.m., 17 July

'Carrie who?'

The deep voice right next to my left ear makes me jump. 'Tim!' Trust him to appear just when he smells a whiff of a story. Good journalists are like that, aren't they? They manage to be on the spot, and listening, at just the right time. 'You made it!' I wrap my hands round his waist and our lips meet. Just the right amount of snog for a party like this. Pleasant.

Oh my God, I need to stop thinking like this. But it *is* a bit like kissing a middle-aged relative, or somebody you've been married to for decades (not that I have been, but it's how I imagine it can get if you're not careful). Although I have to admit after a few drinks, and not sharing a bed for longer than seems acceptable, I'd quite like something a bit more intense. Shouldn't sparks be flying at our age? Right now, we couldn't set a bone-dry field of straw in a drought on fire.

'What do you mean, eviction?' He is actually giving me his intense stare, but it's the version linked to work, not sex. He's definitely not thinking about sex, maybe a vodka will help.

'Bloody hell, don't you love a man who's passionate about his *work*.' Drawls Frankie. 'So sexy.' Her one visible green eye narrows and she rests her chin on her knuckles. I wish Tarquin was here to distract her.

I am tempted to kick her on the ankle, but shockingly Tim is actually preening. He has totally missed the sarcasm and thinks she fancies him, I swear he does. He puts on just the same face when Ruby, the agony aunt (who is nothing like any aunt you have ever seen – she looks about 15 years old), asks if she can 'run a problem past him'.

I dare to glance Uncle T's way – he's faintly amused. Watching them spar.

'Frankie, great to see!' Tim grins and gives her a thumbs up. 'You are looking stunning, even better than last time we met.' This might actually go alright. I was worried he'd hate her, go on the defensive and she'd shred him to pieces before telling me to dump him. All for my own good of course. Instead he likes her, he's trying to charm her.

This is good. I'm not the insecure type who is scared her friends might steal her man, and I know that he's so far away from Frankie's type that she'll be amused and entertained rather than turned on. So, this is brilliant.

'You've no idea how great it is to see you too, Timbo. I was beginning to think you were Daisy's dirty little secret, she just keeps you all to herself.' She leans forward. 'Tell us about your naked men!'

They've only met a handful of times, just after I started working with him, and briefly at the flat, but every time I see her she drops hints about meeting him properly. So this is supposed to be the opportunity, but I'm not sure I trust her in this mood.

She says she wants to delve into his mind and decide if his intentions are noble. I reckon she wants to inspect his body and give him an energy rating. I am now very worried that asking about naked men is her lead in to other trickier topics.

'Not a lot to tell. Ladies of the WI had draped them in dock leaves and roses by the time I got there, an allotment holder had some bolt-cutters and another had a chainsaw.

Great photo opp. Just trying to frame a headline.' He frowns, he's thinking.

'Well I hope it wasn't Steven Dunlop with the chainsaw, he's got very shaky hands you know! I wouldn't let him touch my dahlias, let alone my lady garden. Salmon blinis, anybody?' Mum is very good at using food and drink as a way into any conversation. She is looking at me expectantly, and angling her head in the direction of Tim.

He is staring blindly at the morsels that have been shoved under his nose, his mind still on work I think. 'Invasion of Lady Lane allotments? Too much?' He stops staring at the plate and glances my way. I shrug.

'Fuck me, Ladies Lane, it's called Ladies Lane?' Frankie laughs loudly, the quiet hum of conversation dies. 'You couldn't make this up! This is better than binge watching Vera or Midsomer Murders. My ladies lane has been invaded.' She is struggling to breathe, she's laughing so much.

'It's Lady Lane.' I point out.

'Anybody?' Mum squeezes in between us, her back to Frankie, and shoves the plate so far under Tim's nose he could practically inhale the contents.

He flinches and pushes the plate away, rather violently. 'I don't eat fish.'

'Oh, it's not proper fish, it's smoked salmon!'

He rolls his eyes, I am expecting an outburst any moment. 'Tim, meet my mum, Mum meet Tim, my boyfriend.' I add the last word rather more strongly than I intended to. To make sure he is polite.

'Oh, how wonderful, that's wonderful! I was thinking she'd made you up! Call me Wendy!'

'He's vegan, Mum.'

'Oh dear.' She looks confused. 'V what? Can't he call me Wendy?'

'Of course, he can call you Wendy.' I try not to roll my eyes. 'Tim is vegan. I told you! He can't eat salmon.' My insides slump. I have told her, several times. I've even printed off a list of do's and don'ts, which I bet she used as scrap paper for her shopping list.

'Oh, that nonsense. Don't fuss, dear.' She waves a dismissive hands and smiles. 'I'm sure it's not worth fussing over. Come with me to the buffet, Tim. You can tell me what you really don't like then I'll get it right for when you come at Christmas. Daisy used to be so funny about olives and mushrooms, but she grew out of it so I'm sure we'll be fine. So nice to see Daisy with a man, she brought a dog to the last family party you know. And her lesbian friend.'

'All going okay?'

I glance at Frankie, whose eyes have lit up in such a way that even if I wasn't totally familiar with Ollie's deep tone, I'd know it was him.

'Great!' I grin up at him. He does look good. He always did, and now I've realised that he has to put up with the same kind of 'mother pressure' that I do, and he isn't really that much different to the kid I shared a paddling pool and baby Jesus with, I can forgive him his perfection. In fact, I've rather begun to enjoy it. What would you prefer, a gross part-time flat mate, or an attractive one? See. Shallow, but true. Ollie and I have already swapped 'you look nice' comments before we left home. We're beginning to behave like some old married couple. I put a hand out to stop Mum dragging Tim off to look at canapés, 'What about Carrie?'

Tim looks at me blankly.

'You know, Carrie! I was just talking about her.'

'The one who runs the dog rescue place?' Says Ollie. We share a conspiratorial look, which I then feel guilty about. It's not Tim's fault he wasn't brought up in the village and doesn't know every bit of gossip.

Tim is still looking confused.

'She's being evicted! She's behind on her rent, and she's got far too many dogs to feed. She's got until Christmas to sort it, and then she'll be turfed out. And Christmas is her worst time!' When Carrie started the shelter, it was to help street dogs like Stanley from abroad, she's got a friend out there who rescues them and then sends them over. The problem is though that she hasn't the heart to turn away all the other dogs that are found abandoned locally, or that just need new homes.

I'll do anything I can to help her. Every penny she's given goes on the dogs and given a choice between dog food and a sandwich for herself, she'd plump for the dog food every time. Which is why when I visit I go armed with a coffee and junk food – she'd never, ever give that to the dogs!

'I was thinking maybe you could start a campaign.' I look from Tim to Frankie and back again. 'You know, put something in the paper, and you're ace at ideas and talking people into doing stuff Frankie.'

'Not sure it's headline grabbing, unless she's going to barricade herself in?'

Mum is gently tugging his arm, and I can see his attention is on the buffet and drinks.

'Dogs are headline grabbing, people love animal stuff, and it's local.' I try not to sound needy and pleading.

'Homeless people.' States Tim.

'Pardon?'

'Homeless people. What people want, not dogs.'

'But there aren't any homeless people in the village!'

'Might sell to the nationals.' He holds up a hand, headline style. 'Village of shame, poverty strikes rural idyll, lost souls nobody talks about.'

'Well Carrie might be homeless soon if somebody doesn't help, and so will a load of dogs!'

'That's the time to do it.'

'That's when it's too late Tim!' I grit my teeth and fight the urge to throttle him. I've always known he's quite ambitious, and he only wants to write on-trend pieces that might make the nationals take notice. His Instagram account shows he is an achiever, mine shows I'm a drifter. We are different in so many ways. I have always thought he's a very nice, kind boyfriend, even if I've not been convinced that he's my happy ever after. But right now, I could shake him.

'Why can't you do it yourself?' Says Ollie, to me. 'Write a piece? Kick things off.'

'She does reviews.' Says Tim, holding a 'whoa' hand up. 'No offence, but it's not the same. Can't step on people's toes.'

Wow, Ollie is standing up for me! A little tremor of something that could be mildly sexual but is probably just normal excitement makes me want to clench my fists and jump up and down like a small child. But I don't.

'Not the same as writing about naked men on an allotment?' Ollie says drily. Then he looks at me. His gaze steady, and I feel like I should be saying something strong, something positive, but I don't know what. I just blink back at him, feeling like I want to hug him, and shout thank you. Ollie thinks I can do this – even if Tim doesn't! 'It's what you're good at.' He says softly.

'No offence, mate.' Tim practically elbows his way in. 'But take it you're not in the biz?' It's the first time I've noticed *he's* the one that can sound pompous. A bit of a smart arse.

'He's a doctor,' says Mum, 'a consultant no less!'

'No, I'm not in the biz, but you are, aren't you, Daisy?' Ollie is a bit like a ship in a storm, well a rock, or a lighthouse. He's been buffeted from all sides, but he's standing firm. Ignoring all the commotion. Still looking at me, as though nobody else exists. It has taken my breath away.

'I wouldn't know where to start.' I say lamely. My idea had been to get Tim roped in, not to launch a campaign single-handedly.

'There's no start.' Tim says, quite firmly. 'End of. First step is knowing if there is an actual story or not.'

'Can't argue with that, Dais, the man has a point. Anyhow why rock the boat and fuck up your job, I thought you liked it? Shouldn't you be concentrating on that, not some pie in the sky idea? It's less than a year since you ditched the ads job and started again!' I stare at Frankie. It's quite nice that she's agreeing with Tim over something – but not nice that they're both dissing my idea. Why does she keep have to keep reminding me that I'm new at all this? And calling my idea 'pie in the sky' is just nasty.

I feel all hollow and empty inside. Surely friends are supposed to help each other, at least offer some support, not just shoot each other down?

Even if she is right, and I should stick to what I know, she could at least be diplomatic about it.

Is she right though? Is it really a lame idea, am I wrong to want to try everything I can to help Carrie?

'And I need food, lead me to the buffet!' Frankie has got bored with the lack of entertainment and has decided to stand up. Which leaves Tim open mouthed. She has that effect on people, when she unfurls to her full magnificence. She has these never-ending legs, she might not be one hundred per cent conventionally beautiful, but Frankie is stunning.

'I'll join you.' Tim smiles, then strokes my arm absent-mindedly. 'Sorry, Daisy. Lovely idea, but you know James, all about the distribution figs and job descriptions. Nibbles?'

'Lovely.' Mum can sense she's finally going to be able to get his attention and interrogate him. 'Let's grab your canapés! You can tell me all about what you do and don't eat.'

'Beard definitely has to go,' whispers Frankie in my ear. 'Christ, that must tickle your fancy!' I'm sure Frankie didn't used to be this rude, she seems to have sex permanently on the brain since I moved out and Tarquin moved in. 'C'mon let's go and find out what your mum's saying to him! Not sure she should be allowed to grab his canapés.'

'Daisy.' There's a staying hand on my arm, and I know before I even glance up, who it is. Ollie.

'I'll catch you up.' I say to Frankie, who rolls her eyes. 'Is there a story?'

'There is for me.' I sigh, I can't help it. 'Maybe I'm being stupid, I mean Tim's the one with all the experience ...'

'And you're the one with the heart.' He half smiles, and it's so beguiling I stop listening to his words and watch his lips. They're very kissable. Very. Mesmerising. 'Daisy?'

'Sorry.' Oh my God, I must *not* kiss him. 'Yeah, well, I mean he's probably right, there's no real point, no story.'

'But there is to you? Come on, you're the girl that breaks in and rescues dogs in peril,' he winks, 'that place means something to you, doesn't it?'

At this point I could come clean – but I don't. Carrie rang me the day after we rescued Stanley.

'Great rescue, very professional!'

'You knew? You were watching?'

'Of course I was bloody watching!' She'd laughed. 'I paid a lot of money for that CCTV. I do have an, er, confession.'

216

'What kind of confession?' I asked suspiciously.

'Well,' she paused, 'an hour before you broke in, I had a letter through the door. That family who adopted him hadn't got the guts to call or speak face to face, but they did say they didn't care, I could do what I wanted with him. Or words to that effect.'

'Yay, that's brilliant, Carrie!'

'I spoke to the vet, he reckons the threat of legal action was all it needed.'

'So I didn't have to rescue him?'

'Nope. You were having so much fun though, seemed a shame to stop you.' I could tell from the tone of her voice that she was grinning.

'Git! So I can keep him?'

'You can keep him, but maybe you need to formally adopt him?'

'You bet! Carrie, promise me something?'

'What?'

'Don't tell Ollie? I reckon he enjoyed being all heroic, not quite the same if you tell him you were watching.'

'Gawd, you've got it bad, haven't you babe?'

'I don't know what you mean!'

She'd laughed. 'I won't tell him. I have er, got a bit of a problem though,' her voice had lost its humour, 'could do with your help. Have you got time to pop in for coffee tomorrow?'

'Sure.'

And that's when she'd told me.

'You really want to help her, don't you?' Ollie is watching me intently.

'Well yes, Carrie's my friend for a start, and she does such a brilliant thing. I mean,' I gulp, it's hard to concentrate when he's gazing at me so intently, 'dogs can't stand up for themselves, can they? We all need somebody to be kind to us, don't we? We all need to be listened to, talked to, hugged ...' My words tail off. Strangely, all I can think is that Uncle T was right, we need passion. I need passion. I need something to feel passionate about, like Carrie has her rescue centre.

'We do.' Ollie has somehow edged us into a cosy nook between some bookshelves. It's a Harry Potter wonderland, on the shelf behind him is a hat. I pick up the wand from the table and run my finger along its knurled edge.

'If Carrie loses the dogs it'll destroy her, after what happened to Evie.'

'I know.' Ollie squeezes my hand. It's nice, I might be staring at him all doe-eyed like no doubt his patients do. 'Evie really was her one and only, wasn't she?' This is one of the nice things about living in a village. The 'knowing about Evie' bit, not me being doe-eyed. Although that's quite nice. He's got very warm fingers.

We're so close together in this quiet corner, and he really is quite attractive, and he's looking at me in a way I can't remember anybody ever looking at me.

And if it was Christmas, and Uncle T had put a sprig of mistletoe in this corner, I think I might just ...

I suddenly realise he's disentangling himself, so I let go abruptly. I hadn't realised I was hanging on. Or thinking about snogging him.

Bloody hell, what is wrong with me? I have a boyfriend! I feel so confused.

He sticks his hand in his pocket, and I feel strangely lost. I must just be missing Tim, where the hell is Tim?

'You love her, you love helping people, Daisy. You're in the right place to do it, so why not?' Luckily, Ollie is oblivious to my mixed-up brain, which brings me back down to earth. I rearrange the pile of books slightly, take a couple of deep breaths, and try to concentrate on his faults. Which is tricky, because they don't seem to be coming to mind right now. Apart from the fact he's too neat and tidy. And has posh and totally unsuitable girlfriends.

'Daisy?' He sounds slightly exasperated and puts a hand out to stop my book sorting, which is a bit unnerving. I leap back, which makes him start and step away, which sends the magic sorting hat flying. In typical Ollie fashion, he catches it neatly in one hand.

'I'm a book reviewer, I don't write features and ...'

'But you could. You wrote a couple before, that's why they gave you the job, promoted you out of the hell that was small ads!'

We share a smile, the awkwardness of the finger grasping forgotten. He even takes his hand out of his pocket and picks up a mini Harry Potter figure.

'And those ads were a work of literature.' His words are teasing, and I'm very tempted to kick his ankle.

'Now you're getting cheeky!'

He raises an eyebrow, just a little bit. But when he speaks again, his voice is surprisingly gentle. 'It's one story, pitch it to your boss, James Masters isn't he called? Uncle T will help if you need him to, I know he will. Though you don't need anybody's help, Daisy. It's time you trusted yourself, believed in yourself again, isn't it?'

I think I'm staring up at him in the same way Stanley gazed at me when I brought him back home. Adoringly. 'I do trust myself!'

'Well do it.' His eyes are sending out a challenge, and it's making my heart go all jittery. 'Just write from the heart, like you do when you write your reviews. Nothing clever, just being you.'

Nothing clever! Ha! 'I do love books, I love doing my job.' I stare at the display, the magical Harry Potter. 'Tim's got a point, he knows much more about this than me, he knows what the paper will print. And what if Frankie's right and I fuck things up?' I can't risk my job. I like it, it pays well. I've got enough money to pay rent once I find my perfect home, a steady job, a dog. I'm finally getting things together. 'I've got what I've always wanted.'

'What you've always wanted?' Ollie is looking at me in a strange way. 'Is this all you ever really wanted, Daisy? Or is it all you'll let yourself want?'

Is it?

I stroke down the spine of a book with my finger. I've spent so long denying myself everything, that I've no idea what I really want. I look him in the eye. 'I'm not sure,' I say quite truthfully. I have to start being honest with myself, with everybody. 'But it's a good start.'

'Promise me you won't let it be the end?'

I nod. My heart pounding. Ollie has this way of saying the right things, asking the right questions, marching his way through the me I've been as though he's determined to ignore her and reach the me I used to be, the me I could be. I want to beg him not to walk out of my life again. But I don't. I nod again and smile. Positively.

I look around, at Mum trying to persuade Tim to at least try the mini toad-in-the-holes, and Uncle Terence catches my eye. He smiles and raises his glass, and I automatically lift my own. Ollie follows my gaze and nods at Uncle T.

'I promised I'd have a chat to Uncle T about something, I'll catch you later?'

'Okay.' I put the wand back down on the pile of books. Magic. Passion. I love books so much because they've got everything I want. Even the stuff I won't let myself dream I should have.

'Dais, you care more about people than books, you know you do. You could do this. You can be,' he pauses, searching for the words, 'authentic. Do it for Carrie, even if you won't do it for yourself. Tell James Masters it's a one off. I dare you!'

Then he leaves me, in my little cosy nook with Harry Potter.

Frankie and Tim are wrong, and Ollie is right. There is a point, and there is a story – well at least there is to me.

Chapter 16

2 p.m., 18 July

'What's that?' I point at the pinkish-brown sliver of something that Mum is artfully piling potatoes on top of.

'A bit of lamb won't harm love!'

'Yes, it will!' I whisk it off the plate and put it in a bowl at the side. If Tim can as much as smell meat, let alone see traces of animal fat on his plate he'll be marching off for a lie down.

'It's not like proper meat.'

'Of course, it is! It was standing up in a field not long ago, bleating.'

'But it's only a tiny bit.'

'That's Stanley's bowl! Don't put it in there, I'm giving him his own food!' She flicks the slice of meat onto another plate. 'Your father can have it. I'm disappointed Tim won't at least try it, when you were little we made you at least take a taste, and he does need building up.'

'It's different, Mum. It's not that he doesn't like the taste—'

'Well it's a shame not to have a bit then. He can have a chicken vol-au-vent later before you go, they're so small and a little one won't harm, it's mainly mushrooms and sauce after all. I made them especially, I won't tell if you don't!'

I would try to explain, again, but I know I'll be wasting my breath.

Despite the food thing, I can't believe how well Mum's 'real' birthday is going, and we've barely started. But I am part of a couple! I have a date, and a dog. Sadly, mother is finding it hard to come to terms with what 'vegan' means. She thinks Tim's just in denial and longing for something meaty to get stuck into. Her plan seems to be to sneak bits onto his plate thinking that the rest of us won't notice, and Tim will be thrilled.

He won't. He'll be sick.

At her big party at Uncle T's, Mum and Tim became so attached she insisted I bring him round on her actual birthday for a meal. It's just a shame that I am suddenly starting to feel a bit detached from him. It's weird. I thought this was what I wanted, but now I am almost pining for the 'hasn't got a man' comments.

Maybe I have matured to the extent that I now realise having the right man is more important than just having any man.

'Well here we are then!' Mum holds out a plate for Tim and I try to check she's not sneaked a cutlet back on there. I don't think she has. 'I've given you plenty of carrot batons, Tim, don't you love batons? We normally have rounds, but it is my birthday! And broad beans, I've given you extra, love, nobody is keen on them not even the dog so it's thoughtful of you to eat them up! Do you like sprouts as well?' she plonks the plate down, 'Stanley was quite keen at Christmas, wasn't he, Daisy? Very smelly, I must say. Now, are you sure you won't have some gravy? It's made from proper lamb stock, this vegetable stuff is very thin, it's not normal.'

'It's fine, thank you Wendy.'

'Wine?'Dad waves a bottle of red in one hand, and a bottle of white in the other. Apparently, many years ago he did try to make Mum a birthday dinner, but he said it upset the harmony (then whispered that he was scared he'd be dead and buried before the day was out if he didn't keep out of Mum's way) so he'd stick to pouring the drinks.

'Thank you, Stuart.' Tim winks at me and squeezes my knee under the table.

If we go home and have sex after this, it will be the first shag after a family dinner that I have had for a decade. Well, ever.

I stare at my broad beans. The thought should make me happy, but strangely enough it doesn't. I feel like somebody else should be here, not Tim. I would also much rather he just drop me off home tonight with Ollie and go back to his own place.

This is very worrying.

'Well now, Tim, tell us about your job! It's so exciting having a real journalist in the family.' Mum smiles at me. 'And my very own trainee, isn't Daisy clever?'

'Definitely.' Tim pats my hand and looks at me adoringly. I smile back, but I think it's a bit false. Very false. Right now, I'm not sure I want to be with Tim at all.

I don't want a man who just pats me, like he'd pat a dog. I want somebody who believes in me, who wants to support me, who loves me.

It's not like I've always thought he was 'the one', but I did at least think he was 'one of the ones that was fun along the way'. I'm not even sure about that now.

I've finally got my plus-one at my parents' house for dinner – and I'm wishing I was on my own.

Chapter 17

8 p.m., 8 October

'I'm sorry, Daisy. Really.'

'Go away.' I go to slam the door shut but Tim shoves a bunch of red roses towards the gap, and I haven't the heart to crush them. I can't remember the last time somebody bought me red roses.

'Chat? Truce? Pretty please?' In his other hand he has a toothpick. A snapped toothpick.

I can't help it. I smile.

Last night, at the office bash to celebrate James Masters birthday, we had our first big row. This was bigger than the tiff we had by the water cooler just after I started, but it was by the water cooler again.

It started with a ham sandwich. And ended with a mini trifle. Both were in Tim's face – the first in his mouth, the second on his nose.

The first was nothing to do with me. I was just totally

shocked he was not only eating processed pig (he always tells me to think about Peppa Pig when he catches me tucking into a bacon bap) but he was practically orgasmic. I haven't seen him with that look on his face for months, which quite frankly pee'd me off quite a lot.

When I'd asked him what he was doing he started to hiss at me about going behind his back, being a sycophant and not knowing the meaning of the word loyal.

I said he didn't seem to know the meaning of the word vegan.

He called me obsequious and a flirt.

I did a good impression of a goldfish out of water (lots of flapping about and mouth opening).

He made some comment about my lack of eloquence which could give me problems in my save a dog campaign.

So, I behaved in an adult way. I told him to stop using long words and being pompous, tipped his drink over his head, kicked him in the shin and said, 'well at least some men don't offer a toothpick before they snog me'. And walked off.

Like I say. Mature.

Luckily it was actually quite late, and the party was winding down, so it wasn't rude of me to leave.

But how could he do it? Eat the sandwich, accuse me of making eyes at another man, and say I wasn't up to helping Carrie?

He's pretentious, silly, and not a vegan.

And now he is on my doorstep. He flicks the toothpick

over his shoulder. Then starts to sing. 'I can't live, if living is wi—'

'Oh, for God's sake, come in. You'll upset the neighbours.' He comes in and wraps his arms round me.

His beard is a bit tickly and I've got roses tangled in my hair.

'Got a bit wound up!' He looks a bit shamefaced.

'About what?' I frown as I take the flowers from him, and he follows me through to the kitchen, looking around.

'No Ollie?'

'He's not here. You know he's not often here.'

'I felt undermined.' He sits down on a stool by the breakfast bar and stares at me like a sad puppy.

'Undermined?'

'You talking to James about your story. I am your boss you know.'

'But I was only chatting to him!'

'Pitching.'

'Well I might have ...' My cheeks have started to burn. 'I was just fishing, you know see what he thought. Helping Carrie means a lot to me.' Since I first heard about her threatened eviction, I've helped her stick leaflets through doors, left collection tins in shops and put ads in the paper, but it's hopeless. She did manage to pay back some of the debt, but she's limping by month by month. Putting off the inevitable. We're both broke, and she needs something big. A boost that will keep her going over the winter – when the bills are at their worst, and the kennels are cram-packed.

After Mum's party, in a post-sex languor, Tim did say he'd have a word with James, if it meant that much to me. Then nothing happened. And then he said it was a definite no-go again. But when I thought back about it the other day at the party, I started to wonder if it was worth one more try. By somebody who believed in it. I like James Masters, I was just convinced I could make a case and he'd listen.

'And you mean a lot to me.' He takes both my hands, and stares into my eyes.

'You ate a ham sandwich!'

'That's how much you mean to me.'

I'm not quite sure I follow.

He's still clasping my hands, and his are slightly clammy and over-warm. Moist is not a word I like, but it fits this situation. 'I made you turn to meat?'

'I wasn't thinking straight. Shit, I'm sorry. Too much to drink.' He pushes his sleeves up, displaying those fabulous forearms which I fell in love with the first time I met him. I know that might sound a bit kinky, but I'd just wanted to touch them, feel the soft downy hairs against his firm hard muscles. I stare at them and swallow.

I can't let a slice of ham come between us.

The problem is, after my chat with Ollie at Mum's surprise birthday party I've not felt settled. It's been niggling at me. I might have a more organised, better life. I might have more job security and a lovely home. I have (I think, though not sure on this one) still got a boyfriend. But is this really what I want? Is it really what I've always wanted?

Much as I adore good books and a funny movie, is writing about them what I want to do for the rest of my life? It's hard to be witty when you're writing about mass murder or a herd of nutcase zombie bulls who are taking over the world (yes, really), and that's what comes naturally. Being funny, not pithy and meaningful. James said only the other day that he thought my latest theatre review was lacking my normal oomph. I think it's because I'd known even as I was writing the words that they weren't really me. I was trying to write what I thought I should.

Maybe I'm just a crap journalist after all. Maybe this isn't the career for me.

I think I want more than just the perfect life. I want an imperfect, but better one.

Tim strokes a finger down my arm. Normally it feels sexy, today it is mildly irritating. 'I'm a stupid twat, I should believe in you. I do. Honest.' He is looking at me so seriously, I have to believe him. 'If you get the go ahead for the story, I'll help you, then back to normal eh? What you're good at.'

I'm not sure we're completely on the same wavelength here. But he definitely seems sorry.

'I'm also jealous as hell that you're living with another guy.' He gives me a twisted smile but avoids looking directly at me. He seems fascinated by my forearms. Maybe it's just our arms that should be in a relationship? Anyway, it's handy right now because all of a sudden I feel a bit hot and bothered.

'I don't live with ...' it comes out strangled and reedy. 'You know there's nothing between us, Ollie just sometimes sleeps here, and not often.' And not with me, although recently he did feature in a startlingly realistic dream.

'You nearly kissed him!'

Okay, I made an error of judgement here. As I was mushing a trifle into his nose, I might have mentioned that close-up to Ollie in the Harry Potter aisle had been sexier than most of my encounters with Tim recently. Ollie was a man who didn't insist I floss then pass an animal-product free breath test.

'I did not nearly kiss him!' I did. But it didn't happen, so it doesn't count. And Ollie didn't know anything about my lustful thoughts. But this is why I am now glowing with embarrassment and shame.

It was just weird how it felt when Ollie's fingers brushed over my arm. All tingly, it left me buzzing and feeling a bit trembly. Although I think that had to be adrenalin, I was a bit worked up at the time, about nobody wanting to help me help Carrie. That's it, it explains the lot. A bit like when I get shaky and it's because I've got a sugar low. I'd got an adrenalin high.

It meant absolutely nothing at all ...

11 a.m., 9 October

'Right then, what's the plan with this idea of yours? Any progress?' James Masters is sitting behind his big desk in his small office. He's quite a big man actually, which makes it all feel even more cramped. But he's nice and smiley.

I smile back, all tongue-tied, slightly in awe of the big boss. I've hardly spoken to James since I started working for him and now he's summonsed me into his office!

'Sit down, sit down, coffee?'

He's the only one with an office, and everybody else is trying to watch us and lip read whilst still appearing to concentrate on their laptops and work.

The coffee is brought in by Maureen who answers the phone, and generally keeps a close eye on us all. She gives me an encouraging smile. 'Biscuit?'

Bloody hell, I've arrived! It's normally make your own coffee and keep a snack in your drawer. I am being offered custard creams! I take one, to hell with my no-carb diet, I am not going to pass up on this. It might never happen again.

Tim's desk is just outside the office, and he keeps rubbing his upper (hair-covered) lip with a finger. It's one of the things he does when he's anxious.

'Can you hit today's deadline? There's a slot on page 4, not much but we can always expand if the online hit rate is good.'

I start to choke on my biscuit, which I think I've inhaled out of shock, and follow it with a sip of coffee which is so hot I think my tongue has melted.

I grab a tissue and pant into it, my eyes watering, heaving for breath. 'Sorry, it went,' another crumb tickles my throat and sets me off again, 'down the wrong way.'

Today's deadline? A slot?

'Happens to us all!' I bet it doesn't happen to him. 'The more I've thought about it, the more I think it's a brilliant idea, there's nothing like helping the local community.' He leans forward looking at me earnestly from behind his glasses. 'That's what we're supposed to be doing, isn't it? That's partly why we brought you in.'

I nod. And then it clicks. I realise what he is talking about.

'The dog rescue centre.'

He looks at me, as though he's expecting me to expand on the statement. What am I going to do? Shit, what's the plan? The plan. He's expecting me to have a plan.

'Another tissue?' He smiles encouragingly. 'Take your time.' He grins. 'But not all day, we have a deadline!'

I can do this. It's easy. I do have a plan. 'A fun day, an open day. That's what the centre needs.' He nods. 'We need to build up interest,' bloody hell, how do we do that? 'I thought maybe a feature on a few of the dogs?' Funny features, that's what we need. 'Where they came from?' I've got it! 'The saddest, funniest, ugliest ones!'

'A series then.' His fingers are steepled and he's watching me keenly.

'Series?'

'Of articles, start now do one a week.'

'Really?'

'Have you got enough material?'

'Oh heaven's yes, there's lots of stuff, I mean some of

the places they've come from, and some of them are real characters, and then there's Carrie, she was brought up in foster care you know, which is probably why she feels like she does, and she lost her partner and ...'

He frowns and hold up a hand to stop me. 'I can't see why Tim had any doubts about running this, it's dynamite. Well maybe not,' he smiles and it's slightly mischievous, 'in the eyes of a national, but this is gold for a local paper. Do it girl! Go on, scoot!'

'Now?'

'Now.' He bangs the desk with the flat of his hand and I jump. 'Let's do this!'

I stand up clutching my coffee, but in my head I'm dashing round squealing. 'But my reviews?'

'Cut back but do those as well. I'll work out how many words you need to run with and email you. Anything else?'

'Er, well, no.'

'Photographer?'

'Oh, that would be great, yes, thanks.'

'Get Maureen on it, check the diary and make sure next week's piece has some heart-breaking photo's, right get going then, you don't want to miss the deadline, do you?'

'This week's? You mean I can start ...'

'Straightaway. And, Daisy ...' his voice stops me as I reach the door – 'take the biscuits; I'm on a diet, according to my wife.'

Oh my God. It is happening!

I grab Tim's arm and pull him over to the water cooler.

'He said I can do it! Now! Straightaway!' I might be jumping up and down a bit, it's hard to keep still. This is it, my career is moving on!

'What?'

'Write about Carrie, run a feature!'

'Fantastic.' He squeezes my arm. 'Get it right though, don't screw up the proper job!'

Okay, maybe my career is only making a temporary leap and normal service will be resuming soon. 'I won't.' Yay, I've been given free rein to help.

'Talking of which,' he taps his watch, 'deadline looming!'

I take the hint and go back to my desk. Slightly deflated. At times I could strangle Tim. But I don't. I find myself picking up my mobile and hitting the speed dial button.

I know exactly who will be pleased with this news, exactly who I want to share it with. 'Ollie?' I lean forward and lower my voice to a conspiratorial whisper.

'Dais?'

'Are you busy? Shall I call back?'

'No, it's fine, fine. You just sound a bit strange, stranger than normal!'

'Ha-ha, I'm whispering, I don't want to get the sack now I've got the go ahead!'

'Go ahead?'

'You were right! You were right all along, I talked to James and he said yes! He said yes, Ol! I'm going to write a feature about Carrie, well several, a series, and I get a photographer, and an open day!'

'Hang on, slow down.' He's laughing, his deep chuckle infectious, making me laugh with him. 'That's amazing! You're amazing!'

I'm glowing and feel fit to burst. I want to hug him, do a silly jig, dance round the office.

'I knew you could do it, Carrie will be thrilled.'

'Oh God, yes, I've got to tell Carrie. She doesn't know yet.'

'You told me before you told her?' I can imagine his lifted eyebrow, the quirk of his mouth, the dimple. 'Thank you.'

Two words, just two words but he says them so softly, so genuinely that they send a shiver down my spine.

'I'll bring some bubbly home, unless you want me to take you out to celebrate?' Bloody hell, his voice is even deeper and sexier on the phone than in real life.

'Home is fine.'

'See you later, Dais. Well done!'

I put the phone down slowly, my cheeks glowing. In fact, I'm glowing all over. I did it! And Ollie thinks I'm amazing.

I want to high-five him. But I can't. So I pick the phone up again and pick out another number. I have got to tell Carrie that she's holding an open day and dog show!

Chapter 18

6 p.m., 15 December

'Oh my God, that was brilliant.' Carrie hugs me, and her eyes are glistening. It's very unlike Carrie, who never shows weakness of any kind. She sniffs and wipes the back of her hand over her face. 'It was awesome, thank you so much you lovely lady. You're the best friend ever.'

'How much money did we make?' This has just got to be one of the best days of my life. I cannot believe just how many people turned up to Carrie's Fun Dog Show and Open Day.

'God knows! But so many people have filled in forms to adopt, or sponsor, look!' She holds up a sheaf of forms and laughs, letting them fall to the table. I've not seen her look this happy and relaxed since, well since Evie was here. 'Your friend Frankie is so brilliant at persuading people to do stuff.'

'I know.' I grin. 'She sees a weakness and she's in there.' She does. There's no hesitation with Frankie, she knows what you want before you do. I'd hoped she'd hang around at the end and get to know Carrie a bit better, but dogs' homes aren't really her thing. She probably shot off to go to some grand opening of something or other, or a night with Tarquin, I didn't get time to ask.

Carrie winks. 'Wow, really moving up the ranks these days, no stopping our small ads girl! You should ask for a promotion, or a move, or whatever it is. The features you did were amazing. I mean, even before today we've had so many donations sent in, and tons of enquiries! I've been able to pay the arrears plus put money aside to cope with the Christmas rush! You are awesome!'

I'd been quite excited once James gave me the go ahead, and really pleased with my first attempt which I'd thought was quite witty. I'd even had emails and readers letters about the dogs! 'I'll be quite sad to just go back to writing reviews.'

'They won't do that will they? Can't you have a column, you know write about pets or local businesses or something?'

'I don't know, Carrie.' I hug her. James hasn't suggested anything, he'd just accepted my plan for the features and that had been it.

I try to smile brightly. 'It's all good experience though, and I'm so pleased I could help. This is about you, not me!'

She hugs me. 'See you soon?'

'Definitely.'

I stand at the gate and take a deep breath and wish Tim hadn't had to rush back to file his copy and check the photographs. It would have been nice to stroll down to the local pub together and celebrate my tiny success. But I guess to him it's just another job.

'The girl did good, eh?'

I spin round and grin. I haven't seen much of Uncle Terence lately and I've missed him. It's strange how quickly I've got used to our little chats, and his advice.

'Wasn't it great!'

'It certainly was. I take it you are going back to your parents?'

I nod. 'I'm staying for tea then heading back into town.'

'I'm sure your mother is dying to hear how it went, she's very proud you know!'

'That makes a change!' I smile, but I know she is. 'Poor Mum, she's always tried her hardest to find something to boast about, but Vera has had so much more material to work with!'

He chuckles. 'I'm going that way as well. Come on, dearest Daisy, let's walk together.' Uncle T inclines his elbow, and I slip my hand through it.

It's a beautiful evening, a clear sky and a crispness to the air that takes my breath away but makes me feel full of energy despite how hectic the last week has been. The perfect end to one of the best days of my life.

'Thanks for coming.'

Uncle T smiles. 'My pleasure, it was a triumph!' He kisses my cheek. 'Wouldn't have missed it for the world. And it was so lovely to see young Carrie with a smile on her face.'

'She's going to make it an annual event. Plus, do a summer one, one in July would be brilliant wouldn't it?'

'And so she should, a triumph! No small thanks to you and your publicity campaign.' We walk on for a few minutes in silence. 'Lovely to see your interesting friend again. She's quite a character, isn't she?'

I laugh. Interesting is one word for Frankie. 'She's lovely underneath all that flash exterior. She really helped me when I was living with her and pushed me to apply for my job.' I shrug.

'Smart girl.'

'Well she actually suggested I go for the marketing manager job, you know, aim high, but then Tim said they had the other vacancy, which is tons better.'

'Indeed it is.' He pats my hand.

'Frankie was a bit shocked I got it!'

'I wasn't, none of us were.' He smiles. 'It's so wonderful to see the old Daisy blooming again. No pun intended.'

I frown at him.

'You're reaching for the sun, going after you want. If you believe in yourself, anything can happen dear girl. Surround yourself with positivity. That's what Ollie does.'

'Hmm.' In the past, any mention of Ollie used to make me feel all defensive and cross inside, but I've just realised that I'm not feeling like that at all these days. Maybe because I'm beginning to see the real Ollie, underneath all the hype. Which he didn't create in the first place – our mothers did.

241

I also realise with a jolt that I've really missed him today. I would have loved him to be here, after all it was him who encouraged me to go ahead. When I get home, I will text him, tell him all about it, and say thank you.

'You and Ollie are quite alike you know.' I glance up at Terence, and he's looking quite smug and happy.

'We are?' He sounds more interested than surprised.

'You are. And you've both really helped me.'

'I'm glad. You get on then now? No Chinese burns and pushing each other under the water in the bath tub?'

'He's not coming anywhere near my bath tub!' I feel myself redden. 'But, er, yes. I'm not sure he likes all my stuff cluttering up the place, and I'm not sure he's that keen on Tim.'

'Are you? Keen on Tim.'

'He's nice.' I say, which sounds a bit defensive (and lame) even to my own ears. If I am keen, I seem to be the only one. Frankie makes the odd snide comment even though she's only met him a handful of times, and Ollie is wary and keeps out of his way. But am I? Or are we just a not-so-good habit?

'Ollie is probably just giving you space.' Says Uncle T, but he's got that thoughtful edge to his voice.

'I wish I was more like Frankie.' The words are unexpected, but I can't stop them. I do, I really do. I want to be interesting, different. I want to challenge the world like she does.

'No, you don't, darling Daisy.' I grind to a halt, so Terence has to as well. He looks me in the eye, then encourages me to walk on. 'You need to want to be more like you. *You* is the very best there is. Ah, here we are, home sweet home!'

7.30 p.m., 17 December

'What the hell is this?'

I glance over at Tim, who is dangling something black in the air and looking at it disdainfully.

'T shirt? God, I have nothing to wear!' I rake through the hangers in my wardrobe again. We're late and we're going out with Frankie and Tarquin and I have decided I need to make an effort. Frankie and Tim got on so well at the fundraiser for Carrie we arranged another get together as soon as we could.

I've been doing my best to follow Sasha's fashion advice since July after she picked out my outfit for Mum's party. Ollie had told me I looked nice for the first time, and even Mum had been impressed.

In fact, Ollie often makes comments about my clothes in a nice way, and I've even started to ask his opinion. Though he did get a bit stuffy and mutter something about it not being in his remit to tell me if my bum looked big, and maybe I should ask my boyfriend.

Sasha says I need to find my own style, so I've been trying. But secretly I think my style is more jeans, shirt, cowboy boots and hat – a combo that doesn't always work, especially in December at a posh wine bar. But it does

Zara Stoneley

kind of suit my messy blonde hair (which is currently in a very messy bun) and blue-grey eyes.

'Are you nearly ready?' Tim is looking at his watch. 'We're going to be late.' He taps it. Actually taps it.

He's not normally bothered if we're late, so I give him a look. 'Can't you wait in the lounge? Watch TV or something, I'm not going to be long!' I hate being watched while I'm trying to pick an outfit out. Mainly because I want to be able to put one on, strip it off, put another one on, strip it off, until I've exhausted all possibilities and gone back to option one, and tried adding a necklace, or belt, or something. I'm self-conscious if he watches.

'I like watching you.' He sits on the bed. 'It's sexy.'

'But we haven't got time for sex, you said we were late!'

'I just want to think about it, for later.' Tim does a lot of this, thinking about it for later. Then, after an evening out he's usually so drunk he just has a quick fumble then falls asleep before he can remember why he's doing it. I'm going to have to be more organised and get ready earlier if I want a sex life with him. But he takes so long in the shower, and hogging the mirror, I'm always last minute.

'We could do it now?' I check my own watch. I'm sure we can fit a quick romp in, it's not like it takes hours, is it?

'I can't just do it, I'm a man not a machine you know! And the pompous prick might come back.'

I cringe. He won't stop calling him that, ever since he heard Frankie say it. 'Ollie's away at a conference, I told you.'

'Or your bloody dog will want to join in.'

I have to admit, Stanley does find the sight of Tim's bare bum fascinating. It's a bit unnerving when he jumps onto the foot of the bed, sits down, and stares. His little head bobbing up and down in time. I laughed once, which completely ruined the mood.

'So, you don't want a shag?' I turn back to the mirror. 'Messy hair okay, or too messy.'

'It's fine.' He sighs and stands up. 'So,' his tone is now slightly belligerent, 'whose is this? It's too big for you!'

I stop trying to do flicky eyes and look at him. 'It'll be Ollie's, you know it will.'

'In your bedroom?'

'I told you, the washing sometimes gets mixed up. I just grab a pile and shove it in the drawers without paying attention.'

'Hmm.' He drops it on the floor and marches off into the lounge.

'Bloody hell!' I've just made a real mess of my right eye, after doing a perfect black flick on my left. He's completely wrecked my concentration. I can tell he's cross and my tummy has done a bit of a dive. He seems to thrive on winding me up, causing an argument, and then making up. He can be hard work at times.

'Tim.' I drop the eyeliner and follow him into the lounge. 'You know there's nothing going on. He's not even here most of the time, I live on my own!'

He's sat on the sofa, sulkily messing with the remote control.

'Even Frankie thinks you fancy him.'

'Since when did you talk to Frankie?' We hardly ever see her when we're together.

He shrugs. 'Your mum's party? Dog show? She always makes comments!'

'Because she fancies him!'

'Bollocks.' He looks a bit less sure of himself though. 'Does she?'

'Definitely. That's why she's always so scathing and insists on calling him pompous prick, to cover up the fact.'

'But she's got Tarquin.'

'I know.' I sigh, slip off the arm of the sofa so that I am sitting next to him. 'I don't think she's sure about him though, she wouldn't let him move into the flat until she didn't feel she had a choice.'

'Really?' He looks more interested now, than argumentative, which is good. Then he sits back and stares at me, then sits forward and grasps his hands together, then ums and ahs in a very un-Tim like way.

'Are you okay? You still want to go out?'

He moves closer, which is a bit alarming, and cups his hands round my face. He strokes his thumb across my cheek, and I wonder if this happens to everybody after being in a relationship with someone. Not the thumb thing, but the fact that it is no longer sending a thrill of anticipation into my knickers. I'm not dying to grab him and kiss him. Instead I'm wondering if it's a crumb in his beard or a grey hair.

'We've been together a long time now haven't we?' He pauses. It is a long time. Well, it has been on and off a bit, but still. 'Sometimes you have to take the plunge I guess, pop the question.'

Ooooh, Holy Shit! Not *the* question. I always thought this relationship wasn't for life, it was for Christmas!

He shifts nervously, but doesn't let go of my face, which means I can either follow him across the sofa or stay and be stretched.

'How about it then?'

'It?' I squeak.

'Moving in with me. Trial?' His eyes twinkle, his eyebrows rock comically.

Phew. Thank fuck for that! It's the living together question, not the forever-together question. My heart was hammering a bit for a moment there.

'Nothing too serious, see what it's like to share the toothpaste.'

I gulp. 'It's a bit sudden.' And laugh slightly hysterically. 'Didn't expect that!'

'But you want to?'

I don't know. How do I say I don't know without changing this relationship forever? Saying no will change everything. Well, actually so will saying yes. Whatever I say, there will be no going back.

Why did he have to ask?

'Tim, this hasn't got anything to do with the T-shirt has it?'

'What do you mean?' I reckon he's trying to look innocent, but instead he looks shifty.

'It's just, I mean if it's just that you'd rather I wasn't living with Ollie.'

'Rubbish! Do you really think that?' He gives a harsh laugh. 'I'm not exactly the jealous type, but I don't for one minute imagine he'd want—'

Tim is literally saved by the bell. I'd have ignored my ringing phone, but he sweeps it up and answers.

'On our way, soz, Frankie!' Then he grins at me and stands up. 'C'mon, gorgeous, taxi awaits. Did I tell you how beautiful you look? Don't do it enough!'

He doesn't. He also doesn't tell me he loves me very often. I haven't minded up until now.

'What were you about to say?'

'Say? Nothing. Come on, chop, chop, want to sort out that eye?'

I rub my flicks off and draw a quick line with kohl eyeliner. And pull my checked shirt on over my head. It's what I want to wear. I know Tim's not keen, but it is what I want to wear.

What the hell was he about to say? That he didn't for one moment think Ollie would be interested in me?

He might be right, but what kind of boyfriend says that, just after they've asked you to live with them?

I stare at myself in the mirror. Yep, he might be right. Ollie might call me amazing, he might be wonderfully supportive, he might be funny and entertaining – but that doesn't mean to say that he'll ever want to kiss me again, does it?

Which is a slightly depressing thought.

Because I'd really like to kiss him again. Even though I know I shouldn't.

1 a.m., 18 December

I shut the door and lean against it. As evening go, it wasn't the best. Okay, Frankie was on form, but I couldn't stop thinking about what Tim had said.

It's not just the moving in question. I mean, he's kind of taken it that I will (I think) which is a bit worrying. But it's the fact that he seems to have asked because he just doesn't trust me. Surely relationships are all about trust?

Not about finding suspect T-shirts.

How can I even think about moving in if I think it's just his way of controlling what I do and who I do it with?

Why doesn't he trust me?

I can't think of a single thing I've ever done. Well, there was the time I was very tempted to kiss Ollie. But I didn't. And he wouldn't.

Oh yeah, and what the fuck was that about? How dare he say (or nearly say) that he thinks Ollie wouldn't want to kiss me back? He is supposed to have me on a pedestal, he is supposed to think everybody in the world would want to kiss me! Well, maybe not everybody, but you know what I mean. Or maybe you don't. I am a bit drunk.

But you're supposed to be proud of who you're with, aren't you?

And he obviously isn't. He doesn't think I'm all that brilliant. Or lust-worthy. I am not good enough in his eyes, not for Ollie, or who knows who. A bit like when he didn't think I should stretch myself and write a feature to help Carrie.

I don't think he's ever really meant any harm, but he just doesn't understand me. He never has done. In his head, living with him, doing my safe little job and living a neat little life is all I need, all I want.

But it isn't.

Uncle Terence understands.

Even Ollie understands.

I think *I* finally understand as well. I can't move in with Tim.

I stand up.

I can't even date Tim. What's the point? All he's done for me is what I've been doing for myself since I fucked up my 'A' levels – undermining me. Telling me what I can't do, rather than what I can. And if I'm brutally honest here, I've not put him on a pedestal either. I was worrying about what was in his beard, rather than admiring his manliness.

I'm not sure all this will make quite as much sense in the morning, when I'm sober, so I think I need to text him now. Tell him.

It's over.

ACT 3 – NOTHING'S GOING TO STOP ME NOW

Chapter 19

'Happy Christmas, Daisy!' James Masters, my very nice boss, perches on the corner of my desk, which is quite a feat considering the amount of crap piled up. Anybody would think offices would be practically paperless these days, wouldn't they? This one isn't.

I love paper though. I never want to switch to full-on electronic. I like the piles of books with pages you can smell and flick, I like printing my copy off and being able to red ink it. I also like my dog mug, the picture of Stanley, the packet of Pringles and the mini Christmas tree I spotted for a bargain 50p. Okay, I admit it, I just like crap. Stuff.

Anyhow, my boss has managed to find a spot big enough to park a bum cheek on and smiles across at me as I close the lid of my laptop and slip it into my bag.

'Anything exciting planned?' James is holding his own laptop in one hand and has the other in his pocket. He looks like a man planning his escape from the office.

253

'Family party at Terence's bookshop!' I am rather looking forward to Uncle T's party this year. When I got up this morning and went through my mental list of things that I needed to do, it went better than it ever has done.

1. Buffet food – check (smoked salmon blinis, chilled bubbly and fancy nuts)
2. Christmas jumper and antlers found – check
3. Stanley washed and dressed (he's not keen on his jumper but I told him he has to enter into the spirit) – check
4. Sparkly Christmas nails – check
5. Boyfriend primed about what to expect (i.e. my mother) – check. Uncheck! BF has now gone, and I'm happy to be going on my own, so there!
6. Last review of the year written and subbed – check

'Sounds good. Have fun!'

'I will do.' I double check I haven't left any chocolates in my desk drawer and smile at my boss. 'Have you got much planned?'

'Oh, the normal, five kids, a mother-in-law an ex-mother-in-law and having a vicar for a father makes life interesting! See you at the bash I hope?' He stands up, pauses to wait for an answer.

'Definitely.'

'Fantastic.'

The bash is our works Christmas do, and is held two days after Boxing Day – which is perfect timing to my mind. I will have recovered from Christmas, and be bored, in that lull before New Year. It's that time when you've eaten far too many chocolates, but feel obliged to finish them all off, and you're totally sick of turkey, but pick at the leftovers anyway. And you're worrying if your charade was really as inappropriate as you think it might have been. And you really need to get back to work or at least talk to some real people i.e. not family.

'All geared up for another animal feature in the New Year?' He winks, which rather takes me by surprise, the wink and the words.

'You want me to do another one?' I move my mini Christmas tree to one side, so I can see him more clearly. This year's tree is rather on the big side, but it was a bargain price and it flashes. It's got a bit competitive in the office actually, we've all been trying to see just how much tinsel, and how many baubles we can get away with.

'I certainly do, if you want to?'

I nod vigorously.

Tim has been rather grumpy since we decided to call it a day. So next year I think I am going to have to think about asking for a promotion, or a new boss.

'Great! Right, I suppose I better be off, last minute shopping to be done, and all that. Have a wonderful Christmas, Daisy.'

255

'I will!' For the first time in years, I actually believe I will. 'Happy Christmas, good luck with all the mother-in-law's and the vicar!'

'I might need it!' And he strolls out of the office, grabbing his coat off the rack as he goes.

I skip down the stairs and pause halfway down to look out of the window. It's part of my health drive, the skipping down the stairs bit, not the pausing. I really have to stop the pausing, which happens all the time – to chat to people, stroke dogs, tie my shoelaces. You know, all those things you do when you're knackered and need a break, but you're trying to kid yourself that it's unavoidable and not your fault.

Today though I just need to look. It's truly beautiful outside, a real winter wonderland. The perfect Christmas scene.

There's a gorgeous thick blanket of snow draped over the roof of the café opposite, the place I met Uncle Terence when I first got offered the job, it looks like a cute gingerbread house that's been iced with a heavy hand, and I can't help but smile.

Wow, it's nine months since I stood here for the first time, after my interview with Tim. Is it really that long? You can have a baby in that time! Although in a way I feel like I've done something a bit similar to giving birth, but it's the new me that has been born. I feel like I'm living a different life now.

I love living with Ollie. Well not *living*, but you know what I mean. When he is there, he's great company, and he never brings girlfriends home (which is a huge bonus, I was rather worried about being the gooseberry). In fact, he doesn't seem to have had a girlfriend for ages which shouldn't, but does, make me happy.

And now, after my huge success with the features I ran for Carrie, James has asked for more! This is totally amazing! There's a real chance I'm starting to move up the ladder, and I don't want to get ahead of myself here, but maybe one day I'll leave the review column behind! Wow, I've not stopped to think about all this until now, but I really am making something of my life at last.

I give myself a little hug, that's another thing I love about Ollie. He insists we celebrate every achievement, 'sharing is caring' he said the other night – before nicking the last bit of pizza. Cheeky bugger, that bit of him definitely hasn't changed!

Next year is going to be even better, I just know it is.

Stanley has flatly refused to entertain coming to Uncle T's party tonight, he hid when I got his jumper out and refused to come out from under the bed, even though I'd got him some lovely new flashing antlers.

So, I'll be partner less again, but, to be honest I don't particularly care. Does it matter? I do not have anything to prove to anybody – including my mother.

I am a bit sad that Ollie won't be there. I've not seen him for a while – he's not been home much (I love calling our apartment home), there has been an end of year rush of conferences, meetings and emergency ops. But he has promised he'll be around for Christmas day. And we're friends now, so Mum and Vera can be as competitive as they like tonight because I know exactly what Ollie is like – and Mum will have some totally un-exaggerated good things to say about me! This is going to be the best party ever!

5 p.m., 24 December

'They look almost edible!'

'Shit!' I drop my tea strainer, which I've been using to scatter icing sugar snow on my mince pies with, then rap the back of the rather large hand that is trying to snaffle one. 'Stop it! What are you doing here?'

'Happy Christmas to you too, Virgin Mary, and you Stanley boy!' Ollie pats Stanley, who is sitting by the table, his mouth half-open with expectation, on the head. He got over his Christmas jumper aversion when he smelled food.

'You're supposed to be in London!' I try not to grin. I'm disproportionally pleased to see him. Which is a bit worrying. I only spoke to him on the phone yesterday, and he's only been gone three days this time! I try not to ogle him too openly. How can a man look so gorgeous? His hair is longer than he normally lets it get (probably because he's been so busy), and the ends are just tipping under leaving me with a sudden longing to see the curls he used to have as a child. His cheekbones are tinged pink by the bitter cold wind outside, and he's grinning, his cute dimples nestling at the sides of his generous mouth.

Good enough to eat.

'In London? Says who?'

'Juliet!' Juliet has come back into our lives. When I say 'our' I mean Ollie's, but I seem to be spending more time than he does answering the door to her.

'Really?' He looks surprised.

I was surprised as well when I answered the door to her at 10 p.m. last night.

'Hey, Maisie! Just popped in to sort last minutes! Isn't it exciting?'

'Daisy! It's Daisy!' I am tempted to swear loudly, but I desist.

Not a lot is exciting at 10 p.m. on a week day in my life. Unless I've won a lucky dip on the lotto, Wolverine is on TV or I've managed to dye Ollie's white shirt pink (it happened).

Anyway, Juliet was looking all slim and sleek, and practically purring as she tried to edge round me into the apartment. Like a black panther, but pale pink. With high heels.

I was all cuddly and half-comatose, more black-bear in the middle of hibernation. With hair in ringlets that were all mussed up at the back because I'd been lying flat on the sofa. My big jumper has got to the over-fluffy stage, and my old joggers are for my eyes only.

I was a make-up free zone. Which is fine if you aren't

knackered from a day in the office, and still feel 'radiant', but I felt puffy eyed and sallow.

I mean, who just 'pops in' at that time? 'Last minutes?'

'Oh God, hasn't Ollie told you? Oh wow, well it's secret, but, well ... Is he in?'

'Nope.'

She gazed down her long sleek nose at me, giving me the once over, then giggled. 'Oh, I guess not.'

I was about to point out that I do not dress to impress him, but then decided not to.

'Well, you'll know soon enough, but don't tell anybody I told you!' She whispered confidentially, even though I'm sure Stanley wouldn't tell on her.

'We're going to have an announcement.' She beamed. 'You know! Pop the ...' Her eyes opened wider than I have ever seen eyes open (apart from Gollum) and her neat eyebrows shot up to her hairline. 'Oh God, I shouldn't have said! But it's so exciting! Don't tell him I told you. Can you give him this invite though? Here.' She fished in her massive tote bag and flourished a very expensive looking envelope under my nose. 'I think this is where he's going to do it! Tomorrow!'

Then she was off before I could shut the door in her face. Pop the question? How can Ollie pop the question to somebody like her? I slammed the envelope a little too forcibly on the table and Stanley whimpered and shot into his basket.

And tomorrow? How can he miss Uncle T's party? How dare he miss the party to propose!

260

'*Aww*, sorry Stanley, come here.' He can't marry her! It's all wrong. We've been getting on so well, whenever he's been here, and I like living with him – I actually really miss him when he's working away. The apartment feels strange, it's much more 'home' when he's here. He helped me save Stanley, I nearly kissed him. Oh hell, I nearly kissed a nearly married man.

Except I didn't know. I mean, Juliet had been off the agenda for a while.

I feel sick. I sink down onto the floor and Stanley crawls onto my knee and licks my nose.

I am not feeling sick because I nearly kissed him, but because I'm about to lose him.

He's one of my best friends, he's not pompous at all. Ollie believed in me when nobody else did. Ollie encouraged me to go for it and talk to James about my ideas. Ollie is the one who has never doubted what I can do. Ollie is the first person I've wanted to tell when I've got good news, the only person I want to talk to when things haven't gone quite as well as I'd hoped. Because I trust him. I value his opinion. I know he knows me, understands me, better than anybody else.

Oh bugger. I don't want him to marry her. He can't.

That sounds awful, and selfish. And I can't say that, it sounds like I'm just bitter and jealous because I have split up with my boyfriend.

'Why do I feel this bad, Stanley?' I had been feeling so positive about things, so happy that it was Christmas and my life was finally shaping up.

261

Do I say something to him, even though Juliet told me not to? Do I ask, check, beg him not to?

I need Frankie. Frankie will know what to do.

So I phone her, and tell her.

'I don't want to lose him!'

'You really fancy the arse off him, don't you?'

'No!' I shout, then make an effort to lower my voice. Stanley is looking worried, he doesn't like loud angry noises. 'It's not that, I don't fancy him, but I do like him, and I like living here and ... shall I ask him? Shall I check?'

'No.' Frankie is using her firm, don't mess me with tone.

'No?' I am using my why not? Little girl tone.

'Definitely not. You'll sounds like a needy pathetic weakling, you don't want that, do you?'

'Well no, but, I could just ...'

'He'll know you fancy him, you'll make yourself look an idiot.'

'Surely it's reasonable to just ask, and then I know if I'll have to move out.' An image leaps into my head, of Ollie carrying Juliet over the threshold into *our* apartment. Obviously, he's practically skipping in, because she's light as a feather. If it had been me, he'd stagger in then drop me in a heap on the sofa and collapse on top of me. A string of bellboys waltz in after her, with all her posh designer cases and soon there's no room for my stuff or me. I'm consigned to the tiniest of tiny box rooms. Stanley squashed into a corner.

Except it's not Ollie's place. It is Uncle Terence's. And Uncle T wouldn't let that happen to me, would he?

'Dais, are you listening? I know if you ask him, you'll end up getting upset. Don't!'

'I won't get—'

'Yes, you will!' I haven't spoken to Frankie for quite a while, I've been busy working, and I'd forgotten how assertive she was. 'Do not ask him! You'll know soon enough if he's getting hitched when you get the invite.'

'But ...'

She sighs. Heavily. 'It was bound to happen sooner or later to a dish like him, wasn't it? And you knew you hadn't got a hope, you just like to fantasise about him.'

For a moment I am speechless. She sounds just like bloody Tim! Is it really true, does everybody feel they have to tell me that I'm just not good enough for him?

'No, I don't.' It comes out a bit strangled, because I feel all choked up – and angry. Frankie is my friend!

'Shame though, I'd have liked a play with his stethoscope. Oh well, maybe in a year or two when he's bored of her.'

'Frankie!' I put down the phone and stared at the wall.

'Juliet?' Ollie has that puzzled look that Stanley gets, when he's pretending he doesn't know what 'get off the sofa' means.

'When she came round last night?' Frankie might have told me not to discuss his proposal (which I want to do purely to establish facts), but she didn't say I shouldn't talk about *her*.

'Did she?' While I'm distracted he takes the opportunity

to grab a mince pie, unfortunately I mistime my grab as it is heading up to his mouth, and somehow end up smashing it into his face.

I freeze. We stare at each other aghast.

A bit of pastry falls from his eyebrow, and he blinks.

There is a slurping noise, as Stanley Hoovers up the floor around our feet.

A piece of sticky dried fruit slides down his nose. For a moment it sticks on the very tip, and I make a grab for it just as he does. We end up in a sticky hand grasp, our faces nearly touching, and it's a bit like when we were six, but different. It's making me feel a bit breathless and peculiar. We stare at each other. Swap breath. Then he grins and the world clatters back to normal. And I realise. He's actually got the most amazing eyes close up, all brown and liquid-y and flecked. 'Did you know your eyes are the same colour as,' I pull my hand free from his and hold it up triumphantly, 'sultanas? I won!'

'Give that here, you little ...' He's grabbed my hand again, and we're back in those arm-wrestling days. Except we're not. His touch is so firm, and warm, and I suddenly feel like I might not want to fight, I might not actually want to escape ...

But, oh God, he's about to get married. I can't do this.

'Shit, bugger.' I forget thinking of what I can and can't do. My feet are slipping backwards from under me and I'm scrabbling with my feet and flapping my free arm, and somehow end up hanging onto him for dear life, then slowly sliding down him. Sinking down onto my knees as I clutch the waistband of his jeans and hope they don't fall down, because my finger tips are against his red-hot skin, and my eyes are fixed on the band of his designer trunks.

And now I'm nose to nose with Stanley instead.

'Eurgh, my God, Daisy, what have you stuck down my pants?' He's fishing very close to the spot I've just been pawing at, and his finger emerges, with that sticky sultana – now thoroughly squished.

'Some people would quite like me putting my sticky fingers down their knickers!' I probably shouldn't have said that. Luckily, I can hide my red cheeks by staring at Stanley. Who appears to have a cherry on his head.

He licks his lips, licks my nose (I really hope he's not recently been licking anywhere else) then burps. Then sniffs his way along my legs.

'Ouch! You bugger. Bloody hell.' I scramble sideways. Stanley has mistaken my little toe for something savoury and tried to eat that as well. He backs off, licking his lips and looking far too pleased with himself.

'Oh bugger, quick, quick, get all the bits!' I scramble round on my knees, sweeping up the fruit and crumbs with my hands. 'It's poisonous! I'm poisoning him with a mince pie!'

'I would have thought eating your feet would have been more of a threat to his health!'

'He likes my feet, even if you don't!'

'I didn't say I don't like your feet.'

I look up at him, my hands full of fruit and squished pastry, and I think I've just rubbed some into my hair.

Ollie grins, then guffaws, then very deliberately wipes the pie from his face and tries a bit. 'Mmm, not bad for a beginner.'

'Sod off!' I shake my head at him. Baking has never been my thing, but I thought I'd make a special effort for Uncle T this year and actually do some home baking rather than just pretend I had. 'Are they really okay?' I'm worried now. 'Maybe I should dash down to Waitrose before they shut?'

'Definitely not!'

'Not okay?'

'Not Waitrose. These are great. Obviously, I would prefer one not mushed into my face, but not bad as a deconstructed thing.'

'Deconstructed is so in.'

'It is.' His eyes light up, he's got that mischievous look I know I need to fear. 'We could always deconstruct the rest?'

'Don't you dare!' I drag myself back to my feet, using his legs for purchase and pick up the rolling pin. 'Touch them at your peril!' I grin back though, almost forgetting that he is about to get engaged.

'Shouldn't that be eat them at—'

'Stop being cheeky! Anyway, you knew Juliet came round.' I can't help it. I can't not mention her.

'I did?'

'You did. You asked her to!'

'Did I?'

266

'She brought the invite for you!'

'Ah.' He sits down at the kitchen table and eyes the food up in a way that is very similar to the Stanley stare. 'That invite. I'm not going to London.'

'You're not?' He's not! This is fantastic – he can't propose if he's not there. Can he? Surely proposal by Skype or Facebook isn't acceptable, even for busy people?

'It's a medical do, she wants an escort.'

I know that feeling. 'And you are her boyfriend,' about to be fiancé, 'so ...'

He shrugs. 'I told her I didn't fancy it, but she said she'd drop the invite off in case I change my mind.' This is a bit weird. 'Can't miss Uncle T's do though, can I?'

'Really? You can't? No, you can't!' So, are they about to get engaged, or not? I am confused. I am very pleased he's coming to Uncle T's, but there's a hard lump in my chest, a pain.

I've lost him. Even if he does come to the party, he's practically married. I'll never have another kiss.

'Highlight of the year!'

I decide not to point out that for many years he did indeed miss it, and attend either other countries, dying people, or medical parties in London. Or Birmingham, or Manchester. I also decide I have to put a bright smile on my face. I am not going to let this spoil things. I am still going to have a wonderful time.

'It certainly is.' I start to pile my mince pies into a tin. 'I know how many there are, so don't even think about it!'

He looks at me with what I am sure he thinks is an innocent look, but I know better.

'I'm going to get showered and changed, keep your hands off!'

'What time are you meeting Frankie?'

'I'm not, sorry, she called off. I can give you her number though, for new year? Next year?'

He gives a wry smile. 'Uncle T will miss her stunning presence.'

I want to ask if *he* will miss Frankie's presence, but don't. And after all, he has got Juliet.

'Would you like to come with me then, Dais? I can give you a lift?'

'Juliet isn't coming?' I need to double check.

'Nope, the bright lights of London, and lots of rich consultants are beckoning her.'

'Oh.' It's on the tip of my tongue to ask him if he minds, but I don't. It's also on the tip of my tongue to point out that she has high expectations of the evening. But I don't. Instead I joke. Joking is safer.

'No trying to kiss me, giving me a Chinese burn, arm-wrestling, or mussing up my hair?' He has an annoying habit of ruffling up my hair after I've spent ages trying to smooth it down.

'Not if you don't want me to.'

'Deal then. But you still don't get a mince pie.'

'Carriages at 7 p.m. my lady?'

I turn, and huff off, I have to, so he doesn't see the big

smile on my face. I can't help it. Ollie makes me smile even
when he's breaking my heart.

8 p.m., 24 December

'Oh my goodness Uncle Terence, it's amazing!'

I can feel hot tears prickling at my eyes, I'm not quite
sure why except it really does look amazing, it's magical.
'Wow, this is the best ever! You've surpassed yourself this
year!'

He smiles broadly, and wraps me in a bear hug, blocking
my view of everything but a very jazzy black and gold
brocade waistcoat. Then he lets go, and the real world
returns. Except it's not really the real world, it is Uncle
Terence's bookshop decorated in the most festive way ever.
And I do mean *EVAH*.

I mean, he does always make an effort, but this year
he's really gone to town, and it's making me feel quite
tearful.

'The old devil still has it in him, eh?' Ollie laughs, and
Uncle T grabs his hand and they have a man hug.

'Less of the cheek young Ollie!'

Something nudges my calf, and I bend down and pick
Stanley up. He's feeling left out. I give him a cuddle, then
look around more carefully.

Each pane of the beautiful old shop windows has an
artful fallen snowdrift, despite the fact that so far the real
snow has barely settled outside, and the snowflakes falling

down the windows look so real I have to stare to make sure they're not actually moving.

Stanley suddenly makes his little whiffling noise and struggles free, haring over to the window on the left of the doorway. He stands there wagging his tail and making excited little barks. There's a little scene from 'The Snowman', and it is animated! The snowman is swooping as gently as a moving cloud in a high circle above the prettiest snow-covered village ever, and it's a copy of our own little church, village green and cottages.

I grab Stanley's collar. 'Don't you dare eat the snowman!' I can see it now, one crunch and the magic of Christmas will be destroyed for ever.

'Listen!' Uncle T is grinning when I look up from the scene. 'Move closer.'

I lean in, listen carefully and can just hear the haunting music.

'It's all in the detail, darling Daisy. It's the little things that count, the bits we miss if we don't care enough to pay attention! Now, come and see my cauldron!'

I glance over my shoulder not really wanting to leave the scene, and Ollie catches my eye. He doesn't smile immediately like he normally does or make a cheeky comment. He just looks, his gaze unreadable for a second. warm brown eyes locked onto mine. Then the gentlest of smiles appears, and he lifts his hand. 'Go on, he's dying to show you the rest. It's taken him ages this year! I'll go and put this food with the rest.'

We pass Dobie, peeping out from behind the pile of Harry Potter books, a slumped very real looking Scrooge sat by the fire at the end of the nook that houses the classics, another book aisle where a very lifelike Mr Darcy has his shirt plastered damply to his chest and an artfully placed sprig of holly over his privates (I suspect Mabel has been at work) and then Uncle T throws open a door that has never been there before, and we're in Narnia. With the snow, the signpost, the lion ...

'My God, how did you do this?' I laugh and turn on the spot.

'With a little help from my friends! Isn't it the best? You've no idea how many people it's brought in this month, and I just titivated it up a bit for tonight!'

'Daisy, darling! No, Tim?' Mum peers round me.

'Nope. Ditched him. I told you!' I'd been um-ing and ah-ing about whether to admit to my dating disaster but had decided to bite the bullet.

'I was just checking darling, in case you'd changed your mind again. I know what you're like!'

'I don't change my mind!'

'Well I know you don't like to disappoint people. I was worried you'd insist on joining Tim's parents for Christmas dinner just so that they haven't got an empty chair. Are they vege whatever as well?'

'I don't know. I haven't met them.' This fact should have been forewarning that we were not going to live happily ever after.

'Well I'm pleased! He was rather annoying dear, pretentious is the word isn't it? I really didn't like to say, it's not my place, you know I don't like to speak out.'

'No, Mum.'

Ollie, who is passing with a plate of mince pies grins at me, and it is very hard to keep a straight face. It's okay for him, he just keeps on walking.

'But I am glad he's gone. He was very controlling as well, I thought. Was that Ollie?'

'It was, Mum. Anything else?' I say mildly. I'm not bothered, she can slag Tim off all she likes.

'Well he did try the chicken vol-au-vent on my birthday, I mean I didn't think he was supposed to do that, and he said it was nice and moist!'

'He ate a ham sandwich at the office party as well.' I admit glumly.

'Well there you go then. A man who can't resist forbidden fruit is a man not to be trusted!'

'Where did you get that from Mum?'

'Oh, some daytime TV thing dear, one of those judgemental things where they pretend they're trying to help people but really they're making an example of them. That reminds me, where's your pillow princess?'

'My what?' I nearly choke on my mulled wine. Mother slaps me heartily on the back, and I am so glad Ollie moved on and didn't hang about to hear more.

'I heard that on TV as well, apparently you're a baby dyke!'

'No, Mum. I am not.' I put my glass down, for safety reasons. 'And nor is Frankie, if that's who you mean?'

'That's the one! You see, she's even got one of those ambidextrous names.'

'You mean ambiguous.' I shouldn't have put my drink down, it's better to consume more, not less.

'She was such a funny girl! What was it she called Ollie?' She pauses, she knows full well. 'That's it! A pompous prick. Oh, she did make me smile,' she leans in, so she can lower her voice confidentially. 'I mean, he is such a nice boy, and I don't blame Vera for being proud. I mean she is his mother, but to be honest, dear,' she cups a hand in front of her mouth to make sure she's not overheard. 'I do get a bit sick of hearing his achievements being drummed out by her, day in day out, at every opportunity. I mean, I balance what I say about you. Wonderful as you are, I do recognise that none of us are perfect and we all have low points. But Ollie? Oh, I ask you. I bet he's not even got a single pimple on his perfect buttocks!' Then she gives me an assessing look. 'Unless you know otherwise?'

'Mum!' I am slightly shocked, not by the thought she needs to check I've not been inspecting his bare bottom, but by the fact that whilst I have spent the last few years never feeling good enough to meet my mother's expectations, because of Ollie, she's actually been slightly pissed off about the whole competitive-mum business. If she'd told me this a couple of years ago it would have totally made my day. But it hits me now, I'm surprised, but not half as bothered as I expect to be.

In fact, Ollie *is* pretty close to perfect, so I can understand Vera being like she is.

I smile. Broadly. I can't help it. Okay, I now know Ollie much better, and know he's as human as he ever was. But I also am beginning to realise I can win at this life business. Or at least give it a good run for its money.

Mum thinks it's because of her pimply bum comment. She shrugs and gives me a conspiratorial wink. I don't want to burst her bubble. I'm quite enjoying this moment of solidarity.

'Well, anyway, that Frankie girl was amusing. She'd make you laugh you know. That's what's important in a relationship, being with somebody who makes you laugh.'

Oh God, we're back on her lesbian theme. Just when I was thinking we had common ground. 'Take me and your dad, well, you wouldn't think we have a giggle looking at us together would you?'

I don't know where this is going, but I'm scared. Very scared.

'But right from our wedding night when we had a giggle over his dingle dangle I know we'd be okay!'

Dingle dangle? This is heading downhill fast. 'Need a top up, Mum? Canapé? Wine?' I don't manage to knock her off her stride.

'You know they call it wedding tackle? Well we think it's because they looked just like two bells, hanging there! He said all I had to do was pull the rope and we'd be ringing out all night. Oh, he did make me laugh!'

Kill me now. I am not ready to hear this. I never will be.

'Anyway, enough about us, I'll be embarrassing your father if I'm not careful.'

'What about me!?'

'Oh, at your age you must have heard it all before! Now, so if you're not keen on Frankie, are you and Ollie an item yet then? You do live together!' She ignores the fact that he has just walked up and is standing right next to her. He has a bottle of something in his hand. I shove my glass out for a refill, right now I don't care what it is as long as it is not alcohol-free. 'He's free isn't he? You are, aren't you? Well isn't this lovely?' I don't know whether it's the drink that's lovely, or the prospect of matchmaking. She lets him top her glass up as well. I hope it's something strong. 'Vera says that the Juliet girl is after him again, went to their house she did looking for him!'

'She didn't?' Ollie looks shocked, and slightly annoyed.

'Oh, she did, didn't she Vera?' Vera who was passing by on her way to the buffet is stopped in her tracks and dragged into the conversation. 'The Juliet girl? What on earth is. this, it's rather delicious, Ollie! Aren't you clever!'

'Rhubarb and ginger gin liqueur with Prosecco. I didn't make it, Terence did.' Ollie frowns. 'Why did—'

'Rhubarb? Good heaven's and there was me telling your father to rip ours out of the garden. It's unsightly you know.' Vera looks at Mum, who nods.

275

'Very, wild, you can't stop rhubarb when it's on the rampage!'

'Mum, why—' Ollie is looking a little bit impatient and flustered.

'I wonder how difficult it is to make this, it can't be worse than jam can it?' Vera knocks the rest of her glass back, and my mother sips hers thoughtfully.

'Well it doesn't have to set, does it? Pectin can be such a problem, that's why it won't set you know according to an article I read in the paper. Jam not gin, that is. So, last time I boiled mine up again, added a whole packet of pectin and it was still wobblier than a jelly on a bicycle. I was at it for three hours, added the whole box of the stuff and then Stuart turned round and asked why I didn't just buy a jar! Honestly!' She pauses to draw breath. 'Do you think you have to buy that proper knobbly ginger?'

'Mum, Juliet! Why did she come to your house, you never told me!'

Vera blinks. 'Don't shout, Oliver dear. She wanted some ideas for your Christmas present!'Then she squeezes his hand, 'don't worry darling, I didn't tell her about your obsession with flying toys.'

'Flying toys?' I think this gin stuff is working, I have instantly forgotten about my mother's match-making attempts and want to know more. This is a side to Ollie I did not know about!

'It's a drone, Mum!' He blushes, does an eye roll and looks incredibly little-boyish, not at all serious consultant.

I want to hug him. 'And I've only got one, it's not an obsession!'

'And I certainly didn't tell him about your crush on that Lara Croft girl!'

I start to giggle, I can't help myself. After the last few heavy days at work, I think I'm slightly hysterical. 'Lara Croft?'

He is even more embarrassed now, and the desire to hug him is even stronger, so I grab a handful of cheese straws instead.

'That was years ago, Mother!'

'He had a poster!' She says in a confidential whisper that everybody can hear.

'Can we talk about my career or something instead?' says Ollie. 'I like talking about my career!'

This party is turning out to be the best Christmas Eve party ever!

Vera and Mum seem to have joined forces rather than competing (Mum has probably given up and decided she can never win). It just seems so much more chilled than the last few, but maybe that's because I'm more chilled. I'm enjoying myself.

'Daisy had a poster of that *Poldark* character!' Adds my mother, 'and that was only last year!'

'It was at least five years ago!' I give her the evil eye, but she just laughs.

'Ah but he did have such a glorious scythe!' Uncle T pats my shoulder. 'Mulled wine anybody?'

Much later, as my feet begin to ache from the standing, and my face starts to ache from all the laughter, I catch up with Stanley who has discovered my favourite bookish corner and is curled up with a cuddly reindeer which I am sure Terence must have given him.

He has already chewed both antlers off and pulled its squeak out. But he looks so contented wrapped around it, a little bit of brown felt sticking out from the corner of his mouth.

I sit on the chair next to him and he clambers onto my knee, as the classical string trio in the corner play the most amazing renditions of Christmas tunes ever. This is Uncle Terence's latest surprise, he's really pushed the boat out this year – with live music. And it is beautiful. They've gone from 'White Christmas' to 'Silent night' to 'Last Christmas' effortlessly and now a few people are even dancing on the mini patch of floor space between 'Fantasy fiction' and 'Self-help'.

'Help me!' At least I think that is what poor Ollie has just mouthed at me. I smile back at him contentedly, too warm and comfortable to do more.

My mum has him in a firm grasp. She spins him round, rather inappropriately I'd say, given that we've just switched from a rather lively 'I Wish it Could Be Christmas Every Day' to the much gentler 'Have Yourself a Merry Little Christmas', before grabbing his hand as though she's about to charge down the centre of the shop. Instead, she loses her balance, treads on his toes and sends him careering backwards into a pile of books. Before landing on top of him. I can hear the oomph as all of the air is expelled from his lungs.

There is a crash. The hum of conversation stops, but the music continues after the very slightest of hitches. The shoulders of the violinist closest to me are shaking, I think she's trying not to laugh.

'Oh goodness gracious me, this is fun!' Mum is on her hands and knees staring down at Ollie. She is looking at him like Stanley looks at me in bed, before he tries to French kiss me. I hope Mum isn't about to do that to Ollie.

She doesn't. She straightens the tinsel she has tied around her head. I'm beginning to wonder what Terence put in the mulled wine this year, she is rather flushed. 'Oh look! I've always wanted to fondle Rupert Campbell Black's bottom!'

For a moment my heart is in my mouth as she reaches down, and I have visions of her turning Ollie over, and debagging him so she can check for pimples.

Instead after a heart-stopping moment when she is nose-to-nose with him, and even from this distance I can see panic in his eyes, she straightens up and waves something triumphantly in the air.

Phew.

'Haven't we all!' Says Vera, bending down beside her.

She picks up a book from the collapsed pile, which appears to be some rather racy Jilly Cooper novels.

That's the thing with Uncle T and this place, it's full of surprises. You never know what you'll find around the next corner.

They both stroke the covers of the books they are holding.

'Something tells me I should have stocked up on hang-over cures!' Says a voice in my ear. It is my dad, seldom seen out in the open at these parties – he has his own favourite nooks to hide in. 'Are you having a good time, darling?'

'Perfect thanks, Dad! All ready for tomorrow?'

'Well we were, I think. Not sure your mum will be up to boiling sprouts if she carries on much longer. I think it's time maybe we made a move.'

'You could be right, Dad.' We share a smile. I guess I've always been a bit of a daddy's girl. He's never been particularly touchy-feely, but he's been a quiet steadying figure in the background. I've always known he's been there for me if I need him. 'Lovely to see you so happy, Daisy.' His arm is round my shoulders, and he squeezes then kisses my forehead.

'Oh Stuart, come and dance, they're playing our tune!' Mum is still grasping Rupert to her chest but is now swinging her hips suggestively in time to 'Frosty the Snowman' and beckoning him with one finger even more suggestively.

'Your tune?' I raise an eyebrow.

'It's not, honestly!' He takes a step forward, smiling at her. They're so different, but they love each other for the differences. I watch them for a second, then sidle over to Ollie – who is busy reassembling Jilly Cooper and looking rather flushed. I straighten his hair, I can't help myself. I've never seen him looking so dishevelled and flustered.

'Vera?' Uncle Terence offers her his hand, and she hands me her copy of the book before kissing him on the cheek and joining him.

I've never seen Uncle Terence dance before, but with Vera in his arms he looks a natural. They're cheek to cheek, and both of them have soft, dreamy smiles on their face. Her eyes are shut as she moves to the music, and they look like a couple from the movies. Elegant, graceful, perfectly in tune with each other.

I'm distracted as Dad steers Mum our way. He's had enough, he never was very keen on dancing, but he'd do anything for her. 'We're off darling.'

'Oh, we are, early to bed you know!' Mum grins at me, mischief dancing in her eyes. 'Ding, dong, merrily on high and all that!' Then she lurches forward to kiss me. 'You should try it! I bet Ollie is game, aren't you?'

'Mum!' I think I am now the colour of a well-cooked beetroot. Luckily Ollie is still busy crouched on the floor with the books and hasn't heard.

'See you bright and early tomorrow!' She winks in a very leery and lopsided way. 'Maybe!'

'Yes, Mum. Good luck, Dad!'

Phew, I feel exhausted. All I want to do is sink down into my favourite corner and watch the world go by. And maybe catch up on a little bit of reading.

There are many lovely spots in the shop, but the little nook I've left Stanley in has always been the best, and Uncle T has made sure it is today as well. Nothing over the top, just tasteful swags of holly and berries, clove studded oranges hanging from the shelves that fill the air with the perfect Christmas smell.

I've just taken a step back in that direction when my arm is grasped very firmly.

'Daisy, darling!' It is my mum.

'I thought you'd gone?'

'Oh, my goodness, I am going to, I'm worn out!' That makes two of us, but I really feel that as I'm one of the younger partiers I need to stick this out a bit longer. 'But come on, come on darling, don't sit with the boring books and be a grump, join in, promise me! It's Santa Baby, I do love a bit of Eartha Kitt, don't you? Oh, yes, yes, Stuart I'm coming! Oliver? Ollie, over here! Daisy needs you!'

He dusts his knees off, waves her goodbye and makes his way over, an enquiring look on his face.

'You need me?'

'No, I don't.' I bite my tongue, to stop myself mentioning Juliet.

'But ...'

'Well, maybe I do.' He's here, in front of me, and I *would* rather like to join in and have a dance. Because this party has been too good to end without one. And I do actually like a bit of naughty Eartha Kitt. And it can't do any harm. And books can wait for another day.

'You do?'

'Well I'd look bloody silly dancing on my own, wouldn't I?'

'Ah, using and abusing again, eh?'

'In your dreams, Joseph. Come on!'

So he does. He offers his hand, Uncle Terence style. And Terence smiles at me over Vera's head as we find a small space in a dark corner next to the musicians.

'Happy?'

'Very.'

Then he moves in slightly closer and I can't help it, I respond. It's automatic, I can't stop myself from slipping my arms round his neck, though I do bury my face in his shoulder so that I don't have to meet his gaze.

I am so totally aware of every inch of his body, it's weird.

He smells clean, spicy. I can even smell a hint of whisky on his breath, and his jacket smells of holly and evergreens, the greenery he's no doubt brushed against as he's sorted the pile of books out.

His arms are so warm against my back it's as though there's no fabric between us. Skin on skin, a thought which makes me shiver.

'Cold?'

'Oh no, I—' I make the mistake of glancing up as I answer, and then I'm lost.

I never believed that this really happened to people.

That you could look into somebody's eyes and see only them. That the rest of the world faded away, the sounds receded. Only their heartbeat, their breath, their look existed.

His lips meet mine and my eyes close. I don't consciously

close them, it just happens. I can taste the whisky now, taste the spice of mulled wine, the fruit of mince pies, and then I can taste only him.

'Shit, sorry.'

The tune has changed, and he's pulled away. And I'm glowing redder than ever and he's blinking as though he's just come to. 'Christ, Daisy, I'm, I know, well, er, bit embarrassing.' We both look round wildly. But the only eye I catch is Uncle Terence's. Nobody else is looking our way.

And Terence just looks thoughtful, as though he's got other things on his mind.

And then he falls to the floor.

It's in slow motion at first, a waiver, a slow, slow spin, then a sudden heavy clunk. Abrupt. Frightening.

'Terence! Oh God, help him, somebody.'

It takes me a minute to realise it isn't my voice, I haven't had time to say the words. It's Vera, high pitched and frightened. 'Terence, Terence, darling.' She's on her hands and knees beside him, stroking his face, shaking him gently.

'Mum, mum, stop. Go and call an ambulance.' Ollie is there almost before I realise he's left my side. 'Give him some space.' All I can do is watch, my hand to my throat, every last bit of Christmas cheer evaporating into the air and away as though it never existed.

Chapter 20

6p.m., 28 December

Uncle Terence looks so pale and small in the big hospital bed that for a moment I'm not sure it's him. Stripped of his peacock finery – the colourful waistcoat, the bowtie, the cheery smile he just looks like an old man.

I'd never thought about just how old he was, his age hadn't seemed to matter. Logically I knew he had to be around the same age as my parents, as Ollie's. But he was different and always seemed so full of energy and life. I'd never thought for one second about one day losing him.

Uncle Terence isn't even my uncle, but I'm closer to him than to most of my own relatives. What do they say about being able to pick your friends and not family? Well, Uncle T is honorary family, and I'd have picked him any day of the week.

'Sit down, sit down dear. I always imagined this moment as rather different. The whole family gathered around my bed, clutching my hands, sharing fond memories. Rather over-inflated opinion of myself, don't you think?' His eyes open and he winks at me.

'That's on your death bed Uncle T, I'm just stopping by to visit.'

'Oh, well that explains it. Consultant not declared I'm about to expire then?'

'Not yet.'

'Wonderful.' He coughs. 'I was beginning to wonder seeing as they wouldn't let me out! I do hope you haven't brought grapes? Look at the bloody things.' He waves a hand to encompass the bedside cabinet, and the table at the foot of the bed. 'Fruit is no good to anybody, until it's fermented! Wine, whisky and women have always been more to my taste, and a spot of good literature.'

'Well, I could bring you some books, but I'm not so sure about all the W's.'

'Oh bugger.' He manages to put on such a sad, morose face, I laugh. He's obviously feeling much better than he looks.

I had been planning on popping in to see Uncle T tomorrow and attending the after-Christmas work's bash at my office tonight, until Ollie had rung just as I was gazing at my wardrobe and trying to decide what to wear.

'Couldn't do me a favour, could you?' He'd said.

Ollie has never asked me for a favour, so it must be serious. 'Sure, if I can.' I am tempted to wear my little black dress, but that is just boring. I shift the hangers along, only half-listening. Sasha has told me to let my true character shine though, but as I think that involves wellingtons, a big jumper and hair that hasn't seen straighteners for a while maybe not. I need to find my inner true professional character. If I have such a thing.

'It's Uncle T. I'm concerned.'

'Oh.' I stop shifting clothes around for two reasons. One, Uncle T, because he's important to me and he's still ill, and two because Ollie is concerned. He's only ever concerned when people are really ill (he's used to distinguishing between the stuff that might not be nice but is easily got over, and the real stuff). I sit on the bed. 'Is he okay?'

'Medically he should be, but he's really low.' He pauses. 'Mum was quite upset when she got back from visiting him this afternoon, she was agitated. It's not like her.'

It's not. Vera is not an 'agitated' type of person. She's like Ollie; sensible and grounded, able to find the positives and not get het up and overreact. Like I do.

'I can't get away from this conference unless it's an emergency, so I was wondering if you could pop in, cheer him up?'

'Of course, I can! Er, now?'

'It would be good, if it's not too much trouble?'

'Of course, it's not.'

'I mean, if you've got anything on, don't worry.'

'Nothing on at all.' I shut the wardrobe door. 'I'm on my way. I'll give you an update later!'

'You're a star!'

I quite like being a star. It's making me feel all warm inside. But I also quite like being able to repay Uncle Terence in some, however small, way.

After all he has done for me, no way can I let him down if he needs me now. And there will always be another office bash, won't there?

So here I am, bearing sweets and smiles. But luckily no soft fruit.

'I was rather hoping that I'd die full of good whisky and in flagrante with Stella from the Bull's Head, or a much younger wife.' Says Uncle T, shaking his head.

'But you're not on your death bed, there's plenty of time to arrange that!' He's always been so positive, I can't believe he won't stop talking about dying as though he's already resigned to it. 'Copy of the local newspaper, mint humbugs, liquorice pomfret things any good?' I wave the newspaper with one hand and pass the sweets over with the other. Determined to cheer him up and stop him talking about death. It must be being in hospital that's caused that.

'Ah splendid.' He pops one of the black sweets in his mouth and sighs. 'Good girl. Knew I could rely on you, takes away the taste of this food. Damned hospitals, I can't believe they've not let me go home.' He tuts, and sounds quite disgruntled, which isn't something you can often say about him. 'You'd think over Christmas they'd want shot of people, wouldn't you? Instead it's wait for this test, wait for that, wait for the flaming results.'

Ah, maybe Ollie did have a point when he said Uncle T was a bit low and a visitor might do him good.

'You don't seem very happy, is it really horrible?'

'Oh no, no not at all. The staff have been top notch, and Ollie has kept them on their toes! I'm just not used to being cooped up. Being tied to a bed is fine under the right circumstances if you know what I mean.' He gives me a knowing look. It would appear that when you get to his, and my mother's age, you turn completely randy and full of double entendres. Personally, I'd rather not know. 'But they won't even let me up to go to the lav! Talk about adding insult to injury, wouldn't even treat a dog like this. Talking of which,' he looks around, 'you didn't bring little Stanley to cheer me up did you?'

'I don't think they'd let him in.'

'Get one of those 'therapy dog' vests for him! If you look in the back room of the bookshop there's a fluores-cent jacket that used to belong to my old Labrador. You can make Stanley a jacket! There's plenty of black marker pens there as well.'

'I don't think you've got enough to think about.' I grin at him. 'Anyway, a Labrador would be way fatter than Stanley.'

'And old Bully boy was rather stout.' He sighs. 'Just a thought, it's so flaming boring in here.'

'And he doesn't act like a therapy dog.' I'm dubious about this idea. He'd be up on all the beds, chewing up those horrible cardboard sick bowls and weeing on the bedside cabinets. I narrow my eyes. 'Bully boy?'

He grins, raises an eyebrow, and for the first time looks more himself. 'Couldn't really call a Labrador Bull's Eye, could we? If you know what I mean?'

'Nancy, Will and Oliver? Oliver Twist?' I giggle.

'Little bit of fun between Vera and I. Not intentional mind, but once we realised what she and Charles had done, we couldn't help but laugh! Too late to change their names though, far too late. But you mustn't tell eh, mum's the word.' He taps the side of his nose and I see a whole different side to Uncle Terence.

For years he was just Uncle Terence, and I was obliged to go to his Christmas eve party. But lately he's turned into my fairy godmother (is there such a thing as a fairy godfather or is that just weird?) who has found me somewhere to stay, helped me out when my confidence has dipped, and shared in-jokes with Ollie's mum. I wonder how many other pies he's got a finger in?

A lump lodges in my throat.

I hope I haven't found out too late. Like he said the other night it's the little things that count, the things you don't always notice if you're not looking.

The people you don't always appreciate.

'I'll bring Stanley in tomorrow.'

'Good! Vera said you would!'

'Vera?'

'It was lovely that she insisted on coming in the ambulance with me. It was quite nice having my hand held, and she really hadn't the heart to object when I asked for a kiss.'

This is not the version of the story I had. The paramedics were working on him all the way to the hospital, and all the heartbroken Vera could do was watch and will him to hang on.

'Now, I need you to promise me a few things.' He shifts on the pillows. 'You couldn't help me sit up a bit more, could you?'

I catch the eye of a nurse, and together we lift him higher on the pillows.

'You must smile.'

'I do smile! I'm smiling!'

'At the service. Pay attention, keep up, and you must make sure the others all smile with you.'

'But, you're not ...' I'm at a bit of a loss to know how to head him off from this line of thought. I am failing Ollie. He was relying on me. But Terence seems to have decided he's nearing the end of his days.

'I never had time for being miserable. No regrets, isn't that what they say? I trust you to stand up for me, tell them I've had a bloody good innings and I'm proud of it!'

'Terence, I ...' But he isn't listening.

'Wear what you want my dear girl, be yourself! But not your whole self, obviously. Not advisable for anybody at these sombre occasions, please don't wear that bloody awful orange and green ensemble that you wore a few years ago. I didn't like to say, but you looked like a satsuma that had come to a sticky end.'

'I didn't!'

'Oh, you did, and I can say that without getting into trouble. I am impervious. Just look at the photographic evidence dear girl, you are so much more beautiful now you've gone back to the Daisy I've always adored. You were such a sweet child, so soft, gentle, but clever. Oh, you were clever.'

'I was—'

'But far too easily crushed. Wear your cowboy hat and checked shirt with pride my girl! Kick ass! Isn't that what they say? You were quite an ass kicker in your day.'

'I was?'

'Oh yes. I remember those boots you used to wear.' He smiles fondly. 'You made Ollie be your horse and you gave him hell!'

'I did?' This is embarrassing. I am so glad Ollie's at work and I had to come on my own.

Or maybe Uncle T is more ill than he realises, maybe he's delirious.

'You smacked him on the arse with your hat!'

Oops, I do remember now. Which is even more embarrassing. But rather funny. Ollie between my thighs, though of course it was totally innocent back then. I realise now why he says I used to be bossy. I was. And he let me be. He's always let me be myself.

Oh God, I mustn't think about Ollie. Or the fact that he kissed me again.

'Right, where was I? Orange, satsuma, stand up ...' Terence mutters, staring over my left shoulder, deep in concentration. 'Stanley! Invite Stanley! Can you remember all this, Daisy? I would write it down but can't find my bloody glasses.'

'I can remember, but you'll have plenty of time—'

'Stanley must run riot, invite the cat as well if you have to, to ensure there is mayhem and laughter. The buffet should be at his head height so that all dogs can help themselves, it concentrates the mind. No time for being morose and mooning around if the buffet is in peril, eh? And be yourself, did I say that?'

'You did, but Terence, don't talk like that, you'll be here for ages yet, Ollie said you're fine.' I think about looking at the medical notes hung from the bottom of the bed. That's what people do, isn't it? But as I won't understand them, and probably, if the consultant has handwriting like Ollie's I won't even be able to read them, it's a waste of time. Ollie once left a list in the kitchen that he swears said 'milk, steak, beans' but I'm convinced said 'meh, stench, gremlins'. I'd thought he was commenting on my hygiene. I still don't know if I believe him.

'We can write all this down, you can tell Ollie.'

'Oh no.' He stops his musings then and looks at me. His gaze is as clear and sharp as it ever was. Then he reaches out and covers my hand with his own.

The skin looks papery thin. Why has nobody noticed? Is he dehydrated, sick or just old?

It's dried out and tired, and all of a sudden he reminds me of the white freesias that he always kept in the shop.

Still blooming, still spreading their scent, but their petals turning paper thin just before they fall.

'Terence.'

'I'm sorry darling Daisy. But I've had my time and the sands are running out.'

'Don't say that. It's not true.'

'It is the truth, and you know I've always told you the truth. I've always thought of you as a daughter. I've watched you grow and bloom, I've watched you struggle in the drought of summer, be beaten down by the icy cold, and then return,' he smiles, 'pardon the pun, but fresh as a daisy.' I try to smile back, but it hurts, it feels like it's breaking my face apart, mirroring my heart. 'I've loved, I've lost, I've hurt, and I've mended and I learned to live with what I could have.' He strokes the back of his hand down my cheek. 'But I don't want that for you. I want you to learn you can have it all, and only the brave learn that lesson. Only the brave and the kind.'

'You knew, didn't you? You knew you were ill before Christmas?'

'Oh, I've known for a while my darling, Daisy. Dicky ticker! But I had so much to do, so many loose ends to tidy up.'

'That's why you made the party so fantastic.' I bite hard on my lip, trying to stop it wobbling. Because if it wobbles my whole face will collapse and I'll be weeping and wailing.

'I've always wanted to go out with a bang, but I wasn't sure I'd make it to the New Year's Eve fireworks.' He coughs.

Something damp blobs onto my cheek and I wipe it away angrily. This is about Uncle T, not me, I can't sit hear blubbering while he's being so brave.

'I want you to manage my bookshop Daisy or sell it. I turned that shop into the love of my life after I lost my other one, but once I've gone it doesn't matter if it dies with me. But words are in your blood, you love them, you play with them, tease them, make them alive.'

I don't quite know what to say. 'I'm not all that good.'

'Oh, you are. Never say that, never ever. I will look down on you and be very angry if you do. I see a little bit of myself in you, dear girl, I always have. So don't let me down, will you?'

'Okay.' I sniff and look at him through blurred vision.

'I always wanted to leave it all to dearest Oliver, so fond of the dear boy. He's always been my favourite.' He smiles, a soft, gentle smile that reminds me of Ollie. 'Parents are not allowed to have favourites, are they? But Uncle's are! He has a very good heart you know.'

'I know.'

'He's not a, what did you call him?' His eyes are twinkling, but tired, like fading stars. 'A pompous prick?'

'I know he's not, I was angry, and jealous, and well ...'

'Sick of hearing about how well he was doing?' I nod. 'Your mother didn't mean to undermine you, Daisy. She was just proud of him, like Vera is. And she's proud of you. She always knew you'd work things out. But it's hard to step back from the people you love and let them carry on without you. You always want to step in, guide. Interfere.' He is looking through me, thinking about somebody else. 'Your heart aches, but you know it's not about you, your choices.'

'Who is it about Uncle Terence?'

'Vera.' The word is faint, and then he looks at me more directly. 'No one darling girl, just an old man rambling. Would you pass me a glass of water? Then maybe I need a rest.'

I pour him a glass of water. Watch as he takes tiny sips.

'Come back tomorrow, Daisy. Promise you'll bring little Stanley.'

'I will.' I lean forward on impulse, kiss his cheek. Then smile. I've come here to smile, not be sad.

I can't help it. I glance at the board at the foot of his bed.

Hieroglyphics, as I thought.

10 p.m., 28 December

'He said Vera. I could have sworn he said Vera. Why did he say Vera?' Stanley blinks at me. 'Did he say Vera? Mira, lira, neara, near, maybe he said nearly a, not Vera?' Stanley is not convinced. Neither am I.

'Will you fit in my rucksack? I need to smuggle you in to the hospital?'

He has been curled up in a rucksack shaped blob, but now he stretches out on his side. Toes pointed, even his tail extended as far as it will go.

Maybe not.

9 a.m., 29 December

'You're here!' Terence is sat up in bed and looks so much more cheerful than I remember him being yesterday. I must have imagined it, or maybe he just felt a bit tired. He's going to be okay! 'I will be going home tomorrow, all being well!'

Ah, that's it! He was upset about not being allowed out and is now feeling much more his old self.

'So, dear girl, what have you brought me today? Whisky?'

'Er no.'

'Wild women?' He winks, and I can so picture him in his bowtie and waistcoat I laugh out loud with relief.

'No!'

'A dog?'

'Yes! Stanley!'

'Bravo! I knew you'd do it. Where?' He frowns.

'Here.' I point. 'Shit!' Stanley is not at the end of his lead. All that is there is a collar, dangling. 'Stanley!'

I had shown him the rucksack and he'd gone rigid when I tried to pick him up. Totally un-bendy. And as I didn't want to snap him I'd decided the best option would be to try to wing it and pretend he is indeed a therapy dog, or parcel him up in my coat.

There's no sign of him. I bend down, panicking, and look under the bed. Look under all the beds, crawl on my hands and knees and check under the cabinet.

Uncle T is guffawing, and coughing, but mostly

297

guffawing. So at least somebody is happy. I have achieved something.

'Have you lost something?'

I spin round, relief surging through me like an electric shock.

The nurse is holding up a fluorescent vest with 'therapy og' written on the side. The D has disappeared. So has the dog.

'Anybody lost a—'

'Yes, me! Me!'

'—colostomy bag?'

'Sorry, I thought you meant, I've lost my dog. You haven't er, seen a dog?' The nurse scowls at me. 'Maybe not. Never mind.'

'You can see my puppies!' I spin round again, and the woman in the bed opposite Uncle T laughs and lifts up her sheets.

'Now, now Enid. Don't you be naughty!' The nurse tucks her sheets back in.

'Daisy, dear.' I look at Uncle T. He nods his head towards the end of the ward.

Stanley is there. Next to what looks and smells like a food trolley. There is an empty tray at his feet, and I swear he has a smile on his face. He licks his lips. Then licks the tray again, before spitting out a piece of carrot, and then jumping up to rest his front feet on the shelf.

'Oh my God, come here you rascal. Sorry, Uncle T, back later, got to ...' I run as fast as I can, slip on some cabbage and end up rugby tackling him. We slide out of the ward on a slick of gravy and veg and come to a stop at a pair of feet.

Behind there is applause and laughter. I glance up, hanging on to the wriggling Stanley for dear life.

'And there was I thinking hospitals were sterile environments.'

It is Charles, Ollie's dad. Looking stern.

'Hi.'

He shakes his head, but there's a hint of a smile. I'm sure there is. Or at least I like to think there is.

'Oh, Daisy, you really are such a tonic. I can see what Ollie sees in you!' Vera is chuckling, her eyes sparkling. She puts a hand out, helps me to my feet. 'SO wonderful to hear Terence laughing, I'd recognise that sound anywhere.' And before I can thank her, she's off, hurrying onto the ward. Charles striding behind her.

Vera and Terence? Really? Could that be a thing? I am slightly dumbfounded, but I can't shake the thought from my head.

Or the image of them dancing together at the party. Harmonious, happy.

Or the love letter I found in the bookshop, hidden inside the special editions. The one to V.

Until Stanley licks my chin.

'Well at least somebody enjoys the hospital food, Stanley! Come on let's get off before you cause any more problems. Therapy dog my foot!'

Chapter 21

3 a.m., 1 January 2019

'Daisy, I didn't wake you, did I?'

'Wha?' This is the best I can do. In the absence of a flat mate, a boyfriend or a friend who wanted to see me, I saw the New Year in with Stanley. It was rather nice actually, we watched 'Love Actually' followed by an episode of *Poldark*, a James Bond film and then fireworks on the Thames all from the comfort of the sitting room, covered with a nice warm blanket. Stanley had a pigs ear, doggie popcorn and pawsecco (he's not a beer kind of dog) and I had a pizza, Prosecco, giant bowl of Bombay mix and a whole packet of Pringles. I was not seeing in the new year as I meant to go on, I was seeing out the old year with a massive celebration for all I have achieved.

I now don't feel hung-over, I just feel a bit sick, and very tired. Because I finished the night with a dance off, which I think Stanley won by jumping over the back of the sofa, racing round using the backs of chairs as a racetrack and then puking up pigs ears all over Ollie's game controller. I washed it, but I think that might not have been a wise move.

'Sorry, I can call back, I never thought ...'

'Ollie?' I struggle up onto my pillows and self-consciously pat my hair down. I am turning into my mother. 'Another phone call, turning into a bad habit, ha-ha.'

He doesn't laugh back or make a clever comment.

'It's Terence.' There's a long silence. He didn't say Uncle Terence, he said Terence. Why did he just call him Terence? There is a dead weight in my chest, a lump blocking my throat, and yet the rest of me feels like I'm not here. Like this is unreal. 'I'm sorry, I thought you should know straight away, he's passed away.'

'He's ...'

'He was peaceful they said, happy.'

'Ah, right, thank you.' It comes out all stilted. Not sounding like me. Not feeling like me.

'Daisy, I ...'

I put the phone down and stare ahead. Uncle Terence has gone.

The phone beeps with a message. 'Will you be okay? Be back home tomorrow eve, earliest flight I can get x'

'Will be fine x' I put the phone down, then pick it up again. 'Are you? Xx'

'Fine. Can you go to your parents?'

I feel numb, as though this isn't happening to me.

Maybe I will get up tomorrow and discover it was a dream.

9.30 a.m., 1 January

Uncle Terence did make it to New Year's Eve, he must have hung on until the last firework had lit up the sky and dropped to the ground. He hung on until the last chime of Big Ben bid farewell to the old year and welcomed in the new. And then, very quietly, like the gentleman he was, he told the nurse on duty that he felt as fit as a flea. He closed his eyes, smiled and he died.

I swear he still has a soft smile on his face when I see him.

Vera is sat at the side of the bed, looking distraught, Charles looks very upright and in control. I feel like I am intruding.

'I'm sorry, I shouldn't, I just wanted to …' I shouldn't be here. I'm not family.

Vera looks straight at me, but her eyes are clouded over, and I don't think she really knows it's me.

'He would have wanted you to come.' Charles' voice has a lightness I don't expect, and when I look at him there's a faint lift to the corner of his mouth. It reminds me of Ollie. 'He wouldn't have wanted to go quietly, unnoticed.'

We share a smile. He knows what Terence was like. They were brothers, after all.

'Ah yes, he left this for you.' He picks up a letter from the bedside cabinet, hands it over almost reluctantly, his hand lingering until manners make him let go.

'He left us all a little note.' Vera blinks, not seeming aware of the tears on her cheeks She gulps, grasps his hand.

Strokes it. 'He was such a lovely, kind person. Oh Charles.' She looks up at her husband, her face twisted with pain and he pulls her tight against him.

I blink away my own tears. Feel like I shouldn't be here.

I take one last look at him. He's not Terence any more. His face looks different, slightly puffy around his jowls, the edges of his face softened. No longer animated. His skin is so pale, his lips slightly parted as though he has more to say. But his eyes are shut and he's still. So still it fills me with a hollow, emptiness inside.

I sit at a small table in the canteen and open the letter. The writing is spidery, faltering in places, letters slightly smudged and written over twice where the first time they were faint, leaving a ghost image.

My darling Daisy, these words are for you. Please humour an old man, and at least read to the end.

You asked who my heart ached for, who I'd made my choices for, who it was about. It was Vera. Ah, you are not shocked! I saw the look in your eye, I knew you'd heard. I knew at the party you'd seen something you recognised but hadn't been able to put a name to.

That name is love my dear! Love, romance, infatuation! Passion!

Vera was my day, my night, my stars, my sun. The day she stepped into my life she sowed a seed inside my heart – even if that love was doomed, and we could never be together.

You should have seen her when she was young. So beautiful, such poise and yet so kind. Not unlike you, my darling Daisy.

Which brings me to the point of the ramblings of an old man.

Listen to your heart, Daisy. Don't let somebody else steal your happiness away and leave a hole that cannot be healed. Never ignore the tiny things, Daisy. Never let them grow unheeded and realise too late. They fill you with regrets each day, and sap your strength, and leave you floundering for answers that will never solve the problem.

When you were a tot you sat on my knee and asked about all the pretty ladies, and why I didn't stay with them. I didn't stay with them because they didn't hold the key to my heart, darling girl. And it would have been wrong to have pretended they did. My God, I tried. I tried to live a full and happy life, and I loved every one of my beautiful wives. But I wasn't in love with them, Daisy. And they knew, they knew so they let me go with their blessings because they knew I wasn't leaving them for somebody I would love more. They knew that this old romantic held a torch for another man's wife. An unrequited love. I never thought that Charles would ask her to marry him! I thought he was just having fun. But you know what thought did. The day they announced their engagement was the day my world stopped, the day I had to don a façade to hide my heart from the world. So, this is my message to you, my dear. Think not, Daisy. Act!

You have a passion inside you, I have seen it. Now give yourself up to it, and don't let anybody or anything stop you. In work, in play, in life! Do not try to live up to other people's expectations, live up to your own.

It has been bloody hard work writing this down without my reading glasses, so do not disappoint me. And look after my nephew for me. He has been like a son to me.

And now I have other notes to write and then I can move on to whatever is in store for me next. After, of course, I have had a little nap!

T xx'

I close my eyes and can see him on the hospital bed. The half-smile on his lips, and I like to think his last thought was of Vera, the one he loved and lost. That they're holding each other close, dancing to the music. He can smell her perfume, hear the tinkle of her laughter, and know she loves him, too.

8 p.m., 1 January

I'd got home from the hospital in shock, and just curled up on the sofa with my knees to my chest and stared at the wall for a while. I was glad I'd gone to see him, that I knew he'd gone. That the man I had adored was just not there any more.

And then I'd started to cry.

I couldn't stop.

Who was going to read over my reviews and give them the thumbs up? Suggest new books I should read? Tell me that I was good at what I was doing?

What was going to happen to the lovely apartment I was living in?

Who was going to agree that Tim was an arse, and laugh at my dress sense? Take me for afternoon tea, and make me and Ollie laugh with his easy sense of humour?

I was crying because I felt adrift. I'd been so certain that I was finding my way. I'd got a new job, was comfortable in the apartment, had owned up to stealing Stanley and officially adopted him (I had responsibilities), had held down the same job for long enough to know I liked it.

Now I wasn't sure I was sorted at all. What was I going to do without him? And how I could not disappoint him?

Ollie wasn't there to talk to, but I knew just who would listen to my wailings, hug me, offer me wine and talk common sense. The person who always had. Before Terence. Before Ollie.

Frankie.

'Oh, Daisy! Shit! What a surprise.' Frankie stares at me in surprise. 'Did I miss a call? What's up?'

I bowl into the apartment as though I still live there. It's a hard habit to break. Slump down on the sofa then stare.

There is a man sitting on the other sofa. With a beer in his hand, and a crisp part-way to his mouth. And it is not Tarquin.

'Tim!'

'Hi!' He waves his crisp half-heartedly, stuffs it in his mouth and looks a bit queasy. I don't think it's the crisp that has upset him. Maybe I have just forgotten how washed out he is? I've got used to Ollie, all tanned and healthy looking.

'Meat free flavour!' Tim grins weakly. I blink. Did he always grin like that? Or did he have a full-on cheeky grin with dimples, like Ollie has.

This is wrong. Why do I keep comparing him to Ollie? For one, Ollie is not my boyfriend, and for two, neither is Tim – he is my ex. So, I frown to cover up my confusion.

Then I realise that this is a lot more confusing than the mess in my head. 'Why are you here?' I look from one to the other, they both look a bit uncomfortable. 'You two don't even like each other!' Oh God, they're not ...

'I didn't say I don't like him,' says Frankie, and slumps into a chair, 'I said he's a bit wacko.' She picks up her glass, and looks at me, her head tilted on one side. As though it's me that is the weird addition here.

Tim looks a bit taken aback. 'Wacko?'

'Freaky?'

That doesn't seem to go down any better.

'In a nice way. Normal is so bloody boring. Are you okay, Daisy? You look a bit pale.'

'Where's Tarquin?'

She shrugs again. There's a lot of shrugging going on, considering how much Frankie likes to talk. 'Shit, you two aren't?' I motion between them. 'You are.' I feel a bit queasy myself. 'Fuck! Frankie!'

I'm trying to drag the door open without opening the

latch properly when she catches up with me. I'm blowing hot and cold, a sweat has broken out on my brow.

'How long have you ...?'

She grimaces. 'Got chatting at that dog thing I guess. We clicked, what can I say, and it was a bit tedious.'

'Tedious? It was not, it ... You said all kinds of stuff about him, you didn't like him!'

'Love, hate.' She shrugs. Again. It's fucking annoying. How can she be so bloody nonchalant about this? All the time I was going out with him, she was putting him down. And now ...

'You just wanted him for yourself! We're supposed to be friends!'

'Friends?' She looks at me blankly, and there's a dull ache in the middle of my chest. 'We were flatmates, Daisy!'

'But we went out, you came to Mum's party, to Uncle Terence's, you helped me, you ...'

'It was a laugh. Oh, for God's sake, Daisy, listen to yourself! We had a good time, then you moved out, moved on, started going on and on about the pompous prick.'

'I did not!'

'Yes, actually you did. All the bloody time. And your new job. It's always about you!'

I gasp. Mouth open. I can't believe what I'm hearing. 'How can you say that?' This hurts, I thought we were friends. I had no idea this was what she thought.

She shrugs. 'You're always so fucking perfect.'

'Me?' I blink at her.

'Some of us have to put effort in, and you know what, it fucks me off that you're such a mess and you still have half the men after you. Well now, darling Daisy, Tim is after me! Turns out I'm his type, and you're not.'

I stare back at her; my brain has been emptied of words. Then I finally manage to wrench the door open and storm out. I am shaking. Really shaking, pretty violently actually, even though I'm clutching the door of my car. Which is a bit scary.

Frankie was never my friend. I was entertaining. I was her flat-mate.

Which means ... I close my eyes. Feel the cold metal beneath my fingers. Try to take those measured in-out breaths they tell you to do at yoga, the ones that normally make my head spin because I've overloaded on oxygen. Right now, I'm not very good at it, so I'm not overdosing on fresh air. It's actually helping.

My chest isn't about to explode any more.

My teeth aren't chattering.

I take a couple more breaths. I can let go of the car without falling over. Which means I can get in. Sit down. Hang onto the steering wheel instead, which is less likely to give me frost bite.

Did Frankie ever say anything for my benefit?

Frankie told me that small ads were my thing, not to try to step out of my comfort zone. Frankie wasn't pleased when I told her about my new much better job. I nearly turned it down because of her!

Frankie wasn't pleased about me launching support for Carrie – the only time she did help was when it meant she could stand next to Tim. Were they seeing each other even back then? Because they both told me to concentrate on my review job, not try to move into features. They both had a chip at the little self-confidence I had.

Frankie is a complete fraud. A selfish bitch who has never actually given me any real support, even though I thought she was.

I don't want to be like Frankie.

It's not just the nastiness, it's the high heels – all day – and the need to hold your tummy in, and take your makeup off EVERY single night, and iron your hair.

And, basically, only think about yourself.

Terence was right. And at that thought the tears well up in my eyes again and I start to cry. But these tears are different to before. They feel good. They feel healthy, if that's a thing? Healthy tears. I need to be more like me, like Terence told me to be.

Oh God, I miss him.

10 p.m., 1 January

'Bloody hell, Daisy. Are you alright?' Ollie jumps up from his spot on the sofa and places his warm hands on my upper arms, as though he thinks I might fall over.

'Do I look rough?'

'Total mess.'

I can't help but smile, which is probably what he intended. 'Total?'

'Total. Smudged make-up.' He wipes the ball of his thumb under my eye gently. 'Eyes as red as an albino wombat.'

'Do you get albino wombats?'

'Yup. Drenched clothes.' He slips my coat off my shoulders, which sends a shiver through me. I'm not sure if it's the dampness, the air against my shoulders, or the brush of his fingers against my skin. 'Rat's tails.' He twirls a lock of my hair round his finger, which brings me closer to him. I stare into his eyes. Sadly, his are not black with lust, more warm with concern. Which is good. Falling into his arms would just be a rebound, a shock reaction after all that's happened.

'What happened?' He read my mind. 'Apart from losing …' He doesn't finish the say the name, but he doesn't need to. He also obviously knows this is not grief at losing the man we both loved. This is a different type of grief. An anger. It wouldn't take a psychologist to spot it, I think I am still fuming so much there is steam coming out of my ears as well as off my damp clothes.

'Frankie.' I scowl. 'Frankie happened!'

'Ah.'

'What do you mean, ah?'

'Well, just …'

'You knew she was fucking Tim!'

'No!' He looks startled enough for me to know it's the

absolute truth. 'You have to be kidding me. She isn't?' I nod vehemently, and the water flicks off my hair onto his face. 'How long's that been going on?'

I shake my head sadly. 'Not a clue. I thought she was my friend!' I eye him up thoughtfully. 'Did she try and get off with you?'

'Nope.' He half-smiles, which is cute. My heart does a little flip, obviously because I am relieved nothing has happened between them, no other reason at all. 'Should I feel slighted?'

'You must have been a decoy!'

'Oh great, thanks for that. You really know how to boost a man's ego!'

'She did say you were hot, and she did mean it.'

'Maybe she thought I was out of her league?' He winks, so I thump his arm.

'Your ego does not need boosting!'

'Feeling a bit better now?'

'Yeah.'

He takes my hand and leads me over to the sofa. We both slump down in our favourite spots and stare at the blank TV screen.

'It was just a shock, and on top of ...' I sigh. 'I needed somebody to talk to, and you weren't here and ...'

'I know, I'm sorry.'

'So,' I give him a puzzled look, 'why are you here now? You're supposed to be in Scotland, you couldn't get a flight until tomorrow!'

'I hired a car and drove back. I thought maybe you'd want some company, seeing as you didn't go to your Mum's.'

'How do you know I didn't go to Mum's?'

'I asked her.'

'Oh.' I snuggle a bit deeper into the sofa, feeling a little bit pleased and warmer inside. 'Well I've got work, and Stanley, and ...'

'You wanted to be here?'

I nod. I'd just been trying to explain, but he'd said it for me. I'd wanted to be here, the place Terence brought me to. 'I used to think I wanted to be like Frankie.'

'Oh, you don't, you really don't.'

I smile. 'I know. Uncle Terence said that. He said I need to be, no not to be, I need to *want* to be me.'

'Wise man.' Says Ollie.

'He was.' I realise our fingers are linked. He squeezes. I squeeze back.

He let's go of my hand, and I feel lost, then he drapes his arm over my shoulder and suddenly I feel safe.

'I know a lot of people who'd want to be you, Daisy.' I look up, and he's studying me, then he drops a kiss on my forehead. Feathery light. I want to put my hand up, touch the spot, but I don't. 'Gorgeous, strong, clever, funny.'

I stare into his eyes. Swallow hard. 'Er, is this okay? I mean, I,' I try to pull away a bit, but his hold is firm. 'Should you be with Juliet, it's not fair ...'

'What's not fair?'

'On,' I gulp, 'her.'

313

'Daisy, why's this not fair on Juliet? What's she got to do with ...'

'Well, if you're getting married.' I realise I am pleating my top with my hands. He stops me. We have a bit of a silent tussle as he tries to free my clothing from my fingers.

'I'm not marrying Juliet.' He rakes his fingers through his hair, distracted. 'It's all in her head, she likes to imagine stuff. My God, who's she told?'

'Just me I think.'

'I bet she hinted at Mum when she went round for present ideas, thought she was acting a bit edgy.'

'So, you're not?'

'I'm not.'

'Oh.' I blink away the tears that are threatening. I will have rivulets etched into my face if I carry on like this. I should have asked him straight away, I should have followed my instincts, made up my own mind. Not followed Frankie's advice. She probably didn't want me to know the situation, she didn't want me to find out if Ollie was single or not.

There's still a hard lump in the middle of my chest, like bad indigestion, so I'm blinking like mad and breathing a bit heavily, but I feel relief. He's not getting married! I'm not cosied up next to somebody else's fiancé, wishing he'd kiss me.

No, I didn't think that. Not at all. He's just being nice. 'Er, I was thinking,' I will concentrate on work, that will solve the problem. 'After the Tim thing, I mean it was awkward anyway, but it'll be worse, and, well ...'

'Well?'

'Do you think I should ask James if I can be more involved in features? You know do more stuff like I did for Carrie?'

He smiles. A gentle smile that shines from his eyes, that parts his lips. 'Is that you, what you want? Not just because of Tim.'

'It is. I just didn't think I was ready.' I think I'm leaning in towards him, and I'm practically whispering, even though I'm definite about the words I want to say.

'You've always been ready, Daisy.'

'I'm good enough, I could do it, I'm sure I could.' God, we are so close I'm practically speaking the words into his mouth.

'You are, I never ever said you weren't, I've never doubted you.'

'But I did.' I've never quite felt good enough since that day I realised I'd failed my exams. My life. Let everybody down. I've never felt confident enough to commit to anything, because then I might have failed again. But sometimes you have to pull your big girls pants up and risk it, haven't you? Because nobody else will do it for you.

'Then you've been a silly girl.' He traces his finger over my lips. Stilling them, stopping me from speaking, from breathing. 'You've always been good enough, Daisy. More than good enough.' And then I feel the tug of his fingers in my hair, the touch against my scalp, holding me steady. His gaze never falters. He doesn't say anything. There's no question in his eyes. He just does it.

Ollie Cartwright kisses me.

This time I don't hit him over the head with anything.

Chapter 22

3 p.m., 18 January

'Bloody hell, it's packed!' I don't know why I'm surprised, because Uncle T was an exceptionally nice man, but the church is full to the rafters. I've certainly never seen it this chaotic, and I'm sure the vicar hasn't either. I mean, okay, I know this isn't Westminster Abbey, but it's quite a good-sized church.

Ollie squeezes my hand. 'Okay?'

'Good.' Apart from the embarrassment. 'Why do I have to sit right at the front?'

'Because we're family.'

'Why didn't we get here early?' It hadn't seemed important before, I'd thought the crowd would have been the size we normally see at Uncle Terence's Christmas Eve parties.

'Because we're family.'

If I had been on my own, I'd have tip-toed down the aisle and hardly been noticed, I wouldn't have been following the coffin, been walking next to a very tall dark handsome man, or been expected to go to the very, very front.

Strictly speaking, I am not actually family. But Ollie and I did agree to come together, and Uncle T apparently decided where everybody should sit.

He'd decided everything.

In detail.

Which is why the mourners are dressed in what can only be described as diverse styles. A few must be bloody freezing because they look like they're heading to Ladies Day at Ascot; one is in a ball gown, there are a good number in jazzy waistcoats (nobody did it better than you Uncle T), and some actually look like they're attending a funeral.

I don't. Today I am being me. Sasha might think I have taken her advice too far, but I think I am doing what Uncle Terence would have wanted me to.

Vera had sent a note out with the funeral arrangements, which, in true Terence style he had arranged in advance.

'Dress like nobody is watching and you will be unique and gorgeous. Dance like everybody is watching and you will always have an invite to parties. Drink only the best and there will never be a bad morning after. Follow your heart and love like you'd want to be loved, and your life will have been lived. And then, dear boy, die a good death. Nobody likes a messy one.'

Words that my grandfather said before he dropped like a stone. He would have been proud of himself.

I failed at only one, because sometimes life can be

a contradictory bastard. Just like my brother, who I still managed to love. But I trust you will honour the sentiments today. Humour this old, romantic fool.

There was also a note to say we should '*dress for life, not a funeral. Donate to charity if you will, but still send flowers as they are joyous.*' Ollie had said he thought the flower bit was a Terence joke, as he'd suffered from hay fever and so did most of the family.

The top of the coffin is teeming with them, they are literally falling off. A florist wouldn't have had a better send off. Most of the immediate family were sneezing and struggling for breath, their eyes streaming, before they even got in the church. I have never seen hay fever in January before. Hopefully nobody has asthma and will drop dead in the aisle.

'You look pretty, darling!' Mum and Dad are already sitting in the pew. 'I didn't think you still had that cowboy hat.'

What she means by this is, she thought she'd thrown it out. She had. I had rescued it and kept it in the top of my wardrobe. It had progressed to living in the top of many wardrobes, though Ollie hadn't spotted it in his until I'd clambered on a chair to get it last night. On impulse. But Uncle T had mentioned it, so I was bloody well going to wear it.

'I am expressing my true self.' I'd said to him. We had both been a little bit tipsy, preparing for the nasty day ahead. 'My inner cowgirl.' This had caused him to choke on his beer, splutter and turn a funny colour I thumped his back helpfully.

'You didn't tell me that last night!' He'd said, when he finally recovered enough to speak.

We have progressed over the last few weeks from gentle snogging, to full on hot action. This is totally incredible, but also totally scary. It is everything I ever dreamed it might be – and more. A year or so ago, scary might have put me off, but right now the passion and feeling of anticipation I get every time I see him is worth the occasional twinge of fear that 1. I am not good enough for him (as Frankie the floozie and tiresome Tim kept telling me), and 2. We will never get a happy ever after because of what really sent my life off the rails.

'I think you better put it on and give me a demonstration.' I looked at him, blankly probably. 'Ride 'em cowboy?' He lifted an eyebrow, and I got all hot and bothered. Partly with embarrassment, partly with lust. Ollie had put his glass down, pulled me in close to his body and wrapped his arms round my waist.

'Is it too much?' I wriggle free. 'For a funeral?'

'Well I wouldn't wear the spurs or the leather chaps, might give the vicar a heart attack. Now stop talking, and come here, woman.'

So I had done as I was told.

'And your hair is all natural.' Mum bounces it about with her hands, what is it with mothers and their need to tidy hair? 'I thought you'd lost your curls!'

'I iron them out, Mum.'

319

I'm not quite sure what to do with the hat, so I put it on top of Stanley, who clambered up onto my knee the moment I sat down.

'Room for a little one?' Somebody edges past my mother and plonks herself between us.

She is dressed warmly in a big donkey jacket, hat with ear flaps, boots and trousers. She takes the hat off.

'Carrie!' I give her a quick hug, really pleased to see her sat in the front pew.

'Don't worry, Terence sent strict instructions that I should sit next to you!'

Stanley, who has been asleep under my hat, suddenly recognises Carrie and leaps on her, offering French kisses and wriggling delight. Lashing my face with his whip-like tail. Which is good. It gives me a chance to wipe the dampness from my eyes and pretend that it was the dog's fault anyway. And not the fact that Terence had instinctively known who should be at my side today.

Then a thought suddenly occurs. What if he's arranged for Frankie to be on my other side? Panic courses through me, my palms are sweaty. But she wouldn't come, would she? She would. Nothing stops Frankie.

'Are you okay?' Ollie nudges me, pretty hard.

'He's not invited Frankie has he?' My throat is dry. I can't. Not today. I need Ollie, not Frankie.

He squeezes my knee. 'It's okay, she's not on the list. I checked.'

'How did he know?'

Ollie smiles, and gives a little shrug, then kisses me on the tip of my nose. 'Terence knew everything. Though she could always have seen the notice in the paper and turn up anyway.'

There's a nudge on my other side. 'What happened?' Carrie, half-buried under dog, hisses in my ear. She tips her head not at all discretely in Ollie's direction and nudges me viciously in the ribs. The violence is because I've ignored the gentler nudge, and she believes in being direct. She says that dogs appreciate things being black and white. I don't. I'll be black and blue if she carries on.

'Nothing!'

'You said you snogged!' I had reported to her the other day that we had indeed shared quite a long, passionate kiss, 'Well?'

'Shh. It's a funeral.'

'You dirty mare!' She grins, gives me a quick hug, then let's Stanley settle on her knee. Ollie's hand creeps back, and gently takes mine, under the hat, as the vicar clears his throat.

'How bloody fantastic to see you all here!' A familiar voice booms out, and I jump. Stanley barks in alarm, and Ollie clutches my hand so tightly I have to kick him on the ankle.

We both knew that Terence had prepared a video for the service, but it is still a shock to see him on a big screen larger than life, behind the coffin. His coffin.

The hum of conversation that started up when the vicar

321

stopped talking halts abruptly, and there are a few gasps, a low moan, and a high-pitched squeal which makes Carrie and I turn in our seats.

I'm not quite sure who the squeal came from, but it was definitely from one row behind on the other side of the aisle.

Which is totally packed with women!

'Who the hell are they?' Hisses Carrie in my ear.

'WAGs!'

I hadn't noticed on the way in as I hadn't been able to take my eyes off the coffin. I'd been on edge, waiting to grab any flowers that were lost along the way, but the aisle opposite is filled with Uncle Terence's wives and girlfriends.

One of women glares at me. Which is fair enough, if she heard me calling her a WAG. It's not very flattering, to be grouped along with *all* the other women your ex has loved.

They all look amazing though. Uncle T always had an eye for a beautiful woman, and these have beauty in all its forms. As in buxom, slender, joyous, kind, and flamboyant. Obviously, they don't each have all of that. But the one thing they have in common is that they are all gorgeous in some way or other.

'All of them?' Carrie opens her eyes wide dramatically.

'Bloody hell.' Ollie has turned around to see what we are looking at, then turned abruptly back. 'I didn't realise there were so many! Is that Stella from the Bull's Head?'

Carrie and I both turn round again. 'Bugger!' I've cricked my neck, which means it might not have been as discreet as intended. 'He said he would have quite liked to have died in bed with her!'

'Really?' Ollie frowns. 'Not Louisa?'

'Louisa? Was that the young one he met at the book fair?'

Ollie nods. 'The one in pink, don't turn round again!'

We both turn around. Louisa is younger than me, petite, has a make-up free tear-strewn face and is dressed in jeans, a black leather jacket and a low-cut pink top. I want to go over and hug her.

'Oh, Vera said he was very fond of Louisa.' My mother pipes up. I'd forgotten she was there, she'd been quiet for more than five minutes. 'He said she was too young to be a widow though, so he let her down gently.'

'*Shhh.*'

'Ouch!' Something hits Ollie on the head, which is a bit unfair seeing as it was Mum talking. I lean forward a bit, so I can look past him. It is Ollie's sister, Nancy, who is an opera singer so projects very well (she also throws very well). Which means everybody hears her shushing and looks her way. I wave. She waves back, but her smile looks sad.

'Has somebody halted the vid?' Carrie is nudging me again.

I shake my head and can't help but smile. It's typical Uncle T. He is beaming at us from the screen, pausing theatrically, knowing full well the effect he's having. This could well be his finest moment.

Stanley realising our attention is elsewhere and Carrie's

not gripping him as tightly as she was, leaps off her knee. 'Stan!' We both stand up, but it's too late. He's bounded up to the coffin, he makes a giant leap and a rose bouquet shoots off to the side and is caught rather neatly by the vicar. Who is in the first X1 village cricket team.

Charles applauds.

Stanley skids, sending some freesia to the other end of the coffin, where they teeter for a moment before stopping. He sits down, eyeing up the screen. His head tilted on one side. He is gazing at Uncle T with something like adoration, then he very slowly lies down and lowers his chin to his paws and whimpers. The flowers in front of him are practically brushing his nose, the freesia drop with a small plop onto the floor.

The funeral director edges over as discreetly as he can, picks them up, then rearranges the top of the coffin again.

The church gradually falls silent.

Stanley sneezes.

Uncle Terence beams at us, then takes a deep breath. His timing always has been perfect. He looks larger than life in his fanciest turquoise and black waistcoat with gold and black bowtie. He guffaws and pats his chest – almost as though he's seen the reaction.

Stanley whines. I stand up, thinking I should get him, but he rolls over showing his tummy and male-bits which isn't a sight you should see in church, so I sit down again.

'Leave him.' Ollie whispers, squeezing my hand again.

Uncle Terence clears his throat. 'Well, I say thank you

all and I bloody hope you have all turned up or my last attempt at a party will be a flaming disaster, and I've put a lot of effort into it!'

There's a ripple of amusement.

He looks so *alive*, that it brings home the fact that these really are the last words I'll hear him speak. Suddenly, it's not funny. Not funny at all. I miss him *so* much.

There's a heavy weight lying across my chest, making it hard to breath, my throat is blocked, and my eyes are prickling, and the cold dampness tells me the tears are spilling over.

I'll never see him alive again.

'My dear brother Charles, I am sure you have noted my request and come dressed as yourself. Is there a noticeable difference between that and normal funeral attire? Bravo! I know I can rely on you to bring a suitable sombre air to proceedings.'

I glance sideways, over to Ollie's dad. He's in a very elegant silver-grey three-piece suit. He catches me looking, and winks. Which shocks me into looking away, then back again, and flushing. I've never seen him do that before, and it's got a certain cheekiness that reminds me of Ollie.

'You have always been the brown sauce to my tomato, the steady scholar to my flights of artistic temperament, the reliable family man to my fickle romantic heart.' He turns slightly as though he can see us. 'Vera, my beautiful sister-in-law, how I always wished you had been my bride.

I trust you are wearing something stunning in emerald or turquoise to show off your eyes? As that is the image of you I have in my heart.'

I glance at Vera. Her eyes are glassy with unshed tears, and she's staring straight ahead. Fingering the necklace at her throat. Beneath her coat I spot a hint of emerald and I just know she'll be as stunning as Terence imagined her to be as he took his last breath. Because I am positive he would have been thinking of her.

I wonder for a moment if she loved him a tiny bit as well?

I'd been right about Uncle T though, he was a true romantic, he loved to love, which is why he'd kept marrying after he'd lost the one who meant everything to him. But he would never have waded in between his brother and Vera. Uncle Terence was a tragic hero.

'Nancy, Will, and Oliver you have made an uncle very proud. Nancy if you are not in an opera gown now then I insist you wear it for my wake darling girl! William wear that barrister wig with pride, and Ollie, throw off your consultant's coat and weight of responsibility, cast off that cloak of stuffiness,' he's starting to throw his arms about as though he's starring in some Shakespearian tragedy, 'and let sweet Daisy show you a trick or two about letting your heart rule your head!'

Somebody sniggers. It sounds like Frankie. If she is here, I am going to drown her in the font when Terence has finished talking.

Ollie and I have both bowed our heads and sneak a

look at each other. This is the most embarrassing funeral I have ever been to. We had rather cast off our cloaks and abandoned all trace of stuffiness last night – and so had one of my cushions, which had exploded under the weight, scattering its innards everywhere and sending Stanley into one of his mad runabouts.

'I didn't realise they'd prescribed him hallucinogenic drugs!' Ollie says drily, which makes me splutter.

'He thinks you've been choosing girlfriends you know you won't ever really love.' I whisper back, my voice tailing-off as I wonder if I should have said that. As although I don't think I am a girlfriend exactly (we haven't been on actual dates), this could mean I'm putting myself in that category. Which isn't a very nice thought.

Ollie raises an eyebrow.

'To protect your hea—'

'Now, darling Daisy!' Interrupts Uncle Terence, and it's my heart that needs protecting. It plunges down to my feet, which is where I'm now staring. I'm not family! Why talk about me?

'I hope, my dear, that you have done as you are told for once.' I think everybody is staring, I can feel it on the back of my neck, the hairs are prickling. Maybe I can just slide off the seat and hide on the floor? 'And have turned up as yourself.' I give a feeble thumbs up. 'A skirt is never too short,' I had been wondering how short is too short for a funeral, had agonised about whether jeans were just too informal, and then had finally plumped for my midi brown suede skirt which I have loved forever but don't often wear. I have come true to myself, and it's not as bad as it sounds. My boots are long brown leather ones, that are smart and not really cowboy boots at all, I have a long brown tapestry coat, and a cream blouse that is flecked with delicate flowers. And when I looked in the mirror I saw a smart version of cowgirl Daisy, and one which I rather liked.

'And never too bright,' continues Uncle T, 'unless it is tangerine and green.' Definitely not tangerine.

'My lovely Adrienne ...' I'm pretty sure she was his first wife, which means this might go on for quite a while, so I switch off and worry about Stanley nibbling the lilies – which are probably poisonous to dogs. He doesn't appear to be though. I think he's dozed off. Must make sure we remember and move him before Uncle T goes off to be cremated.

'And lastly,' there is a loud clap, which reverberates from the speakers. Stanley yelps, falls off the coffin and dives for cover at my feet. 'For those that are still awake ... I have now used up my quota of words, if I had been born of the opposite sex I would have been allotted many more so may have lasted a few more years, but alas not. So farewell my dearest friends, I love you all. And now I get the last word. Ashes to ashes, dust to dust and Terence to Torquay.' He raises an arm in salute, and I find myself returning it. Then the picture slowly fades and music filters in.

Goosebumps race along my arms as I realise it's Frank Sinatra and My Way.

I clutch at Ollie as we listen to the words.

They could have been written for Uncle Terence.

I close my eyes, not trying to squeeze the tears away, just so that I can hear the words properly. And I can see him, in all his glory. Watch him dance with Vera, hear him chuckle as he stirs the mulled wine, feel his hand over mine as he talks about some wonderful book he's discovered.

The pall bearers lift the coffin. We all stand up.

The loves of Terence's life all seem to be hugging each other and wiping each other's tears away. Vera is biting her lip, oblivious to the tears streaming down her face.

Ollie looks at me, pulls a lopsided smile. 'I think I need a stiff drink.'

'At least he didn't want you to get up there and speak.' Terence had been quite strict about this one, he said he'd do the talking as he wasn't feeling too emotional – but he expected eulogies at the wake after a few glasses of decent malt whisky had been knocked back.

We stand outside in the cold winter air. 'What did he mean about Torquay?'

Ollie smiles. 'Mum said all will become clear when the will is read, apparently we are joint executors.'

'You and me?' He nods. 'Why?'

'Haven't a clue, Daisy. But Uncle T never did anything without a reason, did he?'

Chapter 23

3 p.m., 3 February

'He said what?' I have never been to the reading of a will before, it turns out that this one is pretty informal, and not at all like the image I had in my head. The solicitor is not old, imposing, looking over his glasses at us and striding around an impressive office reading out something we can't understand.

'Call me Trev' is not much older than me, has a tiny office up a poky staircase in what probably used to be an impressive town house, but is now the home to sixty million legal types. Well, probably twenty-two, but you get the gist. They don't have very impressive offices. Or toilets.

'He said,' Trev glances down at the will again, 'please scatter my ashes in Torquay. The place where I was born and expected to spend my days.' He looks over his glasses at us. 'He was initially fostered in Torquay, by the Granthams, and then,' he looks at Ollie, 'your grandfather adopted him as a baby ...'

330

'I thought Vera was his only secret!'

Ollie and Trev stare at me. Oops, maybe I shouldn't have said that.

'... as your grandmother was his biological mother, but he was born out of wedlock.' Trev completes his sentence, the word 'wedlock' sounds curiously formal.

I think my mouth is hanging open. It is. So, I close it. Wow, who knew there were skeletons in the Cartwright closet!

'Your grandfather brought Terence up as his own, along-side your father Charles.'

'What about his real dad?'

'Undisclosed.' Trev moves his finger down to the next paragraph, which is a shame as my brain is still coming to terms with the first bit. 'The next point relates to his assets, namely the bookshop and apartment. The apartment will be passed to you, Oliver, with the proviso that Daisy be permitted to live there for one further year minimum. At the end of this period, an allotted sum of money (see below) shall be provided for her to use as a deposit on a property of her own if she so wishes.'

I shoot a sideways look under my eyelashes at Ollie to see how he's taking this. Having to live with me for another twelve months! Though he doesn't have to I suppose, he could move out. I am there more than him, it's just an extra for when he's working locally – which actually seems to happen more and more these days.

Ollie winks. Which makes me blush.

'My bookshop should be retained, financial records and my tax returns will demonstrate it is viable and in no way a burden, until after Christmas. It is my wish that during that period, Daisy decide how to manage the business, and Oliver and Daisy continue the Christmas Eve party tradition together for one final time. After which Ollie may decide its future.' Trev looks up. 'There are a few more legal clauses about what to do if you can't reach agreement, etcetera, etcetera. I do believe he's covered every eventuality. I've taken the liberty of taking copies for both of you, and I've read out the bits he asked me to.' He smiles and pushes the paperwork across the desk. Neither of us move. 'If you'd like a quick look, then I can answer any questions? Otherwise get back to me any time. The only time dependant act is the er, scattering, and we've been instructed to sell certain shares and so forth, apply for grant of probate, complete the tax forms etcetera. All takes time, so no hurry.' He stood up, held out his hand for us to shake, then suddenly remembers something. 'The keys!' He takes them from his desk and holds a bunch out for each of us.

'What did you mean about Mum?'

Without even discussing it, we head straight to the nearest pub after we come out of the solicitor's office. It is all a bit mind boggling. It was very kind, and typical of Uncle Terence to make sure I would have a roof over my head for the next twelve months. And very generous of him to also bequeath money for a deposit on my own place, but weird that I am not allowed to have it yet. Maybe he wanted to make sure I had sorted my job out, that I could afford to pay a mortgage. Yes, that was probably it.

But the Torquay bit was an eye-opener! It seems Terence had many hidden sides, but hopefully no more secrets. Talking of which ...

'I, well.' How do I explain this one? Oh my God, my heart starts to race, doesn't Ollie know about Terence and his mum? Uncle T didn't tell me it was a secret. I'd kind of assumed it was family knowledge. 'He left me a note and mentioned how much he really liked your mum.' Really liked is okay, isn't it? Unlike 'adored', 'was infatuated with', 'loved to bits'.

'Ah right, that's it?' His tone is even, so I dare to glance up at him.

'Well, yes, but ...'

'She was his sister-in-law.'

'I think he might have wished she was a bit more than that.' Do I show him the letter? This is a bit awkward.

He smiles. 'Well, okay, let's say it's not a huge surprise. He did always treat her like a goddess, you know, the compliments, the way he held her a little bit longer than most people would when they hug.'

'Ah, good. And you're er, alright with that?'

'I've caught him watching her from the side-lines often enough, but dad just humoured him.'

'Fine.' I feel slightly miffed, on Terence's behalf, that

his grand passion was just something to be humoured. But there again, it was an unrequited love. Charles was his brother.

'I'm just a bit surprised he's told everybody but me.'

'I'm sure he's not told everybody, and maybe he just didn't tell you because it was a bit weird? You're his nephew! And he just wanted me to be more passionate I think, that's why he told me.'

Ollie chuckles, and raises an eyebrow, which leaves me all hot and bothered. 'More passionate, eh?'

'You know what I mean!' I scrabble in my handbag and find the bit of paper. Slightly crumpled but safe. I sigh. Torn. Then make a decision and push it across the table towards him. 'He knew he hadn't got long, didn't he?'

'I think he must have, from what Mum's said, he's been ill for a while.'

'It just seemed so sudden.' I feel the choking start up again, and bat it away, swallowing hard. 'But he wouldn't have told me, talked to me like he did about your mum, and the funeral and everything, if he hadn't known he would ...' I take a gulp of my drink, which goes down the wrong way and has me spluttering for different reasons. Then I look at the letter, which Ollie hasn't touched. 'He only told me about your mum so that I could learn from it, not because he really wanted me to know, or anything.'

Ollie smiles. Gently. I love it when he smiles. 'It's fine. He trusted you, that's nice. You're nice.' He touches the tip of my finger gently with his own, and I stare into his eyes and wonder if Uncle T was warning me about this. Me and Ollie. Was he telling me to throw all my energy into work, warning me off making the same mistake he had?

Ollie has always been my friend, have I risked losing that forever? Spoiling things because he's so frigging gorgeous I've not been able to resist him?

'I think I have though, learned from it.'

Ollie finally picks up the letter and reads it, his face paling as he does. It's horrible, the colour washes away like a wave on the shore, and just as I'm about to reach out and take his hand, it comes rushing back. Stronger, an angry colour that contrasts strongly with the white of his knuckles.

'You've got to be kidding? This is crazy.' His voice is tight, restrained. I don't know what he expected, but it obviously wasn't this. Maybe he just thought it was some 'in' joke between the two of them, a little secret – like Oliver Twist, which I'm pretty sure I should not mention.

'He's probably exaggerated, you know, to make a point.'

'They were in love! For God's sake, Daisy, wouldn't you want to know if one of your parents was mad about somebody else?'

'They weren't in love, Ollie. That's the point.'

He stares at me.

'He was infatuated with her, he totally loved her, but he didn't do anything about it.'

'How do you know?' He gives a short laugh. It's brittle. Not nice.

335

'Because I know Terence, and so do you!' He stares back at me. 'And your mother didn't love him she married your dad! Nothing happened.'

There's a long silence, which I want to fill. I want to babble. But for once I don't. All I can think about is the love letter I found in the bookshop. The letter addressed to 'V'. I've not thought about it at all since he died, and now I can't *not* think about it. I don't think this is the time to mention it though. And it was in the shop, he hadn't actually sent it.

'And your dad knew, I'm sure he did.'

'Why didn't you tell me earlier? I didn't think you and I had any secrets.' He looks disappointed, his words are formal, stilted. I hate people being disappointed in me. I hate Ollie being disappointed especially. It's important he's not.

'We don't.' I swallow hard. Is this our first tiff? It feels different than all our scraps and hard words when we were kids. It's stomach churningly different. It's scaring me. 'I just thought maybe you knew, and there hasn't been the right time to ask, not so soon ... Don't be cross with me, please.'

'I'm not.'

He is.

'Oh God, I don't know what I am.' He dips his head, puts both hands on top, his fingers digging into his scalp. I wait, hardly breathing, then he slowly looks up, the heels brushing over his eyes, until he rests. His palms cupping his chin, his gaze on me. 'It was a bit of a shock.'

He pushes the letter back towards me. Closes his eyes. Takes a deep breath and then re-opens them. 'I thought I knew him.' For a moment he looks broken, before he reins it back in.

'You did.' The words creep out of me, softly. I put my hand over his. 'You did know him, Ollie.'

This is grief. This is the heavy cloak that today is weighing him down so that he can't move, so that he wants to strike out rather than weep. I've not seen him cry yet, but I know Terence was like a father to him. I know he misses him like hell, maybe even more than I do. Tomorrow I know he'll cast it off, not feel the frustration and sadness. Be able to forgive Terence for going. For everything. Until it swoops down again.

At least I hope so.

I jump and he blinks as a jarring noise interrupts us.

5 p.m., 3 February

'Oh bugger.' Ollie looks at his pager. 'I'm really sorry, I'm going to have to go. Looks like an emergency. Will you be okay?' He stands up, holding my coat out for me to slip on, and I fumble about trying to get my arms in the right sleeves. His voice still has a stilted edge, but when his fingers brush against the back of my neck, a little frisson of happiness nudges away all the sombre thoughts that have been hovering inside me since we left the solicitors office.

'I'll be fine.'

'I'll drop you by the apartment.' He's already got his own coat on and has fished his keys out of the pocket.

'No, don't worry. You go. I'll get the bus.'

'Sure?'

'Positive.'

'I won't be back tonight.'

I stand in the doorway of the pub, watch him stride off to his car. He hesitates for a moment before getting in. He looks back at me, and I'm sure he's on the verge of saying something. Then he changes his mind, waves and is gone.

I catch a bus.

But it isn't the one that will take me home, it's one that takes me to the bookshop.

On the door is a 'Closed temporarily. Re-opening soon' sign.

There's a weird stillness when I open the door, but it isn't unnerving. It's comforting, as Uncle T would have wanted.

There's a lingering scent of Christmas – of mulled wine, cinnamon and evergreens, and all the decorations he so lovingly put up are still there.

But he isn't.

The loss is so deep down inside me that it really feels like somebody is stabbing my soul, the very essence of me, and it takes my breath away – catching me unawares. It hurts more than any hurt I've felt since he went.

I somehow find my way to my favourite nook and sink down on the leather chair, out of sight of anybody passing the shop. My eyes close and I let the distant sound of cars, the smell of new books, the calm still air surround me and my racing heartbeat gradually slows, the world stops tilting crazily and the hot and cold flushes leave me be.

I open my eyes and concentrate on the gentle tick-tock of the grandfather clock. I've never heard it before! I've always known the clock was there, but the sound has always been masked by other sounds.

The clock is slow, a few hours out. I can't help myself, with a smile I unlock the door – Uncle Terence would have hated it to be wrong, he liked everything 'just so'. Everything from the buffed tips of his shoes to the angle of his bowtie. A small twinge catches me as I can't help but picture him in his peacock finery, but it passes. It's not the pain of a moment before, just a slight ache that comes with remembering.

When I open the door, wondering how to alter the time, I see them straight away. The letters tied with a red ribbon in the way only somebody like Uncle Terence would do.

My darling Daisy, it's so wonderful to know you're here! I hope you enjoyed my video, it was an absolute joy to make! Your father helped me, so please forgive him but he was sworn to secrecy – I also asked him to tuck this letter away for you, as I suspect you are not a stranger to my scribblings! You have wonderful parents, Daisy – take care of them. It's very true that we never know how many more times we will see our loved ones.

Now, I very much hope I have not shocked you when

I spoke of Vera (and I very much hope she shone at my funeral).

Some things are not to be, and I learned that as I grew older – I'm not bitter. I loved my Vera's loud laughter, she was so full of life … she knew, she knew of my infatuation, but I was too late. She said 'I do' before she knew I meant it, while I was dallying on the sidelines. I should have taken a risk earlier, believed in myself. It is always better to risk it all and lose, than to never have dared in the first place – and never known what might have happened. That is the worst. Not the fear of the unknown, but the sadness of knowing you failed to act. The not knowing if it could have been a different life.

I had a lifetime of idolising the most beautiful woman in the world, and I hope you can forgive an old man for his monotony and repetition. These letters are ones I have written and never sent, for fear of causing upset. But they are yours, dear Daisy. Maybe you should burn them and release them with my ashes, let the wind decide where they rest?

Read them, or not, at your leisure.

Be your best 'you', Daisy! With warmest wishes and love. T x

More letters! How many did he write? Did he realise I'd found the other one before he died, that I already had my suspicions?

I run my finger over the ribbon, then very gently place the letters in my bag and gaze around at the books.

And I think I know what I need to do.

Uncle T helped me, inspired me, encouraged me, and was a far better mentor than Tim when I first moved jobs. It is my duty to not let him down. He might have missed his chance with Vera, but I must not miss any of my opportunities. I have to do something with my life. I have to live the life I really want.

And I think I know what it is.

Chapter 24

7.45 a.m., 11 March

'This might seem a totally off the wall suggestion.'

I type the words into the chat facility we use at work before I have a chance to change my mind. As it is my heart is pounding, my mouth is dry and tastes like the inside of a running shoe and I feel a bit sick. Probably because of the running shoe. Or the fact that I came in very early and have sat here chewing my nails while I waited for my boss to appear.

Nail cuttings and sweaty feet aren't a good start to the day.

'?' The reply is almost instantaneous. I am striking while the iron is hot, and the workload hasn't yet built up.

I dare to glance across the office. James lifts an eyebrow. He's a busy man, words might be his job, but he keeps them to a minimum if they're not going into production. He's not one for idle chatter.

'I move out of the office and work from the community, you know writer in residence style?'

'Go on ...'

'Invite people to come and chat, like an MP's clinic, but without the MP, obv.'

He chuckles. It carries across the office and spurs me on. 'People will feel involved and bring the real stories they want to read to us?'

'And where exactly are you planning on taking up residence?'

'Terence's bookshop.' I have thought about this long and hard. It's only March, and Uncle T wants us to keep the shop going until Christmas at least. He asked when he was in hospital, if I'd look after it. And I want to. That bookshop is the most magical place I have ever been. To just bring in a manager who doesn't care about the place could be disastrous.

I have decided living the life I want to involves this bookshop.

And it isn't just because it is Uncle Terence's bookshop, it is because I must not let him down. I therefore sat down and tried to write a list of the things that are most important to me, the things I am passionate about. I googled 'passion' first and came up with:

- a powerful feeling, for example of sexual attraction, love, hate or anger,
- a strong belief in something,
- something that challenges, motivates and intrigues you.

And then I wrote a list of everything that might be my passion.

1. Books – I have loved books for as long as I can remember, largely because of Uncle T. I have never called them a passion before, but they are.
2. People – writing a feature on Carrie, and supporting the fundraiser was the best thing I've done since starting my job at the newspaper. Features like this are exciting and fun, I just like to help people. This was a bit of a surprise, I blame mind-mapping for pointing out that although living in a village can be a pain, it can also be wonderful. Uncle T has always championed his community, and I think it's about time I do too.
3. Stanley – who needs no justification.
4. Ollie – Ollie comes under many of the words used to describe a passion. In fact, probably all of them. Which is a bit worrying. He's my friend, he's always been my friend, and I'm still scared that by admitting to the world how much he means to me might jinx things. I don't want to lose his friendship, the thought of us splitting up and never seeing each other (except at family gatherings and feeling awkward) is horrible. The fact that I have a secret of my own, that might change his view of me forever makes my stomach churn. Maybe I should never have let him become my passion.

344

'As in your Uncle Terence?' I glance up again, and James is watching me carefully. 'His bookshop?'

I nod, and type some more. 'I want to start off with a feature about the shop and its history, and Terence of course, invite people to bring in photographs, memories, talk to me about books. I can rope Mark in as well to write a few snappy book reviews?'

'Well, it's a novel idea, ha-ha.' James doesn't often joke. He's grinning now and looking slightly embarrassed. 'Come and chat over a custard cream!'

6 p.m., 11 March

Ollie is home. It has been quite nice having the company, I think he's got used to my soft furnishings and dog, and I've got used to his piles of case notes and the hours he spends staring into the distance and asking me medical questions that I clearly have as much hope of answering as I have of conducting brain surgery. He says it just helps, asking things out loud.

But then, after the 'Vera' conversation he'd distanced himself a bit. I'd hardly seen him for days, though he had sent regular messages asking how I was. Like a doctor might. Which seeing as he's a doctor, figures. He was taking care of a patient, not the girl he'd shagged senseless in the bath, under the TV and on the kitchen worktop.

It was bloody awkward for nearly a fortnight, then he'd turned up one night looking totally knackered after a long gruelling operation, and asked if we could watch something 'inane, romantic or just plain stupid' on TV.

Then he'd held me. And we'd talked about Terence, and he'd cried.

And we'd nearly gone back to normal, except I felt that he was holding a tiny part of himself back – and as I'd known him for most of our lives it was hard to ignore.

But Carrie told me to be patient, and I'm trying. Because, after all, I've held a tiny part of myself back as well, haven't I? But when the time is right to share, I think we'll know. 'I've had an idea.'

'Mmm?'

'I'm going to be writer in residence at the bookshop.'

'Right.'

'James has agreed, and it means we can keep the shop running properly and I can still do my job.'

'Okay.'

'I'll work from there, and manage it, and we can keep Mabel on and the student that does weekends.'

'But how can you do both properly?'

I take a deep breath. 'I'm not going to be a staff reporter, I'm going to be freelance.' I feel myself flush under his scrutiny. I am throwing everything at this, at what I want to do. I am risking my nice safe job, that could become permanent if Sally decides not to come back after her maternity leave comes to an end. I am deciding once and for all that I am not going to return to 'small ads' or 'reviews'. I am doing what my heart is telling me to, and my head says it's okay too. 'James has offered me a weekly feature slot that will concentrate on people-stories, real community stuff.' What I'm good at, what matters to me. 'Starting with the bookshop. I can do it.'

He smiles. The first proper Ollie smile I've seen for a while, and my air comes out on a whoosh. 'I know you can.'

I grin at him. I can't help myself, that smile has lifted a little sadness in my heart that I hadn't realised I was holding. 'Er, there's more.' I have to tell him the rest, because the bookshop is actually his, really. I am at his mercy. I know Uncle T wanted me to manage it until Christmas, but after that it is up to Ollie what happens. And even if that wasn't the case, I still want to share my idea with him, I still want him to think it's a great one, to work with me on it. If he says no to all this though then I have screwed up royally and will have to go back to James on my hands and knees, kiss his feet and beg him to reverse all his decisions.

'Tell me something new.' He gives a wry smile. 'Go on, spit it out.'

'We should sell coffee and cake!'

'So you want to be a barista after all?' He chuckles. It's nice. It makes me feel all warm and fuzzy. And dirty and needy. 'Your mum will be pleased!'

'I knew you'd help!'

'Hang on you cheeky monkey I didn't ...' He's edged a little closer along the sofa.

347

I grin up at Ollie. No regrets.

'I guess you need me to check the deeds?'

'I guess so!' Our arms are touching, which is little bit unsettling. 'You think it could work?'

'Isn't it a bit dodgy, selling drink where there are books?'

'Not at all, people who want to buy books are careful with them.' He gives me a look, and I sneakily close the book that I have left upside down, pressed open, creasing the spine.

It's a bad habit I know. And so is my impossible-to-resist urge to read the last chapter of a book sometimes, when I'm only a quarter of the way through, just to see if I've guessed the twist. I tend to keep that to myself, it can really upset some people.

'And it doesn't make it more like a library, you know, people just coming in to sit and read over a coffee? It won't stop them buying books?'

'Oh no, no. No!' I hope. 'It just increases the time they browse, makes them more likely to actually buy.' I cross my fingers under the cushion. I haven't actually checked the stats on this yet, but other bookshops do it successfully, so why shouldn't we? 'We can only fit in a few more seats in the big nook where we have the Christmas buffet laid out, and there's no free Wi-Fi so it will be for people who come in on their own and want to look at books, it won't turn into a café where they come to meet friends and just chat.'

'True.'

'And the little nooks are perfect for sitting with a drink and browsing.'

'True.' His arm has somehow sneaked along the back of the settee and rests on my shoulders. His fingers are stroking the top of my arm and it is very distracting. 'You don't need to persuade me, Dais. You've sold it.'

'I don't? I have?' I make the mistake then of looking up. Which is totally, completely distracting, but not really a mistake at all. He's dipped his head and his nose is now so close to mine we're practically Eskimo snogging.

'You don't need to persuade me of anything at all. Christ, I fancy you, you know.'

'I do—' I don't get to finish what I do and don't know, because his mouth covers mine. He tastes delicious, forbidden, forgotten fruit. It's like I've been on a diet and been doing my best to ignore my cravings, but now I'm faced with a big bar of chocolate and I want, I need, to wolf the lot down in one go.

'Easy tiger.' He chuckles and swings me off my seat so that I'm on his lap, straddling his strong thighs. 'Take it slow or this is going to be over before it's started.'

'Don't care. We can do it again.' I'm breathless, tugging his sweater over his head, then his top. 'Bloody hell, how many layers have you got? It's like pass the parcel.'

'Nothing like high expectations eh?' He chuckles, it's muffled under the layers that are still half over his head.

'I won't set the bar too high seeing as it's you!' I poke his ribs while he can't protect himself.

'You think you're funny eh?' He throws the clothes free and stares at me. Eyes twinkling. 'You'll pay for that.' His grin suddenly slips. 'God, Daisy, I'm sorry, about ...'

'Shh.' I put a finger on his lips. 'Not the right time, buster.'

You know that bit about living the life I want? Well it includes this. Him. Ollie.

Carrie had told me that maybe he'd hit out at me because he'd felt vulnerable, because he'd felt grief right there in that pub. She'd said it hits you when you least expect it, with the daftest of triggers, and for somebody like Ollie – and her – it's that point when you are scared to admit it, to let somebody in, because they'll be closer than anybody has ever been before. Because grief strips you of normality, grief takes you to your lowest. You're naked. Exposed. So you push them away.

Carrie said she'd let me in, when the whole world was knocking at the door, because I'd been genuine. I'd really cared, about the things she did. And I'd not said it would get better, and I'd not told her it would pass. I'd just held her hand, shovelled up dog shit (though not both at the same time) and waited.

'Didn't you say that Terence told you Ollie was protecting his heart by picking women he knew he wasn't truly in love with?' She'd said. *'Well maybe he's protecting it now from you.'*

And then I knew why it hurt so much that he'd backed off. And I knew what I really wanted. And I knew why Terence had told me everything he had.

I strip my own top off while Ollie is fiddling about

with a belt that seems completely beyond my fumbling fingers right now.

It's the most natural thing in the world, when he suddenly pulls me close and kisses my stomach. A little shiver of anticipation filters through my body, then he looks up and the look in his eyes make me sink lower onto his lap and cradle his head in my hands.

He kisses his way up my body, between my breasts, my collar bone, that sensitive spot on my neck that always sends a shiver through me. And then his lips take mine again.

His tongue circles inside my mouth, teasing, playing, and then it skates over my teeth and every nerve ending seems to jar with expectation. His thumb rubs gently over my nipple and I gasp into his mouth.

And then he's rolled me beneath him on the couch. His hard hipbones against mine, the warm heaviness of his body covering me, the heat of his lips making my heart beat race, and I know.

Deep in my heart I know that this is really what I want and if I lost everything else right now it wouldn't matter.

And I understand.

Chapter 25

10.30 a.m., 18 May

'Oh shit. You're kidding me?' I think my face has fallen, it feels that way. It feels like I'm an emoticon sad face. 'They can't!' I'm an angry face with horns now. And I want to stamp my foot like a toddler and say it isn't fair.

Luckily, it's Monday morning, which is always quiet, so there's no one else here to see my amateur dramatics. Apart from Stanley, who whines and goes to hide under the desk.

'We did know this was a possibility.' Ollie puts the coffee, cream cake and letter on the table and hugs me. It's an official looking letter, which I could tell was going to be bad news even before he opened his mouth to tell me. Well, maybe my sixth sense isn't that well developed, it was probably the anxious look on his face and the fact he was bearing gifts that really gave it away.

'I know, but ...' I had decided to look on the positive side, and trust that the village would be behind me, would see this as a positive. It would appear that certain elements of the village were not.

'The planning officer we chatted to at the start was right, the café up the road objected straight away.' He waves the letter.

'But we're not taking their business away!'

'Their argument is that they're paying the same rates and only have food and drink as their livelihood, we've got books as well.' He holds up a hand to stop the objection that's on the tip of my tongue from spilling out. 'I know. I know, it's different. But the town council voted to object to the application.'

'But they can't! That's only one person who's objected!'

'They can.' He grimaces.

'So that's it? Everybody who comes in is so excited at the idea, and one person can ruin it?'

'Don't give up yet, it'll have to go to the county meeting.'

'But, isn't that the same?'

'Yeah, well,' he sits down, points at the coffee he's bought for me and takes a bite out of the cake. 'Hopefully not.'

'I thought that was for me!'

'Share and share alike.' He grins. 'Hey, cheer up, we've still got hope. And it is going well without the coffee, isn't it?'

'Yeah, but.' I sit down next to him and grab the cake before it disappears all together. Stanley clambers up onto Ollie's knee and stares at it. 'Stop it! Honestly, you men are all alike!'

Things *are* going well.

Uncle Terence, and his shop, were popular and people flocked back when we re-opened the doors. And soon they tentatively started mentioning stories that I might be interested in. They'd chat, then stay for a while and browse the shelves. Delighted when they discovered that we didn't just stock old favourites and new chart toppers – we stocked all kinds of treasures.

Mark is brilliant as well, James came up trumps with him. He truly loves books and the review column took on new life after he took over from me. I do love to read, and I am addicted to the smell of old leather bindings, and fresh off the press new books, but Mark has a way of analysing and questioning that I don't have at all. He can ask a question that makes you read a book in a totally different way. Which is what he's been doing. The column, which also goes onto his blog, now features a complete mix of old and new. Rediscovered treasures he calls them, and they're all books he's discovered in our book shop. And we get a credit each week, which has been amazing for business.

The new part-timer I took on has been busy labelling the shelves so that people can find 'Mark's favourites!' and her recommendations, and 'If you like that, you'll like this'. I also think there might be something starting up between them, after she'd nervously suggested that maybe he might like to look at a book she'd found hidden away, I found them both hidden in a corner. Heads together, with a lot of giggling and whispering going on.

I would have used it for publicity if I'd found them in

the 'Romance' section, but unfortunately they were between 'Horror' and 'Self-help'.

And I've had no trouble at all finding new interesting stories each week for my column (I like saying that – 'my column') and passed lots on to the other guys on the 'paper. James seems quite pleased with the results in such a short time. He said that after the merger, he'd been worried that we'd start to get more distanced from the actual communities we were supposed to be supporting. In fact, he's so chuffed he's thinking about sending other journalists out to be 'writer's in residence' in the other villages that we cover.

I love working here.

But happy as I am, I really wanted to open up a little cake and coffee corner in the bookshop.

'We'll sort it.' Ollie squeezes my knee. I like the squeeze, and I like the 'we'. I honestly do feel that it's a joint venture. Ollie is the first person who has actually supported me however mad my ideas seem and has had total faith in me.

'Oh hell, sorry, I'm going to have to go. I've got an appointment.' He stands up, drops a kiss on my head, which kind of slides down my face as I choose that moment to stand up.

'I suppose I could try and drum up support? You know get some letters or something from people who want this?'

'Worth a try, in fact I'd say definitely. Yep, brilliant idea. See, I knew you'd come up with something!' He kisses me on my lips, properly this time. 'This might be a wild idea, but ...' He hesitates.

'What?'

'Well, I was just thinking, book club?'

'Sorry?'

He runs his fingers through his hair and looks a bit embarrassed. 'Mum used to be in a book club, they met up every few weeks, had refreshments, coffee, cake, wine, whatever. Can't you do that while you wait for planning permission? Book club members only? They pay a sub, that covers the cost of the drinks so you're not actually running a café, you're not selling the stuff? You could have more than one club on the go, one each week? And,' he grins, 'they all buy a copy of the book you're reading as well!'

'Wow, who knew you had brains as well as beauty?'

'Cheeky girl.' His smile broadens. 'You think it's got legs?'

'Definitely.' I grin back at him. 'That's brilliant, why didn't I think of it?'

'Well, I hate to say this, but I did used to come top in more tests than you at school!'

'Rubbish!' I swing for him, but he dodges, then grabs me round the waist and kisses me on the nose. 'Hell, I really have to go. Look at the time!'

'Come back soon?'

He winks, then grabs his jacket, and strides to the door. I like to watch him walk, he's got this masterful, long stride. It looks good, though it's bloody annoying if I'm trying to keep up with him whilst I'm wearing high heels. We've adopted a code for the different speed limits I need him to apply. So far we've got flats, flip-flop, heels and Oh my God slow down, these are new and they're rubbing!

'Off to Barcelona for that conference this afternoon. I'll call you.'

'As soon as you land!' I'm turning into my mother, I like to know he's got there safely.

He gives a thumbs up. 'You can tell me your action plan.'

'If I've got one.'

'You'll have one, don't forget to include me in book club!' He chuckles. I stare back, with what is probably a drippy smile on my face. There are deep dimples at the sides of his mouth, laughter lines fanning out from his gorgeous eyes and the kind of dark shadow on his chin that I love to run the tips of my fingers over.

His jacket is slung over his shoulder, and his shirt hugs his chest, the sleeves rolled up to show his tanned, softly muscled arms.

I like to look at him properly, before he goes.

Then he strides back and grabs me. 'Have you any idea how hard it is to walk away when you're looking at me like that?' This time it's the kind of kiss that normally leads to us ripping our clothes off.

His jacket is dropped on the floor, my hands slip into the waistband of his trousers, so I can feel his warm skin beneath my fingers as he threads his fingers into my hair, holds me still so that he can kiss my lips, my neck, my throat.

I honestly do not know what I had with Tim, or any of my boyfriends. But it wasn't this. Oh yeah, I might have felt a bit horny after a few drinks, but this is on a whole different level. One kiss, one touch, and I desperately need to rip my clothes off so I can feel his skin against mine. So that I can taste him, so that I can feel his fingers wander over my body turning me into a squirming mess.

'Ahem.' Mrs Gray from the post office coughs. 'I've brought those photos in of the sewage plant, like you asked for. I'll go through to the back shall I?'

'Er, yes please. Shit.' I make wide eyes at Ollie, and whisper. 'Didn't hear her come in!'

'Shit indeed.' He grins. Naughtily. Which makes me clench my thighs and jiggle about in an attempt to dispel the rush of warmth I can feel in my nether regions.

He cups my face in his hands, his skin warm. The humour drifts from his face and his dark eyes are gazing at me intently. 'I'll miss you.'

'I'll miss you too.'

'One thing I can't work out, why did we waste all those years?'

'Because I didn't know Uncle Terence properly.' I reply softly.

He frowns.

'I'll explain one day, aren't you going to be late for your life-saving?'

I stand and watch him walk down the street. My fingers resting on my lips. I'm pretty sure my cheeks are burnished pink, and half my messy bun is actually just messy un-bun. But I don't care.

Mrs Gray might though.

'Well my dear, bit of a kerfuffle at the planning meeting, wasn't there?'

'Sorry?' I pat my hair down, in the manner my mother would, and hope I don't look flushed.

'About your application? I mean, you know why they voted to object to your application, don't you?'

'Well, I don't ...'

'It was that stupid woman at that new café on the corner of my road. I mean, nobody goes in there because she's a miserable cow!'

'Really, well I can see she might—'

'You serving a cuppa here won't make a blind bit of difference to her, she's jealous you know! That's what always does it with folk like her. Can't bear to see somebody else being popular and successful. Mark my words, she'll be gone by this time next year she will.'

'She will?'

'You can always apply for temporary change of use you know, by the time it's run out she'll have scarpered.'

'I can?'

'You can!'

'Well I was thinking about asking for local support, seeing if anybody would mind writing to the council in support, do you think ...'

'Well I'm sure most people will be right behind you my dear. Terence wouldn't have done anybody any harm, and I'm sure you wouldn't either. Now, I wanted to talk to you about the change in allotment rules, but don't you want to know about my sewage problem?'

'Of course, I do, I'm dying to hear about your sewage. I'll just grab a pen.'

11.30 a.m., 18 May

Up until now I've avoided using Uncle Terence's big old antique desk at the back of the shop. He used to sit here to go through his accounts, to order new books, to put his feet up and chuckle over a new book he'd discovered, and it still feels like an invasion of his space to sit there. But Mrs Gray has 'gone through to the back' and sat in front of the desk, clearly expecting me to go round and sit opposite her just like Uncle T would have done.

So I do.

By the time she's shown me all her photos of the sewage plant, talked to me about the new rules for the allotment and explained to me all about 'temporary change of use' I'm exhausted.

'You should go to more council meetings my dear! Terence did, he was quite the one for objecting!'

'Really?'

'Oh yes, he kept a finger on the pulse. Just look in that top drawer, there.' She points across the desk. I look down at the drawers on the right-hand side and hesitate. It seems wrong to go through Uncle T's personal belongings, although I know Ollie or I'll have to do it at some point.

360

'Open it dear.'

'But ...'

'What on earth are you expecting to find? That's his council drawer, dear. The second one down. Go on, just look. There's a buff manila folder in there with every meeting he went to.'

I give her a look. How does she know?

'Well we went together!' Remind me never to play poker. I swear I only thought that and didn't actually say anything.

I open the drawer. Reluctantly. And take the folder out.

'There, what did I tell you! Now you catch up on your reading with that dear, don't you reporters go to the meetings any more?'

'Well it's not really my ...'

'You'll find out more about who's who and what they're up to at those meetings than you will in a month of Sundays anywhere else. Now I better be going, you let me know if you want any more information, won't you?'

I nod, slightly dumbly.

Out of the corner of my eye, when I took the folder from the drawer, I saw a hint of red that looked familiar.

I walk with her to the door. Promise she'll be featuring in my column soon and go back to Uncle T's seat behind the desk.

The drawer is still open, as I left it. And at the back, tucked away behind the 'council matters' are some letters, tied with red ribbon. Just like the one I found in the grandfather clock.

I've never read those letters. It seemed wrong, even though he'd given me permission. But now, I suddenly feel compelled to read them and these new ones. I want to look after them, burn them (as Terence suggested) if that seems the best thing to do. Along with the letter I found with the special editions before Terence died.

Or give them to the person they were intended for: Vera.

8 p.m., 18 May

'Oh my God, Stanley!' I reach blindly for another slice of pizza, and munch on it as I read the letters, being careful not to smear them with sticky fingers. 'This is so sad.' I wipe the back of my arm across my eyes, and sniff loudly.

The letters I found in the clock, are so wonderfully romantic they would make me blub even if Uncle T hadn't been abandoned for another and left with a broken heart.

He had been totally infatuated with Vera. A love that started well before she married Charles, from the sound of it.

'He says here that if he had only one breath left to take, he'd give it to her!' Stanley licks my hand, and edges closer in an attempt to lick the pizza crust while I'm not concentrating. 'Stop it.' He sneezes, which puts me off completely, so I have to get a new slice out of the box. '*I spend the night hours staring at your photograph, not daring to close my eyes and waste a single moment of time that could be spent gazing at you. No dream could be more beautiful than your image, my darling.*' I turn the sheet over. 'And listen to this, *I sit* by the stream and the tinkling of water is nowhere as sweet as your laughter, if I could capture your voice and hold it close to my heart forever I would feel complete.' Infatuation is too small a word. The word passion barely touches on what Uncle Terence felt.

Normally I totally miss Ollie if he's not here, but tonight I wanted to be on my own, just until I know what's in the letters. And I'm so pleased I am. This is all a bit mind blowing for me, so how is Ollie going to feel about it? Suspecting his Uncle fancied his mum 'a bit' and reading this are two totally different things. Are they better burned, scattered where we scattered his ashes, so that he might be reunited with his words in death and nobody will be hurt?

I can't help it. I carry on reading.

Terence had remarked on every outfit she wore, her hair, her skin, her laugh, the gentle warmth of her fingers. The dimples he adored, her slim shoulders that he longed to kiss.

There were letters that commented on her bloom in pregnancy, the way her eyes were alight with happiness and the pride she took as she cradled her bump.

There were photographs that he'd taken, where he seemed to have transferred his love to the camera so that she was captured in perfection.

The sadness and poignancy of loss ripped through the one he'd written to congratulate her on her engagement, his pain clear when he told her what a beautiful bride she had made. So this was the version he'd thought was acceptable – but he'd hidden the even more true-to-his-heart one amongst his special editions.

I could picture him writing these letters, his hand trembling, his heart broken, can imagine him folding them up carefully then re-writing a version that would be acceptable to Charles if he ever saw them.

One confuses me a bit.

'*I saw the look in your eyes when you glanced my way,*' he said in one, '*and the yearning had gone, leaving behind only remorse and guilt. One mistake, my darling, one mistake, but not one we should ever regret as it has always brought happiness to you. The pain and loss has all been mine to bear, and bear it stoically I will.*'

I put it to one side and untie the bundle I've found today in the desk.

It's obvious immediately that these are more recent. The envelopes look new, in fact there is a date on the top one, which was written shortly before his death, just before his final Christmas Eve party. Which is a bit shocking, I'd never for one moment have thought they were carrying on a secret affair, I thought this was all in the past, before Vera married.

And then I spot one envelope bears Terence's name. All the others had been blank, never addressed, never intended to be sent. I spread out the ones from the desk.

Terence's name is on several.

I stare at the first one I'd picked up for a long moment before slipping the letter out.

The handwriting is different. '*I agree, my darling. The time is right, it would be unfair to put this off forever. It has been on my mind for some time, he needs to know.*'

I hold the letter up, hardly believing my eyes, the letter is not from Terence. It is from Vera.

I spread a handful of the letters out, they're all in the same handwriting. All from Vera.

'*My darling Terence, Charles and I are in agreement. It would be wrong for us to tell him without you being there, but equally wrong for you to break the news alone. We propose that we all start the year with a clear slate. I have checked with Oliver, and he is not on call on New Years Day, so this would seem the perfect opportunity. Do you agree? A quiet evening at our house, just the four of us?*'

My heart is pounding as I put the letter down with shaky fingers. What is going on? Was Vera about to leave Charles, and run off with Terence? But why would they only tell Ollie, why would his brother and sister not be invited as well?

There is one more letter.

One unaddressed envelope.

I take the single sheet of paper out.

'*My darling Ollie, of all the letters I have written, all the words that I have spoken to you. These have to be the hardest. How to explain to a son why you kept his parentage secret for so many years? How does one justify a secret like mine, like ours?*

You have been my greatest triumph Oliver, the highlight

of my life, the peak of my achievements. I have glowed with parental pride as you have flourished, and hated that your mother and I agreed not to tell you our secret earlier. I love your mother, I love your father – my brother, and I love you, my dear boy. Sometimes love is complicated. I hope you can forgive me my secret, I hope we can get to know each other better in the time I have left.

Charles has given you a far better upbringing than I ever could have. He is the stable, safe, reliable representation of our genes, that I am not. But I hope I have been a good Uncle, a good friend, and that you will allow me to be more.'

I drop the sheet of paper as though it is alight.

Terence was Ollie's father? Terence was going to tell him the day he died?

Oh. My. God.

I lean back and stare at the ceiling.

Buggering hell. What on earth do I tell Ollie? But more to the point, how? When? He was upset enough to find out that Uncle T was madly in love with Vera, how is he going to feel when he finds out they had taken the 'un' out of unrequited love for at least a short time?

11.30 p.m., 18 May

The ring of the phone makes me jump guiltily.

'How did you get on with Mrs Gray and her sewage?' Ollie chuckles.

'Fine, er great.' I must not mention the letters. I must NOT. I have to see him face to face. Or talk to Vera first.

'You okay? You sound a bit strained?'

'Tired. You've no idea how much that woman knows about sewage!' I say brightly. 'And council meetings.'

'Oh, she knows about council meetings?'

'And appeals. She told me who's put in the objection and she told me all about Uncle T going to the meetings, he's got a file full of details in his, er, desk. She forced me to look.'

'Oh, right. Fascinating stuff, yet another little fact we didn't know about him! Full of them, wasn't he?'

'Full of what?'

'Secrets, stuff we didn't know about.'

I choke, have a splutter. 'Oh, I'm sure not really, well, yes maybe.' I'm not doing very well on the not being honest front.

'Are you sure you're okay, Daisy?' He sounds worried. 'I can try and come home a bit earlier, if you like?'

'Oh no, no. I'm fine Ol, really. Just knackered I suppose, and rooting through Terence's desk was a bit ...' I leave that to hang in the air.

'Oh, Dais.' The warmth of his tone makes me feel even guiltier. I close my eyes. 'Are you sure you're not overdoing it?'

'I'm fine.'

'I'll be home as soon as I can, day after tomorrow.'

'Good.'

'I'll call you tomorrow, get a good night's sleep, eh?'

'I will. And I'm going to put together a poster to promote our new book clubs!'

'You're so lucky having a man like me to make suggestions like that!'

'I am. Very lucky.' I think my words get lost in his laughter.

'Night, Daisy. Sleep tight, talk to you tomorrow.'

'Night Ollie. Stanley says goodnight too.'

I'm not sure I can keep this up even one more day. I need to talk to Vera tomorrow, or at least tell Ollie we need to talk.

This is horrible.

Chapter 26

I have made a decision. I've done very little but think about Ollie and Uncle Terence and the need to have a plan since last night but standing here in the shower I have come to a conclusion.

First, I need to talk to Vera. Surely these letters are hers? And surely, if she'd been planning on dropping the bombshell herself, she should have some say in all of this?

I towel dry my hair, pull on my pyjamas and head for the kitchen, feeling relieved and rather proud of myself.

Then see Ollie.

I feel sick.

He is sitting at the breakfast bar, with letters and red ribbon strewn over the surface. The inside of my mouth is dry.

'Hi.' I can't think of anything else to say. My head is empty. All I can see are the letters.

'So, were you going to tell me about this soon?'

'As soon as you got home, after I, er ...'

'You?'

'Talked to your mum.'

'Which you haven't? She doesn't know you've got these?' His voice is even. He doesn't sound particularly angry, or shocked. But Ollie is good at controlling his emotions when he really wants to.

I shake my head, clear my throat, croak some words out. 'You weren't due back yet.'

'I changed my flight, came back early. I was worried about you.'

'About me?' I feel a bit light-headed, I think I need to sit down. I stumble my way to the stool.

'You sounded strange on the phone. Awkward. As though there was a problem with us, me.'

'It was ...' I incline my head towards the letters. 'I didn't want to tell you on the phone, it didn't seem ...'

'Right?'

'Fair.'

'Oh, Daisy.'

'I thought you might be angry, or sad, or upset, or shocked.' I hardly dare look at him, but I have to.

He shakes his head slowly, then puts his hands over his eyes wearily.

'You were angry about their,' I can't say affair, 'about Terence being in love with your mum.'

'I was just a bit shocked, surprised he'd told you and not me. A bit taken aback, but this ...' He sighs. 'Mum had words,' he pulls his mouth into a wry smile, 'about it, after I told her about your letter.'

He puts his hands down and looks at me properly then, shakes his head again, spreads the letters out.

'This is still a bit shocking though, the extent, the ...'

'You've read them all? I've only been in the shower ... How long have you been here?'

'Not long. Twenty minutes, I probably got in just after you went into the bathroom.' He smiles. 'I'm a quick reader.'

'I couldn't tell you on the phone.' My voice sounds pleading even to my own ears.

'I know.' He nods. 'I know, thanks, Daisy.'

'You're okay?' I dare to move a bit closer, until our shoulders touch.

'Mum told me they had a fling, she said we needed to talk more when the time was right. She was so upset about his death, I think she needed time to grieve first.' He shrugs his shoulders. 'She said she'd loved him, but she loved Dad more. That he was a beautiful man inside and out, but irresponsible, and,' he smiles, 'flighty.' His tone is dry when he speaks again. 'Not a trait I seem to have inherited.'

'Oh, I don't know.' I smile back. Put my hand on his knee.

'I guess from the bit she said I had my suspicions, or else why talk to me about it, and not talk to Nancy and Will?'

I nod. Not chatting to his brother and sister, just to him, would have struck him as odd. He's not daft, in fact he's very smart.

'And he did always spoil me a bit.'

'He said in that letter to me that you'd been like a son to him.'

'I know.' I don't say it, but it's typical Ollie would know, he never misses anything. 'I saw that bit.' He drapes his arm round my shoulders. His tone thoughtful. 'He was a great man to have in my life, but as a dad?' We grin at each other. 'He'd have made a shit dad, wouldn't he? Well, wouldn't he?'

I laugh I can't help it. 'Maybe.'

'There's no maybe about it! Come on, admit it?'

'Okay, he'd have been a shit dad.'

'It was him I have to thank for my middle name, I mean I ask you, Zane?' He raises and eyebrow and we grin at each other. 'Mum said he was quite insistent, strange choice though, she hasn't got a clue why he picked it!'

I think about the email from him, when I thought it was from Oz, and have my own suspicions. Uncle T and Vera seemed to like a bit of mischief making over names.

'He'd have never made school sports day,' Ollie continues, 'he'd have been off on a jaunt when he should have been taking me out. I mean, let's face it, can you imagine him changing a nappy?'

'Nope.' I shake my head. Smiling. 'But he was a great man. He was kind, generous, caring.'

'He was. But Dad was all that and more, and he's always been there for me. He wouldn't dream of divorce, I was always secure, part of a proper family. He's supported me, encouraged me at school, uni, the lot. He's been there, Daisy. Always. He's been my dad. He is my dad.'

I nod. 'You've thought about this, haven't you?'

'I have. I just had a what-if moment after Mum chatted to me. I couldn't help it. Terence was more fairy godmother than dad though, wasn't he?'

'He was, but without the wand or tutu!'

'And he was a bloody good Uncle.'

'Definitely.' I nod.

'What were you planning to do with these?' He lifts a letter up, waves it in the air.

'I don't know really. I was going to talk to your mum, then you, then,' I shrug, 'maybe we should burn them, scatter them where we scattered his ashes? I don't know.' I look at Ollie. 'I think they were mine to find, but yours and your mum's to decide the fate of.'

'Sure.' He starts to fold them up. I help. 'I'll let her know.' He puts his hand over mine, and when I glance up, our gazes lock. 'I miss him, don't you?'

I nod. 'I miss him like hell.'

Then he wraps his arms around me. I know my eyes have filled with tears, I think his have too.

Chapter 27

3 p.m., 20 June

'You won't wear that dress you wore to your cousin's wedding, will you?'

I am over thirty, have a career, am celebrating the fact that I have challenged a planning application refusal successfully and my mother is still telling me what to wear?

'Which dress, Mum?' I know which one, I just want to hear what she has to say about it.

'The one where you can practically see your ovaries! Talking of which,' we were? 'I was so glad you dumped that Tim fellow, have I told you that?'

'Yes, you did Mum, at Christmas.'

'I didn't like his beard, and his eyes were too close. They always say you can't trust a man with his eyes too close together. And you couldn't trust him, could you? The moment he took a turkey vol-au-vent I knew! Didn't I Stuart? Didn't I say?' I can hear my dad mumble in the background.

'So, have you got anything you want to tell us?'

'Well, er, no.' I am confused. 'You rang me, remember? About tonight, maybe?'

We're having a little get together in the bookshop to celebrate the fact that planning permission has been granted! We will soon be selling coffee and cakes alongside murder and mystery, and we'll be running book clubs as well – which have proved very popular.

We'd thought a little celebration would be a good practice run before we have to hold the Christmas Eve party. To be honest, I'm pretty nervous about it, Uncle T put on such a brilliant party last year, it will be hard to live up to expectations. I've already started to think about how I'm going to transform the shop into a cosy winter wonderland, full of surprises, like he did.

'Exactly, about tonight! Any little surprises coming our way?'

'Sorry? Mum, are you alright?'

'Of course, I am, dear! I just wanted to make sure I looked the part if there were any little announcements.'

'You know what the announcement is! We've won, we're going to be able to sell cappuccinos, lattes, hot chocolate,' I pause, racking my brain, 'chocolate brownies?' I'm not sure in what way any of these qualify for looking the part. 'Mini cupcakes?'

'Buns? Buns in the oven?'

'I'm not making them myself, Mum! I've been far too busy, I've got the newspaper, and sorting the party, and—'

'Well that's fine then. I just thought I'd ask. *Ring* dough-nuts?' She emphasises the 'ring'. Ah, my totally un-subtle mother seems to have a theme going here.

'Er no. Do you think I should have? I mean I've gone for cupcakes, and cocktails with a picture of the shop floating on the top.' I try not to grin. It might be mean, but I am going to act the innocent and refuse to be drawn for once. I have to give her credit, though, she's never given up on her dream of Ollie and I walking down the aisle together. But, I mean, honestly!

Ollie and I have been closer than ever recently. We've worked together in the bookshop, and since finding out that Uncle T was his father the understanding between us seems to be deeper than ever.

I love him, I guess I probably always have. I can't imagine life without him, but getting married?

'Cupcakes, lovely.' Mum's tone is slightly disappointed, but I'm pretty sure this isn't the last time she'll try! 'I'll be off then now darling. We'll see you later. Love to Oliver!'

'He's not here.'

'Oh.' There's a long pause. 'Will he be coming to the party?'

'Of course, he will, Mum. It's his bookshop! He's just operating this afternoon.'

'Well we'll see you both later then, together! How nice!'

'How nice indeed.' I say to Stanley after she's rung off. 'Now, what do you think about this, any ovaries on show?'

7 p.m., 20 June

'You look gorgeous.' Ollie kisses the nape of my neck and sends a shiver not just down my spine, but to every erogenous zone in my body. My nipples are on high alert which is a bit worrying. Maybe it would have been better to have had my ovaries on display?

I peer down my front surreptitiously, hoping nobody is looking. I think I still look decent. I've opted for a beautiful silk dress, with bright multi-coloured swirls. I loved it the moment I saw it. It's nipped in at the waist, swirls out over my hips, and sits just above my knee. And it's got a nice V at the front that kind of hints at boobs but doesn't shove them in your face. Which is handy, as mine are not exactly a big handful, they are subtler than that.

When I tried this dress on it made me feel light, and happy, and carefree – so despite being very expensive, and also the type of dress you can't hide in, I had to buy it.

I am also wearing ridiculously high shoes which you just *have* to buy when you see them because they are gorgeous, elegant, leg-lengthening and the sexiest thing ever, then realise they're really only good for posing in. I have had to teach myself to walk again, and despite spraying my soles with some stuff that will totally stop my feet aching ever again (ha-ha) I already feel like they've been stripped of skin and beaten with a hairbrush. Or something like that anyway.

'Cocktail?' He hands me a delicious looking drink that we have brought a barman in to make to order.

'Oh, Daisy, darling!' Mum kisses my cheek. 'Don't you look the part! Well I always said our Daisy was special, didn't I Vera? She's always had so much gumption, takes after me, just had to succeed! She sets her mind on something and just goes for it ... oh, oh my goodness it's the chairman of the golf club, Mr Hepworth, Mr Hepworth did I tell you, I'm her mother!' I have never seen my mother flap so much.

She's already claimed that my looks, brains, sex appeal, success and even the fact that my nails grow quite long before they break, are all down to genes. Hers.

She's also inspected the coffee machine, had three cocktails (lethal) and hugged anybody who doesn't move fast enough.

'She's happy though,' says Ollie, and he's right.

'Oh, there's no stopping young girls these days is there?' I'm not sure Dad will ever dare show his face at the golf club again, 'I mean in my day you were expected to get married, have babies, not go out and have a wonderful career. We always knew she would, did I tell you she wanted to be a vet? This is Ollie,' she grabs his arm, 'he was her first crush!'

'He was not!'

'You kissed!'

'We were six years old Mum.' I say, blushing, remembering the rather hot kiss and grope we had just before unlocking the front door to let the caterers in. They weren't happy about the fact they'd been balancing cupcakes and crab rolls on the doorstep for ten minutes. 'You made us!'

'Oh nonsense, there was no stopping Ollie!' It's his turn to look uncomfortable. 'So sweet,' she hugs him, Dad grins, and I want the ground to open up and swallow me, 'we're just waiting for him to pop the question, aren't we dear?'

'No, we're not! Can you excuse us please?' I smile as sweetly as I can at the mayor who has just wandered over, and steer my mother away, towards the crab rolls. She needs to eat. I need to drink. I also need to dunk my head in an ice bucket.

'Well done, Daisy!' James catches me unawares and kisses me on the cheek. 'You've helped me turn this news-paper round, we're so much more community centric now, you've made me realise that we need more reporters who are interested in where they are rather than where they want to be. Like young Tim, excellent journalist, but he's after a headline he can sell to the nationals, and that's not what it's about, is it?'

'Er, well no.'

'We want our journalists to get out and about, catch—'

'Crabs?' My mother shoves a plate under his nose. He looks rather startled.

James looks startled. 'Well, er, that wasn't ...'

'Crab roll, they're really rather delicious! And you must have one of those cocktails. Daisy didn't make them herself

379

you know, she's busy these days. She's important! Her boss has her slaving away, and she's fighting the council and reading books! Isn't she amazing?'

'She certainly is.' He grins. 'You must be her sister!'

I leave them to it.

9 p.m., 20 June

'Terence would have been really proud, you know.' Vera smiles, and glances over at Ollie, who is deep in conversation with his father. 'Of both of you.'

'I miss him.'

'So do I, Daisy. So do I.'

'This place isn't the same without him.' I feel a bit awkward. I haven't talked to Vera since I found the letters, since Ollie read them. But I know he's taken them to show her.

'It's not supposed to be the same, it'll never be the same, Daisy. You've got to let it become a new version, your version. And you're doing that.' She pats my knee gently, looks me in the eye and says it all without saying a word. Stanley edges over and licks her hand. 'He'd have been so proud of you and loved it all!'

'The Christmas Eve party won't be the same, I'm not sure I'll be able to cope being here without him. I'm just going to be waiting for him to walk in.'

'Well, you have to do it your own way, don't you? Don't try and do what he did, make it yours, yours and Ollie's, and there won't be quite as big a Terence shaped gap in the proceedings. We can remember him, we're never going to forget him, but we've got to make a new different version of life without him.'

'Did you love him?' There's a long silence. 'Sorry, sorry I shouldn't have said, it's none of my bu—'

'I did, Daisy.' She kisses the top of my head, then squeezes my hand. 'For a brief time, I really, really did. He was quite irresistible, wasn't he? But I loved Charles as well, and he knew that. It's a shame you can't live your life twice over and have double the magic, isn't it?'

'I think I'd be happy just to have one magical life.'

'Wise girl! And you will have. You've just got to be brave, and as Terence would say, do it your way.' She smiles then, and there's a trace of familiar mischief. Ollie style mischief. 'And hope nobody with different ideas doesn't cock it up! Now, one more cocktail for the road, before that gorgeous barman tries to escape from your Mum?'

11 p.m., 20 June

'That seemed to go well, didn't it?' Ollie shoves me along the leather sofa in my favourite nook, and squeezes in beside me. Just the way he did when we were eighteen. He tilts his head to one side. 'Happy? You seem a bit quiet.'

'It was something your mum said.' I look down at the book on my lap. I've always turned to books when I want to escape. But maybe now I need to stop running away.

I owe it to Ollie. I know his secrets, his mother's. But he doesn't know all of mine. 'She said I had to be brave, do it my way.'

Ollie chuckles, and I look up, straight into those gorgeous eyes. 'I think you've done that, this place is a triumph.'

'It's not just this place.' I look down at my book again. 'It's me.'

'Daisy?'

I put the book down, lean back and close my eyes. 'You never asked what happened after I got pregnant.'

'You said you didn't want to talk about it. I knew you'd tell me when you were ready.' His voice is soft, he slips his hand into mine and I close my fingers round it. He feels warm, solid.

'I think I'm ready now.' I take a deep breath, lean into his firm, familiar body and he wraps his arm around my shoulders, and rests his chin on my head.

'I found out just after that Christmas Eve party, you know, when we kissed?' I can feel the vibration of his nod travel through my body. 'I'd already stopped seeing Josh, it had just been fun, a bit of a joke, we only slept together once, and it was a bit rubbish really. And I was going to uni and he had other plans.' Oh, I had so many plans. My future mapped out. No time for boys or serious relationships. I pause, to let the words form in my head. 'When I missed a period I didn't really think about it, then I missed another and I panicked. I was supposed to be starting my revision, I had a plan and everything.' I know he's smiling, even without looking up. He squeezes my shoulder. 'I did a pregnancy test, then Mum made me go to the doctors to be sure, and we tried to come up with a way to have the baby and for me to go to university as well. I mean, Mum was great, she said it was modern times, she thought we could sort it all, you know go somewhere with a crèche or something.' We had had a plan. I had thought I could cope, anything was possible. I'd catch up with my revision, the work I'd missed when I was flapping. 'Then I lost it.' I blink away the tears that are stinging my eyes, and this time they do go. This time I don't start crying so hard I feel like I'm never going to be able to stop. Like used to happen. This time I feel strangely relieved to say it all out loud. 'I miscarried, and it felt like I'd got this massive, gaping hole inside, and I couldn't stop crying. Nothing was right any more, I felt a complete failure.' It had been the failure of losing my child that had thrown me completely off course. The loss. I hadn't been able to think, to concentrate, to make head nor tail of anything. I hadn't felt a fit person, a person who should succeed or be able to do anything.

'You weren't a failure, Daisy.' He kisses the top of my head.

'It felt like it was my fault.'

'But it wasn't.'

'I suppose not.' I'd needed to grieve. I know that now, but I hadn't at the time. Now, after losing Uncle Terence I've learned a bit about mourning, about grief, but back then I was just a child. I'd expected myself to just be able

Chapter 28

6 p.m., 3 December

'Bloody hell, Daisy!' Carrie is lounging on one of the comfy leather chairs, by the beautiful leaded window that looks over the street. Luxury hot chocolate in one hand, my list in the other, her feet up on a crate that doubles as a book display table (when it is dressed appropriately – at the moment it is naked). 'Why not go the full hog and invite one hundred and one Dalmatians to run riot?'

I'd like to think she is exclaiming with delight about the fabulous drink I have just let her have for free from our café in the corner, but I know she's not. The dog reference gives it away a bit.

I hunker down on the window seat, wrapping my hands round my own mug, and gaze out onto the festive scene that is both warming my heart and terrifying me in equal measure right now.

Christmas really is one of the most fabulous times of

385

the year to live in a place like this. Disagree with me if you want, but there are times when country villages in the UK are unbeatable. And December is one of them.

When it's cold, damp, windy, with grey skies the colour of a white bra fresh out of a wash with a black jumper, then maybe not.

Unless you're in Cornwall, and the grey sky is actually nearly black, and thunder is rolling in, the waves crashing violently against jagged rocks, and Poldark is brooding, his eyes darker than the night sky. Then it's fine.

I got distracted.

Today the pavements are silvery white, sparkling under the glow of the street lights. Across the cobbled road, the higgledy-piggledy buildings that house the butchers, bakers and Claire's Accessorise have window displays that could melt the iciest heart and rival any shop anywhere in the world for pure old-fashioned festive cheer and heart-warming quaintness.

Further up the street, the cobbles merge into the sea of tarmac, and modern brick and huge panes of glass herald modern day improvements. But right here, in my corner of the world, nostalgia and whispers of yesterday rule.

The small pane of glass has steamed up, and I wipe it clear.

The sweet shop opposite has to be the oldest building, its tiled roof sagging under the weight of the years (a bit like its owner's boobs if I'm brutally honest), and its white walls bulging slightly between the black painted framework that has managed to hold it upright for over 200 years. The leaded windows are lit brightly, jars of humbugs, liquorice pomfret cakes, pear drops, and aniseed twists surrounded by candy canes, snow drifts and a rather strange creature that could be a unicorn. I smile to myself, I think Mrs Bainbridge's grandchildren have been left in the shop unsupervised again.

Even the butcher has a flashing Christmas tree, holly galore (plastic of course) and window decals of a turkey and a pig running away from a farmer wielding a sprig of mistletoe.

It reminds me of Uncle Terence. All that flaming mistletoe.

'So, what do you really think then?' I put my feet up, twist round and smile at Carrie. 'I am totally knackered, I've been trying to come up with something for ages! Christmas is going to be over before I've got my act together, and I've got to plan the party!' It's not the actual party that has been terrifying me – it's the fact that the shop needs to be made ready, it needs to look its best. I need a theme!

'What does Ollie think?'

'We've not really talked. He's been so busy, I've hardly seen him.' I haven't, and when I have he's looked so shattered I've not thought it fair to start quizzing him about party planning. 'He's got in, eaten then collapsed in bed and left me to watch TV.'

'At least he's warmed up the bed for you! I hate not having anybody to put my cold feet on.'

I laugh. Carrie is doing well. She can say things like that now without her face crumpling.

'I don't want to let Uncle Terence down.'

'I know. But,' she looks down at my list. I have thought about all kinds of options, bigger and better, more and more winter wonderland, 'really? Listen! Masquerade ball, Charlie's Chocolate factory, Holiday swap, Love actually, Elf, Grinch, lots of reindeers, too much mulled wine so nobody will remember, North Pole.'

'They're just ideas! I'm brainstorming, I need input! I was thinking maybe go with a movie, or more than one, or have one of those chocolate fountains and turn the place into a sweet factory?'

'Mrs Bainbridge across the road holds that card!'

'A real Nativity?'

'In a bookshop? Really? Have you been hitting the magic mushrooms or something?'

'Oh Carrie.' I collapse at her feet, laughing and pretend crying, then look up at her. 'Help me!'

She giggles back. Then laughs more. Then we both end up laughing until we're clutching our sides and the tears are streaming down our faces.

For no reason at all. I think I might be losing the plot.

11 p.m., 3 December

'Hey, stranger, how are you?' Ollie crashes onto the settee, rests his head on my lap and looks up at me. Then Stanley, feeling left out leaps onto his chest, tiptoes along his body, sits on his face and gazes adoringly into my eyes.

'I'm fine, thank you.' I say, seriously, to Stanley, and shake one of his paws. 'Is this the magic of Christmas, or do I really have a talking dog?'

'We have a very spoiled, attention seeking dog.' Ollie picks him up and deposits him on the floor, then reaches up to tuck my hair behind my ear. 'I need you to myself, we need to get away, make mad passionate love, drink wine and laugh.'

'We do?' I raise an eyebrow.

'We do.' He closes his eyes. 'God, I am knackered, you might have to give me a moment.'

I smile. He's cute when he's tired. I very gently run my finger down his nose, then rest it on his lips.

'Does this mean things are going to get quieter at work?'

'Got a replacement for doc Baz, you know the one that was suspended?'

'That's good then.'

'Excel-*leeeent*.' The second half of the word gets longer and longer and more drawn out. His breathing slows and I watch his chest rise and fall. I've never known anybody be able to just drop off like he does. It takes me ages to fall asleep, even when I'm worn out. I lie there, sure I'll go to sleep. Then get bored and start to do the 'imagine your body getting heavy game' where you work up from your feet and should be out for the count by the time you get to your head. Never works. My feet get heavy, then by the time I've got to my knees my toes are twitching again.

Ollie lies down, closes his eyes and is gone.

I close my own eyes. Think about all the ways I could decorate the bookshop for the party, and Christmas in general. Think about reindeer. Wonder if Ollie will really like what I've got him for Christmas, and whether it's over the top. Wonder if maybe he wants to carry on living here with me, even though Uncle T said we only have to stay here together for a year. Wonder if we'll have a Christmas party again next year, even though Uncle T only stipulated in his will that we have to do it one more time.

I just can't imagine Christmas without the party, I'll have to ask Ollie if he can.

My eyes are still closed but I'm smiling.

I can't imagine Christmas without Ollie now either. He makes me feel so happy, so loved. He makes me feel that I can do anything.

And I think about Uncle Terence, and last Christmas, and him dancing with Vera. Every bit the gentleman. They look so perfect, so elegant and refined. The polished wood bookcases, leather chairs and piles of leather-bound books the perfect backdrop. Like something out of an Agatha Christie movie ...

Chapter 29

5 a.m., 4 December

'I've got it! I know!' I am suddenly awake, wide awake and sit bold upright. 'I know what we need to do.'

'Eurgh.'

I just manage to catch Ollie, who I've nearly thrown off my lap.

Bugger, did we fall asleep on the sofa? How did that happen?

He nestles back into me, his face against my stomach.

'Wake up!' I nudge him hard in the chest and he groans and rolls over and ends up on the floor.

'Christ, what's happening, where ...' he looks up at me. Luckily it is not a big fall from my lap to the floor. He frowns. 'Shit, it isn't time to get up, I feel like I haven't been to bed.'

'You haven't.' He closes his eyes again. 'It's just after five o'clock.'

'Five?'

391

'Ollie, listen, I know what we need to do for the party.'

'What?' His words are heavy with sleep.

'Passion, love!'

'Sorry.' He opens his eyes and frowns. 'Too tired, can't ...' He's fighting to stay awake. 'Maybe tomorrow ...'

I laugh. 'Not you!'

'S'good.' There's a long pause, and I think he might have drifted off, then his eyes spring open. Wide open. 'Who?'

I giggle. 'Nobody, you noddle. I'm talking about me, the shop! We just need to make the bookshop its festive best. No gimmicks, just wonderful. Like Uncle Terence was, wonderful, old-fashioned, traditional. That's it.'

'Good. Excellent.'

'Slightly eccentric, but wonderful. We're going to make it the best afternoon tea ever, with champagne and gentleman relishes as well as ...' I stand up.

'Where are you going now?'

'To get a notepad, or I'll forget. Tiny scones, macarons, he'd like macarons wouldn't he? And mini mince pies, and Christmas cake of course. And tea. Very nice tea. Bubbly, excellent dry bubbly. We're going to celebrate Uncle Terence. Then I'm going to bed, are you coming?'

He's already asleep again. I pop a cushion under his head, cover him up with a throw and start to tiptoe out as quietly as I can.

'Of course I'm coming!'

I squeal with surprise as his warm breath hits the back

of my neck before I've even got to the doorway, and one of his hands touches my waist.

'You were asleep!'

'But I'm not now!' He grins. 'I'm wide awake and coming to get you!'

I scream again, I can't help it – then make a run for it, with Ollie in hot pursuit.

Chapter 30

6 a.m., 24 December

'Wake up, Daisy!' Somebody is shaking my shoulder and shining a light in my face.

'Go away!' I am not a morning person. Anything before 7 a.m. does not exist in my world. Unless I've got to get up early to catch a plane and jet off to somewhere exciting for my holidays, then I can make an exception.

'Come on sleepy head!' Ollie chuckles and doesn't go away. 'Help me, Stanley, come on boy.'

Stanley helps. He shoves his cold nose in my ear, then starts to lick my face. 'Eurgh, bugger off!' I pull the duvet over my head, but he considers that a challenge and burrows under. 'Oh God, what is the matter with you two! It's still dark outside!'

'You said you wanted to know what I'd been up to, so now's your chance to find out.'

'Can I find out in three hours' time please?'

'No.' He's laughing properly now, and it does cause some

kind of stirrings in my sleepy body.

'You can make love to me when I'm half asleep, it's fine. Quite nice.'

'It's not fine.' He chuckles. 'You don't want to know then?'

I can't help it. I open one eye, because I do actually want to know what he's been up to. 'What?'

'Sit up.'

'Can't.' I close the eye again and pull the covers higher.

Ollie has been very secretive the past couple of weeks. He's been guarding his laptop and his phone. 'Anybody would think you're having an affair!' I challenged him one evening after his phone had been beeping with so many alerts, I thought it might spontaneously combust.

'I am – with Ms eBay!' He'd said. 'I just hope she doesn't two-time me.'

'I thought you didn't do eBay?' He doesn't really do any kind of internet stuff apart from research. He definitely doesn't do online shopping.

'I don't, but this is different. Now, keep your hands off, it's a surprise!'

'I don't like surprises, tell me! What are you buying?' I've never really been that keen on surprises, I mean, what if people get it wrong? I hate trying to put a delighted, wow, that's brilliant, face on when in fact the surprise is a huge let down. Like when you think you might get a pony for Christmas (it's what you've always wanted! It'll get you to school quicker! You can give it a name!) and it turns out to be a bike.

'You do like surprises, you just don't like to think you don't know what I'm doing.' This was partly true.

'Ollie!'

He grinned. Don't you hate it when people won't give in? '*Aww*, poor Daisy, never mind it's nearly over!' Two hours later he'd whooped, danced round the living room with Stanley and then poured us a glass of wine.

'What?' I'd laughed, I couldn't help it. He was *so* pleased with himself. So un-pompous prick like, so much more wonderful than I could have ever imagined when we were growing up. My God I love him so much it's scary.

'I'll tell you on Christmas Eve!'

'God you are annoying!'

'I know, good innit?' He'd chuckled and kissed me. 'You have no idea how sexy you are when you're annoyed!'

Then he never said another word, which was bloody frustrating.

Until now. 6 a.m. in the morning.

'Happy Christmas, Daisy!'

'You're a day early, bugger off. Honestly, you're like a little kid at times, that annoying little kid who tried to drown me!'

He chuckles. 'You are so grumpy in the mornings! God knows why I still love you. Now come on, it's for the shop, for tonight.' I open one eye again and grin at him. Hearing him say he loves me has that effect. It's something I don't think I will ever tire of hearing.

'Say it again!'

'It's for the shop.'

'Not that bit.'

He laughs. That wonderful rich, toe-tingling laugh of his. 'I love you, now, open it!' He points to the very large box at the bottom of the bed. 'Quick! I've got to get to work!'

I've always been a sucker for a big box. 'I will kill you if this has got a smaller box inside it!'

I rip it open.

It hasn't. It has got books. Gorgeous, first edition, wonderful books.

'Oh. My. God. Wow!' I feel all choked up, there's a lump in my throat as I reach out and touch the spine of one of the books tentatively, almost afraid they'll disappear.

Ollie grins. Very pleased with himself. 'Did I do okay?'

'You did amazing.' I jump on him, monkey style, and kiss him hard. 'Ouch.' Hard as in, clashing noses and teeth hard. But he did do amazing, he is amazing. 'I love you!'

He grins. 'I love you too, afraid I've got to dash, late for work, but I'll come to the shop straight after.'

'Sure.' I hardly hear him. I know it's terrible, and selfish, but I need to touch these books. I'm holding my breath, hardly daring to unpack them. Five beautiful Charles Dickens Christmas books. They smell incredible, they look totally gorgeous. Red bound, with gilt lettering. 'Uncle Terence would have loved these.'

'I know.' We swap a smile, and then he's gone.

7 p.m., 24 December

'You can open your eyes now!' I feel a bit like I used to feel when I was about ten years old. All shivery and excited inside, barely able to stand still because I just *have* to know what he thinks. But then I'm also a little bit worried in case he doesn't like it. But I know he will, I'm sure he will, so I just want him to see. I want him to smile and clap his hands like Mum used to do when I gave her a nice surprise. Even if it was the most misshapen cake in the history of man with blue blobs of icing on top that could have been flowers, whales or man-eating dinosaurs.

I've spent so many hours rearranging bookshelves, and finding the best holly with berries, and studding oranges with cloves, making mistletoe balls, draping the doorways with heavy red velvet curtains and basically interrogating Google until all the web thinks I'm interested in is having a Victorian Christmas.

Even Ollie has been determined to play his part – he arrived home one evening with a Christmas tree to die for, and of course found the books which have pride of place in Uncle T's favourite nook.

But all the hard work and frustration was worth it. The shop looks beautiful. This is an old-fashioned kind of magical Christmas without the bah-humbug, but with added candy canes.

'I daren't open my eyes!' Ollie chuckles. And the lovely deep sound increases the anticipation that is bubbling up inside me, so that I almost feel like I'm going to explode if he doesn't look soon.

'Do it!' I shout. 'Open your eyes, look!'

'Can't! What will you do to me if I say the wrong thing?' He's chuckling more now.

'You think you're so funny!' I punch him lightly in the ribs.

'I remember having my thumb bent back when I thought your picture of a bird was a giraffe!'

'You'll remember something if you don't open your bloody eyes. You have no idea what I am going to do to you in a moment!'

'Does it involve stripping me, tying me up and having your wicked way?'

'No, it involves prising your eyelids open and glueing them back!'

'Ha!' He grabs me tight round the waist and pulls me against his warm body, but I can tell he's opened his eyes, because he's rested his chin on my head and the little 'ah' vibrates through my body. 'Wow, Daisy, that is breathtaking. Stunning. Not a giraffe in sight.' He spins me round to face him, but his gaze is wandering around us as he slowly turns, taking us both in a full 360 spin. He's smiling broadly, taking it all in, and I'm grinning back at him like a goof. We spin faster, me in his arms and I feel like my chest is going to burst with happiness. 'It is just how he would have wanted.' He stops turning us. Looks down at me. His gaze meeting mine. His face serious. 'You are just how he wanted, just how I want.'

I gaze back, not sure what to say.

'But...' he swallows and looks nervous now. Uncomfortable. 'We need to talk about the apartment.'

'Do we?' The words squeeze their way past the obstruction in my throat. Just when I thought everything was coming together, that it was going so well.

'I think I want to sell it, now the year is up.'

'Oh, but ...' I mustn't cry. I must not.

That isn't what I expected to happen at all. Not today, not now. Some of the magic ebbs away, replaced by something uncomfortable. I go to take a step back, but he holds me firm. 'Well, if you want to. It is yours.' I swallow. I can do this. The new, confident me can cope with this. He's saying the year is up, we've satisfied the conditions of the will and it's time to move on. Tonight is the finale. I will have my money, my deposit. 'What about this place?' The words come out jagged, but I can't help it.

'We can talk about that later, Dais.' The heat of his hands is searing my skin. 'I wanted to know what you thought about the apartment first. I mean, it's been your home,' he looks less confident now. Unsure. 'I know it's a bit rushed, but I've been thinking about it for a while.'

'You have?'

'About Stanley, and the distance I have to commute to the hospital. It's not ideal is it?'

I swallow hard and can't think of a single thing to say.

'What do you think?' There's real indecision in his eyes. 'I don't want to force this, I mean if you don't think ...'

'Does it matter what I think?'

'Well yeah, of course it does! Daisy, if we're going to get a place together then I really want it to work for both of—'

'A place together?' I think I just shouted very loudly. Stanley has yelped and hidden under a chair. 'The two of us?'

'And Stanley, with a garden for Stanley?'

'You and me?' I can't quite process this. I've gone from a happy high, to down in the dumps, back up to a place I can't quite understand. I'm all shaky and excited, and feel tearful, but want to laugh.

In fact, I'm overloading on emotion.

'You don't want to? Shit, sorry, I—'

I put my hand on his lips to stop him talking. Blink. Try to process this. 'No, no I do, I just ...' I clutch his arms. Stare into those wonderful eyes I've grown to love so much. 'I wasn't expecting.' I blink more rapidly, smile in what feels like a very wonky, about to cry, way.

'It's a huge commitment, I know. But,' his voice is soft, gentle. But there's a distinct edge to it, that I think Uncle T might have called passion, 'you mean so much to me, Daisy. I love you.'

I think about all the girls he's dated, the ones he knew

weren't right. The guys I've dated, when I haven't even wanted to share a toothbrush.

But I want to do this with him.

Not for Mum, or security, or to make more sense of my life. Just because I want to.

'So, this together, just one set of bed sheets type of together.' Just to be sure what he's saying here.

He smiles, relief lightening his features. 'One bed, but hopefully more than one set of bed sheets. But maybe not too many cushions?'

'You can never have too many cushions!' There's a tremble in my voice, but it's not doubt or fear.

'There's something else. I think I should have said this first, but I was scared.'

'The great Ollie Cartwright scared of something?' I smile up at him. We're moving in together! Properly together.

He's fumbling about in his pockets panicking a bit. 'Hang on.'

'What?'

'Shit! Oh bugger. Oh, here!'

He is clutching something. He's got a small box in his hand. Oh shit, oh bugger, oh God my knees are about to give way.

'Daisy.' He's blinking now as well. 'Will you do more than just move with me, will you.' He opens the box. The most beautiful diamond and sapphire ring sparkles under the lights from the tree behind me. 'Daisy, will you marry me?'

I stare at his full lips, at his wonderful face. Straighten his tie a bit. Touch his mouth with my trembling fingertips. Then take a deep breath.

'Ollie.' It didn't work. My voice is still wavery and thin. So I clear my throat. Do some more blinking, as my eyes are about to overflow. And it's that very moment that Stanley chooses to start yapping and jumping up at me, then jumps into my arms and starts to lick my face frantically. I laugh. 'We'd love to! Wouldn't we Stanley?'

He laughs, with shaking hands takes the ring out of the box, and very carefully puts it on my finger. 'Uncle Terence left it to me, to us I guess, in his will.'

'Uncle T?' I put Stanley down on the floor and he wanders off, as though he's happy now his job is done. He just wanted to be involved in the decision. I run the tip of my finger over the ring, lift it up into the light.

'He said he'd bought it for the greatest love of his life, and he'd be honoured if I gave it to mine.'

'I'm the greatest love of your life?'

'Without a doubt. Well,' he pauses, 'apart from Stanley of course. It's a draw!'

Then before I can joke, or say anything at all, he pulls me in tight and kisses me.

Thoroughly.

So thoroughly that I am all flushed and hot, so hot I have to take my Christmas jumper off before we carry on.

'Oh my God, Daisy, you look gorgeous.' He groans. 'Put it back on before I have to ravish you!'

'I quite like the idea of that!'

He chuckles, then strokes his strong fingers up my leg, under the hem of my quite short dress, around to the front, to the tender part of my thigh. I gulp. He looks into my eyes. Totally serious. We stop.

He swallows hard. 'You do look amazing. Beautiful.'

'Really? My bum doesn't look big in this?' My laugh is a bit strained, but I think we need to break this up before our families gate-crash the situation!

'Your bum has never looked big in anything. I was just always scared to say anything when you asked before, in case I went over the top and said the wrong thing.'

'You could never say the wrong thing.'

'Really? How about you were a lousy throw at cricket when you were ten?'

'Cheeky.' We're trying, but we're still not out of the lust danger zone.

'You might have hit me if I'd ever said what I really thought. Cow girl!'

I hit him then, but with the back of my hand in a friendly way. Not on the head with a plastic doll in an angry and startled way. 'Later, cowboy!' I wink and grin, and he pulls me back into his arms.

'Promise?'

'Promise.'

His lips this time are gentle, not bruising. He teases mine apart for a moment, but this is tender love not passion. And it's just as nice.

He rests his forehead against mine. 'Shall we sit in your favourite corner, and have a drink before the hoards arrive?'

'Please.'

He opens a bottle of champagne, and we sit quietly in the corner. Our fingers interlocked, and I can't help but keep staring at the ring on my finger.

I want to laugh, and I want to cry. My heart is practically bursting with happiness, but at the same time I'm indescribably sad. I wish Uncle T was here to share this moment, I wish he was here, that he knew I'd found my passion.

He knew about Ollie and me, long before we did. He made this happen. I wish he knew that his plan had worked.

There is so much love in this ring, there was so much love and pain in his life. He was wise and he was clever, and he had romance flowing through his veins. Just as his son has.

'He loved us, you know. Terence.' Ollie swallows, his Adam's apple bouncing in his throat. He brushes away the smallest of tears that has fallen onto my cheek.

'I know.' I blink away the new tears that are filling my eyes. 'There's one more secret, one more letter hidden in the special editions that I have to give you. He had such a big heart, he was so wonderful.'

Ollie smiles and blots away the new tears that have plopped onto my cheek. 'You can show me tomorrow. And you're right, he was wonderful. He loved love, and he loved to give. It was never really about this Christmas Eve party, was it? It was about keeping us together until I realised what an idiot I'd been. I love you, you know.'

'I love you too, you know. Maybe I always have.' I pause. 'Or maybe not, I mean you were a git in the paddling pool, and my birthday candles ...'

'You're never going to let me forget that, are you?'

'Never!'

'Happy?'

'Oh yes, the happiest of happy.' I close my eyes, rest my head on his shoulder and the smell of him is mixed with the leather and wood of the shop, with the cinnamon, cloves and holly, and it's the most perfect smell ever. And in the background, there's the gentle sound of the old-fashioned festive soundtrack I'd put together with Uncle T in mind.

Bing Crosby starts to sing White Christmas and I open my eyes and look at him. My fiancé. My future.

I feel like I've come home.

There's a loud, very jarring hammering noise. It is Mum. Hammering on the door.

'How come she's so early?' I grin at Ollie and stand up. Straighten my dress. It's rather glamorous, but this year I decided that 'me' was a sexy, happy, confident woman who wasn't afraid to kick ass, even if she was a little bit overweight and would never have all the 'A' level results she'd once thought she would have.

The jumper over the top was just a nod to Uncle T's

tradition and I'd always intended to strip it off. But maybe not quite so quickly.

'Your parents are always the first!'

'Really?' I blink at Ollie, who I've just noticed is wearing a truly atrocious Christmas jumper.

'Yep, your Mum is always competing with mine to get here first!'

'*Coo-eee*, we're here! We know you're in there, we can see Stanley!' Vera shouts through the letterbox and there is more rapping on the door.

We laugh, then he takes hold of my hand. 'Ready?'

'Hang on a sec!' I point at his chest. 'You just proposed to me in that!!

'I reckoned if you said yes, we were meant to be!' He grins. 'Ready? Shall we get this party started?'

'Definitely!'

We go to the door together. Stanley between us. Ollie opens it, and we both grin at our parents, all four of them hovering on the doorstep, bottles of bubbly and sprigs of mistletoe in their hands.

'Daisy!'

'Ollie!'

Vera and Mum both shout out at the same time and point wildly – at my finger! My God, how can they be so eagle eyed?

'You've, oh! Oh, well, I don't know what to say!' Mum puts a hand over her mouth melodramatically and Dad grins and winks at me. Vera fans herself wildly, and her eyes are brimming over. I wonder if she's seen this ring before.

'Are you going to put them out of their misery, or shall I?' Asks Ollie.

'I will.' I take a deep breath. 'Guess what? This year I *have* got an announcement.' I look at Ollie, suddenly feeling shy. Then he slips his hand into mine and the full magic of it all hits me. 'We both have.'

We raise our hands and I'm pretty sure they are clapping, but I can only really see Ollie – as he leans in closer and his lips meet mine. And finally, my life is exactly how I always hoped it would be.

THE END

Acknowledgements

Every book starts with an idea – this idea first popped its head above the parapet during a fabulous Christmas celebration with three wonderful friends: my amazing publisher Charlotte Ledger, fabulous agent Amanda Preston, and the very lovely author Jane Linfoot.

In the totally gorgeous festive setting of St Pancras Renaissance Hotel (you may have spotted it in the Harry Potter films), which had not one but TWO incredible Christmas trees on the stairs, we chatted about all those Christmas surprises, disasters and happy moments. And on the walk back to Euston station to catch my train home, this idea was born!

As books do, this one grew, changed and was mulled over for several months. And during another get together (I don't spend all my time eating and drinking – promise!) with Charlotte, Amanda and digital marketing star Claire Fenby, 'the secret' started to take on a new significance. My editor-extraordinaire Emily Ruston then kicked it well and truly into shape!

Zara Stoneley

So thank you, thank you, thank you to my wonderful team – you're always there for me from day one of each book, right through the nail-biting, hair-tearing, sobbing-in-the-middle days, to the happy end!

Thank you also to all the other incredible people at HarperCollins, and One More Chapter, who have helped make this happen. I don't want to name all the names, as I am scared stiff of missing somebody out, but from cover design (incredibly beautiful), to editing, and marketing that started well before this book was finished, I feel incredibly lucky to be able to work with all of you.

Thank you as always to my family, supportive friends, and lovely author buddies (Mandy Baggot you are a star!) without you cheering me on (and cheering me up) I'd never have got to 'The End' (Jules Wake, your wise words sent me sprinting to the finish line). And thanks to Harry, my gorgeous pup, who keeps me sane, gives me much needed cuddles and ensures I get my daily exercise – my bottom would be so much bigger if it wasn't for you!

And last but not least, a massive thank you to you, for reading this story, and being so supportive.